THE MIDNIGHT HOUR

KATE HEWITT

Storm
PUBLISHING

Ebook ISBN: 978-1-80508-701-4
Paperback ISBN: 978-1-80508-703-8

Cover design: Eileen Carey
Cover images: iStock, Shutterstock, Stocksy

Published by Storm Publishing.
For further information, visit:
www.stormpublishing.co

ALSO BY KATE HEWITT

The Last Stars in the Sky

To Caroline, Ellen, Teddy, Anna, and Charlotte, my own cottage kids, and to Jacob, who passed the cottage test with flying colors! I've been so privileged to share the magic and beauty of the cottage with all of you.

ONE
ALEX

We drive for six miles before our luck runs out. I can smell the smoke in my hair, taste its acrid tang on my tongue. My mind is reeling, *reeling*—we have left everything behind. Everything.

Everyone.

Kerry...

"Mom." My daughter Mattie, just fifteen years old and utterly focused, calls out sharply. "*Mom!* There's someone up ahead."

I blink the winding gray ribbon of road into focus. Straight, green pine trees line it like bristling arrows on either side. We are in the backwoods of Ontario, Canada, driving away from oblivion and toward the utterly unknown, nearly seven months after a nuclear holocaust that devastated the world and our lives. A dried trickle of blood runs down my arm from where I was nicked by a bullet, and my heart is still pounding in my chest, hard enough to hurt. Less than an hour ago, my whole world imploded, for a second time. I picture black smoke swirling into the sky, and I push the image away. I need to focus, because now there's another danger.

Up ahead a beat-up truck on monster wheels is parked sideways, blocking the road. A man in a plaid shirt and weathered baseball cap is lounging against its bumper, working over a chaw of tobacco. He is holding a semiautomatic rifle like it's a toy, slack against his hip, but I have no doubt whatsoever that he knows how to use it, and, moreover, that he'll enjoy doing so. I think of the men who have burned down our cottage on Lost Lake, the *relish* on their grimy faces as they came to steal and plunder what was ours. It doesn't take long for the animal to emerge from the man.

"Mommy." Phoebe's voice is quiet, more a question than a wail. She is four years old, and her mother died an hour ago, sniped by a broken-toothed man in a baseball cap. Does she even realize her mother is gone forever? Can she possibly understand? I don't know if any of us can; the reverberations will continue thudding through us for a long time to come, but right now we have a new crisis to deal with.

"Mom... I'm not sure those guys are friendly," Mattie says quietly. She has Phoebe on her lap, her arms laced around her middle, and Ruby, my twelve-year-old daughter, is sitting next to her, as silent and watchful as always. My husband, Daniel, is driving the car ahead of us, with our nineteen-year-old son Sam and Kyle, the kid we picked up along the way, a couple of months ago.

I can't think about the people we've already lost, the sacrifices they made. The cost was high, too high, and it might be about to get higher. It's all too much to take in, especially when there's a guy who is blocking the road and he's holding a gun.

The guy raises the gun a little, like a greeting. *Hello there.* Up ahead I see Daniel veer hard to the left, pulling onto the side of the road with a screech of tires and a spray of gravel. I follow suit, hunched over the steering wheel, keeping low in case he decides to shoot. I hear a pop, and then an exhale like a slow breath, and finally a sinking sensation. I realize the guy must have shot out my front right tire, and for what? Fun?

Stupid, I think, my hands clenched on the wheel. *He could have used the tires.*

Remarkably, I do not feel remotely afraid. Too much has happened today for me to feel any more terror. My house has been burned down by backwoods terrorists; my best friend has died along with my mother; I'm on the run in a world that is on fire. I don't have time to feel afraid of one measly guy with a gun.

Except, I realize when I dare to lift my head a little to peer out the windshield, there's not one guy. There are two. The other one sits in the cab, looking relaxed, his head tilted back against the seat, his expression almost sleepy. These guys are toying with us, I think. They're so sure of themselves, and, more importantly, they're sure of *us*.

Just like before when I've run into this type of backwoods hooligan, they think we don't know our way around a gun. They assume we're city slickers, simply by the cars we drive or maybe the way we look. Daniel is sporting a Patagonia fleece and I'm wearing a striped boat-neck top from Land's End, relics of a former life when we were smug suburbanites and our idea of roughing it outdoors was mowing the lawn ourselves.

Well, things have changed since we came to Canada back in November, when my biggest worry was whether our turkey would defrost in time for Thanksgiving. Things have changed since Daniel made me practice shooting, the first time I'd ever held a gun in my hands, and it took me fifty tries to so much as nick the tin can on top of a stump. Seven months later, I'm hardened to the core; I feel as if I have no more softness inside of me, and I'm glad.

Observing these two cocky guys, I feel only a flicker of nerves, like a ripple in water. It's strange, how calm I feel. Otherworldly, almost like I'm not entirely here. I'm floating somewhere up in space, watching this scene unfold with only a mild curiosity about how it might all go down.

"Mom," Mattie whispers, and she sounds as angry as she does afraid. "What are we going to do?"

Up ahead, I see Daniel get out of the car. I glimpse the flash of Sam and Kyle's scared faces in the back, like pale moons, before they bob beneath the seat. My husband's movements are slow, purposeful, as if he's got all the time in the world. As if there aren't at least a couple of rifles trained on him.

I open my door.

The man leaning against the bumper is still looking relaxed, his gun slack but its muzzle still aimed toward me. The guy in the truck also has a gun, I see; it's propped against the open window, tilted toward Daniel. The air is filled with birdsong, the rustle of wind in the trees. The road stretches in both directions, shimmering in the summer sunlight. It's a beautiful June day, and I have no idea what is going to happen. Whether someone is going to die here.

"Hey there," the man says in a drawl. His finger plays with the trigger of the rifle. Daniel and I have rifles, too; we're holding them in a way that is just as trigger-happy as this guy, but we haven't aimed them at anyone yet. But we will, I know we will, if we have to.

I'm carrying a Colt semiautomatic M-16 that belonged to Phoebe's uncle, before he killed himself because he couldn't take the Armageddon scenario he thought he'd been waiting his whole life for. It shoots thirty rounds and, while I can't claim to be any kind of expert on guns, I think this one will get the job done if it needs to, because more potent than the weapon in my hands is the fury in my heart, the steel in my spine. I'm so ready to shoot someone who is threatening me or my family.

"You want to put your gun down?" the man asks Daniel, and his voice is mild, almost amused. He really believes we're noobs and compared to him we *are*, but it still makes me angry. Guys like this have taken *everything* from me. Everyone. And I'm not letting another one take a single thing more.

"No, I don't think I do," Daniel replies, his tone an unsettling mixture of affability and deadly seriousness. "You're blocking the road."

The man frowns, his brows drawing together as he glances between us, and I know he is re-evaluating the threat we present, and I'm glad. *That's right*, I think. *This isn't going to be as easy as you thought it was.* I raise my rifle just a little bit, like a warning, or maybe a greeting back. *Yes, hello there. I see you.*

"Look..." the man begins, and now he sounds both weary and wary, his finger still on the trigger. "Let's not get carried away here, okay? It would make it a whole lot easier for everyone if you just put the guns away."

And walk right into whatever he has planned? The last time I faced these types of guys, they killed two women. The time before that, they shot at me. And the time before that, they tried to rape me *and* shoot me. I am not putting *anything* down.

"Like I said," Daniel replies, and now he just sounds serious, "I don't think so."

A second passes, taut, sparking with tension. No one moves; no one even breathes. From its perch on a tall birch by the road, a mourning dove lets out its soft, sorrowful coo, and an oriole chatters in reply. A single trickle of sweat rolls down between my shoulder blades, and my arm throbs where the bullet nicked me. My hands don't waver. My rifle is still lowered, but only halfway.

What happens next is a blur of instinct and reaction; I move before I think, and so does Daniel. The guy in the truck moves first, the muzzle of his rifle swinging around to Daniel. The guy by the bumper raises his own gun. And then someone fires.

I don't know who pulls the trigger first, but as my ears ring from the sound of the shots, and my shoulder pulses with pain from the recoil, I see that the guy by the bumper now has blood blooming across the blue plaid of his shirt. He looks dazed, his eyes wide, his jaw slack as the rifle slides from his hands, and then he falls back against the truck before slipping all the way to the ground.

The guy in the truck is slumped forward, and the windshield is speckled with blood like something out of a horror movie. In the second of electric silence, the man in the truck suddenly lifts his head, blinking blearily at us, before he stumbles out of the truck, clutching his arm. His shirt is covered in blood.

"You... you killed him," he exclaims in hoarse disbelief, blood trickling between his fingers, while Daniel and I simply stare. Then he starts half running, half stumbling into the woods, and a few seconds later he is gone.

I breathe out slowly and lower my rifle.

"You okay?" Daniel snaps out, and I nod before I find my voice. I'm numb, yet also shaken.

"Yeah," I croak, "they didn't get me. You?"

"Yeah, me neither."

We are silent, absorbing what just happened, although I don't think I actually can. We just killed a man and seriously injured another, and we are safe. I have to hold those things together, make them work in unity.

Another second passes, and then the back door of Daniel's car opens, and Sam comes out, his mouth slack, his eyes wide.

"Mom... you *shot* that guy."

I can't quite judge his tone; he sounds wondering, but also, I think, accusing.

"They were going to kill us," I state, matter-of-fact. I put my rifle down on the ground; my hands are trembling. I'm not as hardened as I thought I was, I realize, and I don't know if that fills me with relief or disappointment.

"Is he... *dead*?" Sam's voice is hushed as he creeps a little closer.

I don't reply as Daniel dispassionately inspects the guy on the road. His face is expressionless as he turns back to us. "Yes," he tells Sam. "He's dead. As for the other guy..." He glances back at the woods. I know he's thinking about how injured he was, how far he might make it. "I don't know," he tells Sam.

I exhale slowly.

"We need to keep going," Daniel states. "That guy might be getting some backup. We can take the truck. It fits all of us, and I think we should stick to one vehicle. It's safer, and we'll conserve gas."

I nod, still not trusting myself to speak. What are we meant to do with the body? I have yet to look at him properly, and I realize I don't want to. Both men were threats we had to eliminate; that's all I can let them be. I can't look the dead man in the face, check if he has a wedding ring, family photos crumpled in his front pocket. I can't let either of them be ordinary men. They were, I remind myself, ready to shoot us.

From behind me, I hear Mattie get out of the car. I turn and see she's got Phoebe on her hip. Her dark hair is blowing in the breeze, and her eyes are narrowed, her face hard, as hardened as I thought I was. "What do we need to do?" she asks Daniel.

"I'll deal with the body," he tells her. "You all unload our cars. Let's load up again as quickly as we can."

He glances up and down the road, and I'm reminded of how vulnerable we are. The cottage we left burning under a blue sky is less than ten miles behind us. The gang that took it from us might still be roving the countryside, out for revenge. I might have just shot a man in cold blood, but I do not want to meet those sadistic savages again.

"All right," I say, and now I sound stronger. "Let's get going."

We start unloading our gear—crates of food, bottled water, guns and ammunition, sleeping bags, tarps, backpacks of clothes, a first aid kit, flint and steel. We packed it weeks ago, in case we needed to run. It will last us a little while, but not much longer. But hopefully a little while is all we'll need.

Our destination is a military base near Buffalo that Daniel believes might be some kind of safe community. He heard rumors of it, when he'd gone to upstate New York to get Sam, but that's all we've got to go on—a whisper of hope. We have no idea if the base is even there, or if the people will be welcoming. We don't even know how far the radiation might have spread across the country, or if there's any remnant of government still in place, or how many people are left in this world. There are a lot of unknowns, too many dangers, but the only chance is to keep going, because we can't go back.

Phoebe clings to Mattie, silently sucking her thumb as we stack everything as quickly as we can. Mattie moves with brisk efficiency, Ruby more slowly, with care. Sam unloads the other car; Kyle was shot in the shoulder by one of the renegades back at the cottage and is lying in the backseat, his face gray with pain and beaded with sweat. Daniel got the bullet out and bandaged him when we first stopped a couple of miles out, but he still looks in bad shape. He'll need some more medical care, not that anyone is actually qualified to give it, but we'll do what we can.

No one looks at Daniel, who is dragging the man's lifeless body to the side of the road. From the corner of my eye, I see a smear of rusty red on the road and I quickly avert my gaze, focus on the box of canned goods—the last we have—that I'm lifting from the trunk.

We've nearly finished unpacking the cars when Daniel comes up to me. "I'm going to bury him," he says quietly. "I know it might take a while, but... I think I should." He glances at Sam before turning back to me. "There's a shovel in their truck."

I'm startled, because somehow it puts a different spin on what happened. Do you bury your fallen opponents in battle? Isn't that *their* side's job? Unless those guys really were inno-cent. Does Daniel think that, even if he won't say? But even so, we're vulnerable out here, and we need to put more distance between us and the cottage... and the guys who attacked us there.

I don't say any of this, however, because I recognize the calm but obdurate look on my husband's face. He's going to do this, no matter what. "Keep an eye out," he tells me, and I nod.

We finish unpacking the cars and load everything up into the truck. I check on Kyle, who is only semi-conscious, his gaze bleary and pain-filled as he looks up at me. Blood has soaked through the bandage on his shoulder.

"Let me fix that," I say, and I find the first aid kit and change the bandage; the wound looks clean but deep. I've come a long way, I reflect as I carefully wrap gauze around the area, from when I was so squeamish I nearly passed out when I had to stitch up Ruby after she'd nearly severed an artery. A sigh escapes me at the thought; it's a distance I wish I hadn't had to travel. I glance down at Kyle and see that he's passed out.

Twenty minutes later, Daniel is just coming out of the woods when, in the distance, I hear the rattle and hum of some kind of motor. We exchange knowing glances and then we start to move.

"Let's go," he says.

We take the keys from our cars; the last thing we want is to provide transportation for anyone. I glance at the front tire of mine and see that it's flat, but not blown out by a bullet, like I'd thought. I crouch down, and that's when I see it—a rusty nail embedded in the rubber. An accident or intentional? It no longer matters. I straighten and head for the truck.

Daniel and Sam maneuver Kyle into the back, so he is slumped against the seat, his eyes fluttering open and then closed again. Mattie and Ruby slide in next to him, with Phoebe on Mattie's lap. The little girl's eyes are wide, but she doesn't say a word. Daniel, Sam, and I take the bench seat in the front. All our stuff is in the truck bed, covered by a tarp, and Daniel thankfully wiped the windshield clean of blood, although there's still the metallic taste of it in the air, along with a smell of tobacco and someone else's sweat.

I don't want to imagine that man's body buried in a shallow grave, covered by leaves and just a little dirt, to be discovered by foxes and raccoons, and so I don't.

"They had forty gallons of gas back there," Daniel continues in a low voice. "So that's good."

Gas was one of our biggest issues with making this journey. In the last seven months, we've conserved and hoarded as much as we could, but we knew we wouldn't have enough to get from rural Ontario all the way to Buffalo, a distance of some three hundred miles, and that's without considering any necessary detours. Forty gallons will certainly help; it might even get us all the way there, although this thing looks like a gas guzzler.

Daniel starts the truck and I turn to Sam, who hasn't spoken since he told me I shot that guy. His face is pale, and he is biting his lip as he stares out the window. I put my hand on his arm, and he twitches, as if to shrug it off. I return it to my lap.

"You okay?" I ask in a low voice, and this time it's his shoulders that twitch. I have a feeling he is deliberately trying not to look at me, and unease creeps along my spine, settling in my gut. *How did we get here?* I wonder, even as I know how.

Seven months ago, we traveled from suburban Connecticut to rural Ontario in a naive and desperate attempt to recalibrate our family after so much had gone wrong. We'd come to my parents' dilapidated cottage that no one had stepped foot in for seven years, thinking somehow this change would reset us. I'd envisioned a montage of Hallmark moments—bonfires and s'mores and candlelit card games, spontaneous hugs and important, healing chats. What I got was a nuclear holocaust five days after we arrived.

Really, I know it was a blessing that we'd been there at all, away from the disaster, the radiation, the fallout. Nine initial strikes across America turned into dozens more, leaving most of the United States and some of Canada unlivable, as far as I knew, although the truth is no one really knows anything. This is not a comfortably predictable disaster movie or even a smugly certain governmental strategy for a potential extinction-level event; it's reality, and it doesn't unfold the way anyone expects. It doesn't *unfold*, at all; it both explodes and collapses, it trickles away, and it surges up. Endlessly.

Over the last seven months, I know that all the major infrastructure of North America has collapsed, the government has more or less disappeared, the military melted away. Civilized human beings emerged from terrified hiding and some formed into roving gangs while others did their best to protect themselves. And that was in just our little part of rural Ontario. Who knows what has happened elsewhere; Daniel experienced some of it, but so far he hasn't given any details. He was gone for six months, getting Sam from college at my command, yet another jagged piece of our fractured relationship. When he returned, he was a different man, silent and tense-jawed, yet with a resignation about him that seemed to be soul-deep, and scared me... but at least he'd brought back Sam.

Sam, my son, my firstborn, who now is refusing to look at me. And I know the real question I'm asking is not *how did we get here*, but how did *I* get here. How did I come to shoot a man without a flicker of fear or concern, never mind remorse or real guilt? How did I become this person I don't really like, and yet I already know I don't want to change?

I *can't* change, because this is the world we live in now, and this is how you survive.

We drive for maybe half a mile before Daniel slows, and then stops in front of an old iron bridge that once crossed Snake Creek, a swathe of murky green water fifty feet below us. The bridge has collapsed into the creek, a jumble of giant rusted parts. We are silent, realization trickling through us, or at least through me. And not just realization, but the guilt I thought I didn't feel.

Was this why that man had blocked the road? To warn us about a blown-out bridge? Going sixty miles an hour on a back road, we would have sailed right into oblivion before we'd been able to hit the brakes.

It's a thought I can't cope with, not now. My mind rejects it the way a soda machine refuses a crumpled dollar. *He shot first*, I insist in my mind, but I know I'm not sure.

I turn to Daniel, who is staring at the bridge, his hands braced on the steering wheel, his jaw bunched and his gaze distant, almost as if he is thinking about something else.

"Turn around," I say stonily, and, after a second, he gives a jerky nod. No one speaks while I stare straight ahead, not wanting to meet anyone's eyes as Daniel reverses and then we start back the way we came.

TWO

I crouch at the stream's edge and cup my hands, letting the cold, clear water trickle through them as I take a much-needed sip. I close my eyes and splash my face, as the water spills down my chin and throat and dampens my t-shirt.

We drove for three hours, making just over one hundred miles, before we decided to camp for the night. It was, surprisingly and a little unsettlingly, all so much easier than I'd thought. We stuck to Route 28 rather than get mired on some twisting back road, then potentially hijacked by someone with a bigger vehicle than we had, although considering the wheels on this thing I wasn't even sure that was a possibility.

We'd bumped down the road a good twelve feet off the ground, driving down a straight shot of concrete where we barely saw anyone—a few wood cabins or breeze-block ranch houses in the distance, everything locked up tight. Once I glimpsed someone standing on a front porch, watching us blank-faced and unmoving. We passed a town that had burned down, now no more than a ruined husk of blackened buildings —a roofless church, a lone pump standing like a sentry amid the rubble of a destroyed gas station. Other towns had been abandoned, ghostly and desolate, doors ajar, a suitcase dumped in the street, a shopping cart left on its side.

Bancroft, once a tourist destination in this remote part of the world, had become a quasi-fortress, many of its quaint buildings now encircled by barbed wire, with a sign warning us that intruders would be shot. But they didn't bother shooting at us as we drove through it, and I wondered if it was the monster truck, on its intimidating sixty-six-inch off-road tires. The few trucks and cars we passed on the road—three in total—sped right by us, like they didn't want to attract our notice.

Still, I expected *some* kind of obstacle—a blockade, maybe a military presence, some semblance of threat or danger—but all was emptiness and silence, a stretch of road with trees on either side, punctuated by the occasional town or house. Rural Ontario, as it had once been, but surely no longer existed... except here we were. After a while, it became unnerving. Where had everybody *gone*?

Of course I knew the answer to that naive question. As we got closer to Toronto, one of the secondary blast sites, I knew everyone must have either fled or died.

"We don't want to get too near to Toronto," Daniel announced after two hours of driving. No one had spoken that entire time, not even Phoebe. "Not if we can help it."

"Are we going to get radiation poisoning?" Mattie asked abruptly. She sounded matter-of-fact rather than concerned.

"Dude," Kyle muttered, having come out of his pain-filled stupor about half an hour ago, "that would *suck*."

"I don't think we will," Daniel replied after a moment, his tone careful and even. "It's been seven months, after all. Most of the fallout has already dissipated into the atmosphere by now." He glanced toward all of us, his eyes serious although there was also a flicker of his old wryness at playing the expert. "Of course, the fallout has traveled beyond the bomb sites, depending on the wind, but any radiation has most likely been absorbed into the troposphere at this point, especially with seasonal changes, which could accelerate the process."

I barely understood what he was saying, but I did grasp one salient fact. "But if there's less danger of radiation sickness, why is the world still like this?" I asked.

I'd assumed, in my ignorance or maybe my naivete, that a giant radioactive cloud was hovering over the United States like a dark and poisonous vapor, holding us in its pernicious thrall. It seems, according to Daniel's unexpectedly detailed knowledge, that this might not be the case. It should give me hope, but it doesn't, because as far as I can see the world is still on fire, metaphorically, anyway, and that is surely terrifying enough.

He let out a small sigh as he rolled his shoulders back. "Because of all the ripple effects of the initial detonations—the contaminated water, the clouds of soot and ash, the fires, the collapse of all infrastructure, and... well, the nature of man." He paused. "I mean, in an ideal world, people would have rallied together a little more than they have, I guess."

"In an ideal world," Mattie replied dryly, "a nuclear holocaust wouldn't have happened."

Daniel glanced at her, and that wry flicker of not-quite-a-smile passed over his face again. For a second, it felt almost as if we could have been around the kitchen table, arguing about outrageously hypothetical what-if scenarios. Mattie would be insisting she could survive in someone's basement on Twinkies and Gatorade for at least a year, and Sam would be telling her, with relish, that her skin would be flaking off and turning black as she crawled on her hands and knees toward a puddle of radioactive water.

Except Sam wasn't speaking, hadn't said a word since we got in this truck. I glanced at him, wanting to reach out, but decided it could wait until later. Whatever was bothering him, I had a feeling it had to do with me, and the way I'd wielded that gun.

"So the world is actually safe?" I stated, testing out the idea, the way I would have inched out onto the ice, back at Lost Lake. Lost Lake, my parents' beloved cottage, now truly lost forever. "I mean, from the actual nuclear stuff." I sounded like an idiot, but I didn't care. I just wanted to know.

"The blast sites themselves will be radioactive for another few years, I should think," Daniel replied. Another pause, this one heavy. "There are a lot of places we need to steer clear of, but really, I think it's all the other stuff we need to be worried about," he continued. "Contaminated water, lack of food sources or medical care—and of course the people who have resorted to savagery out of fear or desperation or a power trip, take your pick. As far as I know, the government and military have both more or less packed up, although when Sam and I were on the road we heard the president was still alive, hiding out somewhere, so maybe some kind of law and order is starting to emerge. I hope so."

We were all silent, as subdued as if we'd been scolded. It all sounded like a lot to worry about. Too much.

"What about the rest of the world?" Mattie finally asked in a small voice. "What are they doing?"

"I don't even know who sent the first bombs." Daniel let out a sudden laugh, the sound strange and wild, making everyone jump a little. "Isn't that crazy?" he exclaimed, hitting the steering wheel for emphasis, his expression hardening into something almost angry. "We don't even know who, or why this all happened."

Nobody replied because what was there to say? There were probably half a dozen countries capable—and, it seemed, willing—to blast the U.S. into oblivion. Did it matter now which one it was? And yet, I considered, the attack had clearly been tactical

—enough to wipe out the U.S. but not the whole world. Enough to do serious damage, but not forever.

"So what is Asia doing?" I asked Daniel. "Or Russia? Or Africa? Or anywhere?"

He shrugged. "I heard that there had been a couple of humanitarian aid efforts by the international community, in various places, back at the start, but not much. I mean, taking North America out has a knock-on effect on the rest of the world, and I don't even know how many other places were bombed." His mouth twisted. "I think it's safe to say they're doing better than us, though."

I was silent, absorbing the insane idea that the rest of the world might be just getting on with things, going to work, buying food, being bored. They might have had electricity. Internet. Hospitals. Fresh water. It was not necessarily a *Mad Max* landscape of roving gangs and terror. But meanwhile, that was what we had to deal with.

But I don't have to worry about that now, I tell myself as I ease back onto my heels. The woods are quiet, save for the rustle of a chipmunk, the twitter of a robin or chickadee. We turned off Route 28 about a hundred and twenty miles before Toronto, a little while after driving through the fortified town of Bancroft, at Kawartha Highlands Provincial Park, just to be safe. The park is an endless enclave of lakes and woods, a dense sweep of green, its few winding tracks barely penetrating the deep forest. It seemed like a good place to hide, at least for a little while, although I was surprised we didn't encounter anyone else here, at least not for the few miles we drove into the park, past weathered signs warning us about the dangers of forest fires and quad biking without helmets. Surely this would be a good place to hole up—in the woods, with plenty of game, fresh water, even compost toilets and campsites, although we decided not to venture near any of those, just in case.

Canada is a big country, I reminded myself, with Ontario,

outside of Toronto, being a pretty much endless stretch of forest and farm field and lake. And who knew, maybe there were others holed up in this particular stretch of woodland and we just hadn't seen them. According to the atlas we'd taken from the cottage, the park was nearly two hundred and fifty square miles, with seventeen different lakes. That was a lot of space to get lost in. A lot of places to hide... and we'd just found one.

A sigh escapes me, a slow exhale of weary relief. It's good to rest, even though I feel as if there's a darkness hovering over my mind, my heart, like the radioactive cloud I imagined over most of America. There's too much to process—the loss of the cottage, the death of my friends in the fight, the fact that we have sole responsibility for a four-year-old I barely know... and that I killed a man today, and I'm not sure how I feel about it.

A sudden snap of twigs from behind me has me whirling around, the rifle I'd left by my side in my hands before I even realize I've grabbed it. My palms are slick and my heart pounds, but my aim doesn't waver. Mattie stands there, hands thrown up in the air. A rush of breath escapes me.

"Don't shoot," she jokes, but I think I see fear in her eyes.

Slowly I lower the rifle. "I wasn't going to," I assure her, trying to smile and not quite managing it. My fingers tremble just a little as I put the gun back on the ground. "But you can't be too careful."

"I know." She drops her hands and comes toward me, and I feel a certain wariness between us that I really wish wasn't there.

"How is everything up there?" I nod toward the small, wooded hill that leads to the clearing we'd chosen for our campsite. It's near fresh water, covered by trees, and far from the road. To get to it, we drove across a meadow filled with wildflowers, the huge tires making light work of any rocks or bumps. Afterwards, Daniel and Sam brushed the beaten-down grass back up, doing their best to hide the tracks we'd made.

"It's all right." Mattie comes to the water's edge. "The black flies are kind of killer."

"Yeah, they're unfortunate." All around us the world has burst us into summer, greener and leafier than ever, and with it come the swarms of black flies that hover in thick clouds and will leave us all covered in red, itchy bumps. Camping out here is not for the faint-hearted.

"Phoebe crashed out even before she had any dinner," Mattie continues. "I put her to bed in a sleeping bag in the back of the truck. I can sleep next to her in case she wakes up."

"Okay. Thank you."

"There's some leftover stew if you want it. It's just a bunch of dried stuff and some potatoes, but, you know, it's edible." She gives me the ghost of a smile before she crouches down at the water's edge, her hand hovering above the stream's current. "Are we sure this water isn't contaminated?"

"Well, I just drank some, so I hope not." I try to make light of it, even though I know it is a genuine concern. "Dad said it would be okay because the source is further north and any radioactive particles would be diluted now, if there were any at all in the first place. Anyway, if it was contaminated, wouldn't I be choking and gasping right now?" I try to sound wry, and she glances up, giving me the faintest flicker of a smile.

"I have no idea."

"No, me neither."

We fall silent and Mattie trails her fingers through the water. I'm conscious of how much responsibility she bears without complaint or even question—caring for Phoebe, making dinner, organizing everything that I should have. In my previous life, I was the mom who made the class cupcakes, who sent Christmas cards to everyone, even our mailman, who had color-coded to-do lists and listened to podcasts on productivity. Now I just sigh.

"Kyle has a fever," Mattie tells me as she flicks water from her fingers, creating an arc of shimmering diamond droplets over the burbling stream. "Dad gave him some Tylenol, but he's worried about infection."

"We still have some of the antibiotics from Justine." A few months ago, Ruby developed sepsis and I ended up scouring the countryside for someone with access to antibiotics; this led me to Justine, who gave me the medicine and joined our little tribe, along with her daughter. Now she's dead, and I grieve more for Phoebe, who lost her mother, than for anyone else; I don't think any of us really knew her that well.

"Yeah," Mattie says slowly as she straightens. "I guess we'll use those if we have to. We'll keep an eye on him."

I shake my head, instinctively resisting the idea that Mattie needs to be in charge. "You don't have to worry about Kyle," I tell her, and she glances at me sharply, almost a glare.

"What? He's my friend."

"I know," I reply, even though I didn't really know; Kyle came to us back in December, a weedy little kid whose two interests were cannabis and gaming. He's grown into himself over the last few months, but I wouldn't have thought he and Mattie were actually *friends*. Except, who else was there for her to be friends with?

There had been Kerry, I think, with a grief that runs through me in a deep seam of sorrow. Kerry, whom I disliked at the start, with her gallows humor and sharp-eyed gaze that missed nothing, not even my own selfishness. Kerry, who gave her life to save my daughter. I miss her more than I can articulate, even to myself.

"All I meant," I tell Mattie, trying to gentle my voice, "is that you don't have to be responsible for everyone. Or everything. I'm worried about you, Mattie. This is too much for you to take on. You're only fifteen." This comes out in fumbling, staccato bursts that sound like accusations rather than empathy.

Mattie narrows her eyes, her lips pursing in disdain. "Fifteen in Armageddon looks a little different than in the life you remember," she tells me shortly. "I'm fine, Mom." It feels like a brush-off. It *is* one, I realize, as, without a word, Mattie turns around and walks back up to the campsite.

I feel as if I've alienated two of my three children today and getting them back is just as important to me as surviving. The trouble is, I have no idea how to do it.

THREE

I linger by the stream for another fifteen minutes, mainly because I'm sad and scared and I don't know what to say to my children when I see them. It's getting dark, though, the sun a massive orange ball sinking behind the dark fringe of trees on the other side of the stream as the horizon darkens to violet, and so reluctantly I rise and head back up to everyone else.

In my absence, a makeshift campsite has been set up—the tarps fashioned into two tents, a fire pit dug, banked by stones and offering a comforting blaze. A metal pot hanging from a travel hook holds the stew Mattie mentioned. She, Ruby, and Sam are all huddled around the fire; Kyle is stretched out on the bench seat in the truck, already asleep, or maybe just feverish, with Phoebe curled up in the back. Daniel sits a few feet away from the others, studying the atlas with a small flashlight, and occasionally slapping his arm or neck when a black fly or mosquito comes too close.

It looks cozy, almost like something from our past life—a camping trip to the Berkshires, not that we did that more than once or twice. We were never great campers, until we had to be.

Mattie and Sam both glance at me as I come up the hill, and then look away again without speaking.

I know I should say something, but right now I feel too cowardly, or maybe just too tired, to attempt it. I head over to Daniel and hunker down next to him.

"How are you?" I ask quietly. Such an innocuous question, and yet it holds so much import. *How are you really*, is what I want to ask. *How are you holding up after what happened today, how are you coping with whatever happened while you went to get Sam that I still don't know about, how are you feeling about whatever is ahead of us?* And *how can I help you*, because I want to reach my husband, but it feels as if he is continually, determinedly edging away from me.

"Fine," Daniel says briefly, the polite equivalent of *back off*.

I nod toward the map. "What are you thinking there?"

"I'm not sure." Wearily he passes his hand over his face. "I wanted to go as far west as we can get because I'm pretty sure the bridge is closed at Thousand Islands, but there just aren't that many points to cross, and we'd have to go miles out of our way around the Great Lakes. But if we go directly south..." He traces the route on the map with one finger, to the edge of a blue swathe that is Lake Ontario. "To Port Granby or thereabouts," he continues, "which is about a hundred miles from Toronto, we could maybe find a boat in one of the marinas, sail across... it's about thirty miles, I think. But we'd be landing on the other side between Buffalo and Rochester, both of which I think were hit."

I swallow hard. "That doesn't sound good."

"No." Daniel is silent for a moment, his forehead furrowed as we both gaze at the atlas with the gridlines of Toronto, Rochester, Buffalo all laid out, and now all most likely destroyed. He pauses, his gaze trained on the map. "The safer thing, perhaps, would be to keep making our way north and west." With one finger, he traces up from Kawartha to Sudbury. "Along the eastern shore of Lake Huron, and then up over the top and down the other side," he continues, his finger marking the proposed route. "There would be a bridge to cross here, at Mackinaw City, between the two lakes, and then down through Michigan and across."

I stare at the roundabout route he's mapped out, the meandering length of it. "Daniel, that has to be at least two thousand miles. We're only a couple of hundred miles from Buffalo now."

He scrubs at his face. "I know."

"We can't... it would take us all summer," I continue, panic creeping into my voice although I'm trying to keep my tone level. "If not longer. We'd run out of food, out of gas, and then we'd still have to cross a bridge that might be closed or barricaded or whatever, go around cities..." The route he's just traced skirts Detroit, Toledo, Cleveland. Detroit was definitely hit; I don't know about the others. Such a journey feels enormous, insurmountable. *Impossible.*

We can't do this, I think suddenly, the force of my feeling like a smack in the face. I haven't actually thought about the future since those terrorists attacked the cottage, sent us running through the woods for our lives. I've been operating on numbed autopilot, but now the future looms in front of me, in front of *us*, and it is both utterly unknowable and completely terrifying. Where will we find food? How will we survive? The supplies we brought from the cottage will last a week or two if we're careful, and that's on practically starvation rations. If we can't make it to Buffalo... what on earth are we going to do? "We can't," I say again, insistent this time.

"Alex, I *know*." His voice contains more despair than irritation, but I fall silent, feeling chastened. Of course he knows. He's come much closer to all this than I ever have, when he went to get Sam. But is this route really our most viable option? He takes a deep breath before continuing. "It's just... if we go south from here... I don't know what it will be like, between Buffalo and Rochester. How bad."

He sighs, knuckling his forehead as if he's trying to push something out of his head. "It's not just the radiation, Alex, it's the other dangers. The *people*. That little redneck gang that took on the cottage?" He shakes his head. "That's nothing compared to some of the stuff happening in the more metropolitan areas. People have got ahold of major weaponry, huge sites they've turned into fortresses—malls, hospitals, hotel complexes... Ex-military and police and some prepper types who have gone totally rogue. It's... it's not good."

Which sounds like the biggest understatement ever. I open my mouth, but no words come out. Daniel's gaze is distant and unfocused, and I wonder if he's reliving whatever terrible things he saw on the way back to me. I want to assure him that he can tell me whatever it is that is so clearly haunting him since he came back with Sam. I want to promise him I will understand, and I want to believe that I would, but the truth is I just don't know.

"But those... things... are going to be in other places, too, aren't they?" I finally say quietly. "The gangs or fortresses or whatever. We're likely to find that stuff anywhere."

"They might be," Daniel allows. "But in the cities..."

"But we won't be in the cities," I persist. "Not that close, anyway. And two hundred versus two thousand miles...? Do we really have any choice?"

Daniel is silent for a moment, his gaze shuttered. "Maybe not," he says, and closes the atlas. It feels as if the conversation is over.

"Daniel..." I begin, wanting to have the courage to say something of what I was thinking before, but I feel him tense and so I let that trail away. "Do you think Kyle will be okay?" I ask instead, which feels like the safest subject at the moment.

"Hopefully, in time, as long as his wound doesn't get infected." He shrugs. "We'll keep an eye on him, let him rest. There's no real reason we can't stay here for a couple of days, make sure we're all fit and ready to go." He tries to smile, but it's like his mouth doesn't quite work.

"And Sam?" I make myself ask. "He's been so quiet."

Daniel shrugs. "I think our shoot-out on Route 114 freaked him out a little." The words are wry, but his tone is grave.

"Daniel..." I don't want to ask, but I know I have to. "Do you think those guys were actually all right? I mean... do you think that maybe they weren't trying to hurt us?" Daniel is silent and so I continue stiltedly, "I mean, the bridge being out. Was that guy trying to warn us about it?" The notion, if I let myself dwell on it, torments me. Did I kill not just an innocent man, but a good one?

"That would have been awfully nice of them," Daniel answers after a moment. I can't gauge his tone, whether he's being sarcastic or serious or sorrowful. "Just parked in the road, waiting for people to come by so they can give them a heads-up."

"I guess..." I have a feeling he's just trying to make me feel better. "But what if they were stopped for another reason—hunting or having a pee or whatever—and they heard our cars coming and decided to warn us about the bridge?"

Daniel shrugs, his face expressionless, revealing nothing. "That's a lot of ifs, and the facts are, they were both armed, and they asked us to put our own weapons away without doing the same. He didn't say anything about the bridge or that he was friendly, and in this world there's no way we would have assumed it."

"Maybe." Heaven knows, I *want* to be convinced.

"Sam will get over it," Daniel tells me. "I think it was just a shock, how it all played out. And he hasn't really seen anything like that before."

Somehow I have trouble believing that. "Even though it took you four months to get back to the cottage?" I counter skeptically. "Daniel, you were just telling me how bad it was out

THE MIDNIGHT HOUR   27

there." Although I still don't feel like I really know. "Both of you must have seen some pretty awful—"

"No," Daniel cuts me off, his tone absolute. "Sam didn't. Not that much, anyway. Not the worst of it. At Clarkson he was protected because some billionaire alum had brought in the Marines. It was almost unreal to him, at the start, like it was a movie or a... a video game." He breathes out heavily, resting his hands on his thighs like he has to brace himself. "But what he did see was bad enough, trust me. We were carjacked at the beginning, and then later..." He's quiet for a moment. "And he saw things from the car—gangs, violence, crowds begging and pleading..." He swallows and then shakes his head as if to clear a memory—of what, exactly, I don't know, and I'm pretty sure he's not going to tell me. "But nothing that close, that personal. Not me or you or anyone he cared about, which is different."

He's hardly told me anything, and yet it's enough to fill me with unease, even dread. Those four months he spent traveling from Massachusetts to Ontario are a swirling blank to me, a vague haze of unwelcome possibility. What did my son endure? What did my husband *do*? I'm not sure I'll ever know, but what I do know is that it has changed Daniel, maybe forever.

"Okay," I say at last. "So we're going to Port Granby, and then across Lake Ontario?" I make it sound like a vacation jaunt, when I know it is absolutely anything but.

Slowly Daniel nods. "Yes. But we'll rest here for a few days first. I think we all need it."

I glance back toward my children, gathered around the campfire, their heads close together although none of them is speaking. In any other normal-life scenario, it would be a scene to warm the battered cockles of my heart—my three children huddled together in stalwart camaraderie, having a moment.

But looking at them now, I feel only despair, that it has come to this for the children I'd give my life for, and gladly. They're so *young*—only twelve, fifteen, and nineteen years of age. They've seen so little of life, and yet far too much. What kind of future can they possibly have? What kind of future can I forge for them?

Because that is what I hope from this unknown, semi-imagined military base near Buffalo. A future... not for me or even for Daniel; I'm forty-four but I feel like my life is over, and I don't even mind. But for Ruby. For Mattie. For Sam. And, I realize with a sinking sensation, for Phoebe and Kyle. *Five* young people Daniel and I are responsible for. How can I ensure they have something to look forward to, to hope for and to believe in? How can I make sure they let me, considering they don't seem to even want to talk to me now?

I turn back to my husband. "What exactly do you know about this military base?" I ask, a plaintive demand.

He doesn't answer right away, taking a moment to consider, his hooded gaze fixed on some undefined point in the night that laps our little firelit camp like the dark water of a dangerous sea. What is out there, I wonder, in that endless night? Can anyone see the smoke from our fire? Are they creeping closer, waiting to jump on us, to *attack*? I suppress a shiver.

"I know it's somewhere southwest of Buffalo," Daniel says slowly, and I turn back to him. "And that it's protected. And that the people there are trying to eke out some kind of civilized existence." He turns toward me, his expression resolute. "But all that is only what I've heard from other people. I have no idea if any of it is actually true. If the base even exists. But people were talking about it, on the road. Not just one group, but several. I got the sense there was someone in charge there—some ex-military guy."

I let out a huff of hard laughter. "This sounds like a bad action movie."

Daniel smiles faintly, his eyes creasing at the corners in a way that reminds me of how things used to be. How *we* used to be. "Yeah," he says. "What do you think happens when we get there—they take away our weapons and turn us into slave labor?"

I give a considering frown. "That would be the best-case scenario."

Daniel raises his eyebrows. "And the worst?"

"They shoot us on sight," I answer promptly. "Or they don't let us in because they don't like the look of us."

He cocks his head. "If they were going to make us slaves, that second option might be no bad thing."

"True."

We smile at each other, barely a flicker, before we both lapse into silence as the reality of what we're facing, the utter unknowability of it, hits us all over again. We can joke about it, and sometimes that feels like the only thing *to* do, but it's real and it's serious. We don't know what's out there. We don't know how bad it is going to be.

"I don't know what else to do," Daniel says after a moment. "Where to go to be safe."

"We've got to try," I reply, an agreement. "Maybe everything will be better than we think." Daniel does not bother to reply to this, and I explain a little doggedly, "I mean, I wasn't expecting the drive here to be so quiet. We saw hardly anyone. And this park... if we had amnesia, we could be on vacation."

He lets out a huff that *almost* passes for laughter. "Except we're in a monster truck. Even with amnesia, we wouldn't own a vehicle like that."

Which brings us right back to what I can't bear to think about, the two men we killed. Daniel must see something of this on my face, for he lays a hand on my arm. "Alex," he says quietly, and his voice is almost tender. "I was the one who shot first."

I'm pretty sure he's just trying to make me feel better, but I nod in acceptance like I'm buying it. He squeezes my arm. "We should all get some sleep."

I nod again, and then rise from where we were both hunkered down, casting my gaze over the flickering shadows of our campsite. Ruby, Mattie, and Sam are all still seated around the campfire, and I give them a smile that no one seems to acknowledge before I go to check on the others. Kyle is stretched out in the front of the truck, sleeping soundly; I rest the back of my hand against his forehead and, while it's not cool, it's not burning hot, either. With a few days' rest, he'll hopefully be well enough to travel. Phoebe is curled up in the back, her thumb tucked firmly into her mouth. I wonder how much she can understand; does she realize her mother is not coming back?

Justine. *Kerry*. My mother, too, dying in her sleep only last night. I can't think of them yet, can't open the floodgates to that tidal wave of grief, and so I turn back to the campfire, and my own children, knowing I can't put off some sort of reckoning with them any longer.

"Hey," I say softly as I sit down next to Ruby. "How is everyone doing?"

Ruby gives me a fleeting smile but doesn't speak, Mattie shrugs, and Sam gets up and walks away. It feels as deliberate as a slap. I glance at Mattie, who raises her eyebrows.

"He's *processing*," she explains in a tone that suggests I should understand this already, and for a second, fleeting and precious, I can picture her on the sofa back in our old house, legs stretched out as she glances up from the phone that was practically surgically attached to her hand and tells me some pithy, dismissive thing, a *well-duh* moment for a middle-aged mom. I would take *that* Mattie, with all her aggravating eye-rolls and hair-flicks, over this one any day, I realize, as much as I admire how strong and resilient my daughter has become. I want those petty problems back so much it hurts. Cannabis in her locker? A deadbeat boyfriend I don't like? Fine. *Fine*. Bring them on. I'd welcome them compared to this.

"Right," I say, because how else can I respond? We're all processing, to one degree or another. "Well... we should get ready for bed," I tell my girls. Daniel and Sam have set up two makeshift tents with the tarps; Ruby and I will sleep in one, Sam and Daniel in the other, while Mattie stays with Phoebe and Kyle in the truck. It's not ideal, but it will work.

"Yeah, okay," Mattie says, but she doesn't move. The fire casts dancing shadows over her face, her dark eyes serious, her arms wrapped around her knees.

I turn to Ruby, who is so still, so silent. Ruby has gone through phases of selective mutism for most of her life, but she'd started to come out of herself, once we'd settled into this strange new life. She had her home-made greenhouse and her books, and I think she was happy, or as much as anyone could be, all things considered. Tentatively, I put my arm around her, and am relieved when she doesn't shake it off.

"Okay, Rubes?" I ask softly, and she leans her head against my shoulder and closes her eyes. I squeeze her shoulder, grateful for this moment. At the edge of the camp, I can see Sam moving away, into the darkness, and I wonder what tomorrow will bring—for the world, but also for this ragtag group of survivors that we are going to have to form into a family. No matter what my children think of me now, I'm determined to keep us all together and safe, even if I already know it's a promise I don't have the power to make, never mind keep.

FOUR
DANIEL

December, six months earlier

"*Dad!*"

Sam breaks into a run, a huge smile splitting his face, as he catches sight of Daniel sitting in the SUV he stole from some teenaged boys twenty minutes before. For a second, Daniel can hardly believe this is real, that he's actually made it here, to his son. It took him three weeks to get from rural Ontario to this part of upstate New York, between Utica and Syracuse—he's been threatened, shot at, has both starved and nearly frozen to death. He feels like a jumble of broken parts, rusted and useless. His lips tremble as he tries for a smile.

"*Sam...*"

Sam jogs to the passenger side and throws open the door. He's got a backpack over his shoulder and he's carrying a duffel bag in one hand. Daniel could be picking him up for an impromptu father–son weekend in the city—catch a football game, steaks for dinner—save for the unsmiling Marine holding an assault rifle and standing next to the car.

"I knew you'd come," Sam says, and he sounds jubilant.

Daniel can't make sense of it. He's glad, *so* glad, to see his son, but who can be happy in this brave new world of desolation and destruction? How can Sam be smiling? Daniel realizes he is not; he's just sitting there, gaping.

Abruptly, he lurches over and embraces his son as tears crowd his eyes. "Sam," he says again, like a blessing, hugging him tightly. "*Sam*."

"Sir, you need to move on now." The Marine waves his rifle meaningfully.

Daniel nods his understanding. When he arrived here, he thought the Marine might shoot him just because he could. But then he explained about Sam, and the soldier's weathered face softened with understanding as he gave a brusque nod. He sent someone to get Sam, warning Daniel that they would not be accepting anyone back into the guarded community if they left. Daniel glanced at the tree-filled campus, the limestone buildings, the low stone walls, and nodded his understanding. They would not be coming back.

Now he reverses the car as Sam throws his bags in the back and puts on his seatbelt. Daniel can't believe how *normal* this feels. Nothing has been normal for over a month, since he first saw the nuclear attacks on the TV—no more than an orange blaze, clouds of billowing smoke. Three days later, he'd left to find Sam. He can still picture Alex's face, the *hardness* in it, as she'd told him to go. Of course, he would have gone anyway, but the unyielding look in her eyes, the hint of blame or even threat in her voice, well... that had stung.

Maybe he had deserved it, after everything that had happened. Everything that he had done. Losing his job and then, far worse, lying about it for so many months. Taking out a second mortgage without telling her. Losing their home. Yes, there was great deal Alex had blamed him for, and he didn't blame her for blaming him, but by God he was going to bring their son back safely, no matter what it cost him, and already he had a gut-deep feeling it might cost him everything.

"So what have you guys been doing?" Sam asks, and again the words sound incongruous, even wrong, as if Daniel has picked him up for Thanksgiving break and they're heading home. They might hit a little traffic, grab a Starbucks, shoot the breeze. Daniel imagines his reply: *Nothing much, your mom's baking up a storm, Mattie and Ruby are excited to see you, I got tickets to the game...*

He shakes his head slowly. "I couldn't really say. I left Mom and the girls three days after the attacks, to get you."

Sam's eyes widen as he sits back in his seat. "Whoa... it took you that long to get here?" He sounds so surprised that Daniel lets out a hollow laugh.

"Yes, it did," he replies briefly. He doesn't want to go into it —the illegal, midnight trip across the St. Lawrence River, being shot at by the Canadian Border Control, spending a week in bed, delirious with fever, cared for by strangers who thankfully were kind. And then after... two weeks riding on a child's bicycle, foraging for what food he could, avoiding the roving gangs and militias, and then, just moments ago, being hijacked by a bunch of teenaged boys. They'd wrecked his bike just for the hell of it and in response, he'd shot one of them. *In the shoulder*, he tells himself, but he's not entirely sure how bad it was. He left them on the side of the road with no vehicle, ten miles from anywhere. That alone could have been enough to kill them all, never mind the gun.

The worst part is, Daniel thinks, he doesn't even care.

"Tell me about you," he tells Sam. "Clarkson looks like it was a pretty safe place to be?"

"Yeah, they closed everything off right after the attacks. Some rich alumnus sent in the Marines. A few kids left, to go back to their parents. My roommate, Tim, went, and some other guys on my hall... but the rest of us just stayed. It was okay." He shrugged, rolled his eyes, as if to invite some kind of commiseration that Daniel already knew he would struggle to give. "It was all pretty strict, you know? Rationed food, you only had certain time in the sports hall or gym, two minutes in the shower, all that kind of stuff..."

You poor baby, Daniel thinks with a sudden, savage bitterness, and then he bites his tongue hard, hating that he is thinking this way about Sam, his son. Of *course* he's glad Sam had an easy time of it, relatively speaking. He's *grateful*. And yet something sharp has lodged in his soul, a splinter of resentment he doesn't fully understand and really doesn't want to feel, but it's there, already tearing him apart.

"I'm glad you were safe," he says, and knows, despite the tangle of his own emotions, that he means it utterly.

"It's just... wild, isn't it?" Sam remarks as he looks out the window. They're driving toward Utica, down a straight road with barren fields on either side, interspersed with a few trees, leafless and stark. Right now, it's hard to believe there has been a nuclear holocaust; there's no sign of it in this bleak and wintry landscape, but Daniel knows they'll come across something soon enough. An abandoned house. A shot-up store. A gang. "This is the first time I've been off campus," Sam continues, studying the empty fields as if looking for clues. "They wouldn't let us out. And we never got any news. It was like they thought we couldn't handle it." He turns back to Daniel, his expression matter-of-fact. "How many cities were hit?"

There's something close to an eagerness in his son's voice that makes Daniel bite his tongue again, just as hard. He does his best to keep his voice measured as he answers, "Nine, to start. And then more after. Retaliations, as well. But I haven't heard anything definitively." *Has anyone*, he wonders.

"What about the radio? Is anyone transmitting?" Sam speaks knowledgeably, but Daniel suspects he's relying on video games for his understanding of this brave new world—the one about a zombie apocalypse, maybe, that they forbade him playing when Ruby was in the room; Daniel vaguely recalls a scene on the screen of an NPC transmitting with a radio.

As for the radio now...? "I don't actually know," he admits in surprise. He hasn't even thought about the radio; he's been on a bike for the last two weeks, and before that, when he'd been driving from the cottage to the border, he'd had no reception. A few days ago outside Utica he'd met Tom, a kind man, who had a ham radio and had given him news about how military reserves had been called up, then had refused to serve and dispersed. Not a good sign, Daniel had reflected at the time, of things to come.

"You could try it," he suggests to Sam now, and his son gives him the wry and slightly patronizing look teenagers have perfected for their parents, as if Daniel is so outdated and dumb for not thinking of this, but it's still kind of cute and amusing. *Parents*.

Sam leans over to turn on the car radio, and a burst of static issues from the speaker like gunfire, making Daniel jump a little.

"Easy there, Dad," Sam chuckles, clearly amused by his over-the-top response. "You know, you're looking kind of rough," he adds, his amusement now laced with sympathy. "When did you last shower?"

Shower? Daniel turns to give him a look of complete incredulity. "Were there showers at college?" he asks, recalling Sam had just said something about showers limited to two minutes, but he hadn't really taken it in. Showers. It feels like an alien concept. "After the bombings?" he clarifies.

"Yeah, I mean they were *limited*," Sam replies. "But Clarkson has this whole eco thing going on. They had these rainwater harvesting showers that were totally off grid. I mean, they were *cold*, and you got, like, ten seconds in them, but yeah." It's more than Daniel has had in a month.

Sam twiddles the dial of the radio. More static. "I was wondering if the radio circuitry was destroyed by an EMP," he continues conversationally. "An electromagnetic pulse," he explains kindly, and Daniel forces a smile.

"I know what an EMP is."

"But they were saying that didn't happen," Sam goes on, as the static continues on various volumes. "And cars are still working too, even though an EMP is supposed to take them out. At least, the modern ones."

"How did you learn that?" Daniel asks mildly. "Playing *Atom RPG*, or *The Last of Us*?"

Sam glances at him, momentarily confused, and then a flash of something like hurt crosses his face before he turns back to the radio. "Actually, those video games are pretty realistic," he says in a voice that to Daniel sounds deliberately mild but still needled with hurt. "A lot of research goes into making them."

"I know." Daniel feels he should apologize, but he can't quite make himself, even though he didn't mean to sound so cutting. "You're probably more prepared for this kind of thing than I am," he tells his son, an olive branch offered. "I'm getting all my information from disaster movies."

"Yeah, those aren't very realistic," Sam replies sagely, as if video games are so much better. He straightens. "So, what did you see here on the way down? I really don't know anything. Tell me what's been happening."

"They really didn't keep you informed at Clarkson?" Now he is the one keeping his voice deliberately mild.

"No, they didn't like to tell us anything, at least not after the first blasts." For a second Sam's seemingly unconcerned manner drops, and he looks serious, even sad. "Too many deaths, and you know, some kids were, like, *really* freaking out. They were worried about their families and stuff and just generally... 'this is bad for my mental health' took on a whole new level, you know?

They just couldn't cope. There were some suicides, even, but not anyone I know." He falls silent.

"I'm sorry." The wellbeing crises of just months ago that had dominated student services of most schools now seem lamentably laughable.

Sam shakes his head, all traces of vitality gone; he looks, Daniel thinks, like the little boy he still, in many ways, is. "New York, Boston, DC... it's so weird, to imagine," he says. "Like, is the Statue of Liberty just *gone*? I keep thinking about that, for some reason. And, like, I don't know, the Met. The Lincoln Memorial. The White House..." He trails off, his expression distant. "Do you... do you think people back home were affected? I mean..."

Daniel knows what he means. *Are they dead*? "I don't know that they were affected by the bombs themselves," he replies carefully, "but everyone has been affected now, Sam. No water, no electricity, no internet, no government..." He trails off, too tired to go on.

"No government? For real?" Again Sam's voice lilts a little with something like interest, making Daniel grit his teeth.

"As far as I can tell. There are roving gangs, homegrown militias, that sort of thing. I saw some redneck guys with AR-10s and a lot of camo gear holed up in a Walmart." He lets out a huff of laughter even though nothing about it is funny. Maybe Sam has the right attitude, he thinks. Maybe the only way to survive is to view this new world as a video game. Unfortunately, in this version, you only have one life. There's no reboot to reality.

"Someone told me the army tried to take control early on," he continues, "but there just wasn't the will. We've got out of the habit of sacrificing ourselves for a greater good no one seems to believe in anymore." He thinks of the years, decades, of disaffection with government, with religion, with any kind of authority. This is where they have all ended up, and he's not sure how they're going to get out of it.

Then he recalls Tom and his family who he met outside Utica, their quiet faith and kindness, and he wonders if he might be able to stop by and see them again. Show them he managed to find his son, after all. The thought of such a reunion almost makes him smile.

"Wow," Sam breathes, sounding awed. "The whole military just... *bailed?*"

"Well, I don't know exactly," Daniel backtracks as he accepts the near limitless extent of his ignorance. "Probably some died attempting to contain the blast zones, or help people affected. And others could be mobilizing somewhere else, away from the radiation. All my news has been very much local." And very, very limited. "But," he adds, by the way of agreement, "it's all been pretty crazy and intense." He keeps his voice mild, hating that, now that he has finally found Sam, he is struggling with some weird kind of resentment. What is *wrong* with him? Sam is nineteen years old, has been isolated on a college campus for the last three and a half weeks. He can't possibly grasp the enormity of what has happened, or what it means, and Daniel is glad of that. Of course he is.

A sudden change in the static from the radio has them both jumping this time, and then they still as a voice comes on, in the middle of a speech: "...in affected areas, windows and doors should remain closed and individuals should only go outside if it is absolutely necessary. Electricity and running water will be re-established as soon as possible in all areas outside of a ten-mile radius of the blast zones. The government is also working on restoring infrastructure for telephone and internet services across the country. Martial law remains in effect, with no one to be outside after seven p.m. at night, but fresh water, food supplies, and medical aid are available between nine a.m. and five p.m. in the following locations: US army base at Fort Drum, US air force base in West Leyden, Elihu Root Army Reserve Center in Utica..." The list goes on, a monotone drone, of places in central and upstate New York.

At the end of the list, the announcement starts again: "This is an announcement regarding the recent nuclear detonations across the United States of America. This announcement serves all areas in central and upstate New York..." Daniel realizes it's a recording played on a loop.

"That's good," Sam says as he turns down the volume on the recording. "There's some organization happening, at least, right? It's not as bad as you thought."

"I guess," Daniel replies. He wants to be heartened by what they just heard, but he feels numb. "We can stop by the one in Utica," he tells Sam. "Get some supplies." A flicker of hope licks through him, a forgotten feeling. Maybe the journey back will be easier than getting to Sam was. Four weeks on, the government is finally getting its act together, offering services and aid. They can stock up on food and fresh water, maybe even gas. Maybe they can drive all the way back to the bridge, at least, before they have to find a way across. Maybe, he thinks, the bridge will even be open; he hopes Sam thought to bring his passport. His mind races with possibility, with the tantalizing prospect of things being normal, even easy, or at least easier.

Another voice, a woman's, ragged and pleading, suddenly comes on the radio, staticky and panicked. "Can someone please help? My daughter has been shot and I'm scared she's going to die. I'm at 1401 Taylor Avenue in Utica... please, anyone... if you have medical supplies, any training, anything, please..." The woman's voice chokes.

"1401 Taylor Avenue," Sam repeats, lurching upright. "Dad, we have to go."

To his shame, Daniel hesitates. They're at least ten miles away from Utica.

"Dad," Sam says again, insistent now, as well as shocked. "We have to go. We have to help, if we can. Someone's been *shot*."

"We can... swing by, I guess," Daniel says, wishing he wasn't so reluctant, but he is desperate to get back to Alex, to Ruby and Mattie. He wants his son, his whole family, safe, and driving into the center of Utica, which he strongly suspects is crawling with homegrown militias and wild-eyed gangs, to help a stranger who has been shot is not on his agenda. But neither is the look of shocked disappointment in his son's eyes.

"Okay," he says, relenting. "We can try to find it. We don't have GPS, and I don't know Utica."

Almost as if the woman on the radio heard him she restarts, her voice sounding stronger. "Please, if someone can help my daughter... I'm on Taylor Avenue, near the intersection with Square Street, across from the St. Agnes Cemetery. Someone, please..."

"We can find that," Sam says with far more confidence than Daniel feels.

"Sam..." he begins, but he doesn't know how to explain all he is afraid of, has already experienced—the barricaded roads, the roving militias and gangs, the violence everywhere, like a ripcord has been pulled on humanity's savagery, and there's no stuffing it back in.

And, he discovers ten seconds later, he doesn't have to explain, because they experience it themselves. The windshield shatters without warning, sending a shower of cubes of safety glass over them. Daniel careens off the road, the SUV lurching wildly from side to side as he realizes they—whoever *they* is— must have shot out the windows. Thank God neither of them was hit. Sam is holding on to the door handle, pale, wild-eyed, his mouth gaping in shock.

The car screeches to a stop, but before Daniel can even

draw a breath his door is wrenched open, and he feels the cold kiss of a rifle muzzle against his temple.

"Get out of the car," a voice growls.

FIVE

ALEX

As the sun rises on the second day in Kawartha, I steal down to the water's edge again, savoring a moment's peace and solitude, although my heart is still heavy, like a leaden weight inside of me. So much has happened in such a short space of time that it's all still hitting me in waves of shock—the attack, the deaths, the loss of my childhood home and the life we'd built there for ourselves in the wake of the holocaust.

I think of the greenhouse that was Ruby's pride and joy, the smokehouse Justine helped us build, the strawberries Mattie and I picked, the ersatz coffee Kerry and I made from cleavers, the beaver I forced myself to gut and skin for meat... so many ways in which we rose to the challenges, and, like Mattie had wryly said, *thrived*. But it's all gone now.

The cottage is nothing but ruins and ash; I burned it down myself, rather than let those redneck thugs take it for themselves. I spent every summer of my childhood at that cottage—running barefoot to the beach, diving deep beneath the water, lying flat on my back on the deck as I gazed up at a sky full of stars. People say no one can take your memories from you, but, in a way, they can.

Already I feel them blurring at the edges, fading the way old photographs do, to a washed-out sepia so the images are barely there. When I think of the wilderness girl I was back then, with bramble scratches on my arms and strawberry stains on my chin, she seems like a ghost, or a character from a story. I reclaimed her a little, over the last few months, because I had to, but she's gone now, just like the cottage, and this person in her place is hard-faced and flinty-eyed. I don't like her much, but maybe it's who I need to be, because, rather than waste time thinking about the past and what *was*, I need to concern myself with the future and what is—or could be.

I sit back on my heels as I gaze at the stream tumbling and splashing over rocks, a stand of slender birches on the other side of the water, and think about the journey we are going to have to make. Two hundred and fifty miles, give or take a few, to the military base fifty miles south of Buffalo, only just out of a potential blast zone, a fact that makes me both cautious and anxious. We'll have to cross Lake Ontario, thirty miles of open water, and we don't even have a boat. I can't imagine it's all that easy to stroll up to a marina and jump in a motorboat just waiting for us.

Plus, we'll have to leave this truck behind, which is something else I don't like. Without a vehicle, we are as vulnerable as if we were naked. How will we travel the last ninety or so miles to this semi-mythical base? By *foot*?

More than any of that, though, is the fear I have at facing the outside world. Every time I've done it before, to investigate or get supplies, it's ended in disaster. What might await us as we travel south to Buffalo? And barring any attacks, will we even have enough food? What if someone gets hurts or sick? Kyle's bullet wound might get infected; Phoebe could catch pneumonia. *Anything* could happen. Disaster feels like it is a mere second away.

I hear a sound behind me, and this time I don't whirl

around, rifle drawn. I make myself turn around slowly, and smile at the sight of my tangle-haired daughter picking her way through the weeds.

"Hey, Rubes."

She smiles faintly but doesn't speak as she joins me at the stream's edge. I watch her, noticing how much she's grown; her long legs are slender and coltish and the clothes we brought back in November don't fit her anymore. I cut off an old pair of jeans for shorts, and she's been living in those and a couple of t-shirts that I can see pull across her shoulders and barely brush her navel. Never mind food, where will we get clothes for her? Mattie can give her some of hers, but after seven months everything we own is already worn and shabby.

There were a few of my parents' clothes in the cottage that we took with us, packed in the car in case of an attack, like what actually happened, but it's not enough. And what about Phoebe? She'll grow and grow, and we only have a handful of toddler clothes Justine had brought that she's already growing out of.

Ruby crouches at the stream's edge and then glances over her shoulder at me, motioning with a hand.

"Did you find something?" I ask as I stir myself to join her. Clothes, I think again, are only one small part of the complicated problem. There are so many other things we'll run out of, and that's if we even have them in the first place—gas, medicine, *food*. You can only pretend-play pioneers for so long, especially when your meals are mainly leaves and roots with a few potatoes, and you're on the run.

Ruby is holding a cattail, its brown, fuzzy head pinched under her thumb. "Is it edible?" I ask, and she nods, smiling. In the last few months, since the start of spring, she's been studying a book on useful plants that she found in the bookcase at the cottage, collecting a few specimens, trying out recipes for food and medicine, along with household basics. She's made dish soap from soapwort, antiseptic from chamomile, and tea from spicebush. Admittedly, I'd much rather buy it all from Costco, but I'm grateful for her interest and willingness, mashing and boiling and steeping various weed-like plants to make something we're all willing to try, even if none of it is very filling.

"So what do you do with cattail?" I ask. "Bake it, grind it into flour, or eat it raw with ranch dressing?" I'm only half-teasing; all three of those suggestions were in the book, for various plants.

"Boil it, I think," Ruby replies, her voice little more than a whisper that the breeze tugs away. I try to think of the last time she spoke, and I can't remember. It's been a few days and so I'm heartened that she answered me at all. "We can make porridge with it."

"Cattail porridge!" I rub my stomach theatrically. "Yum. Shall we pick some? How much do we need?"

"Four or five stalks each," she decides, and we spend a companionable twenty minutes gathering cattails, pulling them up from the muddy bank of the stream with a soft sucking sound as the roots come free. The edges of the leaves are sharp, though, and I give myself several papercuts. Some part of me perversely welcomes the pain.

When we both have arms full of the plants, we head up the bank, back through the woods, to the campsite. Mattie is sitting by the fire, carefully combing Phoebe's dark hair; the little girl is perched in her lap, utterly still. Kyle is still asleep in the truck, his clothes stiff with dried sweat, but he's broken his fever, at least. Daniel and Sam are organizing our supplies in the back of the truck; yesterday we just threw everything in there, but today we need order. We need a plan.

"So show me how to do it," I instruct Ruby, and she glances at me shyly, clearly pleased to be in charge. Wordlessly she sets about her work—stripping the cattails of their outer bark to reveal creamy white stalks that do look fairly edible, if not quite delicious or filling.

She sets a pot of water over the campfire and stirs up the coals, every inch the competent pioneer woman who knows what she's doing. More than I do, anyway.

"Are we eating those?" Mattie asks, making a face, as Ruby starts chopping the stalks.

"We have to use our natural food sources when we can," I tell her, trying to ignore the worry that needles through me as I consider what will happen when there is no food. If we don't make it to the base in Buffalo, or it doesn't exist, or something, *anything*, happens. I keep my voice light as I continue, "I hear they taste just like chicken."

Mattie rolls her eyes. "Mom, they're plants."

"Okay, like potatoes, then. Or actually," I amend, remembering what Ruby said, "like porridge."

She raises her eyebrows. "You have no idea, do you?"

I give her a grin. "Nope."

A smile flickers about Mattie's mouth, and my grin widens; despite all the anxieties that continue to dog me, I feel heartened. Yesterday my children seemed alienated from me, stubbornly spinning in their own orbits, but today I feel as if we're gaining back old ground. I glance toward Sam, but he's focused on the task at hand, stacking plastic crates of supplies by the truck.

I breathe out and turn back to Ruby. "So boiled cattails for breakfast? Maybe I can find some berries to go with them." I glance at Mattie. "Mattie? Why don't you come pick with me?"

Mattie frowns, her arm wrapped around Phoebe's waist as she strokes the little girl's silky hair. "I can't leave Phoebe."

Can't? I glance at the little girl with her straight, dark hair and deep brown eyes; the look on her face is completely expressionless, unfocused, as if she's not entirely here. It worries me.

"Let's bring Phoebe with us, then," I tell Mattie. I crouch in front of the little girl, feeling ashamed that I don't know her better. And even worse, that part of me is viewing her as a potential burden rather than a human being worthy of love, care, and attention.

"Hey, Phoebe, sweetheart," I say gently. "Do you want to pick strawberries with Mattie and me?"

Phoebe gazes at me with her big, dark eyes and beyond that unnerving blankness I see a flicker of wariness, even suspicion. She doesn't trust me, and I'm not sure I blame her. You can't fool a child.

"Well?" I ask, raising my eyebrows, doing my best to sound playful. "What about it? Shall we go find some yummy berries for breakfast?"

Slowly, with firm decisiveness, she shakes her head. A breath escapes me, my exasperation revealed. Mattie gives me a sharp look.

"I don't mind staying here," she says.

"Phoebe can help me," Ruby interjects softly. That's the second time she's spoken in the space of an hour. Today is a good day.

Mattie glances between Ruby and me as Phoebe slips off her lap and joins Ruby by the campfire. Mattie shrugs. "Fine," she says, and rises from the ground.

We leave Phoebe helping Ruby, Sam and Daniel still working by the truck, Kyle asleep, as we head to a meadow further downstream. I don't know if there are tiny strawberries nestled among the long grass, but I hope so.

"How are you doing, Mattie?" I ask quietly as we wade through the grass under a bright blue sky, my tone meaningful enough for her to realize, I hope, that I want an honest answer, considering everything we've endured. Everything we've lost.

"How am I doing?" Mattie repeats thoughtfully. "Well, let's see. Yesterday I was attacked by a gang, my grandmother and two friends all died, my home burned down, and I had to run for my life." She smacks her forehead like she's forgotten something. "Oh, and the other thing is, there's this nuclear holocaust thing going on. But you know, *besides* all that..." She trails off, giving me a look that is half humor, half teenaged *well-duh*, and I let out a little laugh of acknowledgement.

"Yeah, so besides that," I amend, and my daughter laughs, the sound as clear as a bell ringing through the bright morning air. My heart lightens, like a balloon floating up inside me.

Mattie's laughter subsides as she shakes her head, and her expression turns pinched and serious. "I keep thinking about Kerry," she admits in a low voice. "How she saw that guy aiming at me and just *dove* in front of me. I would have died if it hadn't been for her. I would have been shot." Her voice catches, and then irons out. "I feel like I didn't deserve that. She was only in her thirties. She had her whole life to live."

"She made a choice," I tell Mattie quietly. "She'd do it again in a heartbeat, I know she would."

"I know she would too," Mattie agrees on a soft, sad sigh. "But that says a lot more about her than about me."

"Well, the best thing you can do for her now is live your life to the full," I tell her firmly. "Make it count."

Mattie shoots me a dryly disbelieving look. "Did you steal that line from *Saving Private Ryan*?"

I give a guilty chuckle. "Maybe."

She shakes her head, rolling her eyes, and I smile again. The sun is warm on my head, and I am happier—if I can even use that word—than I have been since the attack, or even before that, despite all the sorrows and worries that still dog us like a dark shadow.

At the far edge of the meadow, we find berries—tiny, perfect little jewels nestled deep in the long grass. It's time-consuming and laborious, kneeling on the hard ground and liberating each berry from its nestled home of leaves, but we manage to pick a half a cupful, working in companionable silence as the sun beats down. There's enough for everyone to have a spoonful or two on top of their cattail porridge, which we'll all hopefully be able to choke down.

As we head back to the campsite, I ask Mattie, keeping my tone as casual as I can make it, "How is Sam doing with that processing?"

Once again I'm the recipient of an eye-roll. "Nice one, Mom," she says, shaking her head. "Smooth, really smooth." She lets out a short sigh. "He's okay."

"Does he talk to you?"

She shrugs. "Not really."

"Then how do you know?"

"I just know."

"What... what exactly is he processing?" I hold up a hand to forestall the usual sarcastic reply. "I know the stuff that happened at the cottage, the attack, all that. Obviously those are huge things that have happened. But..." I take a breath and force myself on. "I feel like he's... mad at me, for... for what happened out on that road." It hurts to say it.

"You mean you and Dad killing a guy, maybe two?" Mattie replies with deliberate bluntness, and I can't help but flinch.

"They were a potential threat to us, Mattie—"

"But what if they weren't," my daughter interjects, her tone turning almost gentle. "I mean, I get that you couldn't have known, I thought they were dangerous too, and I said as much, but... I think that's what Sam is upset about. He showed me something he found in the truck, tucked into the visor, on the driver's side. Some Bible verse or something." She is silent for a moment while I absorb what she has just told me, what it might mean. "They could have been good guys," she finishes quietly. "Which kind of sucks."

Of course, I tell myself, a Bible verse on someone's sun visor doesn't necessarily mean anything. I wouldn't be surprised if a good portion of the gun-toting gangs we've run into have had

Bible verses on their walls handstitched by their wives, or verse-a-day calendars by their kitchen sinks. When I went to the little church with my parents up here, at least half the congregation members were carrying.

Still, it shakes me. I'm quiet as we keep walking back, the long grass whispering against our bare legs, the sky so blue it hurts to look at it. The air is full of sound—the chirp and chatter of birds, the rustle of the grass and the wind in the trees, the insistent buzz of crickets a constant chorus.

"Sam'll get over it, Mom," Mattie says after we've walked in silence for a few minutes. "Just give him time."

I nod jerkily, not trusting myself to speak. I feel guilty, yes, but I'm also angry, or maybe just resentful. I might have made a mistake, an enormous one, but I had a *reason*. A good reason, so why should my own child be judge and jury over me, even as I recognize that I'm judging myself? That sense of self-righteousness flares high and hot for a single instant and then burns right out, so all I feel is that wretched, acidic churn of guilt in my stomach. I might have killed an innocent man—and my children saw me do it.

Back at the campsite, Ruby has made a mushy sort of porridge out of the cattails, which taste kind of like a bitter cucumber. The berries help, at least. We all eat it without complaining, even Phoebe, scraping our bowls out. Even though I didn't feel hungry, I realize I was.

Afterwards, Mattie, Ruby, and I gather the dishes to go back down to the stream to wash them while Daniel and Sam continue organizing our supplies. Before we head down, I check on Kyle, and give him some water and porridge. He manages a few spoonfuls before he blinks up at me blearily.

"Sorry to be such a mess..."

"It's not your fault, Kyle." I wipe his forehead, trying not to wrinkle my nose at the smell of him. He needs to wash in the cold, clear water of the stream, but that can wait until he's stronger.

"What's happening?" he asks. "Have those guys... the cottage..."

"The cottage burned down," I remind him gently. I'm not sure how much he took in yesterday, when it was all going down, a blur of chaos and fear. Kyle had been the lookout at the barn, so he wasn't there when they started shooting. "I don't know about those guys," I tell him, "but we're a hundred miles away from them now, and I think they're more of a homegrown gang. I doubt they stray far from their little patch."

He nods as his eyes flutter closed. "Kerry..."

Kerry was the only relative he had left. His parents almost certainly died back in the Miami blast, where they'd had a condo.

"I'm sorry, Kyle," I say quietly. "She was a good friend. A good woman."

He nods, gulping, his brown eyes glassy with tears before he closes them again, and it takes me a few seconds to realize he's fallen back asleep. I glance down at him, filled with a sudden, surprising tenderness for this boy-man. He's only nineteen years old, the same age as Sam, although the two are totally different in personality and experience. Kyle lived by himself in a shabby, dirty apartment in Corville, aimless, jobless, hopeless.

When we found him he was slumped in a chair, having no idea what to do without electricity or running water, just waiting for something to happen. Not every kid who grew up in rural Ontario knows how to shoot game or survive in the wilderness or any of that kind of stuff; Kyle certainly didn't. But he came into his own over the last few months, his weedy frame filling out as he grew both in stature and confidence, learning the skills we all had to, so we could survive in this brave new world. Gently I dab his forehead again and then I leave him to sleep.

Mattie, Ruby, and I lug the dishes down to the stream, with Phoebe following along behind us. The day is turning hot, and dragonflies hover over the stream, the sunlight catching their transparent wings before they flit away, dodging and weaving over the water, an elegant insect ballet.

We kneel on the bank of the stream and start washing the dishes; Mattie rinses, Ruby scrubs with the soapwort she made weeks ago, and I dry. Soapwort is a plant that looks like a weed to me, but, according to her book, when you simmer the leaves and strain the liquid, then whisk it till frothy, it more or less acts like soap. It's what we've been using for the last two months, since the dish soap ran out. I'm glad for it now.

Kneeling there with my daughters, working in harmony, I feel the tight knot of anxiety, guilt, and fear inside me start to loosen, just a little. If I don't think about the past or worry about the future, I can breathe. I can feel, if not quite content, then close enough.

But of course it doesn't last. When we head back up to the campsite, Daniel and Sam have finished organizing the crates, and Mattie and Ruby start playing a game of hide and seek with Phoebe. I check on Kyle again, and see that he's sleeping; and then, steeling myself, I flip down the visor on the driver's side of the truck. A photograph flutters out and I pick it up, blink the image into focus.

It's of a young woman with blond hair and three little kids— two girls and a boy, just like my family. The oldest girl has blond braids, the boy a pie-eating grin and a gap between his front teeth. The littlest girl is little more than a toddler, chubby and rosy-cheeked, sitting on her sister's lap. The mother stands behind them all, beaming but looking a little tired. They're all in front of one of those cheesy photographic studio backdrops, a mottled blue screen.

I stare at that photo, and I taste bile, as the guilt rushes through me all over again, worse than ever. I was so concerned about how *my* kids would see me, how they might judge me. Now I feel the far greater weight of the family I deprived of a father, the wife of her husband. All because I was scared and angry and just a little too trigger-happy... that is, if he really was a good guy. Is there any way for me to ever know?

Still, no matter how I try to spin it to myself as well as my children, right now I know there's no other way to look at it. No other way to feel.

I'm a murderer.

SIX

In some alternate universe, I'd luxuriate in feelings of guilt and ideas of atonement, indulging in various ways to somehow make peace with the fact that I killed a man who might have—maybe even most likely—been trying to help me. Maybe I'd meditate or plant a tree or summon a prayer. I'd let go of my bad feelings, surrender them to the universe, accept my guilt as well as my release from it.

But that is not this world, and so I slip the photo back in the visor, barely glancing at the Bible verse written on an index card next to it. *Habakkuk 3:17–18*, the reference reads, but it's not one I know, not that I know many at all. I'm not about to look up this one.

I walk away from the truck without looking back.

"So, what's the plan?" I ask Daniel briskly, clenching my hands into fists at my sides before I deliberately uncurl them. Sam is standing nearby, watching us both, his expression wary yet alert. "We leave tomorrow for Port Granby?"

Daniel glances at me, his expression both guarded and appraising, clearly trying to gauge my mood. I feel determined but anxious, strong yet fragile, like I could splinter into a million pieces and yet still keep going. I lift my chin as I keep his gaze. "Well?"

"I thought we said we'd stay here for a few more days?" he asks. "Gather food, let Kyle rest, make sure we have what we need for the journey."

"The longer we stay here, the more supplies we'll use," I point out. And we don't have that many, maybe not even enough, to begin with. But it isn't really our supplies I'm thinking about; it's this edginess inside me. I'm not sure why, but I feel an urge to *move*, maybe just to escape the memories that I already know will come with me.

"That's true," Daniel replies equably enough, "but we can live off the land here, for a little while at least. Trap, fish, hunt."

I eye him skeptically. He's a pretty good shot, but he hasn't, as far as I know, *lived off the land* the way we'd been doing before I let the cottage burn to the ground. And while we did bring a couple of rabbit snares and fishing poles with us, it's not like we'll be living large on what we can eke out here in the woods.

A tiny smile quirks Daniel's mouth as he seems to read my thought process with the accuracy that only comes with twenty years of marriage. "You know I've always wanted to be on one of those TV survival shows," he reminds me. "This is my big chance."

A laugh escapes me, an unruly, unexpected sound. "Okay," I reply. After all, the journey to Port Granby and beyond is fraught with uncertainty and danger. Why would I rush into such a thing? I crave safety, and this is probably the closest we're going to get to it... until we reach that base, if it even exists. And yet... we have to catch a lot of fish, and trap a ton of rabbits, just to keep our bellies even half-full. "Okay," I say again, and then, doing my best to keep my voice light and my manner relaxed, and probably failing at both, I turn to Sam. "Can I talk to you for a sec?"

"Wh... what?" He hunches his shoulders away from me, looks both startled and reluctant.

"Just a second, Sam. That's all." I take hold of his elbow like he's a little boy and lead him a little bit away from the campsite to the privacy provided by the drooping boughs of a nearby cedar.

The pungent smell of the needles, with their distinctive notes of balsam and camphor, brings me right back to my childhood, when I'd made a fort under a cedar tree at the cottage. I can picture the little set-up I had—a rough wooden stool, an old medicine cupboard my dad gave me to store my treasures—a pinecone, a smooth stone, a jagged piece of bright blue robin's eggshell. I blink the memories away and look at my son.

"Sam, I'm sorry about yesterday," I tell him. I keep my tone quietly matter-of-fact. "The shooting. The killing." Just like Mattie, I'm going to be blunt. Now is not the time for euphemisms. "I know it was shocking—"

"Mom." He cuts me off, sounding both impatient and disgusted. "You don't know anything."

I blink, doing my best to absorb that statement and whatever it means. "Maybe not," I agree evenly, "but you haven't been yourself with me since yesterday—"

"Mom!" he interjects again, and now he sounds angry. "Yesterday people *died*, our house burned down... I mean, what do you *expect*?"

It's the same sentiment Mattie expressed, but with far more fury.

I take a deep breath and then let it out slowly. "I know all that, Sam, believe me," I tell him levelly. "I just... I just want to make sure we're good." I gesture to the space between us while my son's lip curls. For a second, I experience the dizzying sensation of some kind of time warp; we could be in the basement rec room of our old house, the deep-pile carpet littered with dirty socks and cereal bowls, Sam slouched in the L-shaped leather sofa, the two of us arguing about when he's going to turn off his PlayStation and go to bed.

"We're good," he states flatly, and then he turns and walks away, not back to the campsite but further into the woods. Even though my instinct, my *need*, is to call him back and keep him safe, I let him go.

I'd wanted to clear the air, but I feel like everything I said was wrong and just made things more complicated between us. At least I tried, I tell myself, and I walk back to where Mattie is playing pat-a-cake with Phoebe.

"Do you want a break?" I ask her. "I can play with Phoebe for a little while." I glance at the little girl, who gives me the same serious-eyed, wary look as before. I don't think she wants to play with me.

Mattie shakes her head. "We're good," she says, and I wonder if she overheard Sam say the same thing. My children are brushing me off again, but maybe I just need to let them do it. Everyone *processes* in different ways. Maybe this is part of it, even if it hurts.

I spend the afternoon collecting plants with Ruby; she brings along her book and gives me a tutorial in various specimens, although I feel pretty hopeless at it all. They all look the same to me—green and weedy—but Ruby has a knack for telling the difference between them, even different kinds of the same plant, which is a good thing because staghorn sumac can be used as a spice or made into a tea, but poison sumac is, as the name suggests, poisonous. The only way to tell the difference is from the edges of the leaves. I'm putting a lot of trust in my twelve-year-old daughter, but her quiet confidence both inspires and soothes me, especially after that confrontation with Sam.

By late afternoon, we have collected a whole range of plants with different uses—cleavers to grind into coffee, sumac for tea and seasoning, pineapple-weed to sprinkle on any fresh meat we get to keep it from spoiling, and narrow-leaved plantain, whose leaves can be boiled, its seeds dried and ground into flour. I'm both encouraged by how much there is that's edible and dispirited at just how much effort it all takes. We've gathered enough plantain to make about a tablespoon of flour from its seeds, and a pot of boiled leaves is not, I already know, a satisfying dinner. Still, it's progress, and Ruby seems very pleased with our haul.

Back at the campsite, Phoebe is curled up on a sleeping bag, fast asleep, her thumb plugged into her mouth, and I can't see anyone else around. For a second, panic seizes me like a vise, makes it hard to breathe. Where are they all?

Then I see a dark head in the front of the truck, and I realize Mattie is sitting on the driver's side, Kyle half-seated, half-slumped next to her as they chat. I stride over to the truck and stand in the open doorway of the driver's side, my hands on my hips. "Where are Dad and Sam?" I ask Mattie, my voice coming out sharper than I mean it to because of my fear.

Mattie's eyes widen in surprise and then flash with annoyance. "Dad and Sam went to set some rabbit snares," she tells me in a tone that suggests she wants me gone, *now*. Kyle gives me a half-hearted smile and tries to sit up a little more.

I glance between the two of them and something in me startles, shifts; there's a companionship, even an intimacy, between them that I haven't seen before. Mattie generally tolerated Kyle, had a certain long-suffering sympathy for his general air of patheticness, but she didn't *like* him. They weren't friends, except, I recall, they did work together on the smokehouse, and Mattie taught Kyle how to shoot, seeming to enjoy being the one in the know.

A dozen other memories shuffle through my mind like a pack of cards—Mattie and Kyle having a lively debate about the best *Archie* comics in the loft, relics from my own childhood. Daring each other to jump in the lake a few weeks ago, even though the water was absolutely freezing. Banging out songs together on the very old, very out-of-tune piano on the porch, collapsing into gales of laughter at how bad they both sounded.

I'm stupefied, disquieted too, although I'm not sure why. Why shouldn't they be friends... or even something more? Not that I think that's what is going on here, exactly, but... I suppose it could be a possibility, one day. It's not like there are a lot of others... and yet I resist. I'm not ready, not remotely ready, to deal with that kind of complication.

"Hey," I say to Kyle, several seconds too late. "You seem to be feeling better."

"Yeah." He smiles shamefacedly, like it was his fault for getting shot. "My shoulder's pretty sore still, but I think I'll be up and at it tomorrow. I can help with some stuff, maybe."

"You take your time," I reassure him. I glance at Mattie and see that she is scowling at me. "How long has Phoebe been asleep?" I ask.

She shrugs. "An hour?"

Is that how long Mattie's been in this truck with Kyle? Again the disquiet, and I tell myself not to be stupid about this. I alienated my daughter once already because of a bad boyfriend, back in Connecticut; I'm not about to do it again, and besides, Kyle isn't actually her boyfriend *or* bad. There is absolutely no need to overreact about this; in some ways, it's almost funny, the age-old reaction of a mother to stumbling across her daughter sitting a little too close to a boy, never mind the nuclear holocaust we're living through.

"Okay," I say, and, with Mattie still giving me a stare simmering with resentment, I finally back off.

Ruby and I spend the next hour making dinner, which is another hodgepodge stew of root vegetables we gathered, a potato or two from our limited supply, and a tiny bit of dried meat. I hope Daniel and Sam's snares work, because we could definitely all do with some protein; just as I feared, living off the land is not going to feed us properly for very long, if at all.

I haven't looked in a mirror lately, and I avoided the ones at the cottage after the first few months, because things were hard enough without having to study my grim reflection. I know my hair is now almost entirely gray; coarse too, most likely from a lack of calcium. My skin is weathered and dry, my face seamed with deeper lines and wrinkles, and a few weeks ago I spat out a tooth that had come loose, again most likely from a calcium deficiency. At least it was a molar rather than one in the front of my mouth, I told myself, but it had felt shocking, like something that shouldn't happen to someone like me—a middle-class woman with a very good dentist and a certain appearance to keep up, although of course none of that counts for anything now.

At least I've shed the stubborn ten pounds that had stuck around my middle for the last five years. Thanks to a diet of dried meat and meals like cattail porridge, I'm wiry and lean, verging on positively stringy. I've had to hold my shorts up with a piece of twine; my hips jut out like a supermodel's, without any of the accompanying gloss or glamor.

When Sam and Daniel come back a little while later, they have no rabbit, although they're hopeful there will be something in the snares tomorrow. Daniel is quietly approving of Ruby's industry, rumpling her hair, and is rewarded with a shyly beaming smile. Mattie sidles out of the truck and comes up to me as I get out the plates for dinner.

"Honestly, Mom, you are *so* embarrassing," she hisses. "I could totally tell what you were thinking!" Her face is flushed, her tone melodramatically indignant. "As *if* I'd have Kyle for my boyfriend! Come *on!*"

"Okay," I reply cautiously, but she is already flouncing away.

I shake my head as I catch Daniel's bemused gaze.

"What was that about?" he asks.

"Typical teenaged drama," I reply with a smile, and he laughs, a soft sound that makes me ache because it reminds me of how we used to be, finding humor amid the hardness, sharing each other's thoughts, not even needing to say them out loud. I want that Daniel back, even though I'd been so angry at him for hiding so much from me—the loss of his job, the second mortgage, our house being given back to the bank. None of that matters now. I just want to see my husband smile. I want to laugh with him; I want to feel his arms around me. We've barely touched since he returned with Sam; I'm not sure we'd even know how.

Over the next few days, however, I start to get glimpses of how Daniel and I used to be, and, more importantly, how we *could* be. The warm weather holds, and the days are full of gathering plants, picking berries, grinding seeds into flour, and boiling what still look like weeds to me for whatever purpose Ruby has determined. Daniel and Sam come back with two rabbits, and the next day Kyle, who still moves gingerly, wincing at the pain in his shoulder, is most definitely on the mend, and even manages to catch three small brook trout. We fry them up nice and crispy, picking through the tiny bones for the succulent bits of flesh.

It's not really enough food, but we all act like it is, because we all need a break from the anxiety, the fear and even the hunger. This feels, almost, like a vacation, even though it is anything but. The future looms in front of us, enormous and uncertain, but for a few days everybody is willing not to think about it.

Phoebe sticks close to Mattie, who has taken on all mothering duties; the little girl far prefers my daughter to me. I tell myself I don't mind, but part of me does. *I'm* the mom, I think, except of course when it comes to Phoebe I'm not, and I'm not sure I even want to be.

In the midst of all this busyness, there are surprisingly, and thankfully, moments of both joy and grace. We all go swimming, and Daniel even fashions a rope swing from the branch of a basswood that hangs over the stream that Mattie and Sam both jump on, while Kyle watches, not willing to risk injuring his shoulder. Daniel surprises us all by agreeing to have a try. Watching my husband sail out over the water with a holler makes me laugh; it really is starting to feel like a vacation. As he emerges from the stream, shaking the droplets of water from his hair, he smiles at me.

That night, Daniel and I lie tangled together in our tent, with Sam and Kyle sharing the other one, the girls in the truck. Daniel puts his hand on my stomach like a question, and then, when I let out the tiniest of sighs, slides it upward. I arch into him, craving the feel of his arms around me, the comforting solidness of his body, although as I hold him I realize that, like me, he has become wiry and lean. His lips brush my hair. As we move together, neither of us speaks.

The next morning I'm still lying in my sleeping bag, the sun streaming through the crack in the tarp, turning the makeshift tent into a sauna, when I hear it—the sound of a motor, a distant purr, barely audible. I'm out of the tent in seconds, wild with panic, fired with purpose. Daniel, I see, is half-dressed, rifle in hand. No one else is awake.

"A car?" I ask in a low voice, and he nods.

"Or something."

"How close?"

He shakes his head. "I don't know."

We both dress quickly as the sound of the engine, wherever it is, fades in and out. First it seems to be coming from the east, then the west. It feels as if we are being circled; perhaps it's going around the main road that rings the park. There's no reason to think they'll find us; we drove across a field and parked in the woods. We haven't seen a sign of anyone in all the time we've been here.

And yet the sound of the engine drones on.

My skin grows clammy and my heart rate, which has leveled out these last few days, picks up its panicked pace. *We were so happy here*, I think, *so briefly*. Why does it have to end?

As the noise of the vehicle, whatever it is, continues, Daniel and I decide to wake up the others just in case. The dazed sleepiness of early morning is replaced by instant alertness and a focused kind of panic. Ruby gathers our food supplies, and Kyle and Sam pack up the tents, Kyle moving slowly thanks to his shoulder. Mattie, with Phoebe on her hip, tosses the sleeping bags into the back of the truck. The sound of the engine is getting louder, fading out less. Whoever it is, they're definitely getting closer.

Are they looking for us?

Daniel, Sam, Kyle, and I all act as lookouts, while the girls are ready to go, sitting in the truck.

"I can shoot, too," Mattie argues, but I shake my head, firm, as I guide her inside.

"Phoebe needs you."

My daughter doesn't argue with that; the little girl's arms are wrapped around her neck.

Daniel crouches behind the open door on the driver's side of the truck; Sam is perched in the fork of a nearby birch tree. I stand on the other side of the truck, half-hidden by the bumper. Kyle is behind a thicket of sumac. He's not healed enough to hold a rifle but Daniel, Sam, and I are all armed, our rifles trained on the stretch of open meadow we drove across to get to this hidden woodland by the stream, our brief oasis in this desert world.

The grass that had been flattened by the truck has sprung up now; there's no way to know anyone was here at all, and yet we can hear the steady hum of a vehicle, growing louder with every second, and yet barely audible over the rush of blood in my ears. It's as if they *know* we're here, hidden by the trees, yet how could they?

Then a vehicle comes into view—a gleaming black SUV, like something from the Connecticut suburbs. It bumps along the meadow straight toward us, and my finger twitches on the trigger.

I'm not going to make the same mistake twice, I tell myself, and yet, if I hold back, will it be too late? Whoever is driving the car can't be a friend. They're coming right at us. They *must* have been looking for us, I think, even though that doesn't make sense—and this car doesn't look like it came from Corville. It has New York state plates, for one, and, as it turns, I see, incongruously, a bumper sticker that states the owner of the car is a *Proud Parent of a Haldane Middle Schooler*.

I glance at Daniel, but he's focused on the car, which has now come to a stop in the middle of the meadow, a mere hundred yards or so away. The driver cuts the engine, and in the ensuing stillness I hear the trill of a cardinal, like a warning. We all wait, guns ready, hearts beating.

The driver opens the door of the car.

SEVEN

My finger is still twitching on the trigger when a tall, dark-haired man gets out of the car, stretches hugely with a jaw-cracking yawn, and then looks around him with apparent interest. I almost start to laugh. He's wearing khakis and a polo shirt, and he looks like he came for a day out in the countryside. I can't see a weapon.

What on earth?

I glance again at Daniel, and this time he shrugs back, a look of something almost like humor on his face. Neither of us was expecting someone like this. This guy is not a threat... but I don't lower my rifle. There's no point in being stupid.

The passenger door opens, and a woman emerges, glancing around more warily. She's slender and blond, her hair pulled back into a low, sleek ponytail. She's wearing expensive-looking workout gear—matching yoga pants and a zip-up hoodie in form-fitting teal Lycra. This is getting weirder and weirder.

"Come on, Ben," the woman calls, sounding tired, and the back door on the driver's side is flung open, hard enough to almost make it bounce back. I'm pretty sure a teenager is going to emerge, and I'm right. A lanky boy, maybe fifteen, comes out, shoulders hunched, shaggy blond hair sliding into his face. He shoves his hands into the pockets of his baggy jeans, which are half-sliding off his butt, revealing several inches of plaid boxer shorts.

"Where are we?" he asks in a disinterested tone, and a soft laugh escapes me like a hiccup. I'm incredulous, amused, *angry*. Who the hell are these people, and why are they here? More to the point, where have they *been* for the last seven months, that they can look so normal and sound so bored?

"Kawartha Highlands Provincial Park," the man says. His tone is jocular, jollying, a man used to being in authority. "Pretty nice place, don't you think?"

The boy shrugs, tossing his hair out of his face so I can see his dissatisfied expression, mouth downturned into something between a pout and a smirk. The woman fiddles with her rings, her hair. She seems nervous, but not in the way that we've been nervous, alert to every danger. These three people seem like they don't know what to do in the wilderness. How did they even get here?

I glance at Daniel, who is looking surprised but thoughtful, and then at Sam and Kyle, who both seem entirely dumbfounded, their rifles lowered as they stare at these people as if they're exotic creatures in a zoo, which they *are*. How can anyone be like this anymore? They don't even look hungry; they're all thin, but in a pre-apocalyptic way, when intermittent fasting was a choice and not because you didn't have any food.

"Daniel," I whisper, and he glances across at me, his expression sharpening. "What should we do?"

He shrugs in reply, which is no answer at all. We could wait for these people to leave, but they're acting as if they've stopped for good and they're only a hundred yards away from us. As soon as any one of us moves, they'll hear us. Better to take the initiative, I think, and Daniel must think it too, because he steps away from the car, out into the open meadow.

"Hey there," he says in a friendly voice. He's still holding his rifle, but it's pointed downward.

All three of the strangers turn, looking totally shocked, and then in unison, as if they'd rehearsed it, they throw their hands up in the air.

"Please, don't shoot," the man says, managing to sound commanding even when he's basically begging for his life. "We don't have anything."

The woman's face has drained of color, the boy's boredom turned to terror.

"I'm not going to shoot," Daniel tells them mildly. "But who are you, and what are you doing here?"

Slowly the man lowers his hands. "Will you put the gun down?" he asks.

"No," Daniel replies, keeping his tone pleasant. "But like I said, I won't shoot. Not unless you do."

"I'm not armed."

"Are there weapons in your car?"

He hesitates, and the seconds spin out before the woman blurts, "There are a couple of guns in the trunk, but we've never used them."

"Okay," Daniel says after a moment. He's clearly trying to get the measure of this family and failing. "Let's keep them in the trunk, then."

No one speaks and it feels like a standoff, albeit one without any of the tension of that moment on the road I'm trying to forget. This feels more like confusion, like these people don't know what to *do*.

"What are your names?" Daniel asks.

"I'm William Stratton, and this is my wife, Nicole," the man says. "And our son, Ben." They all stare at Daniel warily, clearly still worried he's going to shoot.

"Where did you come from?" Daniel asks.

A second's pause. "Cold Spring, about a hundred miles north of New York City."

Daniel nods slowly. "Why here?" he asks.

The man hesitates, and then shrugs. "We followed the map."

"What map?" The question comes sharp and fast.

William Stratton looks bemused. "Um, the 2022 AAA Road Atlas? I think?"

Daniel lets out a sound that is part laugh, part huff of disbelief. "You haven't answered my question," he says. "Why *here*?"

William Stratton stares at him, blank-faced. I step out into the meadow. His wife lets out a little shriek, and I realize I'm still aiming my rifle at them. Slowly I lower it.

"Who are you?" I demand, and my voice sounds rougher than I meant it to, almost wild. "Where have you *been* these last seven months?"

"Alex," Daniel says quietly. "Let's put down the guns."

I swing my head round to stare at him in confusion, until I realize how aggressive I seem, and how terrified this family is. I can feel Sam's gaze upon me, boring into my back. I release a shaky breath.

"Okay," I say.

Daniel takes my rifle as Sam and Kyle step out of the woods. William Stratton sucks in a breath. "How many of you are there?" he asks.

"Seven," Daniel replies. He takes Kyle and Sam's rifles and stows all our weapons in the back of the truck. I'm almost positive these people aren't a threat, but I still don't feel good about it. He turns to the Strattons, who are looking shocked by our presence. "Why don't we all sit down, and you can tell us how you came to be here," Daniel suggests.

William Stratton looks like he's not sure he wants to agree, but then he nods. "All right," he says, and he reaches for his wife's hand, drawing her forward as the three of them follow us back to the campsite.

Mattie slides out of the car holding Phoebe, and Ruby follows. After a second when no one seems to know what to do, we all hunker down by the embers of the campfire, which Daniel pokes with a stick.

"Rubes," he suggests with a smile, "do you want to make some tea?"

Smiling shyly, Ruby nods, and takes a bucket to fetch water from the stream. Everyone sits in uneasy silence until she comes back, and then fills a pot, sprinkling in some dried leaves—catnip, I think—and then sets it over the campfire, on the travel hook. Hospitality, Armageddon-style.

Then she sits down, and we all look around at each other.

"Maybe you could tell us your names," William Stratton suggests. He has the stentorian voice of a doctor or a lawyer, someone who is used to feeling important but seems to have no idea how to navigate this new world. I know I'm being cynical, but I'm pretty sure I'm right.

As for his wife? I glance at her, my lip curling just a little. She's so *manicured*, seven months after a holocaust. Her hair is sleek and shiny, her nails perfectly filed. Next to her, I feel like something chewed-up and dragged-over. Not that I'm envious. I'm just... disbelieving. It's as if the Strattons have emerged unscathed from some alternate universe, where the United States wasn't devastated by nuclear bombs and overrun by roaming gangs.

"I'm Daniel Walker," Daniel says. For a second, he looks as if he might lean over and offer to shake hands, but nobody moves.

"I'm Alex, Daniel's wife," I chip in, and then the rest of us go through our introductions. It feels like a very weird dinner party.

"How long have you all been out here?" William asks. It seems we're going to do chitchat.

"Just a few days," Daniel replies. "We were at my wife's family cottage about a hundred miles east of here, but we were attacked and so we had to move on."

William nods, his expression turning somberly understanding. So they have *some* experience of the real world, I think, because he's clearly not surprised by the concept of being attacked. "I'm sorry to hear that," he says, and my chest burns with the injustice of it all—losing the cottage to those thugs, Kerry and Justine's needless deaths... all neatly tidied away under the simple and indifferent sentiment of *I'm sorry to hear that.*

There's absolutely no reason for me to be angry with William Stratton, who had nothing to do with any of it, and yet somehow I am.

"So where have *you* been?" Daniel asks. Although his voice is as mild as before, I hear a thread of challenge in it, a hint of the same anger I've been feeling. I can almost hear the questions clamoring in Daniel's mind—*why does your shirt look ironed? Why are your wife's nails so polished?*—because they're the same ones in mine.

William hesitates, and then glances at his wife, who gives a twitchy little shrug in return. My curiosity sharpens; what is it they don't want to tell us? Ben, I see, is hunched over, staring at his feet, not wanting to engage with anyone.

"We were staying in a bunker," William admits.

"A bunker," Daniel repeats neutrally. I picture something made of Cold War concrete, cold and damp. They don't look like they were staying somewhere like that. "What kind of bunker?" he asks.

William sighs. "You remember those stories back before everything, about billionaires who had these luxury bunkers, underground?"

Vaguely I recall reading an article about how a bunker was the latest outrageously expensive gadget for your average billionaire. I don't remember anything about it, beyond my own internal eye-roll at the whole notion.

"So you were in some luxury bunker?" Sam asks, leaning forward, his voice rising with interest. "What was it like?"

"Pretty nice," William replies briefly. He looks guarded, like he doesn't want to tell us the details.

Daniel lets out a short laugh of genuine amusement. "I'll bet. I was wondering why you looked so put together." William gives a grimacing sort of smile, half apology, half embarrassment. "So what *was* it like?" Daniel presses.

"It was nice," Nicole interjects. Her voice is terse, and she doesn't look anyone in the eye. "We paid for a unit. It was *not* cheap."

I glance at her curiously, wondering why she seems so defensive. If we'd had the money to buy a unit in a luxury bunker, we would have. That is, if we could have predicted a nuclear holocaust, which we couldn't have, and in any case we didn't have any money. But I don't blame this family for trying to stay safe. That is the principle, the burning desire, that has guided me these last seven months. It's why I still struggle to look my son in the eye.

"Yeah, I heard those units go for, like, two million bucks," Sam continues with enthusiasm. William's tight jaw is all the answer we need to know his guess is not far off the mark. "And then monthly association fees," he continues. "Like, a couple of grand. I saw a YouTube video on it."

YouTube videos. In this ravaged world, it feels like he might as well have said he read about it on a papyrus scroll. "And they have all kinds of stuff," he continues, seemingly oblivious to our guests' growing tension. "Like, a gym and a movie theater and even a swimming pool. And electricity and even internet... they used this special microwave satellite thing and wind and solar power. The doors to the place were three inches thick of reinforced steel. Nothing's getting through that." I think of the wooden door to the cottage and how that gang blew it right open. "They were able to grow their own vegetables and stuff," Sam continues, his eyes alight, "and even breed fish. Aqua-something."

"Aquaponics," Ben says, the first time he's spoken. He still sounds bored, but now I wonder if that is just a cover. The curve of his cheek and the tremble of his lips remind me of how young he is, how protected he's been.

"Yeah, aquaponics!" Sam nods in enthusiasm. "That is *seriously* cool."

"It does sound cool," Daniel agrees, eyeing the Strattons consideringly. "And like a pretty good set-up." Which is a massive understatement. I'm trying to imagine getting through these last seven months in such a place, and I absolutely can't.

"It was," William agrees, as terse as his wife.

"So why did you leave?" Daniel prompts. The question is an obvious one, yet with no apparent answer.

The Strattons are all silent for a long moment. "The guy who ran it died," he finally says. "Heart attack. And then it wasn't such a good set-up." A silence falls like a weight on us. I'm afraid I think I know pretty much exactly what he means. Maybe a billionaire bunker isn't so much better than a dilapidated cottage in the backwoods, after all.

"So you just left?" Daniel says after a moment, half question, half statement. Nicole is staring at the ground, and Ben is still hunched over, his arms drawn around his knees. I can almost see the cloud of sorrow and fear hovering over them, dark and deadening.

"We were kicked out," William replies. "Someone else took over and they wanted their friends and family to have most of the units, so anyone who wasn't their friend had to go." He makes it sound like they sent them off with a gift basket and a friendly wave, but I doubt very much it happened like that. How it really went down, William doesn't seem to want to say. I don't want to think about how bad a situation like that might get. A three-inch door of reinforced steel is great until you're on the wrong side of it.

"I'm sorry to hear that," Daniel tells him, and I wonder if he is deliberately parroting William Stratton's earlier remark.

William nods, and we are all silent, no one looking at anyone else.

"So where was this bunker?" Daniel finally asks.

"In upstate New York," William replies. "Just north of Watertown."

We might have driven by it, on our way to the cottage. Maybe Daniel drove by it himself, when he went to get Sam, although I have no idea how he got Sam, or what his route was.

"So you left the bunker," Daniel says, "and you just started driving?"

William grimaces, without looking anyone in the eye. "Pretty much."

"Where did you get the car?" This from Mattie, her voice surprisingly suspicious.

"We'd left our cars on the facility site," William tells her.

"And they weren't stolen?" I interject, thinking of my dad's truck.

William shakes his head. "These places are incredibly well resourced, everything behind a huge fence, watchtowers, security cameras... you can't even imagine the level of security and technology they have at their disposal."

"And they let you take your cars?" This again from Mattie, who is sounding seriously skeptical. "*And* the guns in your trunk?"

William's mouth tightens. "They did. We carried the ammunition separately, but... they weren't totally heartless."

Nicole lets out a disbelieving huff, and he amends apologetically, "They didn't want us hanging around."

"That was pretty nice of them," Mattie mutters, and I know she's thinking of my dad's truck, too. For being kicked out of a billionaire bunker, the Stratton family doesn't seem to have suffered too much.

But then I see a flash of something like hatred across Nicole's face, and I wonder if they have suffered, just in a way that isn't obvious to us... yet.

Mattie subsides, seemingly satisfied, and again we are all silent. *What now?* I think. What are we supposed to do with these people?

"How did you get across the bridge?" Daniel asks suddenly, his tone abrupt. His eyes are narrowed; now he is the one who looks suspicious. "At Thousand Islands. You crossed there?"

William stares at him blankly. "Yes... we drove across."

"Drove?" Daniel sounds disbelieving. "The bridge was closed by the Canadian Border Services, back at the beginning."

William shakes his head. "Well, it isn't now. There wasn't anybody there at all. The whole place was abandoned. We didn't see anyone."

"Really?" I lean forward, eager now. If the Thousand Islands bridge is crossable, we can get to this base near Buffalo that way. It will be so much easier than attempting open water, never mind needing to find a boat. For the first time, I'm glad the Strattons showed up.

William looks between us all, his forehead furrowing. "How long have you guys been out here?" he asks. "Without any news?"

His tone suggests he thinks it must have been some time.

"I came across the border about a month ago," Daniel says. "Crossed at Cornwall, but it was manned then. I was traveling up from Massachusetts."

"A month ago..." William's frown deepens. "Then surely you saw some of the stuff I'm talking about."

"What kind of stuff?" I ask. For the first time, I feel like we could get some actual news of the outside world... but do I really want to hear it?

William shrugs. "Just how... abandoned... everything is now. We got news while we were in the bunker, you know, from the satellite radio. We could communicate with some of the other bunkers, too, so we had a little bit of an idea about what's been going on across the country."

"I mostly kept to myself," Daniel says. "On my own, with Sam here." He nods toward our son. He sounds like he doesn't want to say anything more about it.

"Okay..." William replies, like he can't quite believe it, which makes me wonder, far from the first time, what my husband isn't saying. What he's hiding.

Ruby stirs from where she's been sitting very still next to me. "The tea's ready," she says softly, and I rise to get some tin cups. It's time to settle in and hear what William Stratton has to tell us... and find out what the world is really like.

EIGHT

DANIEL

December, six months earlier
Outside Utica, New York

Daniel stumbles to the side of the road, his hands flung into the air, as a man he can't see presses the muzzle of a rifle to his temple. From the corner of his eye he sees another man, grizzly and bearded, pointing a semiautomatic rifle, a serious kind of weapon, at his son, and something in him both breaks and hardens at the same time. He can't believe this is happening already. He and Sam have been together for maybe ten minutes.

"Please," he says, trying not to sound like he is begging even though he knows he is. "Take the car and go."

The man chuckles, a throaty, smoke-filled sound. "Oh, we'll take what we like," he assures Daniel, and presses the muzzle of the rifle a little harder into his temple, chuckling again as he does so. He's clearly enjoying this—not just the stealing, but the inducing of fear, the relishing of control. What a pathetic power trip, Daniel thinks with a sudden, savage bitterness. What a total loser, this guy, to be getting his kicks this way. He doesn't say any of this out loud, but he feels a spurt of futile rage and he closes his eyes briefly before snapping them open, knowing he doesn't have the luxury of either regret or despair. Not now, not when his son's life is at stake.

"The keys are in the ignition," he tells the man. He forces himself to look him full in the face, yet even as he takes in his features they blur before him, so he is nothing more than a faceless body, an automaton with a gun and a grimy baseball cap. Does this man have a soul? Daniel supposes he must, but it is tattered and threadbare, judging from the relish he is showing as he moves the rifle from Daniel's temple to his midsection, prodding his belly like he's an animal at an abattoir. Again Daniel feels that blaze of rage, and forces himself to tamp it down. He's so close to snapping, and he can't, not here, not now, when he's powerless and this wannabe badass would shoot both him and Sam simply for the pleasure of it, because he can.

While the man keeps his gun trained between Daniel and Sam, the other opens the back of the car to inspect their booty. Sam makes some small sound of protest, quickly silenced. They will take it all, Daniel thinks numbly. His backpack and Sam's, along with Sam's duffel bag. Admittedly, it's not much—a couple of Slim Jims and packets of Ritz crackers are all the food he has, plus a change of clothes, a water bottle. But without those things, how will they possibly survive? And, Daniel realizes, they will take his gun. And of course the car.

The only thing they're escaping with in this situation, he knows, is their lives. And that's if they're lucky.

"Empty your pockets," the man commands, and Daniel complies. He's not so stupid as to have put anything important in his front pockets—the car keys to the SUV left back in Canada are in the inside zipped pocket of his coat, his cash, worthless as it probably now is, tucked into his pants. The man takes a handkerchief, a stick of gum, and a crumpled Slim Jim wrapper, and with a snarl hurls it all to the ground.

"Give me one good reason not to shoot you right here," he snaps, and Daniel stays silent.

The man glares at him for a moment as Daniel holds his gaze, even wonders if he sees a spark of something almost like admiration in the man's wild, red-rimmed eyes. He's on something, coke or meth or whatever it is people shoot up these days. It's a world Daniel doesn't know, even as he comes up hard against it, *again*.

The moment stretches on like an elastic about to snap, and then a canny look comes over the man's face and he grabs Daniel by the front of his coat, wrenches it open, and pats down his inside pockets, instantly feeling the bulge of the car keys. "Ah ha, so what are these to, buddy?" he asks, his breath sour in his face.

"A car two hundred miles away," Daniel replies flatly. The man is already unzipping his pocket, taking out the keys. "In a barn near Rockport, Ontario."

"Oh, yeah?" The man sneers at him, indifferent, but he takes the keys, which is so stupid and pointless Daniel could almost laugh—except he feels, suddenly and savagely, like putting his hands around this man's throat and squeezing. He wants to see his eyes pop and his tongue stick out as the breath leaves his body. He closes his eyes, willing the image away, the deep sense of satisfaction it brings.

Shouting to his partner in crime, the man clambers into the car, followed by the other, and then with a roar of the engine and a squeal of tires they are gone, down the road toward Utica. In the ensuing, wintry silence, Sam collapses to the ground, retching.

"I thought..." he gasps, wiping his mouth with the back of his hand, "I thought they were going to kill us."

"They might have," Daniel agrees. He picks up the handkerchief the man threw to the ground and hands it to Sam, who looks at him with a kind of fearful awe.

"Dad, you were so..." He trails off, shaking his head. Daniel does not ask him to finish that sentence. He was so what? Cold? Indifferent? Weary? Hopeless?

All of the above, and not the kind of man he ever wanted to be, but he can't dwell on that now. They need to obtain some kind of vehicle, as well as find shelter. It's late afternoon, the sun sinking lower in a slate-gray sky, and the temperature is dropping. It will be hovering near zero by dark. They can't afford to be exposed to the cold, as well as whoever else is roaming these ravaged wastelands.

"Dad," Sam asks, his voice full of little-boy trust, "what are we going to do?"

Daniel has no idea. How far are they from Utica? Four, five miles? At the very least. "I think we'll check out that army base that has food and fresh water," he tells his son. "Elihu Root Army Reserve Center, right?"

Sam blinks at him. "Um, yeah, something like that, I think. Do you know where it is?"

No, he does not, and Utica is not exactly a small town. A small city, perhaps, with a population of maybe fifty thousand? Or, at least, that's what it used to be. What it is now, he shudders to think, based on what he's already seen while going to get Sam—guys like the ones he just encountered holed up in Walmart, barricading roads, shooting rounds off just for the hell of it, not caring who might get hurt, and no presence of police or military or anyone remotely trustworthy. How has it come to this, so swiftly? There's no point, he knows, in lamenting the state of affairs; it simply is, and they must move forward.

"We'll ask someone where it is," Daniel decides. "Someone we can trust." He thinks, then, of Tom, the quiet, steady man he met who helped and fed him, back on Route 12, just two days ago. It feels like a lifetime already, but it isn't. He can picture the gummy smile of Tom's youngest, Isaac, only a baby, as he banged his spoon on his highchair. The quiet, dark-eyed older children, Hannah and Noah, the calm capability of his wife, Abby. If he and Sam can get there, maybe they can regroup. Figure out a way forward. But that man's farmhouse must be at least fifteen miles away...

That's about six hours of walking, he tells himself. It will be dark by the time they arrive, close to midnight, but it's still doable... and it might be their only option.

"I think I might know someone," Daniel tells Sam. "But we'll have to walk."

Sam nods jerkily. He's clearly scared, but he trusts his dad to think of a plan, to make it happen. His son might be eighteen, but right then Daniel feels as if he might as well be six years old, gazing at his daddy with big, trusting eyes. Doesn't Sam realize how *powerless* he is? They were just carjacked by two hillbillies high on drugs and he couldn't do anything to protect himself or his son.

He glances down the empty road, a cold stretch of concrete under a winter sky. "Let's go," he says, and together they fall into step and start walking.

As the sun sets, the temperature drops, and Daniel's mind slips into a numb haze. He knows he needs to think about what they're going to do, how they can possibly get all the way back to the cottage in Canada without a car or any supplies, but it feels like everything is happening in slow motion, the gears in his mind barely turning over. He's exhausted, near starving as well as freezing, and it's all he can do to put one foot in front of the other as the road stretches on in front of them, seemingly endless.

"Tell me about Clarkson," he finally says to Sam, rousing himself out of a near-stupor. "Before, I mean. I know we Skyped about it, but what was your favorite class? Did you get along with your roommate?"

"My favorite class..." Sam sounds as if Daniel is speaking a foreign language, and in a way, he is. What does any of that matter anymore? It's a world that has been destroyed, perhaps forever. And yet Daniel wants, even *needs*, to hear about it. He wants to be a normal dad for just a few minutes, smiling and nodding as his son tells him how his economics professor is *super* strict.

"Yeah, your favorite class. Was it Econ? Or the history one? What period of history, again?"

"Modern European."

"Right." Daniel nods, the memories filtering through him like shards of broken glass, glinting with a barely held recollection of what once was, hurting him with their painful poignancy. "What is that, like 1850 to present?"

Sam shoots him a look like he thinks he's crazy for caring, but then he continues, his voice growing a little stronger. "Yeah, around then. We started with the revolutions in 1848."

"Right," Daniel says again, nodding, trying to remember what he knows about that dim and distant past. "Were they in Italy and Germany?"

"And France and the Austrian Empire."

"So back then it probably felt like the whole world was on fire," Daniel remarks.

"Yeah," Sam agrees, smiling crookedly. "Maybe kinda like this."

And suddenly they're both laughing, deep, from their bellies, hard enough to make tears come to Daniel's eyes, although maybe they are real tears, because God knows he is so very close to weeping. But he doesn't; he holds it together for his son as they keep walking and Sam, getting into the spirit of the thing, tells him about the climbing club he joined, how they'd hike out into the Adirondacks. Some kids even free-climbed, which was crazy hard, but pretty cool. Sam wants to try it, maybe, one day.

Daniel listens and nods, grateful for the soothing cadence of his son's voice, the rise and pitch of syllables without him taking in all the words, just savoring the seeming normality of the moment, for however long it lasts.

Eventually Sam's monologue trails away, and they both walk in silence. They haven't seen a car or person in over an hour, which is hopefully a good thing, although the silence and stillness, along with the freezing temperatures and oncoming darkness, make Daniel feel uneasy. They need to find shelter, and soon. His face is numb, as are his fingers, even in the gloves he fortunately had in the pocket of his coat, and his toes.

Then Sam suddenly grabs his arm. "Dad!" he says, sounding excited. "Dad, look!"

Daniel blinks through the twilit gloom, a ripple of shock going through him when he sees a sign for the Elihu Root Army Reserve Center.

"We can get food," Sam says, sounding even more enthused. "And water and maybe other stuff. Maybe someone here can help us."

Daniel looks down the empty road now shrouded in darkness; the only sound is the sweep of the wind against the hardened, snow-encrusted ground. There's no one around—no person, no vehicle, not even a light. He does not have a good feeling about this, but he wants to catch Sam's enthusiasm, to feel his hope. "Let's have a look," he says.

Together they head off Route 12, down a smaller road. One side is an empty field, another a stretch of chain-link fence, with a few flat-roofed, concrete buildings of the Army Reserve Center visible behind, cloaked in shadow.

After about ten minutes, they come to the gates of the center; they're wide open, and one looks dented, as if someone drove into it, hard. Daniel's sense of unease deepens, his gut churning as his gaze darts around, looking for any sign of life. He had, like Sam, been half-hoping, almost *expecting*, even, a place of bustling activity—security guards, trucks, warehouses full of food, a smiling doctor in scrubs standing by a medical tent. He'd felt that palpable sense of relief hovering at his finger-tips, that someone could take charge, even if just for a few minutes, so they wouldn't be all alone in this.

Instead, the whole place looks empty and abandoned. The concrete is cracked, the buildings dark and ominously silent.

"Is no one here?" Sam asks uncertainly.

"It doesn't appear so," Daniel replies. He's conscious of their intense vulnerability—no weapon, no vehicle, no food. They have nothing. And no one is here. At least, he now hopes no one is here, because if they are he doesn't think they're going to be friendly. That radio announcement must have been an old recording, from after the first strikes, because what is abundantly clear is that this is no longer a place to get food or fresh water or medical aid. This is no longer a place to get anything.

Still, Daniel walks forward, just in case... in case of what? He knows no one is here... and yet he keeps going.

In the parking lot in front of the main building, a few tents have been set up. They list now, like sinking ships, their awnings ragged and torn. A dozen or so plastic crates, empty, some broken, are scattered across the asphalt.

Daniel moves forward again to one of the tents, and that's when he sees the sprawled body of someone, their legs visible from behind a table. From where he stands, he can't see their face, but they are clearly dead. They have been shot in the stomach, and, judging from the state of what he can see, it happened a while ago. As his gaze moves around, he sees other bodies sprawled across the parking lot, some of them in military uniform. There must be a dozen people or more; all are dead, and most likely have been for some time.

Sam starts to walk ahead, and Daniel checks him with an arm flung out, hitting him hard in the chest. His son lets out a startled *oof*.

"Dad..."

"Let's go."

"What? Why—"

"Let's *go*."

Sam sucks in a quick, startled breath as Daniel wheels around and starts walking back the way they came. After a few seconds, his son follows. They're both silent as they go back through the gates, out onto the street, and back to the main road.

"Someone shot that guy," Sam finally says, his voice quiet.

His son must not have seen all the bodies, for which Daniel is glad. "Yes," he agrees.

"Do you think it was the same guys who took our car?"

"It could have been anybody, Sam." Daniel takes a deep breath. He is recalibrating his plans, his hopes, of how to get from here to the cottage. Right now, it feels like an unfathomable distance. "We need to find the guy I mentioned," he finally says. "Tom." He says his name as if he knows him as a friend, when all he really is is a stranger who invited Daniel in for a meal. But he was kind and honorable, and Daniel is sure he can trust him. If he can get to that farmhouse, he can make a plan. Somehow... somehow he will be able to get back to the cottage. To Alex and Mattie and Ruby.

Together they start walking back down Route 12. Daniel estimates they have about six or seven more miles more to walk. It's dark now, moonless, so he can barely see his hand in front of his face. This is a good thing because it means they can't be targeted... or so he hopes.

After about half an hour, they come into the center of Utica, and he tenses, conscious that there are likely to be people about. They pass looted stores, houses either boarded up or broken into, abandoned cars with shot-out tires and shattered windows, everything possessing an air of emptiness and desolation and violence. They stick to the shadows, and twice Daniel guides Sam to lie flat on the ground, their cheeks pressed to the freezing concrete, as a truck or SUV careens by. When they reach the downtown, Daniel glimpses people outside a hospital on the other side of the street, racing stretchers down a steep hill so they clang hard into the concrete wall of a parking garage at the bottom. He sees a flash of a pale, terrified face on one of the stretchers and tells himself he must be imagining it; surely no one could be that depraved as to treat other human beings that way, for no good reason. This was a civilized country, he thinks, up until about two minutes ago.

He guides Sam away onto a side street before he sees any of it, and they trudge on, one foot in front of another. At times, the world around them feels like an alien, abandoned landscape—at other times, an apocalyptic hell. Daniel can't feel either his fingers or his toes. They're on a side street of shabby, wooden townhouses, most looking empty or others shuttered up tight, when he hears the staccato volley of gunshots up ahead, and then the squeal of tires, the flash of lights. He pulls Sam onto the front porch of a house with the windows blown out; they both lie flat on their bellies, hidden by the porch railing, breathing hard as the truck races down the street... and then stops right in front of them.

Neither of them so much as breathes as they hear doors open and then slam shut, voices that sound both belligerent and jovial. Footsteps, thankfully moving away. A door opening and closing, directly across from them, Daniel suspects. More voices, another car. Wild guffaws of laughter and then the sudden raucous blare of rap music, making Daniel jump a little.

He hasn't heard music, he realizes, since before the first bombs dropped. Already it feels like a relic from another world, harsh on his ears and yet making something in him yearn for all the things he used to take for granted—music, art, fresh coffee, hot, gooey pizza. It rushes at him, a barrage of simple pleasures that now are impossibly out of reach.

Next to him Sam shifts on the hard wooden boards of the porch. "What should we do?" he whispers. A scent of cigarette smoke drifts toward them on the cold air, along with the murmur of voices. The guys, whoever they are, are standing outside, maybe on the porch of the opposite house, maybe on the sidewalk or the street. They could, Daniel realizes, be there for a very long time. It sounds like they're having something of a party.

"We'll have to go around the back," he whispers back. They can't stay on this porch for much longer; it's too cold, and they'll be far more exposed and vulnerable in daylight.

"But if they see us..."

Daniel hears a tremor in his son's voice. "They won't," he says. There are some steps off the porch leading to a narrow alley that runs alongside the house. If they commando-crawl down it, Daniel thinks they won't be seen. He hopes they won't.

Because if they are...

But no. He's not going to think like that.

"We'll stay low," he tells Sam. "Follow me."

Fortunately, the blare of music covers any sound they might make as they crawl on their forearms off the porch and along the alleyway. *Marines make it look easy*, Daniel thinks, and almost laughs. After just a few feet, he's exhausted and breathing hard. He keeps going.

It's maybe fifty feet down the alleyway to the backyard, a barren stretch of frozen grass crusted with snow, a broken picnic table listing on its side. Safely hidden now, they both stand, wincing as they do. Even with the protection of his coat, Daniel thinks his forearms are probably scraped raw.

"Now what?" Sam asks.

Daniel gazes at the rowhouses stretching in every direction, a sea of chain-link or rickety wooden fencing, roof after drooping roof.

"We keep going," he says, and heads to the back of the narrow yard, vaults the fence, and walks on.

Behind them, from the party house, they hear a gunshot. Daniel doesn't look back.

NINE

We all sit around the campfire, sipping catnip tea, waiting for William Stratton to speak, like children waiting for a ghost story, anticipating the delightful chill of terror, and yet it's real.

"As far as I can tell," William begins in his stentorian voice, seeming to enjoy having the spotlight, a man who is clearly used to it and expects it, "things have... died down a little, since the first bombs hit. That was when the military and government more or less collapsed... it was pretty chaotic. A lot of gangs, violence—"

"That has certainly been our experience," I can't help but interject. William Stratton isn't telling us anything we don't already know, haven't lived ourselves. It's less than a week since the cottage burned down.

William nods, understanding, accepting. "It's probably a little different up here," he agrees, his gaze on me. He has very clear gray eyes and a square jaw. He reminds me of that old TV commercial: *I may not be a doctor, but I play one on TV...*

"Why?" I sound petulant, even aggressive, and I don't mean to be. "All the services have been disrupted up here too," I explain in a more moderate voice. "Electricity, internet. There's no government or military up here, either, at least not that I've seen." Now I sound almost accusing. My emotions are too unruly, impossible to manage; I feel like I have to yank them all back, bottle them up.

"No..." William agrees slowly, like he's making a concession. "But it's the radiation that's the real problem."

A silence greets this explanation, akin to a thunderclap. We all gape at him. "We thought..." I begin, feeling strangely foolish, because I already know that I have no idea what I'm talking about. "We thought the radiation was... you know, fairly localized. And would have... dissipated by now."

"I'm no expert in these matters," William replies, sounding like he thinks he is, "but you're right, in terms of the immediate fallout. According to some estimates we heard through the satellite system, about fifteen percent of the U.S. population died in those first nine blasts from that fallout and its resulting movement downwind. And then, around another twenty-five percent died in the following twenty or so blasts." He dismisses forty percent of the population with barely a wave of his hand. "And since then I've heard another fifteen percent died from various causes, minimum, and more are dying every day."

"That's over half of the U.S. population," Sam whispers, sounding awed.

William gives him a somber look. "That's not all, though. The contamination from long-life radioactive isotopes like strontium-90 or cesium-137, through the food chain and into the body, is more severe than anticipated, and can last for up to five years."

"What does that even *mean*?" Mattie cries. Phoebe burrows into her lap, alarmed by the outburst, and Mattie hugs her tightly.

"It means that the contamination continues after the initial blasts," he explains. "You're not going to die immediately, or even notice, but over months and years it will become apparent... and it already has."

"How?" This from Daniel, like a demand. His brows are drawn together, his forehead furrowed, his expression fierce.

William shrugs. "All sorts of ways. This is just hearsay, mind. We didn't have any of it in the bunker, of course. But... cancer, tumors, genetic modification, infertility... I mean, obviously none of that has manifested itself yet, but it's coming. And, of course, it's not just the radiation. It's the lack of medical care, of medicine and treatment... a lot of people didn't make it through the winter, due to starvation." He speaks so unemotionally that it feels as if we could be talking about cockroaches, not human beings. Millions and millions of human beings who died over a cold, stark winter. I think of mothers cradling babies, children wasting away, families huddled together, eating their last meal as the cold steals in.

"Estimates are," he finishes, "that at least eighty percent of the USA's population has died, and more are likely to."

Eighty percent. For a long time, I haven't let myself think about my wider family very much—my brother, my sister. Some stubborn part of myself, I know, has been imagining them all alive, struggling along as we were. But they didn't have the luxury of a cottage deep in the woods to hide away in, fresh water, and game to trap. I'm reminded of how fortunate, despite our hardships, we truly have been. And yet... all those people. All those people whom I've *loved.*

For a long time no one speaks.

"Still," Mattie says eventually, her tone sober but also thoughtful. "That means almost a hundred million people are still alive... right?"

"Sixty million if it's eighty percent," Sam chimes in. He's always been good at arithmetic.

"More than the population of a lot of countries," I add. "Where is the government in all this? The military?" Seven months on, why hasn't the United States of America, if it's not standing tall again, gotten back on its knees, at least? Or maybe it has, and we just haven't heard about it yet.

William shrugs. "Maybe that many, maybe not. There are most likely more deaths every single day. People are getting sicker, hungrier. When we drove here, we hardly saw anyone at all."

I glance at Daniel, whose expression is shuttered. Has so much changed in the three weeks since he returned? He talked of roving gangs, homegrown militias, similar to what we saw up here. Are they still out there? Or has it become a barren wasteland of not just destruction, but death?

"But the government?" I prompt. "The military?"

"I heard they were doing something out in North Dakota," Nicole says. Her voice is quiet and a little husky, and I realize how little she's spoken or even moved since we all sat down. She's seated next to her husband, her knees tucked up to her chest, looking quiet and watchful and withdrawn. "We heard there's some military complex out there that they've made their headquarters, a springboard for whatever is next."

"Yes, we heard that on the radio," William agrees. "Something's happening out in North Dakota, but no one knows for sure what it is. The government and military have pulled out of the whole east coast, though, as far as I know." His face tightens. "That was part of the reason why we were kicked out, because people were starting to believe that it wasn't safe above ground anywhere east of Chicago."

Nicole averts her face, as if she can't bear to look at any of us, or maybe she doesn't want *us* to look at *her*. My curiosity is piqued, along with my sympathy. Every time her husband talks about what happened in that billionaire's bunker, Nicole draws a little more into herself, almost as if she's trying to hide, or even disappear. Does she miss the luxury, or is it something else?

"Surely that's not true," I protest, trying to sound reasonable rather than argumentative or what I actually am, which is afraid. Daniel and Sam traveled through upstate New York less than a month ago. Have they been affected by the radiation? I don't suppose there's any way to know until we see the effects, but that prospect terrifies me. My husband, my son, withering away, suffering, dying... if that's what happens from the long-term effects of radiation. I have no idea. I realize how utterly naive and stupid I was, taking what Daniel said at face value, about the troposphere and dilution and the rest of it, assuming that, seven months past the bombs dropping, we were past all that nuclear stuff.

It's ridiculous, and it makes me angry. I'm not sure I can deal with yet more insurmountable problems.

"I don't know whether it's true or not," William replies, his even tone suggesting he doesn't appreciate being challenged. "I'm just telling you what we heard from the other bunkers."

"How many of these bunkers are there?" Mattie asks, and again William hesitates, looks at his wife.

"I'm not exactly sure," he replies after a pause. "We were in touch with five or six, maybe."

"And where are you going now?" Daniel asks in a mild tone that still possesses an edge. "I mean, you must have had a plan."

William gives a shamefaced smile as he spreads his hands wide. "Not really. We just wanted to get as far north as we could, away from... everything." He glances at his wife, who doesn't meet his gaze, and then looks around the campsite. "What about you guys?" he asks in the same jocular tone he used when he'd first stepped out of the car. "Are you staying here?"

"We heard about a base in Buffalo that's offering shelter," Daniel tells him. "We're making for there."

William is already shaking his head. "Fort Sanderson? That place has had it. Everybody moved out a couple of months ago. People had started getting sick."

We stare at him, dumbfounded. My fragile, fledgling dream of a safe haven has shriveled to ash in a matter of seconds and now the future looms in front of us, even more uncertain. More terrifying.

"What...? Why? I mean... how?" Mattie asks, a tremor in her voice.

"Too close to the blast centers. Fears of radiation."

I swallow hard. Sam and Daniel *must* have been affected, I think, in some way, even if they don't know or feel it yet. I'd let myself be lulled by Daniel's reassurances, when they must have been lies. Lies he told to protect me.

So what other lies has he told me?

Nicole stirs then, almost as if she's coming out of a stupor, and William springs to attention. Ben lifts his head and looks around at everyone blearily. What, I wonder, are we meant to *do* with these people?

"If you don't have anywhere to go," Daniel says, as if he's read my thoughts and maybe he has, "you're welcome to stay here with us."

"Oh, I don't..." William begins, before trailing off. He glances at his son and wife, neither of whom look at him. "Maybe just for a night," he relents. "We drove through the night and we're all a little tired." He gives us an apologetic grimace before adding, like an afterthought, "thank you."

Daniel, Sam, and Kyle set up the tents again while Ruby and I make breakfast—cattail porridge, *again*—and Mattie gets Phoebe dressed, the little girl standing obediently and silently in front of her as she slips on a t-shirt, brushes her hair. Nicole hovers, not close enough for me to actually speak to, but I'm constantly aware of her in my peripheral vision. I don't think I've ever encountered such a contained yet prickly person; she seems both glossy and brittle.

After about fifteen minutes, she asks me stiffly, "Is there some place I can wash?"

I glance at her, concerned at how fragile she sounds, like she's minutes away from—what? Breaking down? Collapsing? I glance at her face and see a spiderweb of fine lines fanning out from her eyes, etching her forehead. Her eyes look tired, the color of faded denim.

"Yes, of course," I say, as if I'm showing her the guest bathroom of our gracious home. *The tap is a little tricky, there are hand towels to the left of the sink.* "There's a stream at the bottom of that hill, through the woods." I point in the right direction, and she nods and then walks off, her gait as stiff as her voice. I watch her go, and then I turn to Ben, who has also been lurking on the fringes of the campsite, scuffing the ground with his gleamingly white Air Force 1 sneakers. "How old are you, Ben?" I ask, hoping I sound friendly. It's so hard to gauge my tone these days; I feel as if I never have any idea of how I sound.

He gives me something of an incredulous look, that I'm asking such an irrelevant question. "Fifteen."

"Same as Mattie here." I nod toward my daughter, who I can tell is silently seething at this blatant bit of parental social engineering. "Are you in ninth grade?"

Another look of total disbelief. "I *was*."

"Was there some kind of school, in this bunker?" I press, doing my best to sound friendly and interested, rather than as if I'm grilling him for information.

He shrugs. "Sort of, on computers. They'd downloaded all these classes, but they were all really boring."

Mattie lets out a soft huff. Her school was learning how to shoot, skin a rabbit, and generally be a badass. I'm pretty sure she's looking at this pretty boy and thinking how she could take him down in about two seconds.

"Wow," I say, for lack of any other suitable response. I thought awkward chitchat was a relic of a pre-Armageddon age, but apparently not.

. . .

Over the next few hours, we find an uneasy rhythm. The Strattons take one of our tents, at Daniel's suggestion, seeming to see it as something of their due, and bring several leather Louis Vuitton suitcases out of their car. We leave them to settle in as we go about our usual jobs—Kyle fishes; Daniel and Sam check the snares; Ruby and I gather plants, and Mattie minds the campsite with Phoebe.

We've all fallen into these patterns without even realizing it, and they work. How are the Strattons going to upset it all? Upset *us*? Already I feel uncomfortably aware of William's authoritative presence, not quite arrogance, but almost; his wife's tense quietness that is somehow more oppressive than if she talked all the time. As for Ben... he's another child I feel responsible for, even if technically I'm not. I doubt either William or Nicole Stratton can provide for their son out here in the woods. I'm resentful that Daniel offered to let this family stay, even as I accept he didn't have much choice, and it was, of course, the good and right thing to do.

It isn't until later that I learn my husband's ulterior motive.

We are lying in our tent—Ruby is sharing with Mattie and Phoebe, and Sam is sleeping in the back of the truck, along with Kyle—our legs tangled together, our faces pressed close, almost as if we are trying to fuse our bodies, but there's nothing romantic about it. We simply don't want to be overheard.

"I think they're hiding something," Daniel whispers, barely a breath of sound. "And I want to know what it is."

"Why did they come to Kawartha?" I ask, an agreement. Now that Daniel has said it out loud, I'm almost positive the Strattons are hiding something... but what? "They can't have just been driving," I continue. "With no destination in mind."

He nods slowly, his lips brushing my hair. "I think it was a coincidence that they ended up at our campsite," he concedes in a soft huff of breath. "An open meadow close to the road... we probably should have been more careful than that. But... I think they're going somewhere. I think they *do* have a destination in mind, and they just don't want to tell us."

I thread my fingers through his, draw his hand to my heart. I think of what William Stratton said about the radiation, and I want to ask Daniel about it, but I don't. I know he'll lie to me, and I'm not ready for that—or the truth. "Another bunker?" I whisper instead, so quietly I'm not sure even Daniel hears me.

He nods again, his lips brushing my ear as he leans close to whisper, "I think so. And we need to make sure we go with them."

TEN

I wake up early the next morning, while the sky is still clinging to the vestiges of darkness and mist hovers over the ground. I slip out of the tent to stoke up the fire—and make sure the Strattons haven't stolen away in the night. But they haven't; their car is still there, parked under the trees so it's hidden from the road. I can hear William snoring from their tent. I turn toward the fire, and then have to check myself when I see Nicole is already there, a blank expression on her face as she sits by the flames, her knees drawn up to her chest, her manicured fingers laced together over them.

"Hey." I speak quietly, to keep from waking anyone else. I don't think it can be much past five in the morning. "You're up early."

She shrugs in response without looking at me, her zip-up hoodie sliding off one bony shoulder. I decide to go about my business. I head down to the stream to fetch water and put it on top of the stove to boil. The other day Ruby and I roasted and ground cleavers for coffee, or at least the approximation of it, and so I set them to boil while Nicole simply sits, looking blank. I have no idea what to say to her, and so I say nothing, focusing on the job at hand, while she looks remote and beautiful and brittle, in an oversized white cashmere hoodie and steel-gray yoga pants, like a time traveler from another universe.

After five minutes or so, I present her with my poor offering —a cup of brownish, boiled water that vaguely resembles coffee flavor, with no milk or sugar, of course.

She wraps her slender hands around the tin mug, her expression veiled as she remarks without expression, "Yesterday I had a Nespresso."

I have no idea what to make of that, and, while I'm still trying to frame a response, she lets out a dark, bitter laugh, and then drains her cup.

Oh... kay.

"So... did you leave the bunker yesterday?" I ask cautiously as I sit a few feet away from her, cradling my own cup. "And drive right here?"

She nods, not looking at me. "Something like that."

Another silence descends, as oppressive as ever. I don't want to pump her for information... and yet I sort of do. I need to find out where they're going, because I'm convinced, like Daniel, that they have a destination in mind, and it's somewhere we need to know about.

"So why Kawartha?" I ask mildly as I take a sip of coffee. "I mean... it's got to be, what? Two hundred miles from Watertown?"

Nicole looks away, her long blond hair falling out of her ponytail to cover her face. She has to be about my age, I think, and her hair is a perfect platinum. Did they have hair dye in that luxury bunker, along with everything else? Maybe even a hair salon and stylist. "Like William said, we just headed north."

"And west," I add mildly. "I mean, it's not exactly a straight shot, is it?"

Nicole whips her head around, her eyes turning ice-blue as she glares at me. "Why are you asking so many questions?"

"Because I'm curious," I fire back, "and I think you're going somewhere. Somewhere specific."

We stare at each other for a long, level moment, and then Nicole drops her gaze, shrugging as she slips her hoodie back onto her shoulder. "Fine," she says. "We are."

I should feel victorious, or at least vindicated, but instead I'm only wary. There's something dismissive about her tone, like wherever they're going has nothing to do with us, and of course it *doesn't*. But, like Daniel, I want it to.

"Where?" I ask.

"North Bay. There's a Canadian Forces base there, with a huge underground complex. Sixty floors." She speaks almost as if she's unimpressed.

I goggle at her for a moment. "Aren't the Canadian Forces using it?" I ask uncertainly.

"They *were*," Nicole replies with emphasis. "It was Canada's most important air base. But the military has more or less been disbanded, and the place was basically empty, until someone took it over. At least, that's what we were told."

"The *Canadian* military has disbanded? But—"

"After Vancouver and Toronto were hit," she replies with a shrug, "and Montreal, Calgary, Edmonton, Ottawa... I can't remember if there were others, but it's in as bad shape as the U.S., more or less."

"Ottawa?" That was only a hundred miles from the cottage. Have we been affected by the radiation, without even knowing it? The thought is both surreal and frightening, and yet I can't devote any more headspace to an impossible, amorphous what-if. I suppose we'll find out eventually, if we were. I picture myself suddenly starting to cough, or maybe a clump of hair falling out, and then thinking, *yep, must be the radiation, just as expected...*

I mean, everything else has gone wrong, so why not this, too?

"I had no idea so many Canadian cities had been hit," I remark numbly. "Why Canada..."

"Because it's next to the U.S." She lets out a sudden laugh, high and wild, ending on a single, jagged note. "You guys are living out here like it's the Stone Age, and you don't realize the whole world has gone up in smoke?" She shakes her head, disdainful, while I continue to reel.

William Stratton hadn't mentioned all the Canadian cities yesterday. I'd known about Toronto, but I'd assumed it had been hit simply because it was on the border, and the same with Vancouver. But Calgary? Ottawa? Edmonton?

This country is as ruined as the United States... and yet somehow up north is still safe? Well, I suppose it is, if there are sixty stories underground somewhere up by North Bay.

"So this base," I say after a moment. "Are there people in it now?"

"So we've heard." Nicole stares down into her empty coffee cup. "But we haven't had any contact with them, so we don't know for sure. But some people back at the bunker where we were before mentioned it as a possibility, so..." Another shrug. "Where else are we going to go?"

"But surely the military still has some kind of presence there," I persist. It feels too easy, or maybe too alarming, to be able to walk right onto a huge military base, one of the most important in the whole country, and take up residence.

"Not as far as I know," she replies. "The aircraft are gone, and the underground complex was abandoned about twenty years ago. They took all the equipment out back then. I heard it was used to film some sci-fi movie awhile back, but it's basically been empty."

Okay, so not a luxury bunker, then, but somewhere safe.

"How many people does it hold?" I ask Nicole.

"Four hundred underground."

"Do you think it's safe above?"

"I have no idea," she snaps, and now she sounds irritable. "Do you think I actually know anything?"

"Your husband certainly was acting like you both did yesterday," I retort. "With your radio communications with all these other underground condos."

She lets out a laugh, this time a tired huff. "Trust me, it wasn't all it was cracked up to be. Frankly, I'm not sure I want to head down into another one." She presses her forehead against her knees as she lets out a soft moan. "Do you know what I miss?" she tells me. "My *kitchen*."

I have no idea what to say to that.

Nicole lifts her head and looks at me with a mixture of earnestness and despair. "Don't you miss your kitchen? Imagine sitting at your breakfast bar, the sun streaming through the window, sipping a latte, and scrolling through the news on your phone... don't you miss that?" She drops her head back down on her knees and it takes me a few seconds to realize her shoulders are shaking with sobs.

"Nicole..." Awkwardly I scoot over to pat her shoulder. I don't know this woman at all, and I think she's had an easier time of it than most of us, yet in this moment I feel sorry for her. She is weeping as if her heart has shattered into a million pieces and she isn't even going to try to put them all back together.

"Don't." She sniffs, then lifts her head to wipe her streaming eyes. "Don't," she says again, wearily, then she gives another tired laugh. "Thank God I'm not wearing mascara."

I manage a soft huff of laughter, although I'm not really feeling it. I have no idea what to make of this woman. "What was your life like, before?" I ask. "I mean, I know what your kitchen looks like..."

"My life was irrelevant." She sighs. "And I loved it. I was an interior designer, and don't bother murmuring some pleasantry, because I already know you think it's useless. Most people do. It's certainly irrelevant now, and it was more or less irrelevant then as well. I advised people with too much money on what throw pillows they should buy." She shrugs defiantly. "So what? It made them happy. It made me happy."

"I'm sure it was more than throw pillows," I tell her. "I bet you advised on some lamps, too."

She gives me a look of shocked amazement, and then she lets out the first real laugh I've heard from her—deep, from her belly. I smile.

"Oh, yes," she says. "Some really cool lamps." A sigh gusts out of her. "What about you?"

"Oh, I was just as irrelevant," I assure her. "Maybe even more so. I didn't even have a job. I was a stay-at-home mom, because I more or less missed the window for another kind of career. By the time I could have gone into a field I cared about, I was forty, and it just felt... pointless. Too much effort. Or maybe I was just scared." I lapse into silence. Before we lost the house, never mind the nuclear stuff, I'd been toying with the idea of going back to school. Retraining as a teacher, in English or history. Thinking about that barely-there dream is like looking at an old, faded photograph. The evidence is right in front of you, but you can't quite make yourself believe it ever really happened.

"I'm sure your kids were grateful," Nicole says, and I can't tell if she's being sarcastic or not. When are kids ever grateful about anything? "Did you do the whole chocolate-chip cookie thing?"

I can't help but laugh. "Oh, yes."

She nods slowly. "I didn't bake. Or cook. We ordered expensive meal kits to cater for our diet. William was on some paleo thing, I was low carb, and Ben could only eat beige food for a while." She laughs. "I bet you didn't know there was a meal kit for that. 'Fussy Friends.' It's actually called that." She glances at me, somber now. "Don't tell Ben I told you. He'd be so embarrassed. It's for toddlers, and he was eating these 'Tot Pots' when he was thirteen."

"I don't think Ben and I are in the conversing stage yet," I tell her. "I asked him how old he was, and he looked horrified that this middle-aged nonentity was addressing him."

Nicole nods sagely. "You can be seen as a Karen even in Armageddon. Especially by my son." Her voice is full of deep affection. "I never knew I could be so embarrassing until my son became a teenager. Then my mere presence became excruciating to him."

I let out a little laugh, gratified that we can bond over the typical travails of motherhood. "Do they eventually find you less embarrassing?" I muse, and her eyebrows lift.

"Maybe when they're parents themselves? Although then I bet we just become outdated and ridiculous."

"So unfair," I agree.

We smile, and it feels like a moment of surprising solidarity.

"So, do you think you'll get into this place up in North Bay?" I ask, and that moment of camaraderie is forgotten in an instant.

"I have no idea. And I really don't care." Nicole rises from the campsite, depositing her cup by the fire, presumably for somebody else to wash. "Thanks for the tea," she says, and she walks away, back down to the stream, making me wonder if we actually bonded over anything.

The next few hours pass in the usual blur of activity as Ruby and I get breakfast going, and Mattie goes with Phoebe to pick some more strawberries. Sam and Kyle go fishing, and Daniel checks the snares. We all have our jobs—save for the Strattons. They skulk around the camp, silent and wary, and I start to wonder when they're going to head off. Now that I know where

they're going, we don't need them here any longer. It's a mercenary way to think, but it's hard not to think that way these days.
They're using our tent, eating our precious food, and bringing
nothing to the table. As much as I enjoyed that brief moment of
solidarity with Nicole, now I just want the three of them gone.

"So," William says as we are all eating breakfast around the
campfire, his tone that of an announcement, "I thought we'd get
going later this morning. We're very grateful for your hospitality, but we shouldn't use up any more of your supplies."

I haven't had a chance to tell Daniel what I've learned from
Nicole, but I try to give him a meaningful nod from across the
campfire. *It's okay, let them go.* He catches my look and gives a
tiny nod back.

"I wish you safe travels," he tells William. "All of you, that
is. Do you know where you're headed?" His voice is mild,
pleasant.

"Oh, I think we'll just keep heading north," William replies
affably. "Safer."

I catch Nicole's gaze and she rolls her eyes, smiling faintly. I
have to stifle a surprised laugh. Maybe we would have been
friends, I think, but now we'll never know... unless we make it to
North Bay, too.

They leave an hour later, after packing their designer suitcases
back in their SUV. Daniel asks them if they know how to load
and shoot the guns in their trunks and when William admits,
annoyed by his own embarrassment, that he doesn't, Daniel
gives them all a brief tutorial.

"Nice of whoever kicked you out to let you keep some
guns," he remarks as he hands back the rifle.

"He wasn't heartless," William concedes, "and in any case,
these guns wouldn't make much of a dent in the door of the
bunker. They weren't worried."

I glance at Nicole and see she is scowling, and I have the stirrings of a suspicion that her feelings for the man who kicked them out, whoever he was, are different from her husband's. I don't have any chance to explore that idea further, because the Strattons are leaving, giving us half-hearted waves and murmured thanks before they climb into their glossy SUV and head back out onto the open road.

Their departure brings relief, but also a certain flatness.

"When are we heading out?" Sam asks. "And where are we going, now that Buffalo's not an option?" He speaks matter-of-factly, but I can see the tension in his jaw, his shoulders. I don't think my son has looked me in the eye once since we arrived here.

"We need to think about where we're going," I say, and then give Daniel a significant look that no one misses.

"What is that supposed to mean?" Mattie demands. "What's going on? What do you know?"

So much for being discreet. I'm reminded, poignantly, of our former life, when Daniel and I might attempt to speak in some sort of code at the dinner table, while our children, attuned to the merest hint of suggestion or secrecy, would demand to know what we were talking about, how it affected them. Parents weren't allowed to have secrets.

"I need to talk to your father first," I say, and am met with groans. "Mattie, why don't you take Phoebe down to the stream? She loves splashing in the water." I glance at the others. "Let's tidy up camp."

Everyone slouches off, reluctant and indignant, while Daniel draws me to the sheltering boughs of a large cedar tree, the same one I spoke to Sam under, a conversation that was ultimately unsatisfying for us both.

"What do you know?" Daniel asks, and he sounds caught between amusement and intent.

Briefly, I explain to him what Nicole told me about the air

base at North Bay. Daniel is silent, reflective, his gaze distant as he considers everything I've said. The minutes pass and I try not to feel impatient.

"I think I've heard about that place," he finally says. "It was built in the sixties, at the height of the Cold War, and the U.S. paid for something like two-thirds of it."

"We don't need a history lesson here," I remind him as wryly as I can. "Do you think it's real? I mean, I know the base is real, but now... do you think it's a safe place? And will they let us in?"

He shakes his head slowly. "I can't believe the Canadian military has just *folded*... but the U.S. military has folded, more or less, although I guess they're focusing on building something out west, maybe." He sighs, knuckling his forehead, and the slump of his shoulders reminds me of how much he's carrying, for all of us. "I don't know, Alex. It seems like a long shot. But if Buffalo is out of the picture, I don't know where else to go." He sounds despondent, and I long to put my arms around him, but I don't.

"It's only two hundred miles," I say quietly. "We have the gas. We could give it a shot, at least."

My words fall into a stillness that is shattered by a sudden, high, keening scream. Daniel and I stare at each other for one taut second as we recognize the timbre of that particular scream.

Ruby.

ELEVEN

The screaming is coming from the stream, and Daniel starts sprinting down there, while I follow as fast as I can, my heart pounding in my chest, my mind a blur of panic. *Not something else*, I think. Not something more.

I half-stumble, half-skid down the path to the stream, where Sam, Mattie, and Ruby are standing on the shore of the creek, immobile and horrified, Ruby pointing toward the stream, where Kyle is wading out into the water—and soon I see why. Phoebe has been caught in the current and is bobbing along, her face tiny and terrified amid the white-frothed waves.

"What happened?" I cry, which is probably the worst thing to ask, because it sounds like an accusation.

Mattie lets out a sound like a sob, while Sam shakes his head slowly.

"It all happened so fast..." he begins, trailing off as his gaze returns to Phoebe; her head dips below the water and then surfaces again.

"Phoebe—" I call, uselessly. We all watch, transfixed, horrified, as Kyle starts swimming toward her. As he's been shot in the shoulder a mere week ago, I'm not sure he's up to the job; his head bobs under the water more than once. Daniel is already kicking off his shoes. Then, before he can reach the water, Kyle catches Phoebe in one arm, and someone lets out a ragged cheer. Minutes pass as he tows her back to the shore; Daniel wades in to his thighs to grab her and draw her to safety, while Kyle half crawls, half staggers, to shore, blood spotting his shirt where his wound must have broken open again.

To my surprise, as soon as Daniel puts Phoebe down she runs toward me, tackling me around my knees. I hoist her to my hip, a matter of instinct, as she burrows her face into my shoulder. It seems I'm the mom, after all, when it matters.

My gaze moves to Mattie, another matter of instinct, and I catch her glare, half anguish, half accusation. Then she runs to Kyle, dropping on her knees before him while he pats her arm, comforting her, rather than the other way round, although he is gray-faced with exhaustion and pain. His shoulder will need seeing to.

I stroke Phoebe's hair and murmur nonsense endearments as my mind whirls at all the shifts in relationships that have happened in the space of about ten seconds. Sam is watching Mattie and Kyle, and Ruby is looking at me. Daniel comes up to me and puts his arm around my shoulders.

"She okay?"

I nod, still stroking Phoebe's hair. "I think so."

"I'll build up the fire. That water is cold."

Belatedly, I realize poor little Phoebe is shivering. I glance at Mattie again, and see that Kyle has his arms around her. I hoist Phoebe up a little further on my hip, and then up the path to the campsite.

Later, when a warm and dry Phoebe is napping, I go find Mattie. She's sitting back by the stream, hands clasped around her knees, a blank look on her face that reminds me of Nicole.

"Hey." I speak gently, like I would to a skittish animal, as I come to sit next to her on the bank of the stream. The current that seemed so treacherous a few hours ago is now tranquil, sunlight glinting off its placid surface. "Phoebe's okay, Matts. It wasn't your fault."

She turns her head to glare at me, her eyes full of accusation. "Why would you even have to say that?"

"I..." I stare back at her helplessly. "Because you were looking as if you blamed yourself," I finally answer. "And I wanted to let you know that you didn't have to."

She curls her lip, disdainful now. "You don't even know what happened."

I resist the urge to roll my eyes, or maybe even scream. First I'm accused of blaming her, and then of exonerating her. I can't win. But I think I knew that already. "Why don't you tell me what happened, then?"

She hunches her shoulders as she rests her chin on top of her knees. "She was splashing around in the shallows and I was watching her. Sam and Ruby were skipping stones, farther upstream. And I just... I don't know, I just started *thinking*... about what that guy, Mr. Stratton said, yesterday. About eighty percent of everybody dying." She turns to face me again, and now her eyes are filled with tears. "That's like, all our relatives, isn't it? Aunt Sharon and Uncle Matt and Grandma and Grandpa..."

My sister and brother, Daniel's parents. My throat turns tight as I swallow, nod.

"We can't know for sure, but..."

"But probably," Mattie finishes, dropping her chin back onto her knees. "Almost certainly. And what about my friends? And Drew. I don't care about him anymore," she assures me hurriedly, impatiently, "but I don't want him to be *dead*."

"No, of course not," I reply quietly. "Neither do I."

She lets out a huff of laughter like she doesn't believe me,

and I let it go. It's hard enough to think about those we loved
dying, never mind all the incidental people who made up the
complicated fabric of our lives. Randomly, our mail carrier, of
all people, drops into my mind—a smiling, cheerful woman with
curly hair and freckles. If she caught me at the door when she
was delivering a package, she'd always stopped to chat. It
annoyed me a little, made me impatient, to have to suffer
through five minutes of meaningless chitchat with someone I
only knew a little bit. Now I wish I'd invited her in for tea and
cookies.

Mattie suddenly lets out a choked sob as she doubles over.
"I don't *want* this life," she gasps out, the words torn from her,
rending her apart. "*I don't want this life!* I thought I could hack
it if I was strong enough, but I can't, I *can't*, I don't want to."
She's choking and gasping and retching, rocking back and forth,
her arms wrapped around herself as tears spill from her eyes. I
want to hug her, pull her into myself, and give her all the reas-
surance I know I can't, because there simply isn't any for me to
give.

"Mattie..." I say helplessly, tears coming to my own eyes as I
pat her shoulder; I know she won't accept a hug. "Oh, Mattie."

She shakes her head, rejecting what paltry comfort I can
give. She's been so strong, my girl, for so long, that I started to
believe she was okay with it all. She could handle it, even as I
made noises like I was worried she couldn't. I'm angry with
myself, and aching for my daughter, and there's nothing I can
do about anything.

We might both hate this life, but it's the one we have.

Mattie straightens, wiping her eyes, and I feel her retreating
from me, erecting her armor around herself like an invisible,
iron shield. "Don't take Phoebe from me," she states flatly, and I
struggle not to gape at her.

"Mattie, I—"

"You don't even like her that much," she throws at me, and

now I just blink. "I know I should have been watching her better, and she ran to you, but... but..." She sputters and trails away, and I'm pretty sure I know what she's not willing to say. *She's mine.* Phoebe has become my daughter's security blanket, her teddy bear, and can I fault her for it?

"Trust me," I tell her quietly. "I'm not taking Phoebe from you."

She glares at me then, like I've said something wrong, and I resist the urge to throw up my hands. I can't win. We could be back in Connecticut, arguing about her phone. I'm tired of this, tired of it all, but I'm the mom, so I have to keep soldiering on.

"We're going to pack up," I tell her, a little abruptly. "Leave tomorrow morning for North Bay."

"North Bay...?"

"There's a compound there, bigger than Buffalo. It could be a safe place for us."

She narrows her eyes, like she's thinking about asking me a million questions, and then she just gives a terse nod.

"Fine," she says, and she rises gracefully to her feet, striding away from me without looking back.

I stare out at the now-placid stream and wonder why, when we most need to stick together, we all seem to be splintering apart.

We leave the next day at dawn, when the sky is still pink, and Phoebe is half-asleep in Mattie's arms. The truck bed is loaded up, a tarp pulled tight across. There is a feeling in the air, almost metallic, of both expectation and dread.

Last night, Daniel and I lay awake in our tent and whispered the possibilities, like promises or threats, depending on how we felt.

"It might not even exist..." he warned me, or maybe himself.

"I mean, as a safe place. It could just be an empty underground hangar full of Cold War computers and dust."

"Or it could be filled with people we don't want to meet, toting AR-10s and hand grenades."

He rested his chin on my head. "Kind of stupid, to throw a grenade in an underground complex."

I let out a soft breath of laughter. "True. But even if we make it there, they might just throw us out."

"Or they might welcome us in and give us hot showers and a square meal. I'm thinking burgers. Organic beef from Alberta."

It's too tempting to imagine. "Or they might lock us inside," I replied.

"Hmm." With his chin on my head, his voice thrummed through me. "There could be worse places to be."

"That's if we get there in the first place."

Daniel looped his arms around my waist and drew me close. We'd touched more in the last few days than we had in months, maybe even years. I pressed my lips to his throat and closed my eyes.

"You know we don't really have a choice," he said, his voice caught between wryness and a sorrow I didn't want to think about. Even in his lighter moments, there has been a grief in Daniel that tears at me because I don't know its cause.

A sigh escaped me in a soft gust. "I know we don't," I told him. "But I'm still scared."

"I think we'll always be scared. It's just learning to live with the fear."

I smiled against his skin, determined to lighten the mood. "I think I saw that on Instagram, with a picture of someone climbing a mountain or something. Or maybe it was on a coffee mug."

He laughed softly and pulled me closer.

"Daniel..." I felt him tense, even before I'd said anything, and I knew he knew what I was going to ask. "Do you think you and Sam..."

"I can't tell you if we were affected by the radiation," he answered me quietly. "But I did my best to protect him, Alex, I can promise you that."

I inched back so I could peer up into his face, but it was too dark to see his expression. "And what about you? Did you protect yourself?"

His arms tightened around me again. "I did what I could."

Which, I reflected, wasn't much of an answer, but I accepted it because I had to... and the truth was, I didn't really want to know.

Now, as we climb into the truck and leave the little idyll we created for ourselves over the last week, I try not to think about those terrifying what-ifs. The journey ahead of us is frightening enough.

Daniel traced it on the map last night—one hundred and eighty miles on Route 11, heading northwest and then straight north. It's a two-lane highway that cuts through the woods north of Toronto and Barrie; Daniel assured me we'd be no closer than one hundred and twenty miles to a blast site, and we wouldn't go through any town centers.

"We could do it in a couple of hours," he insisted. "It's a fast, straight road, and we have enough gas."

That's not accounting for anyone unfriendly we might encounter on the way, or the very real possibility that the air base in North Bay will refuse to take new people, or isn't a safe place to begin with. There are far too many variables, and yet, like Daniel said, this is our best option. Really, it's our only choice.

I spare one last, longing glance at the little stand of trees that felt like the next best thing to a home, and then Daniel drives through the meadow, onto the empty road circling the park, and then turns right onto the road that leads to Route 118 and then Route 11 north, and to our future... whatever it might be.

TWELVE
DANIEL

Six months earlier
Outside Utica, New York

As soon as they reach the farmhouse of weathered white clapboard, Daniel knows something is wrong. He was here just two days ago—*two days!*—and yet everything has changed. No light glows cozily from within; the whole place looks empty and abandoned, as just about every house they've seen since Utica has been.

Slowly he mounts the steps. It's just past dawn, the light still gray and misty, and they've been making their way, slowly and painfully, through the back streets of Utica, to the relative safety of Route 12. They've kept to shadows and hedges, sidling along, sometimes stopping for as much as an hour, to wait until someone or other—usually in a souped-up jeep or a monster truck—passes. At night, Daniel has come to realize, the vampires come out, looking for blood, dressed in camo and jacked up with weapons. He is hopeful that once they leave the city behind everything will become calmer. The smaller towns won't have these monstrous armies, a crazed infantry waving

AR-1os around, high on coke and power. They might have to walk most of the way, and they'll need to find food, but these dangers, at least, will have passed.

Now, as the front door of Tom's farmhouse, once a haven of warmth and welcome, creaks open, Daniel is not sure.

"Is anybody here?" Sam asks in a whisper.

"I don't think so." Daniel steps into the hallway. The first thing he sees is a picture on the wall, a needlepoint sampler, hanging askew because someone must have knocked it. His heart sinks that little bit further. He imagines Hannah and Noah, the little baby Isaac, and he closes his eyes. They were here two days ago, shy and smiling. What happened?

"What happened?" Sam asks, echoing Daniel's thoughts, and asking as if he knows, but he's afraid he does know, because all the signs are here—a chair on its side, the rag rug in a crumpled heap, cupboard doors flung open. The *silence*.

"They must have left," Daniel tells him. "In a hurry."

Left... or were taken? He hopes, desperately, that it's the former, but he has no idea. Slowly he walks down the hallway, the wooden floorboards creaking under his footsteps, to the kitchen. For a second, he can picture how it was just a few days ago—Tom's wife, Abby, at the stove, the baby in his highchair, their German Shepherd Rocky's tail beating a staccato rhythm on the floor, everyone's heads bowed for grace. An ache starts inside him, deep and wide and painful.

Not this family, he thinks. He can just about handle the strangers—even the pale faces he saw strapped into stretchers, as God-awful as that was—but these good people, who helped him, who only wanted to live a good, simple life? No. Not them. *Not them*, his mind cries out, a prayer, a rant. *Not them, God*.

"Dad?" Sam asks uncertainly, and Daniel's gaze moves slowly around the kitchen. A broken jar of applesauce on the floor, oozing out. A cupboard door nearly wrenched off its hinges. A pot in the sink, maybe the same from which he'd been served stew. A baby's spoon, left on the highchair. He picks it up, wrapping his roughened fingers around it, and then drops it again, with a clatter.

"Dad," Sam says again.

"I'm going to look upstairs," Daniel says. He hesitates and then adds, a command, "Stay here."

Sam, looking troubled and more than a little scared, nods. "Okay."

Slowly, his footsteps now heavy, Daniel mounts the stairs. He's afraid of what he might find, but he knows he needs to look. He steels himself for the worst, but the bedrooms—small and spare—are empty. In the master bedroom, the covers are half-pulled off the bed, the drawers left open, although still with some clothes in them, neatly folded and smelling of soap. Noah and Hannah's rooms are the same—a mess, drawers yanked out, covers off the bed.

Were they pulled from bed? Daniel wonders. He can almost picture it—their rumpled hair, the look of sleepy confusion on the children's faces. Were they made to dress, marched out to a truck? Why? In God's name, *why*? And when—yesterday? The day before? One or the other, because before that Daniel was here and it had been safe.

In the baby's room, the mobile that would have once hung over the crib is on the floor, broken in brightly colored pieces. He sees a rocking chair by the window, an old-fashioned one with a hand-crocheted blanket draped over the back. Daniel can almost imagine Abby there, a sleepy Isaac draped over one shoulder. He didn't even know these people, not really, but they'd felt like family. They'd reminded him, briefly, that he was human, that he was good. Or at least, trying to be good. Wanting to.

He feels so far from that man now.

He takes a step into the room, and that's when he sees it. The grubby blue blanket baby Isaac had held just two days ago, with a bunny's head fashioned out of one corner. It's under the crib, and, when Daniel stoops to pick it up, running the worn fleece between his fingers, he sees it is spattered with blood.

A sound escapes him, more of a sigh than a sob—an understanding, an acceptance. They didn't leave willingly. He sinks into the rocking chair, still holding that little piece of beloved blue fabric in his hands. He stares down at it, bowing his head as if in prayer, but his mind is blank. He can't think anymore. He can't let himself think. He rubs the fabric between his fingers like it's a talisman, the last thing anchoring him to who he was, who he wanted to be.

It isn't until he feels the wetness dripping onto his shirt that he realizes he has been weeping, tears sliding slowly down the seams in his weathered face. He's weeping for Tom and his family, wherever they are, dead or alive—and part of him hopes they're dead rather than suffering—but he knows he is also weeping for himself. He's lost some precious part of himself somewhere between Watertown and Clarkson, and he doesn't think he will ever get it back. And maybe that loss was necessary, so he could make this journey. So he could bring back Sam. He had to close his eyes and his mind to the suffering of others, to the suffering he would inflict, so he could keep his son safe. And the worst part is, he's almost certain that that trade-off has barely begun. They still have over two hundred miles to go, and Daniel has no idea how they're going to manage it, not without making more than a few Faustian bargains along the way.

"Dad?"

He looks up to see Sam standing in the doorway of the nursery. "Nobody's here... are you *crying*?" He sounds horrified.

"I'm just tired." Daniel wipes his face as he feels a familiar hardness settle inside of himself. "It's been a long couple of weeks, and I haven't slept in a while."

"Yeah." Sam hesitates. "There's some food in the pantry.

Not much, but some. And there's a truck outside. I found the keys. It looks pretty beat-up, but we could take it maybe? That is, if no one's here... if they're not coming back..." He trails off uncertainly, clearly unsure how to gauge Daniel's mood.

He can still feel the dampness of tears on his cheeks. Take Tom's truck, eat his food. It feels painfully wrong, and yet also weirdly right. This can be Tom's gift to them. His saving grace. Daniel nods slowly. "That could be good."

"Do you think it's safe to stay here?"

Is it safe anywhere? "I think we need to stay here for a little while," Daniel says in a tone of finality. He needs to rest, eat, make a plan. He's too tired now, too weary in both body and spirit, to keep forging ahead. If he does, he'll make mistakes, and those could be costly. Costlier than he even wants to imagine. "We'll rest for a day or two," he continues. "Figure out what to do."

Sam stands in the doorway and eyes him uncertainly; Daniel feels as if he can't move from this chair. Slowly, everything in him aching, he rises. "Let's have a look at that food in the pantry."

Downstairs, he moves around the kitchen, opening cupboards, finding various cans and jars. He pauses, a jar of raspberry jam in his hand, a woman's neat writing on the front, telling him it was bottled last summer. He imagines the moment —Abby and the children picking fat, red raspberries in the garden, their laughter carrying on the breeze. He can see her standing by the stove, just as she had been when he'd come here two days ago, stirring a pot, the heat flushing her face. He grieves for this family in a way that is unnatural yet still a deep-seated instinct; he is afraid he has already lost his own.

To his amazement, there's enough food in the pantry for at least a few days' meals, as well as propane for the stove. With the truck out back and the clothes upstairs, they should, Daniel realizes, be okay, at least in terms of supplies. He wants to be grateful to Tom, but he feels too sad; it's like a dragging weight, turning every action, every little movement, laborious.

And yet, they eat, and that is a small miracle. After nearly twenty-four hours without food, they're both starving, and he and Sam both wolf down plates of rice and canned beans as if it's a gourmet meal. After doing the dishes—somehow, even in the midst of the empty devastation of the house, this feels important—Daniel decides to do a deeper explore, even though it feels invasive somehow, as if he's violating the family's privacy. He doesn't want to be, and yet he knows he needs to... for Sam's sake.

And so he goes through the house methodically; he opens drawers and riffles through cupboards, finds a flashlight beneath the sink and braves the cobwebby depths of the basement. Sam follows him around at first, but then he gets bored when all Daniel finds is the detritus of a once-normal life—bills to be filed, folded laundry, Scotch tape and a stapler, sixty empty Mason jars in a cardboard box.

While Daniel continues his methodical exploration, Sam retreats to a sofa in the living room, flipping through some *Old Farmer's Almanac*s by the dim beam of a flashlight. Outside the night is still and silent under a cold, wintry moon.

Daniel is looking for guns, but he doesn't find any, and that makes him nervous. It seems that whoever came and took Tom and his family away was more interested in weaponry than food. It's a disquieting thought, and surely the only conclusion he can draw, because he's pretty sure that a man like Tom—he doesn't even know his last name—would own at least one rifle. He was—*is*—a farmer in upstate New York. He had to have had *something*.

Still, Daniel finds other things that are helpful—matches, a flashlight, dried beef jerky, warm sweaters, two decent pairs of boots. They will be vulnerable without a gun, but at least they won't be entirely unprepared. He stacks all the provisions in the kitchen, and then goes to find Sam.

His son is sitting on the sofa in the living room, the flashlight turned off, the room dark, so Daniel can barely make out his face. He comes in and sits opposite him, in an armchair that lets out a creaky little sigh as he lowers himself into it.

"I was thinking," Sam says after a moment, his voice far away. "How we went camping, once."

Daniel blinks at him in the gloom; he can't actually remember when they went camping.

"Do you remember?" Sam continues. "I think I was about eight. We put up a tent in the backyard. Well, you did." He smiles, a little shamefacedly. "I just watched."

"Oh..." A vague memory, sepia-tinted, filters through Daniel's mind. The dutiful effort of putting up the tent. Mattie watching, five years old, her thumb stuck in her mouth. Ruby on Alex's hip. All of it makes him ache. "Yes..."

"It was because I missed the Cub Scouts' campout, because I had tonsilitis. You did it all—the tent, the campfire, ghost stories with a flashlight." He smiles reminiscently, while Daniel struggles to find the memories, hold on to them. "About halfway through the night," Sam continues, "I got tired of being outside and went in, to my own bed. You stayed out, though, in case I changed my mind. And in the morning you made pancakes. Blueberry."

Daniel can't believe Sam remembers all this. He can't believe he *did* all this. "Yeah," he says, smiling. "I remember."

"Well..." Sam pauses, looking a little shamefaced again. "Isn't that a little, I mean a *very* little, like this?"

The question seems to hover in the air. Daniel stares at his son and the realization filters through him that Sam needs to believe that their squatting in the house of someone who is most likely dead—has been murdered—after a nuclear holocaust is, somehow, a little bit like a Cub Scouts-style campout in the backyard.

And maybe it is. At least, maybe they both need to act like it is, to get through it all... or at least to get through this moment.

"Yeah," he says again, and his smile, improbably, widens. "Yeah, it is."

They go to bed a little while later, when it's dark but still early, because they're both exhausted and there's nothing else to do. Daniel locks the doors. He knows how ineffectual such a precaution is, but it seems as if this house has been forgotten; at least he hopes it has.

Daniel sleeps in the master bedroom with its handmade patchwork quilt, the sheets smelling of other people—a faint hint of unfamiliar soap and sweat. Sam takes Noah's room, its wallpaper with vintage airplanes starting to peel off the walls and another home-made quilt on the narrow bed.

Daniel doesn't think he will sleep, with all the dangers and worries clamoring in his mind, but he is so exhausted he falls into a deep, dreamless slumber almost the moment his head hits the pillow, waking only to the wintry sunlight streaming through the windows and the smell of something cooking in the air.

He gets out of bed slowly, all his muscles aching, and moves to the window. Under a deep blue sky, a field of winter wheat sparkles, every single blade and sheaf rimed with a glittering frost. He realizes he doesn't know what day it is, but it must be close to Christmas. It *feels* like Christmas, with the frost and the homely smell of cooking in the air. He dresses quickly and heads downstairs.

Sam is in the kitchen, making pancakes. Daniel stands in the doorway and stares at him, dumbfounded, as his son nonchalantly flips a perfectly round pancake onto the pan on top of the stove.

"I found flour and oil and stuff," he explains, "and some

dried egg powder, and UHT milk. No blueberries, though." He grins. "These people were pretty well prepared, though, huh?"

"Yes," Daniel agrees. "They were." *Were.* Past tense. Where are Tom and his family now? Are they dead? He will never know. "Thanks for making breakfast." He suppresses the spike of frustration he feels that his son is frittering away supplies on a pancake breakfast they don't really need. He gets why Sam is doing it; they're camping, after all.

"There's even maple syrup," Sam says, and brandishes a bottle he must have found in the pantry. "Home-made."

"Wow." Daniel decides to go with it. They can enjoy this moment, this morning; he can let it be what Sam wants, and even needs, it to be. "Smells really good, Sam," he says, and his son shoots him a shyly pleased grin.

"So I was thinking," Sam says, once they're both seated at the table with plates of pancakes, crisp at their edges and soft in the center, drowning in sweet maple syrup. "I think we should go and get Granny."

Daniel, a fluffy forkful halfway to his mouth, stops and stares. "Get Granny," he repeats in a neutral tone, not wanting to reveal the scathing, knee-jerk incredulity. Does Sam not realize what it's like out there? Hasn't he seen enough?

"Yeah." Sam leans forward, earnest now, his pancakes momentarily forgotten. "How far is her nursing home from here? A hundred miles, maybe?"

"Closer to two hundred, and in the wrong direction." Alex's mother's nursing home is between Worcester and Springfield, a mere eighty miles or so from Boston, one of the blast sites, and nearly five hundred from the cottage. It will nearly quadruple their mileage, and bring them closer to any potential radiation or other danger.

"But we've got the gas," Sam presses, insistent now, as well as eager. "The truck has a full tank, and there were a couple of gallons in the barn. I checked. We could do it, Dad."

They'll need all that gas—and more—to get back to the cottage. "Sam..." Daniel doesn't know how to say this any other way. "Granny might already be dead."

Sam's lower lip juts out, like a child's. "But she might not be. It's only been—what? Three weeks?"

"Yes, but..." Three weeks for a dementia-suffering woman in a locked memory care unit with little food or water? Daniel doubts whether Alex's mother could last three *days*.

"I think we should, Dad," Sam says, staunch now, a little sanctimonious. "I know there are a lot of people we can't get to. Grandma and Grandpa are too far away..." His voice wavers and Daniel rubs a hand over his face. His own parents, he knows, down at their condo in Florida, are almost certainly dead, probably in the first blasts. He has tried not to think of them, except to hope that it was quick. "And Aunt Sarah... Uncle Chase... we can't get them, but Granny..." He trails off before he lifts his chin. "We could *try*."

Daniel starts to shake his head, then stops. Something about Sam's willingness, naive as it might be, calls to the better part of himself that he thought he'd already lost. "It's dangerous out there, Sam," he says quietly. "You saw yourself."

"But we've got a truck now," his son persists, excited now. "And we can stay away from the cities. You can take Route 90 the whole way, and the highways don't seem too dangerous, right?"

"We don't know that." Route 90 might be blocked off, barricaded by either the military or lawless thugs. He doesn't say it out loud, but he imagines Sam's instantaneous response. *But it might not be.*

Can they try to get Alex's mother? For a second, Daniel pictures the indomitable Jenny, only five foot two with a carefully kept perm of snow-white hair, blue eyes snapping with fire even as her mind sank into the swirling mists of dementia. She hadn't lost any of her spirit, even in a nursing home, kicking against everything, shooting back with asperity when someone dared to suggest she was in any way feeble or past it. Maybe she *would* survive.

Maybe they could get her.

It's crazy. Daniel knows it's crazy. And foolish, and maybe even a death wish for not just him—he doesn't care about himself, not anymore—but for Sam.

And yet... it feels like redemption, both for his soul and in his son's eyes. If he rescues his mother-in-law, if he somehow, against all odds and expectations, manages to bring her back to the cottage, to Alex...

Will that atone for shooting that boy, for leaving the others, and not even caring if they all died? Will it make up for the many people he's ignored, looking the other way rather than risking his life, his son's life, to save an innocent? Will it somehow soften the calluses that have grown around his soul, so he doesn't even recognize himself anymore, this weary, mercenary, hard-faced stranger?

There is, he knows, only one way he can discover the answer to those questions.

THIRTEEN
ALEX

The sign for 22 Wing/Canadian Forces Base North Bay is made of stone on a concrete plinth, with a tattered Canadian flag on one side and a US one on the other. There are also two guys in camo with semiautomatic rifles, one standing by each flag, unsmiling and at attention. One of them aims his rifle at us while the other one flags us down. All around us the air base stretches out like a small city, surrounded by chain-link fencing topped with razor wire, although this appears to be the entrance.

"Step out of the car with your hands in the air," the guy calls out. "If you are carrying a weapon, concealed or otherwise, you will be shot. I repeat, you will be shot."

His voice is matter-of-fact, almost bored, as if he were telling us to put our phones and keys in the tray at airport security. Daniel and I glance at each other, and I know what we're both thinking. Is this the start of blessed safety—or a trap?

We've been driving along the road from North Bay to the base for nearly half a mile, up a hill, past an airport, empty and abandoned-looking as everything else, the deep blue of Lake Nipissing visible below us, fringed with evergreens. I hadn't quite realized, when Nicole had talked about it, just how *big* this place was, and that was without considering the sixty floors underground somewhere.

I could hardly believe we'd made it here so quickly; Route 11 had been a straight shot, just as we'd hoped, and we'd only seen a couple of cars on the road, and none as big as ours. Some things, it seemed, were still easy.

Was this?

"Out of the car," the man barks, less pleasantly this time, and slowly Daniel opens the driver's side door, weaponless, his hands in the air. "Everybody, follow the man's orders," he tells our motley crew, his voice deliberately calm, and next to me the woman we picked up two hours ago whimpers.

She was the only unexpected aspect of our trip; we came across her fifty miles back, trudging along the side of the road and holding a baby. I thought we'd just drive by, but then Daniel pulled over hard, tires squealing, and got out of the truck.

"Dad—" Mattie began, only to fall silent.

"Let's see where she's going, at least," he said, and there was a steely note to his voice I think we all clocked but didn't really understand. Everybody watched as he stepped out of the truck, and for a second, as he stared at the woman, he looked defeated, even despairing. Then he squared his shoulders and walked over to her, speaking gently, his head bent close to hers. I saw him glance down at the baby, his expression ready to soften into an isn't-he-cute look, only for his whole body to stiffen, his face contorting with shock and then something that looked like a deep sadness, akin to grief, almost as if, for a few seconds, he might weep.

"We don't have room for her," Mattie whispered. "Do we?"

"Ruby can sit on my lap." It wouldn't be comfortable, but I could manage it for fifty miles.

The woman didn't speak or even seem to see Daniel, but

she didn't resist when, with his hand on her shoulder, he led her back to the truck. Sam moved into the back and she clambered into the truck next to me, her face a blank mask, her eyes unfocused. The baby she cradled in her arms looked tiny and wizened and still... and very clearly dead. Shocked, I glanced at Daniel, who pressed his lips together and shook his head. It was clear this woman, whoever she was, wasn't giving up her child, and I couldn't really blame her. Still, it made for an uneasy journey to North Bay, and whatever we found there... which now turns out to be more guns.

With the two pseudo-soldiers pointing their rifles at us, we all slowly climb out of the truck, Ruby sliding off my lap, our hands thrown up in the air. I see Mattie and Sam exchange panicked glances, and Kyle looks both resolute and like he might cry.

I don't think these guys will shoot us; they feel more reassuringly like normal military, although I'm pretty sure they're not. They're dressed in a random assortment of camo and military gear, like two guys playing some serious dress-up. The looks on their faces are serious, too, and their rifles are unwavering as they point them right at us. Maybe I should be more scared, but I'm so desperate to feel safe, to not have to be in charge, even if just for a little while, that right now all I can do is stand there, swaying slightly, my hands up like I'm at a rave.

I glance around at the various buildings spread out along the road—they all look innocuous, flat-roofed and utilitarian, some more modern than others.

"We heard that CFB North Bay was a safe place," Daniel says into the silence. "That you were... accepting people, to... to live here."

"You'll need to come into our decontamination unit," the first man states by way of reply. "Once you're clear, you'll have an interview to determine your suitability for the NBSRC."

"NBSRC?" Daniel repeats.

"The North Bay Survival and Resettlement Center. Did you leave the keys in the truck?"

Daniel nods. The man speaks into a walkie-talkie while the other gestures with his rifle for us to head through the chain-link gates to the parking lot with an aerodrome on one side, a concrete building on the other. We walk slowly, all huddled together, our hands still in the air, each step laden with trepidation. What are we walking into? And should we leave? Get away while we still can?

I'm not sure we have a choice anymore, because already the metal gates are clanging shut behind us, and one of the soldiers gets in the truck to drive it away. We might have just lost all our belongings. I glance at the woman we picked up; her head is bent as she croons to her dead baby, and she seems oblivious to what is going on. Mattie is holding Phoebe's hand, and everybody still looks scared.

As we approach the building, two people emerge, dressed in the kind of inflated hazmat suits, complete with helmets, I associate with disaster movies. They look like a cross between construction workers and astronauts. They gesture for us to come into the building, their faces serious beneath their face shields.

"Who's reminded of the Michelin Man?" Daniel whispers, and Mattie smothers a nervous giggle. I throw him a look of gratitude, that he can make this easier for all of us, but he's not looking at me, and despite his joke his face looks grim.

We are shepherded through a waiting room of what was probably once some kind of health center, into a room that has been cleared of all furniture; before I've fully taken in the barren surroundings, Kyle, Sam, and Daniel are taken into another one. The person in the hazmat suit is a woman, I realize, and she nods at us, her voice muffled by her helmet and face shield.

"You all need to strip. All clothes should be left on the floor.

Try to touch them as little as possible, if you can." Her voice is matter-of-fact, without any sympathy, and we all gape at her, save for the woman with the baby, who, by either miracle or tragedy, is still oblivious.

"Do you think we might be contaminated?" I ask, my voice wavering with nervousness. "We've been in the backwoods of Ontario since—"

"Strip," the woman says again, and it's clear she's not going to engage with any of us more than that.

We all start taking off our clothes as carefully as possible; considering we ran out of razors five months ago, I'm feeling a little less groomed than I would have preferred for an impromptu striptease, but I'm more concerned about some minuscule molecules of radioactive whatever that might be coming off my grubby shirt and shorts—something that hadn't crossed my mind for months, since those first blasts, until William Stratton mentioned it, and now this. Is it a real possibility, or are they just following precautionary procedures? Either way, we're all getting naked.

Ruby, I see with a pulse of motherly shock as she self-consciously slips off her own t-shirt, is looking far more womanly than she did before everything happened, back in the day when I might have helped her rinse her hair in the shower. Mattie, on the other hand, looks as thin I am, long-limbed and bony, shielding herself with her hands as a blush rises to her cheeks and a naked Phoebe clings to her leg. The woman with the baby hasn't moved.

"Ma'am," the woman in the hazmat says to her. "You need to start taking off your clothes. And your baby's clothes—" She takes a step forward, and then does a double-take before recoiling when she sees that the baby is dead. She turns to me, in accusation.

"Why is she holding a dead baby?"

"We only picked her up about fifty miles before the base," I reply, lowering my voice as if to keep the woman from hearing, although of course she still can, even if she doesn't seem to be taking anything in. "We don't know anything about her, but I'm guessing she'd had some trauma." Obviously.

"But..." The woman looks caught between horror and a reluctant sympathy, then she squares her shoulders and takes a meaningful step toward the woman. "Ma'am, you need to let go of that baby. Now." Firmly but gently, she starts to pry the baby from the woman's arms; the woman lets out an ear-splitting shriek in response and takes a stumbling step back, clutching her baby to her. Mattie and Ruby both look transfixed with horror by the macabre scene, while Phoebe stares on, seemingly unfazed. I wince because I think the baby has been dead for at least a day or two, and, no matter what, this isn't going to end well for anyone, the poor dead baby included.

Meanwhile the woman continues letting out a constant, keening shriek, like the human version of a fire alarm. For a second, the woman in the hazmat suit looks like she doesn't know what to do; then she puts one hand on the woman's shoulder and starts steering her out of the cell. We watch, gaping, as the woman is frog-marched out of the room, still wailing and clutching her baby. The door clangs shut behind her, sealing us in this empty cell of a room—alone, naked, and shivering.

"Where do you think they're taking her?" Mattie asks after a few seconds have passed.

"Hopefully somewhere safe, where they can help her." Although of course I have no idea if that's true or not, but I hope it is. I want this place—the NBSRC or whatever it's called—to work. I want to feel safe, and everyone else to as well, and for none of it to be my responsibility.

"Do you think she's going to be okay?" Mattie sounds doubtful, and frankly so am I. That woman did not seem remotely okay, and the woman in the hazmat suit wasn't exactly intent on making her so.

"I hope so, Mattie." I take a steadying breath, determined to believe in this place. "I'm sure they're taking care of her. And hopefully we won't be left here too long."

As if on cue, the woman in the hazmat suit returns, her expression bland but severe. "Your clothes will be disposed of," she informs us crisply, or as crisply as you can sound when your voice is muffled by a face shield and helmet. "You'll need to shower, wash with the soap provided, and then use the far door to go to the changing room, where you will dress in the issued clothing." She gestures to a door on the far wall. "Go through there, down the hallway, and to the showers."

We all hesitate; I suppose no one really wants to walk into an unknown room naked, but what else can we do? Putting my arms around my daughters, with Mattie holding Phoebe's hand, I shepherd us all through the door and down the hallway, to whatever awaits us there.

Fortunately, it is, as we all really should have known it would be, just a shower, much like we'd see at our local gym, albeit a little more utilitarian. Any stalls have been ripped out, so it's just spigots in the wall, but they let out a surprisingly forceful spray when we push a button beneath. We all stand under a separate shower nozzle, Phoebe with Mattie, as we rinse the radioactivity off us—if there was ever any there to begin with; but the truth is, it feels *wonderful*. I haven't had a shower in over seven months. To be sluiced with warm water is a little bit of heaven, and, if they end up ushering us into the next room for our execution, my last thought will be *worth it*.

I meet Mattie's gaze underneath the spray and I'm pretty sure she's thinking the same thing. My hope rushes to the fore, ready to be unleashed. This is going to be good for us, I tell myself. This is what we need.

We wash ourselves with the soap provided in dispensers fixed to the wall, scrub our hair and armpits and nether regions, and I can't remember ever feeling so clean. When we are finished, we walk down the hallway through to an empty room on the other side, where there are cheap, white towels and navy-blue boiler suits waiting for us on a couple of folding chairs.

"What's going on, exactly?" Mattie whispers as she combs her fingers through her damp hair. She's tightened the draw-string waist of her boiler suit, so it actually looks fashionable; weren't these things in style a little while ago? Ruby's been issued a woman's size, which engulfs her, the cuffs hanging far past down her hands. She rolls up the pantlegs as Mattie twists her damp hair into a knot. Phoebe has been given a man's white t-shirt to wear, which falls to her ankles.

"That man said after we'd been—decontaminated, I guess," I tell them both, "we'd have some kind of interview." I'm trying to sound confident rather than nervous. I'm really not at all sure I want to be *interviewed*, but if that's what it takes to stay here...

Mattie shakes her head slowly. "What is this, District 13?" She raises her eyebrows, all sass. "When did my life become a YA novel, and where is my tortured love triangle?"

I let out a snort of laughter. "Ben Stratton and Kyle?" I suggest, my eyebrows raised right back at her, and she rolls her eyes.

'Mom, *puh-lease*," she protests, her tone scathing, but I see the flush on her cheeks, and I know it's not just from the hot shower. I don't mind; my daughter deserves a little excitement in her life—normal, teenaged excitement, and not the kind that gets you either shot or obliterated. Being in a place like this, when we don't have to fight for our survival, will be good for her.

Another door opens, and the same woman, minus the hazmat suit, is standing there, dressed in normal clothes, which make our boiler suits now seem a little ridiculous, but hopefully we'll get to wear our own clothes soon. Her auburn hair is pulled back into a bun and there's a spray of freckles across her nose. I judge her to be in her mid-thirties, but her expression is as severe as a sixty-year-old schoolmarm.

"Come this way," she instructs briskly, and I put my arm around Ruby as we walk through yet another door, into what looks like yet another empty room.

Mattie pauses in the doorway, Phoebe clinging to her, to turn to look at the woman. "What happened to that woman with the baby?" she asks, and her tone is borderline rude, definitely aggressive.

The woman frowns. "We are giving her the help she needs."

Mattie frowns but doesn't press the point. None of us knew that woman. We might feel sorry for her, but that's all. We walk into the next room, and a little gasp of relief escapes me when I see Daniel, Kyle, and Sam all sitting on folding chairs, dressed in identical boiler suits. Sam and Kyle look, in turn, haughty and scared, and my husband only looks bemused.

"Blue's always suited you," he says, and again, improbably, I laugh.

The room is empty save for a half dozen folding chairs, so there are no clues as to what is going on or what this alleged interview will require.

"Did you learn anything?" I ask Daniel as I sit next to him. Ruby sits next to me, and Mattie takes the chair on the end, with Phoebe on her lap.

"That I really missed having a shower," Daniel quips as he smiles at me, his eyes creasing in a way I haven't seen them do in months, since before this all happened, and I'm suddenly struck by how relieved my husband is, to be in a place where someone else is in charge. Where someone else is responsible for keeping us safe.

That's what we both need now.

The door opens and then a man steps in, and I'm pretty sure, judging by the composed but intent look on his face, that he's the one conducting this interview... and deciding our fates.

FOURTEEN

"Good morning."

The man smiles at us, a perfunctory, professional sort of smile, and then closes the door carefully behind him. I'm trying to get the measure of him, whoever he is—he's average height, a little slighter than average build, with thinning dark hair and dark brown eyes behind wire-rimmed glasses. He looks like an accountant, save for the fact that he's dressed in combat fatigues, and I decide there is something comfortingly familiar about his manner. He's an administrator, a bureaucrat, like before the bombs.

"Good morning," Daniel replies, and we all murmur variations of a greeting like unruly children cowed by the new teacher.

He stands in front of us, hands folded loosely in front of him as he surveys us with a faint smile. "You're probably wondering what on earth is going on," he remarks, and I decide his voice is pleasant—pleasant but also restrained, with a hint of the friendly Canadian accent. *Trustworthy*, I think, wanting to believe it. "What we've found," he continues, "is that it's best to have a system in place to process new arrivals. Hence the shower, the boiler suit, and this little interview. I know it might all seem kind of utilitarian and restricted, like something out of *The Hunger Games*, but it really isn't." He glances at Mattie as he says this, and she smiles a little shamefacedly. I'm amused, until I wonder if the shower room was bugged and he heard her make that remark about District 13. Then I tell myself I am overreacting.

"Maybe you could tell us a little bit about this place," Daniel suggests. "What it's like, and who you are. Someone told us about the air base, but the truth is we came in pretty much blind."

"Of course." The man's reply is swift, easy. "My name is Michael Duart, and before the first attacks I worked as a computer engineer right here at 22 Wing, otherwise known as CFB North Bay."

"So how did you go from that," Daniel asks slowly, "to this? What happened to the military presence here? Did they really all just up and leave?"

Michael nods somberly. "Unfortunately, yes. All the military personnel were mobilized after Toronto was attacked." He pauses. "You might not have realized, but this air base didn't actually house any aircraft. The last squadron flew out of here in 1992, when the control tower, airfield, fuel depot, and other base assets were demolished. The airport across the road is for civilians." He pauses, his expression and voice both somber. "In any case, after the mobilization... no one came back."

"No one?" Mattie repeats in something like a squeak.

"There were some reservists still here," Michael Duart allows, "and some non-combat personnel, such as myself. But most everyone was evacuated from the base itself, as well as the city of North Bay, because, as a control center, 22 Wing was thought to be a likely target. It wasn't attacked, obviously, as our enemy focused on inflicting maximum casualties through the bombing of urban areas. But, as you can imagine, or not even have to imagine, since it was probably like this where you were as well, everything was pretty chaotic at that time. If people weren't evacuated, they deserted. Others panicked. People headed west or holed up in their homes. There were, sadly, quite a few suicides." He pauses, as if in memory of those unfortunates. "For a couple of months," he resumes, "it felt like no one was in charge." He spreads his hands wide as if to say, *what can you do?*

"Yes," Daniel agrees, "it certainly felt like that to me." He pauses, his forehead furrowed in thought, and I know he feels he can't get the measure of this man. Is he as trustworthy as he seems? I want him to be. "So what happened then?" Daniel finally asks.

"I realized someone needed to take control." Michael Duart speaks simply, without either pride or modesty, just a statement of fact. "I could see there was a great resource here, even without the military presence. All the infrastructure"—he sweeps one hand out to encompass everything about this place —the barbed wire, the semiautomatic rifles, the security system, the sixty floors underground—"comes in pretty handy. But if it fell into the wrong hands..." He pauses. "Well, maybe you've seen what happens then. Vigilantes and renegades taking over whatever building they can—a hospital, a hotel, a mall." He pauses meaningfully. "It's not pretty," he concludes somberly, "when that happens."

We are all silent for a moment, recalling when we've seen exactly that. No, it's not pretty at all.

"You must have moved fast," Daniel remarks, "to take control of a place this size. How big is it?"

"Well, I didn't do it on my own," Michael replies, sidestepping the question about size. "There were a few dozen of us who saw the need and acted. That was about four months ago. Since then, we've done our best to hone our process and system, for the good of everyone here, and the future we can make for ourselves."

He straightens a little. "You might have noticed this is called the North Bay Survival and Resettlement Center. That's because this is about more than just surviving the next few months or years of whatever happens—the fallout, a nuclear winter, you name it. This is about resettling the country, and indeed all of civilization. And if that sounds grandiose," he continues, sounding defensive even though none of us has said a word, "well, you're right, it is, but that's the world—or lack of it —that we're living in right now, but we here at the NBSRC want to change it. We genuinely do want to make the world a better place."

He gives this stirring speech in the same matter-of-fact voice, but now I detect the slightest hint of pride, and I can't fault him for it. I'm stirred; they *are* doing something grandiose and good here. At least, I hope they are.

"I suppose that's true enough," Daniel agrees with an easy smile, or at least the approximation of one. "So tell us how this works."

"Of course." Michael Duart's voice possesses an eager alacrity that suggests he is getting into his stride. He shifts where he stands, throwing back his slight shoulders like he is settling into himself. "So I'll outline our basic principles and then you can decide if you're on board or not. If you're not, and I'll be honest with you, a fair amount of people have decided that, then you leave here with all your possessions intact, save for the clothes we've had to dispose of due to the potential of radioactive contamination."

"Okay," Daniel agrees after a moment. "Sounds fair."

And maybe too good to be true? I lurch between deep paranoia and wild hope, but I already know which one I want to choose.

"Good." Michael Duart gives a brief nod. "So, the first thing is to assure you that we are not running some kind of Stalinist work camp here. We are not about the state, such as it is, taking control, or the individual giving up his or her rights for the betterment of the community." He gives us the sort of a smile that invites you to share the joke; all that's missing is an eye-roll. "I'm saying that up front because that's what most people are afraid of. The boiler suits don't help, I know, but it was just easier to have something basic for people to change into, and there were stacks of them here already, so we thought we might as well put them to good use."

"Fair enough," Daniel replies equably. "But how does this place operate?"

"I'm coming to that," Michael assures us, with a quick smile. "So, the reason I said all that up front isn't just because it's what people are afraid of, but because of some of the measures we've had to put into place, to make this place function successfully at the current time, which I'm sure you'll be able to understand once I've explained it to you."

"Maybe just tell us what to expect," Daniel suggests, the very slightest of edges to his voice. I think he's tired of all the buildup, just as I realize I am.

"Of course." Michael Duart's voice is smooth and assured. "If you agree to our principles and decide to stay, and, of course, if you're evaluated successfully—"

"What does that mean?" I interject.

"We have rigorous standards," Michael explains with only the barest hint of apology. "Medically, physically, intellectually. We have only space for about five hundred people on site. We can't just take anyone, not if we're rebuilding the world."

Rebuilding the world? All right, yes, he *does* sound grandiose, and I'm not sure how I feel about it.

"In any case," Michael resumes smoothly, "assuming it's all successful, you'll be assigned lodgings here on the site."

"Not underground?" Sam asks, sounding both eager and disappointed. "The NORAD Underground Complex... it seems really cool..." He trails off uncertainly.

"We are in the process of refurbishing the underground complex for human habitation," Michael Duart informs us smoothly. "And, of course, we are monitoring radiation levels. At the current time, the atmosphere is at safe levels. But if that changes, then we will rehouse everyone in the complex." He glances around at all of us as if asking for any questions, and then, after a second's pause, continues. "Now, families stay together..." He glances between us all. "Are you all one family?"

"Yes," Mattie says fiercely just as Kyle admits, sounding resigned, "No."

Michael Duart's eyebrows lift as he waits for an explanation.

"Kyle's not related to us *technically*," I explain after a moment. "But he's been with us for months and he's like family." I sound like I'm pleading, and I'm annoyed with myself. Why shouldn't we decide who we live with? Why have I already handed Michael Duart that power, just because he's acting like he has it?

Already, I know the answer. Because it's safe here, and we'll have food, and a place to sleep, and security. And for that, in this world, I know I'm willing to hand over a *lot* of power.

"I see." Michael Duart is clearly making no promises about us all staying together. "But the rest of you are family?"

"Yes," I say firmly. I'm not about to have Phoebe taken away from us, not after Mattie begged for her not to be.

Michael Duart's gaze lasers into mine and I see a hint of cool appraisal there that unnerves me. "These are your four children?" he asks, and it's like he knows. Yet how can he?

"Yes," I say again, just as firmly. Phoebe has the same dark hair as I do, even if her complexion is far more olive-toned than mine. There's absolutely no way for him to figure out that Phoebe isn't my daughter unless she tells him herself. But why should he even care?

"All right," he replies after a moment, his tone equable, and I relax a little bit. Then he glances at Sam. "You look over eighteen," he remarks in the tone of someone saying, "aren't you a handsome boy."

"I'm nineteen," Sam replies, sounding guarded.

"Well, then, you would live with Kyle"—he gives a nod— "in the single men's dormitory. The rest of you would be allocated housing together." His tone is amenable and yet at the same time clearly brooks no argument. "There are a variety of houses on site, but most families are guaranteed at least two bedrooms and a bathroom. Meals are served communally two times a day; at the present time, to conserve supplies, there's no midday meal. Everyone eats the same thing—I'm afraid we can't cater for any special diets or allergies, not even severe ones. It's simply not possible at this time." He pauses, as if waiting for confirmation, and I wonder if anyone has been turned away because of a peanut allergy.

"Okay," Daniel says after a moment.

"Everyone over the age of fourteen is assigned a work placement," Michael continues after another pause. "Which will be decided by the governing committee based on community needs as well as individual skills and abilities. Children under fourteen will be educated according to the national curriculum." The flash of a brief smile. "We are fortunate to have some teachers among us."

A silence while we all absorb this, but no one objects.

"We also find," he continues, "that it helps the camp to function more smoothly if there's no alcohol or drug use whatsoever."

I let out a huff of disbelieving laughter before I can help myself. "Where could we get either of those things, these days?"

He gives me a thin-lipped smile. "You'd be surprised."

"Any other rules?" Daniel asks. He sounds like he suspects there are, quite a lot of them.

"There's a curfew," Michael replies, like an acknowledgement of an implied criticism. "Nine p.m., everyone is back in their lodgings. Again, it helps with the smooth functioning—"

"Of the camp," Daniel completes. "Understandable."

"I'm glad you think so."

Am I imagining the undercurrent of tension that is suddenly running through the room like an electric wire? For a second, no one says anything.

"The only other rule of note," Michael finishes, "is that we have a zero-tolerance policy. Again, we've found it's the only way to make things work for this number of people—"

"How many people are here?" I interject, curious.

"At present, four hundred, give or take a few," Michael replies. "As I mentioned before, we have capacity for five hundred." Although not underground, I recall. In any case, they're almost full. Quite a few people have agreed to all the rules, which means maybe we should, too.

"This zero-tolerance policy," Daniel asks. "What does that mean, exactly?"

"It means that if you break any of our rules, you and your dependents are required to leave," Michael replies. His tone is utterly unapologetic. "No warnings, no second chances. You just go. And you are not allowed back."

"Not ever?" Mattie asks, sounding like a small child.

"Not ever," Michael agrees. "I know it might sound harsh, but we have to think of the greater good."

Which *definitely* sounds like a Stalinist work camp, and yet... I get it. Sort of. They can't have people coming and going, a revolving door of would-be survivalists.

"Any other rules?" Daniel asks mildly.

Michael gives a little shrug. "No one is allowed off site—again, for the greater good. We are able to monitor radiation levels and they indicate that there's no great danger at the base, but we have no idea how far that safety extends, and, since we can't keep tabs on how far people might go, it's better simply to keep the center contained. We have everything we need here, as you'll discover if you stay."

"How do you have electricity?" I blurt. "And running water?"

The smile Michael aims at me seems a little smug. "Twenty-two Wing operates on a microgrid, powered by solar and wind energy. Neither electricity nor running water will ever be a problem." He makes it sound as if this is his personal accomplishment, but, since he is a computer engineer, maybe it was.

"Do you have internet?" Mattie asks, sounding so eager that I almost laugh. It could be seven months ago, when we arrived at the cottage, and she was bemoaning the lack of Wi-Fi.

"We do," Michael replies proudly, and for a second we all goggle. It's as if we've stumbled into Eden, with all its technological promises—water, electricity, even internet. It feels too good to be true, but that doesn't mean it is. "Although," he continues, "there's very little you can access online right now. Most of the U.S. and Canada's servers were destroyed in the blasts, or the resulting EMP. There are a few other bases in North America that are operating like this one, and we're able to exchange information. Hopefully, as I've stated, one day we can work together to resettle both Canada and the United States."

"Big dreams," Daniel remarks, and for a second Michael looks flinty-eyed.

"Yes," he agrees briefly, and another silence descends on us that feels uncomfortably tense.

"Who makes all these decisions?" Daniel asks. "You talk

about *we*. Do you mean you and the friends who helped you take control of this place?"

Michael's eyes narrow and I resist the urge to grab Daniel's hand and give it a hard warning squeeze. Does he want us to fail whatever evaluation we're given? Maybe it's already started, and this is part of it. Too argumentative and you're out. And I already know I want to stay. Badly. I'm too tired even to think about doing anything else, even if I might regret it later.

"Essentially, yes," Michael replies evenly. "The governing committee is the initial group who secured the base."

"How many of you are there?"

"Twenty-four."

"That's quite a lot of people to weigh in on all these matters," Daniel observes.

Michael's nostrils flare as he smiles faintly. "True. Any major decisions are taken by an executive committee of five." He pauses. "But of course, if you don't like it, you don't have to stay."

"I didn't say anything about not liking it," Daniel replies easily. "It's just good to know what we're signing up for."

"Of course." He glances between us all. "Should I leave you to discuss it? You have fifteen minutes. After that, we'll need these rooms for processing other arrivals, and, if you decide to stay, you'll need to have your medical and ability evaluations."

Medical and ability...? I try not to show my alarm; Kyle looks positively panicked. It's hard to believe more people have already arrived since we did. It can't have been much over an hour. If there are already four hundred-odd people here and only five hundred able to be housed in total...

This place is filling up.

With another faint smile and a small bow that feels a little ironic, he leaves us alone.

"Are we staying?" Mattie demands the minute he's closed the door behind him. She's scooped Phoebe up into her arms and is holding her protectively while the little girl blinks slowly, seemingly unfazed.

We all glance around uncertainly at each other.

"Where else would we go?" Sam asks, the first time he's spoken. I can't tell how he feels about the idea; he seems resigned, but I'm aware—again—that he has not spoken to me or met my eye in several days. Our hurried conversation under that cedar tree did not resolve or even advance our issues at all, and the truth is, I'm not entirely sure what our issues even are, only that they're there.

"It feels a little cultish," Mattie remarks, holding Phoebe even closer. "Like, who *is* that guy? And why does he get to be in charge?"

"They need to maintain some kind of order," Daniel replies in the same mild tone he used with Michael Duart. "But I know what you mean, Mats," he continues as he glances at me. "What do you think, Alex?"

I don't answer right away because I'm feeling a lot of things at the moment. I'm scared of change as well as surrendering choice, and yet... a very large part of me longs for nothing more than to curl up in a bed, in a place with running water and electric light. I crave stability and safety; the idea of two solid meals a day made by someone else feels like a little slice of heaven. Warm showers, barbed-wire fence... it's a trade-off, but right now it's also what I want.

Besides, what other choice is there? Like Sam said, where could we go?

"We can always leave if we don't like it," I point out. "So in that way it feels like a win-win situation, right?"

"We might not even get in, anyway," Kyle ventures, biting his thumbnail as his gaze darts around the empty room. "I mean, what are these evaluations?"

"Kyle, you'll be fine," Mattie tells him, and he gives her a grateful yet uncertain look.

We all fall silent, waiting for someone to give the final verdict, to make us jump, but no one speaks. This is the right decision, I tell myself. It has to be.

"Let's do it," I say, and everyone's relief at having made a decision—*this* decision—is palpable.

I just hope it's the right one.

FIFTEEN

In the end, the evaluations Kyle was so scared of weren't actually that bad. After we made our decision to stay, a man returned, professionally blank-faced; Michael Duart, it seemed, had moved on. He sent us on with an escort—a woman I didn't recognize—to the Health Center down the road, where we would have our medical checks and ability evaluations.

There was something comfortingly bureaucratic about it all; as I waited for my turn with the Center's physician, completing a health form, I felt I could have been at the DMV or the dentist. The building was sunlit and modern, nothing apocalyptic about it at all. There were even a few magazines on the coffee table, admittedly all a year old.

"These were out of date even before the nukes," Mattie remarked scathingly, and I smiled. Had any waiting room ever been any different?

The medical evaluation was more or less perfunctory, given by a professional yet friendly doctor—he even wore a white lab coat—who took my blood pressure and my heart rate and checked my eyesight and hearing, my reflexes and my teeth.

"You're in good health," he told me, "all things considered.

A little malnourished, but that's to be expected. Hopefully it will change pretty soon." He flashed me a reassuring smile as he ticked something on a chart I couldn't see.

Afterwards, I filled out a questionnaire about my abilities—it felt like a cross between a Myers-Briggs test and a career quiz on Buzzfeed. What was my last complete level of education? What jobs had I had? Did I like working with people or by myself? Was I more of a big vision or a small details type person?

Mattie sat next to me, snorting under her breath as she shook her head and ticked off answers. There was something both mundane and ridiculous about it all, considering how wildly dangerous the whole world was, and yet, as Daniel had said, order needed to be maintained.

Filling out forms, I supposed, was part of that.

In any case, we all pass both parts of the evaluations, even Kyle, who was particularly nervous about the ability part of it. None of us needed have worried; we are informed, in a perfunctory sort of way, that our evaluations have been successful and we need to wait for our next orders.

We stay in the medical center for over an hour. Phoebe falls asleep on Mattie's lap while the rest of us slump in our seats before we are told where to go—the six of us to a duplex on a side street, and Kyle and Sam to the men's lodgings, in an apartment building down the road.

The 22 Wing air base is a mix of refreshingly modern buildings, like the medical center, and other ones that, in the pre-nuclear era, could have used a major refurb. There are houses and apartment complexes mixed in with warehouses, supply depots, and massive garages and hangars. All of it is interspersed with parking lots and swathes of green grass, so the effect is part small town, part summer camp. Every so often, in the distance, I catch a glimpse of chain-link fence topped with razor wire, or, once or twice, the flash of blue that is Lake Nipissing far below us.

It is too strange to think about this being our home for however long, and so I don't. I simply follow the woman to the house we've been assigned, telling Sam and Kyle to meet us before dinner, and then walk up the three sagging steps to a sliver of porch and then the dim interior, blinking in the gloom.

The woman leaves us alone, telling us our belongings will be delivered shortly, dinner is at six, and that we will be given our job assignments tomorrow. We crowd into the tiny hallway that manages to smell both of bleach and mold and stand there, no one seeming to know what to do.

Mattie ventures into the living room first, Phoebe on her hip, and then Ruby follows. I glance at Daniel, who manages a weary smile.

"Home sweet home," he quips, and, for a reason I can't really understand, this makes my eyes fill up with tears. "Alex..." he begins, alarmed, and I just shake my head and follow the girls into the tiny living room as I blink the tears back. I don't even know why I'm crying; out of relief, or sorrow for all we've already lost? It doesn't matter; now is not the time to cry.

Mattie has gone on to the bedroom, while Ruby stands in the middle of the living room, where two uncomfy-looking loveseats in faded beige face each other over a coffee table of fake wood laminate. A small flatscreen TV hangs on the wall, and a breakfast bar too narrow to use separates this space from a tiny, dark kitchen. Off the living room are two bedrooms, one double, one with two narrow twins, the standard-issue white sheets and scratchy-looking beige coverlets folded at the foot of each mattress. A tiny, windowless bathroom at the end of a short hallway completes our accommodation.

Home sweet home indeed, and yet it's *safe*.

I sink onto the end of the double bed, gazing around in weary wonder. The entire house is carpeted in electric-blue matting, the kind you'd see in a school or a gym. It reminds me of being at one of those residential activity centers kids were required to go to in around eighth grade, for team-building exercises and organized fun. This whole experience is giving off something of the same vibe, but I tell myself that's not necessarily a bad thing. We're not looking for five-star accommodation, after all. We just want to be safe.

"You okay?" Daniel asks as he comes into the room.

"Yeah." My voice is clogged, and I have to clear my throat.

Daniel frowns. "Alex..."

"It's okay," I say quickly. I don't want to give in to emotion, to *grief*, because I'm fast realizing that's what this is. I can see it coming for me, a towering tidal wave of sadness, ready to crash over me and then drag me under. I can't let that happen, and yet I'm afraid I'm powerless to stop it.

It's been only a week since the cottage burned down, since my mother, Kerry, and Justine all died, since we lost everything. A week where I've soldiered on, focusing on practicalities, but now I'm not sure I can do that anymore. Now, sitting in this bare, ugly little room, I miss the cottage, the life we'd built there, with an intensity that leaves me breathless, a sharp pain of yearning lodged underneath my ribs, so it hurts to breathe.

I think of the sunlight pouring in through the living room windows and gilding the lake in gold. I remember Ruby drawing new, baby-skinned potatoes from the earth, a look of pride and wonder on her face, and Mattie and Kyle fishing by the lake, two slender silhouettes against a twilit sky. I think of glorious sunsets and the sense of peace that seemed to hover over the whole place, of Kerry and me laughing so hard our stomachs hurt, of the comforting crackles of woodfires in the evening and snow heaped on the railing of the deck like mounded icing, the whole world cloaked in white, with the hushed stillness that only comes from three feet of snow over everything.

None of it was what I'd originally wanted, when we'd arrived there last November, but it became something good and true. Something I loved and was proud of because I'd both shared it and built it with my own hands.

And now it's all gone, along with people I've loved, and the future is a depressing little room with a stained mattress and fake wood and a life of obeying the orders of a faceless group of middling bureaucrats.

Yet, I remind myself, we will be safe and fed. We will have *showers*.

I press the heels of my hands to my eyes, hard enough to hurt, so I see flashing lights beneath my scrunched-closed eyelids, but it's not enough to keep the tears in. They seep out anyway, silently trickling down my cheeks. I feel the mattress dip beneath Daniel's weight as he comes to sit next to me.

He puts his arm around me, draws me close, so my cheek is resting on his shoulder. Neither of us speaks; the tears are still coming, now dripping off my chin. I couldn't stop them even if I tried, and I'm not trying anymore. There's a release, in weeping, and one I haven't indulged in for some time. I thought I needed to be strong for everyone, but I think of Mattie crying the other day by the stream, and I wonder if that's what I've needed, too. The release, as well the acceptance of grief... even if it doesn't actually change anything, which I already know it won't.

"Do you think we made a mistake in staying?" Daniel asks after a few minutes have passed. I can hear Mattie and Ruby in the other bedroom, moving furniture around, already making this place a home.

"No." My voice wavers and ends on a sigh. "I don't. I just... wish things were different." Which is so obvious it's absurd, but I don't know how else to articulate how I'm feeling. I miss *everything*—mornings drinking cleavers coffee with Kerry, the smell of the damp spring breeze when I stepped out onto the deck. My mother's fond smile, her eyes dimmed by dementia. The way Ruby's would light up when she found a plant she could do something with, even if the rest of us just saw a straggly-looking weed. Mattie's fierceness in trying to tackle *everything*, the way the cottage seemed to settle at night, the beams creaking comfortably as the fire crackled and blazed.

I want it all back so much, and yet I force myself to remember everything else about those brief months at the cottage—the ever-present fear of something going badly wrong, and the gut-churning anxiety when it did. The constant terror of being invaded, which we were. The yawning sense of uncertainty about everything—where we would find food, what would happen to the whole world.

Here we are safe. We're provided for. I don't need to be scared in the same way, even if the future remains uncertain and unknowable.

I force my head up from Daniel's shoulder. "It's just this carpet," I tell him, as he raises his eyebrows in query. "It's so ugly."

He lets out a huff of laughter and then draws me close again, brushing a kiss against my forehead. I close my eyes, savoring the moment of togetherness, because they've been so few and far between.

"Okay, ew?"

We pull apart to see Mattie standing in the doorway, fists planted on her hips, a look of disgust on her face.

"Sorry," Daniel murmurs. "How's your room?"

"Like, minuscule," Mattie huffs. "We've put the beds together so there's room for Phoebe."

"Let me see," I say, dredging up a smile, and I follow her to the second bedroom, which is just as small as ours. It's not ideal, but it's better than we've had recently. I glance around for Phoebe and see she is sitting on the kitchen floor, pulling pots out of a cupboard, like any toddler might.

I walk into the kitchen and, simply because I can, turn on

the faucet. Water rushes from it and I run my fingers through it, amazed and gratified. Besides the shower today, I haven't seen running water since November. It feels like a miracle.

I tell myself this really is going to be okay.

Mattie, at least, seems energized. She makes up the beds, and then announces that she, Ruby, and Phoebe are going to look around.

"Look around?" I repeat, already alarmed. "What do you mean?"

Mattie shrugs. "This is our home for, like, the *foreseeable*. I want to see what it's like."

I glance at Daniel. "I don't know…"

"I think they're safe," he says quietly. "It's all enclosed and guarded here."

"There are four hundred people in this place," I remind him. "Four hundred people we don't know."

"They've all been vetted the same as we have," he reminds me. "And considering the zero-tolerance policy they've got going here, I think we can give the girls a little freedom."

"All right," I finally relent, "but be back here in an hour."

"How am I supposed to know when an hour is up?" Mattie demands. "I don't have a phone."

"There's such a thing as a watch," I retort, and she lets out an exasperated groan.

"I don't have one of those, either."

"Just estimate," Daniel tells her. He puts his arm around me, both comfort and warning. "And have fun."

The little house feels eerily silent once the girls have all trooped out.

"I don't think they should have gone," I say, already fretting. "We have no idea about this place, Daniel, or what kind of people are here."

"They're people we're going to be living with for the *foreseeable*," he reminds me, wryly echoing Mattie. "I know it's hard,

Alex, but we've got to let them make a life here, just as everyone else has to."

"I know, I know," I say, nodding mechanically. "This is good for them." I imagine Mattie making friends, flicking her hair, and I feel a sense of relief steal through me. I don't need to be scared anymore, but it's hard to let go of the fear.

"How long do you think we'll be here?" I ask Daniel.

"How long? What do you mean?" He smiles faintly. "Are you already thinking of going?"

"No... but the whole resettlement thing. What does that even mean? Are we going to leave here to go somewhere else, somewhere... real?"

Daniel is silent for a moment. "This is real, Alex," he finally says, his tone grave. "More real than anything else right now. The cities I saw—Utica, Springfield, Albany—they were ruins. Wrecks. And... dangerous. I can't see anyone living in them anytime soon. And if what Stratton said about the radiation is true, that the whole east coast is a washout..."

I don't want to think about the radiation. "I didn't know you went all the way to Albany."

He shrugs. "There were some barricades and that was the way around them."

I shake my head slowly. "Why won't you tell me about those months, Daniel?" Now doesn't feel like the right time to address any of this, but I don't know when will be. "Why did it take you so long to get back to the cottage?"

"I told you." He meets my gaze, and somehow that is worse than if he didn't, because there's a remote blankness in his eyes that seems utterly opaque. I don't know what's behind it, or if anything is. "There were barricades and things like that. We had to go the long way around several times." He shrugs in a twitchy sort of way. "Anyway, we don't need to talk about that now. It's in the past, Alex. Better to look forward." A rebuke, and one I accept, because I know he's right, even if it still feels like there's something heavy and immovable between us. Perhaps there always will be. "What happened to that woman and her baby, do you know?" he asks, an abrupt segue.

I shake my head. "I don't know. A woman took her away. She said they'd give her the help she needs, but..." I trail off, not sure how to finish that sentence, or whether I want to.

Daniel nods slowly, in acceptance of what I've said as well as what I haven't. His shoulders slump and he looks down at the ground, seeming moved in a way I don't really understand. Surely he's seen worse things than that woman and her baby. "Poor woman," he says quietly, the words laced with grief. "Poor baby."

"What do you think happened to them?" I ask. "I mean, before?"

"The baby looked only a few months old, but it might have been older, and was simply small from malnourishment. I think it probably starved to death." He is silent, his face drawn in lines of stoical sadness, and his gaze is distant in a way that makes me suspect he's not thinking of that woman and her baby at all.

A knock at the door, a determined rat-a-tat-tat, has us both jumping. When was the last time we heard a knock on a door? I can't remember. Daniel goes to answer it, while I steel myself for whatever's next.

It turns out to be a guy delivering our belongings, and so we spend the next hour unpacking everything, arranging it just so. Our guns have been taken, but there's a note informing us we can collect them if and when we choose to leave the NBSRC.

"It makes sense," Daniel remarks when he reads it. "Even if I don't like it. You can't have four or five hundred people walking around, armed. It would be civil war."

Which makes me wonder if the girls are actually safe, wandering around. "What kind of people are here, do you think?"

Daniel shrugs. "I guess we'll find out at dinner."

After over seven months of virtual isolation, it's strange and more than a little unsettling to think about meeting so many people, making small talk. I'm not really sure I remember how.

Mattie, Ruby, and Phoebe return a little while later, seeming animated; apparently, there's a youth center with a ping-pong table and some board games. They met a few other kids and, although Mattie acts dismissive, I can tell she is excited by the prospect of friends, maybe even a social life, and that gives me a flicker of gladness.

"Where are they from?" I ask, curious now. "Did they come a long way?"

Mattie shrugs. "We didn't go into all that stuff."

I get it; I don't think I want to hear dozens or even hundreds of other people's stories—either what they endured or how easy it was. I'm not sure which would be worse, but I already know I don't have the emotional bandwidth for any of it.

And so it's with something approaching dread that I walk with the others toward the mess hall just down Duxford Road, the main street of the base. It's a sunny day, the sky hazy and blue, although as the sun sinks lower in the sky I feel an oncoming chill in the air, the promise that the night will be cool.

Lots of people are trudging toward the mess hall, a sprawling, one-story building in white stucco with a gazebo and garden area in the back. Kyle and Sam have joined us and say the single men's lodgings are fine, four bunk beds to a room and communal bathrooms.

"Did you meet anyone?" I ask, and they simply shrug in reply. I can't tell if that's meant to be a no or a yes, and I don't press. I think we're all feeling a little battered, as well as unused to social interaction. I glance, with cursory curiosity, at my fellow residents, but it's hard to tell much about any of them. They look weathered, as I do, with a weary resignation in their faces that I recognize all too well. Everyone's wearing an assortment of clothes that look like they came from a garage sale; at least we were able to change out of our blue boiler suits.

"Nothing marks you more as a noob than this suit," Mattie had declared when she, Ruby, and Phoebe returned. She gladly peeled it off to replace with her own t-shirt and cut-off shorts, as did Ruby.

Inside the mess hall, there are long folding tables with benches; it's crowded, and it looks like the space is meant to cater for about a third of the number of people crammed in there. The food is served in bowls in the middle of the table—some kind of tuna casserole, and, while it's definitely not my kids' favorite, it's hot and nourishing and I know they'll eat it.

We sit at one end of a table, squeezed in close together, as others take their own seats. I look around, deliberately not meeting anyone's eye, just as I suspect everyone else is deliberately not meeting mine. There's a weird, muted feeling to the place, like everyone has been turned down a notch. Is that simply a result of the trauma we've all undoubtedly experienced—I suspect most people here are suffering from some form of PTSD—or is it this place itself?

Either way, I don't mind. I can happily be on autopilot for a little while. I can coast along without thinking too deeply about anything, because right now I don't think I can handle anything else.

I'm just starting on the fairly unappealing pile of congealed tuna and pasta on my plate when Daniel suddenly gasps and rises from the table.

"Tom," he practically shouts, and we all stiffen and look around at each other, alarmed, uncertain. "Tom!" he calls again, and this time he really is shouting.

"Daniel—" I begin, only to stop when I see a man walking toward us. He is tall, round-faced, plain but friendly looking.

"Daniel, isn't it?"

"You remember." Daniel's voice chokes. I stare at him,

bewildered. This has to be someone he met on his journey back to the cottage, I realize, but why hasn't he ever mentioned anyone?

Tom nods slowly. "I remember. You found your son?"

"He's right here." Daniel pats Sam's shoulder proudly. "You were so kind. I went back to your house, after, but you'd gone, but..."

Tom nods again, in understanding. "We had to leave in a hurry. We heard about a base near Buffalo that was accepting people. My cousin told us, you remember, the reservist?"

"I remember."

"We didn't have time to pack," Tom explains, "so we just left it all pretty much as it was."

"Isaac's blanket..." Daniel blurts, sounding emotional again, and bewildering me further. Who is Isaac? "There was blood on it. I thought..."

Tom frowns in concern, and then a light of understanding comes into his eyes. "Teething," he says succinctly. "A tooth broke through. Man, he's missed that blanket, though."

Daniel shakes his head in wonder. "It's so good to see you."

"I'm glad you made it," Tom replies, grasping his hand. "We left Buffalo two months ago and came here. The radiation... well, it's all been worse than anyone realized." He nods toward us. "This your family?"

"Yes..." Daniel introduces us and we murmur hellos. It's clear that Daniel feels something more for Tom than this stranger feels for him. He greets us all politely, chats to Daniel for a few seconds more, wishes us all well, and then moves back to his table, where a woman and three young children are sitting.

Slowly Daniel sinks back into his seat. "I can't believe it," he whispers. "I can't *believe* it. All this time... all this time I thought they were dead. I was so sure..." His voice chokes.

I'm about to ask a question when Mattie nudges me hard in my side.

"*Mom.*"

I'm still thinking about Tom and his family as I turn to her. "What is it?"

Wordlessly she points to a table at the far end of the hall, where I see Michael Duart eating, his expression composed and alert even from this distance.

"What..." I begin again and she hisses between her teeth,

"Look who's sitting right next to him."

I move my gaze and my eyes widen in surprise at the sight of the so very self-assured man talking Michael Duart's ear off.

William Stratton, looking very cozy with our esteemed leader for someone who had to have arrived just yesterday. My gaze moves farther down the table, but another man is sitting next to him, and I realize I don't see Nicole or Ben Stratton anywhere. It seems like the North Bay Survival and Resettlement Center holds more than a few surprise visitors.

SIXTEEN
DANIEL

Six months earlier
Between Utica and Springfield

The truck breaks down about sixty miles southeast of Utica, just outside Schenectady. It was rattling for a while, but both Daniel and Sam determinedly ignored the sound. They'd spent three days at Tom's farmhouse, resting and recuperating as well as gathering supplies, making plans, although the truth was, at the end of the three days, Daniel didn't have much of a plan besides go to the nursing home between Springfield and Worcester, get Alex's mother, Jenny, and then somehow get back to the cottage.

At least they had food in the back of the truck—a box of preserves, some cans of tuna, a bag of potatoes, and some dried beef. Daniel had not managed to find any guns at the farmhouse, but they took a couple of butcher knives with them, along with some rope, matches, flashlights, and a change of clothes each. All in all, he feels they did pretty well out of it, although the knowledge of what must have happened to Tom and his family is like a heavy, dragging weight inside him. He can't let himself think about it too much, or he won't be able to keep moving.

They take Route 90 east, and find, to Daniel's relief and surprise, that it is a clear shot, as good as abandoned. The unrest seems to be in the cities, not on empty stretches of road with nothing to steal or destroy. Sam keeps the radio on and occasionally they get a burst of static, a babble of voices; they learn that the president of the United States is "alive and well" at an undisclosed location, and he is going to address the country "any day now." The military have disbanded and then regrouped, and they're now focused on strengthening "areas where there isn't the danger of radiation poisoning or fallout." Eventually they will start with decontamination, rebuilding, but it's all hearsay and hope now; too much infrastructure has been destroyed and too much radiation remains for a clear or immediate way forward.

It's apparent that more bombs have dropped over the last few weeks—some in other countries, as well. Daniel and Sam hear about Paris, London, Berlin. Tokyo and Moscow. In America, Richmond, Asheville, Augusta have all been hit, and, closer to where they are, Philadelphia, Pittsburgh, Hartford. Jenny's nursing home is only forty miles from Hartford. Daniel does not tell Sam this.

According to one tense broadcast, people are still being advised to remain indoors and keep all windows and doors closed—not much of a help if you don't have any food. There's no more mention of army bases acting as assistance centers. The tone is more hold your breath and hope for the best.

At this, Sam looks anxious. "Do you think we've been exposed to radiation already?" he asks. "Are we... contaminated?"

Daniel manages a shrug. "I think we'd know it if we were, at least severely."

"But I mean long term," Sam persists. "Can't there be other effects? Like cancer and tumors and stuff?"

"There can, I think," he allows, "but the fallout from radiation dissipates fairly rapidly, especially if you're farther away from it. I don't think we've been within a hundred miles of a bomb." Yet. The truth is, he doesn't actually know. He knows that wind, rain, the size of the bombs, and how far from the ground when they exploded can all affect the level of radiation in the atmosphere. Or so he recalls from various disaster movies, but is any of that even accurate? Probably not.

"We'll stay inside as much as we can," he tells Sam, and that's when the truck gives its last rattle and gasp, and they roll gently to a stop on the side of the road, under a blank winter's sky, empty, frozen fields stretching all around them, a bleak yet beautiful landscape of nothing.

"That's not good," Sam says quietly. Daniel leans his head back against the seat and closes his eyes. "Dad?"

"Let me think." Except he can't think. His mind feels fuzzy and blurred; is it exhaustion, malnutrition, or something worse? He feels as if everything in him is moving with painful, aching slowness, and he has to keep reminding himself of basic facts— they are in a truck. They are going to get Jenny. There might be radiation everywhere... or not.

Outside all is still and silent. Daniel forces himself to focus. He opens his eyes. "I'll get us another car," he decides. "And I'll drive it back here."

"Where..."

"You stay here with our stuff," Daniel continues. "Keep the windows rolled up and the car locked. Stay out of sight if you can."

Sam looks scared, and like he's trying not to be. "Maybe I should get us a car," he ventures. Daniel can't tell if he is trying to be brave or if this is what he would really prefer. It can be harder, he thinks, to stay behind and wait, to have to be both powerless and ignorant, but he thinks about the warning of radiation, and he wants his son behind closed doors and windows, as safe as possible... if anything can be considered safe in this world.

"No, I'll go," he says, and he takes off his seatbelt.

After giving Sam stern instructions to stay in the truck unless there's an absolute emergency, Daniel sets off down the side of the highway, toward Schenectady. It is a cold day, with the metallic bite of snow in the air, although it hasn't snowed in several days; there's a hardened, crystallized crust on the ground, and no more. Next to the highway is a slate-gray ribbon of river, chunks of ice bobbing in its frigid depths—the Mohawk, Daniel thinks, but he's not sure.

Has he ever been to Schenectady before? He must have driven through it, but he can't remember. It's like half a dozen other small cities in this part of the world—some beautiful old architecture, a little rusted and run-down. Except, of course, it isn't like that anymore, because everything isn't just run-down, it's ruined.

Where, in this destroyed and desolate landscape, is he going to get a car? A car with a set of keys, because he does not know how to hotwire a car and he is feeling far too fuzzy-headed to figure it out. He tries to picture it—the screws he'd have to undo, the wires connected to the ignition and battery he'd need to identify and twist together, the motor wire he'd have to cut off and touch to them to turn the engine over. He knows that much, from watching a YouTube video once out of idle curiosity, but he doesn't think he can actually *do* it all.

So he needs to find a car in someone's driveway, he decides. Someone who is dead.

Strangely, this idea fills him with something almost like comfort. It's not stealing if they're dead, and it means he won't have to hurt anyone.

He keeps walking.

Just past the empty and vandalized Hungry Chicken Country Store, its wooden porch sagging and its windows broken, he crosses the Mohawk River onto Route 5, near an RV park and marina. He hears a noise from the park, and stops, instantly alert. When he left the truck, he took one of the knives with him, stuck into his belt-loop, and he fingers it now, wondering if he'd be able to use it. If he even knows how.

He hears another noise, a sort of gulping sound, and slowly he turns. A little boy, about two or three years old, is standing by some bushes. His face is grimy and tear-streaked, and he isn't wearing a coat even though the weather is hovering around freezing. Daniel hesitates. The boy stares at him and sniffs.

"Hey," he finally says, and his voice sounds rusty, like he hasn't used it much, and he hasn't, not like this. "Are... are your parents around?"

The boy simply stares, unblinking, seeming as if he doesn't even register him at all. With great reluctance, Daniel moves toward him. He scans the area, but all he sees are some dilapidated-looking RVs in the distance. There's an air of abandonment about the place, and he wonders if this boy has been living on his own, and why.

"Where are your parents?" he asks. No reply. Daniel stares at the boy, who stares back at him. He does not know what to do. He has been walking for at least half an hour; he can't bring this boy back to the truck, and neither can he bring the child with him, since he doesn't even know where he's going.

"Look," he says. "Why don't you go inside?" He nods toward one of the RVs. "I'll be back in a little while. I'll look for you then, make sure you're okay." He knows he is telling himself as much as, if not more than, he is this little boy, who looks as if he doesn't understand a word Daniel is saying. "All right?" Daniel tries again. He points toward the nearest RV. "Go in there. Stay warm. I'll be back."

The boy stares at him for another long moment. Daniel

gives him an encouraging smile. Then, thankfully, the boy slowly turns and walks back to the RV. As he disappears inside, Daniel hurries onward, down Route 5, toward Schenectady. He doesn't look back.

Another hour of walking takes him to a promising suburb of the city, older homes with gracious lawns, now weedy and frozen, an air of shabby gentility hovering on the edge of true dilapidation. He can find a car here, he thinks, even as he acknowledges that many of the houses look empty, their cars gone along with their owners. Nearly a month after the first bombs, Daniel supposes people have run out of food. Have they gone looking for it elsewhere? Have they fled this suburb of Schenectady for something that seems safer?

A few of the houses look lived in; there are signs on the front lawns warning people away. Daniel gives them a wide berth. The back of his neck prickles, and cold sweat trickles between his shoulder blades. He's pretty sure he's being watched, and a knife does not feel like nearly a good enough weapon.

The road he's on curves around to the left, and he follows it, keeping to the trees as often as he can. He scans the houses, unsure what he's even looking for. A nice, shiny SUV with a "please take me" sign in the window? Panic starts to cramp his stomach, and he feels dizzy. He's too *tired* for this. He's too spent.

Then he sees it—a house that looks empty, but with a Chevrolet jeep in the driveway, at least twenty years old, but hopefully still drivable. He looks around, and he can't see anyone. Quickly and quietly he walks up to the front door and tries the handle. It doesn't budge. He looks around again, and then peers through the grimy window next to the front door. He glimpses a front hall, a coat stand, a table with a telephone. It looks like an old person's house, judging by the black lambswool overcoat, the old-fashioned telephone.

He takes a deep breath, and then jabs his elbow hard through the window, shattering the glass in one clean break that is strangely satisfying. Carefully he reaches around through the jagged shards of glass still in the window frame; they catch at his sleeve as he flips the lock on the door. It clicks open.

He opens the door and steps inside. The smell in the house is musty and sweet, and catches at the back of his throat, nearly making him retch. Someone, he realizes, is dead in this house, and has been for some time. He is not about to go looking for the body, not when all he wants are the car keys. He breathes carefully through his mouth as he hunts around the hall for the keys —the table, in the pockets of the coat. Then he sees them right by the door, hanging on a hook on the wall. He exhales slowly in relief.

He is just taking them off the hook when he hears a creak behind him, and he whirls around, the knife in his hand before he'd even realized he'd grabbed it. A woman is standing there— tiny, frail, elderly. She trembles as she looks at him.

"Please don't hurt me," she whispers.

Daniel breathes out and puts the knife back in the belt-loop. "I'm not going to hurt you," he tells her. "I'm just taking your car."

Her shoulders slump. "Robert died last week," she whispers. "Upstairs in the bed. It was the radiation that got him."

A chill crawls along Daniel's spine, turns his hand slippery. "We're too far from all that," he says, and he hears the waver of uncertainty in his voice. "And it's been too long." He's sure he read somewhere, before this all happened, that the levels of radiation in the atmosphere are under dangerous levels after just two weeks. They started rebuilding Hiroshima and Nagasaki after just a few months; people reported to work the next *day*.

And yet already he recognizes that this is different. There have been more bombs, over a longer period of time and of a greater power; he recalls reading that the nuclear bombs in modern arsenals are up to sixty times more powerful than the ones that were dropped on Japan. And how many have been dropped now? No one even knows but it's most certainly in the dozens, judging from what they've heard on the radio.

Besides, people are different now. They don't have the same pull-together, can-do attitude of the 1940s, everyone willing to sacrifice for the greater good, a sense of duty and honor more important than safety or comfort. Everyone is an individualist these days, concerned with their own *personal journey*, which, when faced with a nuclear holocaust, means everyone is out for themselves. He has seen the truth of this every day of this hellish journey from Ontario to here.

The woman shakes her head slowly. Her hair is limp and white, her eyes faded into a mass of wrinkles. She has to be well over eighty. "He was out when it happened," she tells him. "He saw the flash. We weren't sure if it was from Boston or New York, but it lit up the whole sky like a firework."

Daniel does not want to hear this. He does not want to imagine that he, and more importantly Sam, might right now be breathing in radioactive particles that are slowly killing them from the inside out.

"What happened?" he asks, with reluctance. "How do you know it was the radiation?"

"He had trouble breathing. Felt dizzy all the time. And then he got all clammy and sweaty and his stomach was swollen... I think from the internal bleeding." She speaks both sadly and knowledgeably, and Daniel doesn't know what to make of it.

"You're nearly two hundred miles from either New York or Boston," he says, almost like an accusation.

She shrugs. "He was outside a lot, trying to make this house secure. Helping other people... he was a good man." Tears come to her eyes. "And he wasn't the only one, either. Lots of people have died. Our neighbors... I heard her screaming, in pain. It lasted for days. And so many people have left, but where are they going? Where *is* there to go?" A tear trickles down her wrinkled cheek, pooling in a deep seam. "I'm just waiting to die. I *want* to die," she exclaims on a moan. "Why couldn't I have gone first?"

Daniel has no answer to this. They're sixty miles closer to the blast sites than they were in Utica, and it seems that has made a difference, although perhaps this level of desolation is coming to Utica and beyond, as well. Perhaps it's just a matter of time, if the bombs keep coming, the radiation traveling downwind, the cloud looming over them all. "I'm sorry I have to take your car," he tells the woman. It's not so much an apology as a statement of fact.

"Robert is the one who drove it." She stares at him sadly. "Where are you going?"

"Near Springfield." He tells himself it will be safe; it's been nearly four weeks now, since the first blasts. Maybe people were dying of radiation a few weeks ago, but not now. He'll keep Sam in the truck or indoors as much as possible. They can still do this.

"Good luck," she tells him, and then she shuffles back into the living room, presumably to wait out the rest of her life. It is a sad yet also moving thought, its own kind of bravery. Daniel is about to head outside, but then he decides to investigate the kitchen. He doesn't feel guilty as he takes two liters of bottled water and another knife, just in case. There's no food left, but if there had been he knows he would have taken that, too.

The car takes several tries to start, but then Daniel is reversing out the drive and heading back to Route 5 and the bridge across the river. He doesn't see anyone along the way, and he wonders how many people here have died. At the bridge, he glimpses the sign for the RV park and marina, and he groans aloud. He does not want to go find that boy. He does not want to have to deal with him.

And yet... can he really leave a child on his own? Resolutely he pulls the car onto the side of the road and heads into the park. It is utterly desolate, the RVs either shuttered and locked up tight or completely abandoned. Daniel picks his way through the tufty, frost-tipped grass as he calls out, "Hello? Anybody here? Little guy? I said I'd come back for you..."

He goes to the RV the boy had gone into before and sees that it is empty; there's a sour smell about the place but at least no dead bodies—and no boy. He stands there for a moment, wondering what to do. Wanting to go.

He steps outside again. "Hello..." he calls. There's no answer.

Daniel stands there for several moments, breathing in and out, imagining the radioactive particles entering his body, his bloodstream. Killing him slowly... or maybe even fast. How is he to know?

"Hello..." he calls out again, half-heartedly. High above him a bird twitters, and the sound comforts him—and gives him the resolve he knows he needs. There is still life—for that little bird, for him, and, most of all, for Sam.

His gaze sweeps around the campsite, searching for a sign of the boy, and then in the distance he sees a woman peek her head out of one of the camper vans. Her hair is tangled, her expression suspicious. She has the dirty-faced boy hoisted on one hip.

"Are you okay?" Daniel asks, and in response she retreats into the van, shutting the door behind her.

Daniel waits another moment, and then he turns and walks back to the car. As he drives across the bridge, all he feels is relief.

SEVENTEEN
ALEX

As we walk back to our duplex, I can't shake the feeling that we're at some kind of family camp, or on one of those low-budget all-inclusive vacations. Dinner was a muted affair, but we got dessert—canned fruit cocktail, swimming in syrup, the kind I haven't had since I was a kid. Michael Duart stood up to make an announcement, welcoming the latest residents. I wondered how many there are besides us. Tom nodded at us as we left, and his wife smiled shyly. I managed a smile back, wondering if one day we'd be friends.

I don't know what to make of seeing William Stratton next to Michael Duart; he can't have arrived much before we did, and yet he was already chummy with the mastermind of this place, which is, I reflect, exactly the kind of guy I thought he was. But where are his wife and son? I think of Nicole, the bleakness I saw in her eyes, the despair that bordered on indifference, and I hope she's okay.

But in the meantime, I have my own family to worry about. Phoebe refused to eat the casserole, despite Mattie's patient cajoling; I'm uncomfortably aware of how silent and withdrawn she has become at only four years old. I don't know her well enough even to guess what might draw her out of her shell, and in any case Mattie is so possessive of the little girl, and seems to resent my poor attempts at interference. Maybe I'll just leave it to her, I think wearily, even if it doesn't feel right, to hand off my mothering to a fifteen-year-old.

As for the others... like Phoebe, Sam seems subdued, and he still isn't looking at me. Ruby has yet to speak today, at least in my hearing. And I'm worried about what we're all going to *do* here—what are these jobs they're going to give us? What if we can't do them well enough? We've found a safe place, but everything about the North Bay Survival and Resettlement Center feels unfamiliar and uncomfortable, like a scratchy blanket I have no choice but to wrap around my shoulders, because I am that cold. I just hope in time I'll come to appreciate and savor its warmth.

That night, I lie on the uncomfortable mattress, the sheets rough, and stare up at the squares of ceiling tile that look like something out of a low-budget office. Next to me, Daniel breathes slowly, already asleep. In the girls' bedroom, I hear the squeak of springs every time one of them turns over, and in the distance the smack of a screen door opening and closing. Everything feels so strange, especially after where we've been, what we've seen and endured. I want to feel relieved, to breathe out an at-last sort of sigh, but I don't yet. I can't. I tell myself it will come tomorrow.

The next morning, just before the first sitting of breakfast, another brisk and bland-faced official taps the door and then hands us "an NBSRC Welcome Pack," which is just a few stapled sheets outlining the expectations of our existence in this place. I'm impressed at the mediocre bureaucracy of the endeavor; in times like these, a typed sheet detailing tedious rules is almost admirable. We don't have time to read all the information before breakfast, but we do discover the jobs we're meant to report to immediately after the meal—Daniel is in accounting, Sam in warehouse, Kyle in farming, and Mattie helping at the school. I'm working in the kitchen, while Phoebe will be in the childcare program, Ruby enrolled in school.

We walk to breakfast feeling a cautious not-quite-excitement at this new phase of life, with jobs we report to, something that feels like a novelty. Breakfast is a cup of watery instant coffee, a bowl of just as watery oatmeal, and a single sugar sachet for flavor. It's still more than I've had in a long while, and I eat every last bite, savoring the sweetness. I look around for William Stratton, and, more importantly, Nicole and Ben, but I don't see any member of that family anywhere.

After breakfast, Mattie takes Ruby and Phoebe to the educational facility—she's made friends with some kids her age, so she knows where she's going—while Sam, Kyle, and Daniel all head off to find out where their jobs are, and what exactly they will be doing. I stay in the mess hall for the second sitting, since I'm pretty sure being on kitchen duty means I'll be working here.

As the building finally empties out, I feel a weird loneliness sweep suddenly through me—I've been cheek by jowl with my family for *months*, all of us working together for a common goal —survival—and it's strange and somewhat unsettling to be on my own now, doing something most likely mundane.

Admittedly, at the cottage I had plenty of alone time; I went for walks, or out to pick berries or check traps, but even when I was on my own we were still all working together, toward a common cause. And while I know that's the kind of thing that is meant to be happening here, right now I feel untethered. Maybe a job will help anchor me to this new life. I take my bowl and cup to the plastic basin by the kitchen hatch and look around for someone to report to.

The kitchen is a hive of activity, and definitely not big enough to serve four or five hundred people, even though that's what it is doing. I hover in the doorway uncertainly until a solid-looking woman with an apron swathed around her middle and a mesh cap covering her salt-and-pepper curls gives me a firm nod.

"New?"

"Yes—"

"You can start here." She nods toward an industrial-sized sink. "Rinse and load," she tells me. "Rinse and load."

I spend the next hour doing exactly that, finding a comforting numbness in the repetitive mundanity of the actions. I'm also more than half amazed that I'm actually running a dishwasher. I wonder if the novelty of having electricity will ever wear off, become commonplace again, the way it once was, but right now I am simply enjoying the ease of it.

There are a dozen women in the kitchen, applying themselves to various tasks, and yet no one really talks. I'm glad; I don't think I'm capable of conversation. For months, conversation has revolved around the practicalities of survival, and when those are taken away it feels as if there's no longer anything important or interesting to say.

By mid-morning, we are finished, and we get a short break before we need to return to start prepping for the evening meal.

I leave the steamy heat of the kitchen for the cool air of outside; it's only as I stand by the door to the mess hall that I realize I have no idea what to do with myself. The idea is novel, both liberating and scary. I could try to find Daniel or Sam or Mattie, check in on Phoebe in childcare or Ruby in school, but I don't know where anything is. All around me bland, anonymous-looking buildings stretch and loom, each one as innocuous and unremarkable as the other. There are no signs to anything, anywhere, and there is, quite literally, nothing to do.

A few moments ago, I was content simply to exist, but already I feel restless, unsure. I decide to explore my surroundings, limited as they are, for, as comforting as all that barbed wire is, it's still fencing us in. As I head down Duxford Road, I also realize that while the base is fairly sprawling it's unremarkable too—flat and mostly treeless, like a giant corporate park. I wander past houses like ours, warehouses that are shuttered, a massive hangar being used as a garage, with men unloading large plastic crates from trucks. I start to relax, a flicker of interest, of curiosity, awakening within me. It is, I realize, a nice feeling, to be both curious and safe. I watch the men for a moment, working in tandem as they unload crate after crate, passing each one along a line to a warehouse. What are they unloading and where did they get all that stuff?

Then a man with a stern expression and a military bearing heads toward me with purpose. "Ma'am?" he barks. "Can I help you?"

"No." I'm startled, apologetic. "I was just walking around."

"It's best you move on," he tells me in a tone that brooks no opposition. "I wouldn't want you to get hurt."

I hurry away because I wouldn't want to get hurt either, but somehow I doubt that's why he didn't want me around. Was there something they didn't want me to see—or am I being paranoid?

This is *not* some disaster movie or spy drama, I think, irritated with myself and my stupid paranoia. There doesn't have to be something top secret and nefarious going on, and there probably isn't. I'm probably being ridiculous.

"Alex?"

I stop at the sound of my voice, and then do a double-take when I see who is coming toward me, carrying a stack of neatly folded sheets. Nicole Stratton.

"You made it," I exclaim, and she lets out a huff of laughter that sounds like disagreement.

"And so did you."

"I saw your husband at dinner last night, but I didn't see you or Ben," I tell her. "I was worried something might have happened."

She arches one elegant eyebrow, clearly skeptical of my concern.

"We weren't hungry," she says flatly, which I find hard to believe, although admittedly she is stick-thin.

"How are you?" I ask. "And Ben? Was your trip here okay?"

For a second, her face softens. "Ben's okay. He's made some friends, which is good." She pauses, her expression distant. "You just want them to be happy, don't you? Even when the world is like this."

"Yes." I think of Mattie, Ruby, Sam, and Kyle and Phoebe too. "Yes, you want them to be happy. And safe."

"Well, this place feels pretty safe." Her tone is so darkly wry that it makes me wonder.

"So how does this compare to the bunker?" I ask, and she lets out a hard laugh.

"It's paradise," she replies, and I can't actually tell if she's being sarcastic or not. She flashes a hand at me. Her once-perfect nails are chipped and broken, the polish flaking off. Considering everything else, this is far from a tragedy, and yet it seems indicative of so much.

I nod toward her armful of sheets. "What's your job?"

"Housekeeping. That's what ten years of experience in interior design gets you in this place. What about you?"

"Kitchen. I think they saw stay-at-home mom and decided that's where I belonged."

"Some things never change."

We both laugh then, giving each other knowing, complicit looks.

"So what does William think about this place?" I ask Nicole. "He got in with our supreme leader pretty quickly."

Nicole's lips twitch at my lame joke. "He always does," she replies, and the edge in her voice makes me wonder—about both their marriage and the man himself. What's going on there that I haven't figured out yet?

"I know it's too early to say," I tell her, "but do you think... do you think being here is a long-term thing? I mean, when is the rebuilding going to start?"

"Who knows?" She sounds as if what she really means is who cares, and really, why should I? If my kids are happy, if I am safe and fed... is there anything more to want? To hope for? I'm not sure there is, and yet somehow it doesn't quite feel like enough, or, at least, like it *shouldn't* be enough. I should want more... but maybe I don't.

Nicole nods toward the sheets. "I need to go make up some beds for the latest arrivals. Do you know, in my former life, I had a housekeeper *and* a cook?" She tosses her sleek ponytail over her shoulder. "But you'd probably already guessed that."

"I had," I admit, and she flashes me a quick smile before moving away.

Feeling weirdly energized by this conversation, I decide to go find Mattie and Ruby. I walk down several streets, all of them seeming the same—a parking lot, a swathe of grass, a building with a number but no other indication of what it is—I pass Building Four, Building Six, Building Eleven. I turn a corner and come across an area with more of a neighborhood feel—modest houses with a playground and basketball court in the middle. I can hear children's laughter and I start to feel a little better. This looks a little more normal, or what normal used to be.

I see maybe two dozen children on the playground—running around, laughing, playing the usual childhood games. It's both heartening and strange to see. One boy falls onto his knees, scrambles up, and keeps running. I glimpse Phoebe on a swing with Mattie pushing her and my heart gives a little hopeful twist. On the other side of the playground, Ruby is standing near but not with a couple of girls who look around her age. The girls are chatting, but Ruby isn't, which is not surprising, but still I want more for my girl. While I watch, she edges a little closer to them, her way of making an effort.

The scene is so normal, and yet so not. If I lift my gaze from the playground to the houses beyond, I glimpse a raggedy fence of barbed wire bordering their backyards. Some of it looks hastily erected but no less forbidding; I'm guessing they tightened the security around the entire base after taking it over.

But if I don't look at the barbed wire, if I close my eyes and let the children's laughter drift over me, I can almost imagine I'm back in Connecticut, volunteering at Ruby's old preschool, and life is easy and good, a thoughtless rolling into the future, one day blurring into the next.

"Mom?" My eyes snap open. Mattie is striding toward me. Another girl is now pushing Phoebe on the swing. "What are you doing here?"

"Just wanted to see where the school was." I point to a single-story building with beige aluminum siding nearby. "Is that it?"

"Yes." She shakes her head, impatient. "It's kind of creepy, to have you just standing on the edge of the playground, you know?"

I try not to feel stung. "I was worried about you."

She frowns, her eyes flashing ire. "I'm fine."

I do my best to ignore her irritation. "You've settled in here, Mattie?" Like Nicole, I want my child to be happy.

She shrugs dismissively. "We've been here, like, five minutes, and you're asking me that? Yeah, it's okay. I mean, better than being killed, right?"

My lips twitch with suppressed laughter. Typical Mattie. "Were those the only options?" I quip, although part of me is serious.

Mattie folds her arms as she stares me down. "Mom, don't go deep on me, okay? We're here. We're fine. That's it."

I nod slowly, accepting. Maybe I needed this metaphorical

slap across the face. *We're here. We're fine. That's it.* This is what I wanted, after all. This is what I chose.

Besides, Mattie *does* seem fine, and so do Ruby and Phoebe. I don't need to poke holes in our happiness, our hope. I don't need to make more problems for any of us, just because I'm having a little trouble settling in, trusting this new normal. I *will* trust it, I decide. I want to.

"Sorry," I tell Mattie. "I'll see you at dinner, I guess."

"Yeah, okay." For a second, her expression softens. "I know this all feels weird, but it's good, right? I mean, we couldn't live in the woods forever, eating, like, weeds."

"No..." That much is certainly true; we were all semi-starving back at Kawartha, even if we tried to act as if we weren't. But the cottage, I think. I could have lived at the cottage forever. Happily, or almost. And I'm not sure I realized that until I burned it down.

Mattie touches my arm, the barest brush of her fingers. "It'll get better. You'll get used to this. We all will."

I manage a laugh. She's being so wonderfully mature, but it's making me feel kind of pathetic. "Yes, I know I will, but thank you for the pep talk."

"Anytime." She lopes back to Phoebe, and I hear her laughter as she says something to another girl who looks around her age. I imagine the conversation—*That was my mom, being weird. Ugh! I know, right? Mothers.*

I drift away from the playground, the children, feeling like a leaf on the breeze, bowled along, going nowhere. I should get back to the kitchen eventually, but I don't want to yet. I don't know what I want, and maybe that's the issue. Everything is finally going right for us, and, as I trudge down the empty street, all I know is that it's taking all my effort not to cry.

EIGHTEEN

Three weeks of summer slide by in a blur of peaceful drudgery punctuated by brief moments of happiness and sometimes, rarely, like a flash of lightning, of joy. It's a surreal, suspended sort of time; life has been reduced to so very little, and yet empirically it's more than we've had in months—fairly plentiful food, running water, hot showers, freedom from fear. Freedom, even, from knowing anything, because there are no radios anywhere, no news bulletins or updates, and no one talks about what is happening outside our barbed-wire enclosure.

It's not that such information is banned; it's more that no one seems to have either the urge or energy to try to find out. No one wants anything more than what we all currently have, and yet somehow, according to Michael Duart, this raggedy band of survivors is going to be the savior of civilization. Most days, I have trouble believing that we'll be the savior of northern Ontario, much less the entire western world.

"Do you think he's got a God complex?" I ask Daniel one evening. We are sitting on the back steps, our legs stretched out in front of us, watching the sun streak its fading colors of violet and orange across a wide, open sky. We are finding beauty where we can, because one thing I've learned over the last three weeks is that 22 Wing North Bay is not a particularly beautiful place, with its parking lots and weedy lawns and prefabricated buildings, although we get glimpses of nature's majesty in the wide, blue expanse of Lake Nipissing far below us. I also saw the tunnel that led to the underground complex; there was a truck parked outside, but that was all the life I saw, and I wondered why it wasn't being used or at least refurbished, as Michael had said.

Daniel knows exactly who I'm talking about. "Duart?" he muses. "It would be hard not to, when you're literally trying to save the world."

I snort with laughter before I subside into a sigh. "But is he saving the world? Really?"

Daniel shrugs, and for a second his wry mood turns dark, the way it so often does, like a cloud sliding over the sun. My husband seems more relaxed in this place, but he's still keeping secrets. "He's saving four or five hundred people, at least," he states quietly, his lips pressed together, "which is certainly more than you or I can say."

I fall silently, slightly chastened, and turn my gaze back to the sunset, wanting to enjoy its beauty, undiminished by our bland surroundings. Everyone else seems to have settled in here well. Daniel is back in an office, crunching numbers; he doesn't tell me much about it, only that he is working out supply systems and amounts needed. Sam hauls boxes and seems to like the biceps he's building as a result; he's played some pickup games of basketball with the other single guys, including Ben, who he has taken under his wing; I was surprised once to see them joking around together. It was the first time I'd seen Ben look anything other than sullen.

Kyle has taken to farming; the NBSRC has several fields out

by the old airport they're cultivating, and Kyle has driven the backhoe, something he's inordinately proud of. Mattie is helping with the kindergarten class, and Ruby enjoys science. Phoebe has come out of herself a little; the other day she brought home a tattered picture book from school and asked me to read it to her.

I'm the only one who's determined to find a problem, it seems, and maybe there isn't one.

"Why are you thinking about Michael Duart?" Daniel asks, nudging my foot with his. I'm glad he's seemed happier here, even if he still has those moments of darkness. I've seen him chatting to Tom a few times, looking both intent and thankful, and I'm hopeful that maybe whatever memories he has been running away from torment him less here.

As for me... when I close my eyes, I still see the affable face of the man I shot dead. In my mind, he looks even kindlier and friendlier than I think he was in real life; soon, in my imagination, he's going to resemble a smiling and benevolent Mr. Rogers. Is he a figment of my imagination, or was he really one of the good guys? Maybe I'll never know.

I walked by the base's chapel the other day—they hold services on a Sunday but so far we haven't gone—and thought about going in and checking out Habakkuk 3:17–18 in a pew Bible, just so I'd know, but I didn't. Didn't want to make the man in my memory any more personable than he already was.

"He's in charge here," I tell Daniel, "so of course I wonder. And what about this committee. Do we even know who's on it?"

"William Stratton," Daniel replies, with a touch of humor. We've both seen him swaggering around here, seeming both pompous and grave, like he's auditioning for president. Maybe he is.

"I'm serious."

"So am I." His tone has turned repressive, slightly impatient. "There always have to be people in charge, Alex, otherwise it's anarchy."

"I know." I sigh as I tilt my head to the sky, wishing yet again I could just be in this moment. This place.

"What are you afraid of?" Daniel asks after a moment. "That he'll imprison us here or something? You know some people have already left?"

"Yes, I know." A couple in their forties, the kind of people who could live in the woods for three weeks with nothing more than a knife and a ball of twine, decided they could do better on their own. They walked out of the gates, got in their car, and drove away, as simple as that, just as Michael Duart had promised.

No, I realize, I'm not afraid of being imprisoned, at least not by the likes of Michael Duart. I am, I realize as I stare at the twilit sky now darkened to indigo, afraid of imprisoning myself. Of letting this be enough—work, sleep, hot water, safety. Life has to be more than that. Doesn't it? Or maybe it doesn't.

As if reading my thoughts—he can be so good at that—Daniel says teasingly, "There's a movie night this week. That's something to look forward to, right?"

Every Friday night since we arrived there has been some organized social activity—a board-game night with battered boxes of Monopoly or Clue; a karaoke and darts night, which didn't go over so well, because the reality is maybe you need to be a little drunk to get up on a table and start singing along to Celine Dion, and of course there's no booze here at the NBSRC.

The social activities have been a nice idea, but generally pretty subdued in atmosphere. People aren't really in the mood to party, or even laugh, but maybe one day we will be. We found the humor back at the cottage; I recall Kerry and I laughing till tears streamed down our cheeks. If we could *there*, when life felt so fraught and precarious, why not here, when it doesn't?

But maybe that is, in fact, the reason why.

"It's just..." I tell Daniel. "What's next?"

He raises his eyebrows. "I heard next week's Friday night fun is going to be tacos and a piñata."

I try to laugh, but I only manage a tired sigh. "You know what I mean."

Daniel sighs right back at me and tilts his head to the sky, staring up at the oncoming darkness. "I'm not sure I even want there to be a next, Alex," he says quietly, like a confession. The words seem to fall in the stillness of the evening, ripple out.

"You're good with this? Life as it is?" I speak with curiosity rather than judgement. Truth be told, I'm not sure if I really know whether *I'm* good with life as it is. I know I'm kicking against the goads when it comes to this place, but that might be all it is. Futile resistance, no more than an exercise in vain autonomy because I don't want to be seen as some kind of mind-less sheep, and yet do I really want to stir myself to do something else? What else is there even to do?

"I'm good with this," Daniel agrees, his tone final. "I like my work, I like having food to eat, I like talking to Tom. You should get to know his wife, Abby—"

"Maybe I will," I say, something of a dismissal. She seems very nice, maybe too nice, the way she smiles and hoists a baby on her hip, all peaceable earth mama. Next to her, I have a feeling I'll be shown up as nervy and selfish and unsure, all of which I know I am.

"Most of all," Daniel finishes, "I like having someone else worry about the world and how it's going." He pauses. "I don't want anything more."

For a second, I picture Daniel back at our house in Connecticut, a sprawling McMansion with tasteful details and four thousand square feet of space I'd made into a cozy and welcoming home. I see him flipping burgers on our deck, opening a bottle of wine at the vast marble island in our kitchen, taking a work call in his study, ensconced in soft leather and dark mahogany, his forehead furrowed in enjoyable concentration.

"Really?" I ask, genuinely curious and a little sad. "Just this?"

He nods slowly, and for a second, no more, a bleak look comes into his eyes. "Just this."

"What about the kids?" I ask quietly. "Don't you want more for them? Eventually, I mean?"

He sighs again and closes his eyes, his face still tilted to the wide-open night sky. "They're happy here, Alex."

Just as Nicole said... but will they be happy here forever? It's a respite for all of us, but is it our future? But maybe we don't need to think about our future. If I'm trying to prove a point, I'm failing, and, I acknowledge, maybe that's a good thing.

But the twitchy, restless feeling still dogs me as I go about my days—porridge and coffee followed by kitchen work, a short break where I wander the site, averting my gaze from the barbed wire yet coming up against it at every turn, because even though the 22 Wing base seemed big when we first arrived, I'm starting to realize just how small it is. My short break ends with more meal prep, dinner, and then back to our house for a quiet evening of nothing much.

I've seen Nicole a few times, going about her business, but we haven't hung out and I doubt we ever will. Daniel chats to Tom on occasion, and I give his wife, Abby, a few uncertain smiles, but that's it.

Sam and Kyle hang out with all the single guys, including Ben, while Mattie often goes out with a group of girls; Ruby happily stays in and reads her book on plants, although I have seen her with some of the other girls in the little school. Phoebe, while still quiet, seems to enjoy preschool, and she lets me give her a bath now and comb her hair; it's a surprisingly sweet moment of my day.

But that's it—day after day. Nothing really changes. A few more people arrive; the days get hotter. Someone tells me about the tiny, winged shadflies that emerge from the lake every summer and swarm over buildings, causing a stink when they're squashed; up at the base, we only see a few, clinging to whatever they can. I exchange banter with a couple of other women in the kitchen, without any of us ever touching on anything serious or even real. No one talks about outside, no one discusses before or a potential after our time at the NBSRC.

The movie night is in the gym, with chairs and a large screen set up. The movie itself is a DVD of a brainless comedy from the 1990s; no disaster or action movies for us, I think a little sourly. We wouldn't want to get ideas.

I sit next to Daniel on a folding chair as the comedian clowns for the camera and the insipid plotline unfolds predictably. No one is laughing at the corny jokes, but I see a few smiles, hear some soft huffs, as if that's all anyone is capable of these days.

Except I find I'm not even capable of that. Halfway through the tedious movie, I walk out of the stuffy gym and into the cool night, letting the breeze from the lake blow over me. Then I see the red tip of a cigarette glowing in the darkness and I hear a woman's voice remark dryly, "I didn't like that movie the first time I saw it."

It is Nicole Stratton, leaning up against the wall of the gym and smoking a cigarette, eyeing me with cool indifference.

"I didn't think smoking was allowed here," I remark. It's banned, along with drugs and alcohol. For a second, I think of Kerry smoking on the deck at the cottage, wrinkling her nose at the menthol taste. The cigarettes had been ten years old, from my parents' time.

Her eyebrows lift. "It's not."

"Then..."

"William got them for me."

"He did?" I'm not surprised, I realize, not really, but it's still unsettling. William is on this governing committee after being here for just a few weeks, and he's flagrantly breaking the rules, offering his family perks? Did I really expect anything else?

"Socialism is always corrupt," Nicole informs me with a hard laugh. "How can it not be? *People* are corrupt, even the ones with the best intentions. They just can't help themselves."

"That's pretty cynical," I remark mildly. She shrugs in response, indifferent to my assessment. "I guess you saw some of that at the billionaire bunker," I venture.

"Yeah. I did." Her voice is harsh, and I'm not sure how to respond. Then she continues, her voice growing so savage that she is practically choking on her own bitterness, "And that experience taught me that anyone can do anything. There are no such things as good guys, not in this world. Not in any world, but especially not in this one."

For a second, I think of the man in the truck. I don't want him to be a good guy, so the thought there aren't any is strangely comforting, but before I can say anything to Nicole a sob escapes her, and then another, as if torn from the depths of her body. I'm shocked, even though I remember her crying back at Kawartha; that had been a silent kind of grief, while this feels like a relentless, futile fury. She hurls her half-smoked cigarette to the ground and grinds it to ash before covering her face with her hands as her shoulders shake.

I stand there for a few seconds, and then clumsily I put my arm around her, the gesture feeling unnatural. "Whatever it is..." I begin, uselessly, knowing there's no helpful way to finish that sentence. She shrugs off my awkward embrace as her shoulders continue to shake.

"Whatever it is?" she chokes through her tears. "*Whatever it is?*"

I don't reply, because I'm pretty sure *whatever it is*, anything I say will make it worse. I feel like I already have. Yet why is she crying like this, saying these things? "Something happened," I finally say slowly. "At the bunker." As soon as I say the words aloud, I realize it is blindingly, and insultingly, obvious. Of course something happened. I think back to when the Strattons stumbled upon us at Kawartha—Nicole's brittle fragility, like she was trying to hold the broken pieces of herself together, like she was no more than a handful of jagged shards. I saw it and I judged her, I realize, assuming she was just reacting to post-bunker life, without her Nespresso and her manicures. Guilt gnaws at me, a corrosive substance.

Will I ever get people right, I wonder. I've made so many mistakes in my judgement—Nicole, Kerry, Kyle, and, most damningly, the man in that truck who I shot dead. They all had to prove me wrong. Prove themselves to be far better, stronger people than I ever gave them credit for. Than I was, and maybe ever could be. I think again of that man on the road, the look of surprise on his face as he crumpled to the ground.

Nicole lowers her hands from her face, then wipes the tears from her eyes with a single finger, like she's making sure her mascara isn't smudged. Instincts from a former life, useless here.

"I was raped," she says flatly, and I recoil slightly, because, while part of me must have suspected in what direction this was going, it's still a shock to have such a violent and ugly thing stated so plainly, without emotion. "By the guy who took over the bunker. It was pragmatic of him, really. A power move, nothing more."

"How could..."

"William was popular there." She gives a short, sharp laugh.

"I know you aren't convinced by him because he hasn't both-ered to try with you. You're not important enough." She says this so matter-of-factly, I find I can't even feel insulted. A weary sigh escapes her, and she carefully wipes her eyes again. "But when he tries," she continues, "he can be so very charming. People are won over, even when they think they won't be. They convince themselves they've got the measure of him, and then they go along with his plans without a peep." She shakes her head, resignedly rueful now. "I've seen it a million times."

"And that's what happened at the bunker?"

"After Ed—that was the original developer—died, people wanted to just continue on as we were. I mean, it was a very good set-up. But then *he*..." Her mouth shrivels up like she's swallowed a lemon, and I know she won't say his name, this faceless rapist, that she can't bear to make him more human. "He wanted some of his family and friends to get in on it. Understandable, I guess, but we'd all paid a lot of money to be there. And William confronted him. There were people who would have rallied around William, because of course they didn't want to be kicked out either, and *he* didn't really have anyone on his side. I mean, if he could throw us out, he could throw everyone out, right? He'd managed to get some guns from the armory, but he wasn't invulnerable. Other people had guns. It could have gotten really ugly. *He* knew he needed William to go, and if he used violence it might backfire. So he raped me."

I'm still struggling to make sense of that terrible, twisted logic. "But surely that would have made William even angrier?" I ask hesitantly.

Nicole throws back her head as she lets out a laugh of genuine humor, hard a sound as it is. "No. Because he said he'd make William believe we'd been having an affair." I stare at her, and then she spells it out in a voice that suggests I'm stupid, which I probably am: "And if William believed that, which he would, he would kill me." Still I stare, and Nicole sighs impatiently. "All right, that might be a little melodramatic. William has never laid a hand on me, although I wouldn't put it past him. I've seen it in his eyes, when he's wanted to, but he's too controlled for that. He prefers emotional violence."

Which sounds terribly chilling. "Why haven't you ever divorced him?"

"Because," she informs me flatly, "he has a watertight prenup and he'd do his utmost to make my life a misery if I let him—and then there's Ben." Her expression softens on her son's name even as her eyes flash with something close to hatred for her husband. "Ben adores him, but William would poison him against me, and Ben wouldn't even realize he was doing it. He'd drip it into his ear and my son would turn against me without even knowing why. I couldn't stand that. I just couldn't." She draws a ragged breath as she wipes at her cheeks.

"I understand," I say quietly. I feel as if Sam has turned against me, quietly but determinedly, but that, of course, is my own doing. Nicole's situation is far more sympathetic... and so very grim. "So you convinced William to leave the bunker?" I surmise. I have trouble believing that such an arrogant man would be willing to go meekly, without a good reason.

"I can be surprisingly persuasive when I play the scared little woman." For a second she smiles, her eyes glinting with humor, and I have that strange sense of complicity that we have shared before and which makes me feel Nicole and I really could be friends. Maybe, I reflect, we already are. "I told him we'd be better off somewhere else, where I didn't have to be scared, and where people would value his intelligence and leadership abilities. Men can be so stupid when it comes to their egos." She sighs. "At least mine can. Your husband seems okay." She glances at me in query, and I find myself blushing—in shame.

It wasn't all that long ago that I was angry with Daniel,

unbelievably angry, and yet it all seems so petty now, especially in light of all that Nicole has endured.

"He's a good man," I state, a fact.

Nicole nods. "You're fortunate, then."

"I am," I agree, and I know I mean it.

We are silent for a long moment; from the gym I can hear the smarmy bleating of the actor in the movie.

"The thing is," Nicole remarks after a moment as she lights another cigarette, "that man—the one who raped me—he wasn't actually a bad guy."

I stare at her in disbelief. "He raped you, knowing you'd never tell your husband, and kicked you out of a bunker into a nuclear holocaust, and he's *not* a bad guy?" And what about there being no good guys?

"I mean before," she clarifies. "He was some tech millionaire, smart and a little nerdy, but kind of charming, too. We knew him socially. He was always kind of self-deprecating, never arrogant, a little socially awkward, maybe." She smokes silently for a few seconds. "But when we were all in that bunker," she continues reflectively, "with the swimming pool and Nespresso machines and all the rest of it... well, you'd think everyone would stay civilized, but it's a thin line, you know? And it's so easy to cross. And it made me realize that most people aren't evil—they're not these Machiavellian monsters you can dismiss as horrible anomalies of the human race, twirling their moustaches as they plot to take over the world. Most people are just small-minded and selfish, pathetic and petty, and when everything else breaks down, well, that's what comes out."

She lowers her gaze from her study of the darkened horizon to gaze at me. "Michael Duart's got this great vision, right? Or so he says. But what's the point of a vision, any vision? How can we possibly build a better world when it's still full of broken, selfish, *stupid* people? And I don't mean intellectually. Just..."

She shakes her head slowly. "No one has the will for anything bigger, and so we'll all hunker down in our bunkers and bases and eke out our days and nothing good will ever happen. Nothing bigger than this, than our stupid little selves, because no one is willing to risk what they have, no matter how small it is." She finishes her cigarette and drops it onto the cracked asphalt before deliberately grinding the butt beneath her leather boot. "Welcome to the rest of your life," she tosses over her shoulder as she walks away, into the darkness.

NINETEEN

A month after my heart-to-heart—or not—with Nicole Stratton, four men, no more than boys, really, are evicted from the NBSRC for drinking. They were friends of Sam's, the guys he played basketball with, some of them only sixteen years old, and they found some booze in the warehouse. One evening after curfew they drank two bottles of vodka and went joyriding around the base in a jeep.

Daniel and I were in bed, holding on to each other for warmth, because now it's nearing the end of August the nights are getting chilly, when we heard them roar past, honking the horn, out of their minds—an act of idiocy, daring, or desperation, or maybe all three. We heard someone speaking through a bullhorn and then a single shot, fired in warning. Neither of us spoke as we waited, clinging to each other now, having no idea what had happened.

The next morning Sam tells us all about it.

"They just chucked them out," he says, caught between disbelief and outrage. Underneath both emotions I sense a deep, pervading unhappiness. "With nothing. I mean, no supplies, no weapons... just the clothes on their backs. It's so unfair. All they did was have a drink."

Daniel and I have been listening to his rant silently, offering neither sympathy nor judgement. It's the first time since we've arrived that we've seen the zero-tolerance policy enacted, and it's immensely sobering. The thought of four young men, none of them over twenty and two of them significantly younger, escorted out of the camp to face the wide world with only the clothes on their backs... well, it does make you straighten up, determined to toe the line and, more importantly, to be seen doing it.

I mention the whole episode to Nicole; we've chatted periodically over the last few weeks, and her cool-voiced cynicism is refreshing and dispiriting in turns.

"What did you expect?" she asks when I broach the subject. "You can't have a zero-tolerance policy and then not enforce it. That's just asking for a *lot* of trouble."

"I know, but..." I hesitate, trying to untangle my feelings. "It just seems so harsh. Couldn't they have given them some supplies? A gun?"

"A gun?" She is incredulous, her elegant eyebrows—despite having been in this camp as long as I have, she looks salon-fresh —arched. "So these kids could use it against them?"

Them, not us, I note. I wonder if Nicole allies herself with anyone. "No, but... some food, then," I persist. "Some supplies."

She shrugs. "This isn't a charity."

"Yes, but it's meant to be a community, isn't it?" I reply, a little sharply, gesturing to the base stretching all around us. "We're meant to be working together, building something here."

Once again her eyebrows lift, and a little smile plays about her mouth. "Are we?" she asks.

· · ·

The question—and the infuriating lack of an answer to it—continues to haunt me as the days and then weeks go by. August drifts into September as the leaves turn shades of crimson and ochre, their edges curling up before they flutter to the ground, turning brown beneath our feet.

I begin to realize that I'm not the only one asking questions, feeling uncertain and even discontented. The mood of the base has shifted with the seasons; as the first frost tips the grass and rimes every dead leaf in white, I feel it like an electric current in the air, rippling silently around everyone as we go about our business—sleep, eat, work, the weary slog of this half-life.

Is it discontentment? Uncertainty? Fear? The boys who were unceremoniously marched to the gate—or ceremoniously, all things considered—remain in our collective consciousness, even without anyone saying anything, ever, about it.

I try to verbalize some of the vague thoughts swirling through my mind one evening when we are all hanging out in our tiny living room; the weather has become colder, the sky the color of steel, the nights closing in darkly so no one wants to be outside much after dinner. I'm sitting in a chair, brushing Phoebe's hair; Ruby is reading a book and Sam is flicking through an old gaming magazine he found somewhere—all vestiges of the former world, the ghostly remnants of what was and all that is left.

"Do you think we're building something here?" I ask, like I'm starting a debate. *This house believes we are all spinning our proverbial wheels, and I'm not sure if I'm okay with that.*

Sam glances up from his magazine, instantly alert, his hair—he needs a haircut—sliding into his face. It amazes and saddens me in equal measure that we have never gotten to the bottom of whatever was troubling him back at Kawartha—and clearly still does. Even now, he is not meeting my eye.

"Building something," he repeats, without expression or, it has to be said, much interest. "Like what?"

"I don't know." Except I do know, sort of. I think back to those admittedly not halcyon days at the cottage, when Kerry's mother, Darlene, taught us how to set a beaver trap, and her trapper friend Joe showed me how to skin and gut the one I'd caught. When we had a garden and a greenhouse and hope, frail as it was.

At the time, it never felt like remotely enough. I was sick with anxiety, apprehension, and grief; I missed everything the way it had been—which, I realize belatedly, I'm still doing. Am I viewing our cottage time through the sepia haze of sentimentality simply because it's gone? Maybe one day I'll look back on our time at the NBSRC in the same way.

And maybe I *won't*, because we'll still be here... and *that*, I know, is the real problem.

Where is any of this *going*?

"What are we supposed to be building?" Mattie asks. She is sitting on the floor, her back against the sofa, because it's so crowded in this little room, and belatedly I clock that Kyle is leaning back against her drawn-up knees in a way that is decidedly familiar, and this gives me the same sort of jolt I experienced back in Kawartha, only more so, so it feels for a second like I've stuck my finger into an electric socket. What is going on there? And for all my daughter's eye-rolls and huffy insistences... doth she protest too much? Do I need to talk to her about it, read her the riot act, or maybe just tell her to take precautions? The thought is most unsettling. I am not ready for that, and I don't think Mattie is, either.

"I don't know," I say a beat later than I should have. "Just... something." Realizing how lame I sound, I continue a little more earnestly, "I mean, remember when Michael Duart gave us that whole song and dance about saving civilization? What happened to that?"

Mattie arches an eyebrow, clearly skeptical. "How do you see that even happening, exactly?"

"Well, we wouldn't be stuck on this base forever," I reply with sudden ferocity, surprising myself with the strength of my feeling. "Going about our business like some—some robot army. We need to wake up out of our—our dream sleep and do something." I think of Nicole. "Start building something bigger than ourselves."

My daughter only looks amused by my stirring little speech. "A robot army that suddenly wakes up?" she muses. "I think you're thinking of that disaster movie that came out, like, ten years ago, Mom. Except it was zombies, not robots, and they'd all been given this electrical charge or something that turned them into killing machines. I think it was with Will Smith? Or maybe—"

Sam suddenly comes to life, his face alert with interest. "What would you rather be," he asks the others, "a zombie or a robot?"

"Are you sentient?" Mattie immediately flashes back, getting into the spirit of the game. "Like, do you know that you're a robot or a zombie? Because that makes a difference."

"If you don't know, does it even matter?" Kyle ventures hesitantly, and Mattie and Sam both turn to look at him with surprised admiration.

"Truth," Sam concedes on a sigh, and Ruby looks up from her book.

"I think I'd rather be a robot," she remarks quietly. "They seem nicer."

Everyone has forgotten the point I was making, even me. Not that I even know what it was in the first place. But to my surprise they drop their robots-versus-zombies debate to circle back to what I was saying.

"We can't do anything," Mattie tells me with authority, "until the world calms down, like, a lot."

"How do we know the world isn't calm already?" I counter. "We've been at this place for over two months now with basically no outside communication. Life could be going on normally somewhere."

They are all silent; I realize they haven't considered this, and yet these are the kinds of concerns it feels like everyone should be having—and some people already are. I see it, I feel it, in various throwaway interactions. The pile of potatoes we are ordered to peel without any discussion about whether other food can be found or grown, or what we'll do when the food we have runs out.

Last week I had to line up with two dozen other weary souls for new clothing for Phoebe and Ruby, as they'd outgrown what they had. All clothes are kept in a warehouse and divvied out by need, a need that's decided by the bureaucrat running the operation rather than anyone who actually needs anything.

When I got to the front of the line, I gave them Ruby and Phoebe's sizes, and they filled a shopping bag for each girl; I came away with two pairs of jeans, a pair of leggings, two t-shirts, a sweatshirt, and a pair of sneakers each. It was all decent stuff, if well-worn—where did it come from? And when the girls both grew again, would there be more? Already I knew I would not be the one to decide.

I didn't ask anything about it, and no one else in the line did, either; we just took our bags and went, but I could feel the questions forming on all of our lips. I continued to see it in the dawning apprehension in everyone's eyes, the silent, pointed looks people shared. The numb blur of the first weeks here was wearing off, and the four boys who had been kicked out were a kind of wake-up call that no one was quite yet ready to heed. So we took our bags of somebody else's clothes and went back to our little lives without a murmur.

"The world *is* calm," Sam says suddenly. "Too calm. It's basically empty. Everything is."

Mattie and Kyle both swivel to stare at him; Kyle is still

leaning against Mattie's legs, and she's got her hand resting casually on his shoulder. "What do you mean?" she asks.

Sam shrugs. "Part of the warehouse crew go out to get supplies from places—"

"What kind of places?" Mattie asks, her voice sharpening.

"Houses, stores, warehouses..." Sam shrugs again. "Wherever."

"I thought all of that stuff would have been looted by now," I remark. I'm thinking of Corville, when we went back in December, and how empty everything was. That was nine months ago. Could there still be stores and warehouses with merchandise now?

"There's still stuff," Sam says. "Because... I guess... a lot of people have died, even up here. Not necessarily from radiation, but from other stuff. Starvation, illness, whatever." He falls abruptly silent, seeming to turn inward. We're all thinking of William Stratton's eighty percent. Two months on from that, is it more? How much?

"But whatever those guys find... it will run out eventually," I point out, making sure to keep my voice gentle. "What then?"

For the first time, Sam looks me in the eye. His expression is bleak. "I don't know, Mom," he says. "What do you think?" He's clearly not waiting for an answer, and so I don't give him one.

It's only then that I realize Daniel isn't in the room. He was sitting in the sagging loveseat across from me at one point, but I don't recall seeing him get up. The kids have gone back to talking about robots and zombies—heaven knows that's easier than dealing with dreary reality—and so I quietly excuse myself and go looking for my husband.

He's in bed, dozing, even though it's only eight o'clock.

"Hey." I sit on the edge of the bed, the mattress springs creaking beneath me. "You okay?"

"Yeah." He smiles faintly as his eyes flutter open. "Just tired."

I study him for a moment, as if looking for evidence, and I find it in the deeper lines of his face, the gray in his hair and even in his skin. He looks tired, and, more than that, I'm afraid he looks unwell.

It's a possibility I push away instinctively, instant rejection, and yet it still hovers, malevolent. I try to think if there have been other signs—has he gone to bed early before? Has he seemed to have less energy? I can't remember. I'm not even sure what I'm looking for.

Daniel must see all this in my face, for he reaches over and catches hold of my hand. "Hey," he says softly. "I'm just tired."

I nod, a knee-jerk reaction. "The kids were having a debate," I tell him a little woodenly. "Robots versus zombies."

"A would you rather?"

"Yeah."

"Hmm." He frowns, giving the matter some serious thought, or at least pretending to. "What's the zombie situation like? Are we talking rotting flesh and eating humans?"

I smile, at least a little bit. "Is there another kind of zombie?"

"Sentient robots?"

"That was one of the points of the debate."

"Hmm," he says again. He's still holding my hand, running his thumb along my palm, and I'm filled with a sudden rush of deep love for him, so that tears come to my eyes and I have to blink them away. Daniel still notices.

"What is it?" he asks, all pretense of robots and zombies dropped.

"Nothing." I shake my head. "At least, I don't know what it is." I wipe my eyes. "I love you," I blurt, and he smiles, his eyes creasing, everything about him so beloved and familiar.

"I'm just tired, Alex, but I love you, too."

It's the first time we've said it to each other in a long time, and it feels rusty, heartfelt but still awkward. He squeezes my hand, then lets it go, and a few minutes later he is back to dozing. I watch him sleep, memorizing his features, wondering if I'm foolish to be afraid. There are enough things to be worrying about, surely?

And yet at the same time, there's nothing to worry about at all. Sleep, eat, work, repeat. Robots, I think with the ghost of a smile, don't have to worry. Maybe zombies don't, either.

Over the next few weeks, the silent, pointed looks become murmurs, and then the murmurs become mutters. A rumor goes around that one of the boys who was evicted has died. No one seems to know how or even if he really did, but the looming possibility of it remains, talked about darkly as people go about their tasks. The rules that we once accepted for safety's sake have begun to chafe. They don't just feel unfair; they feel wrong. And what are we doing, following them all, anyway? For what purpose, if it's just endlessly *this*?

All around us, tense little scenes play out. In the warehouse, as Sam tells us one evening, a fistfight breaks out and the supervisor looks the other way, even though this is, technically, in breach of the NBSRC's zero-tolerance rules. In the kitchen, one of my coworkers doesn't show up—another rule broken—and the head cook just tells her sharply not to miss another shift.

It should hearten me, these little acts of rebellion, but the truth is it just makes me even more anxious. Because if we can't co-exist here in a way that works, what hope is there? The last thing I want is more chaos, more violence, and yet I'm afraid that's where we're headed, as people emerge from their chrysalises of numbness and start to wonder why. Start to want more.

Then, in October, when the trees are all leafless and the base has become a barren and bleak landscape like a frost-tipped tundra, when the very air feels charged with tension and every moment seems expectant, Michael Duart calls a community meeting, the first since we've arrived, and, I suspect, the first ever.

It's in the gym, where the movies and quiz nights are, and as I'm getting ready to go, feeing a strange mix of apprehension and excitement, Daniel comes in our tiny bedroom and stretches out on the bed. Something in the way he settles in makes me pause in my primping—not that there's much to primp with.

"Aren't you going?" I ask, and I hear the wavering note of uncertainty in my voice.

"Tell me your impressions," Daniel replies easily. "Take notes." He pillows his hands behind his head as he closes his eyes.

"Daniel..."

His eyes remain closed as he tells me gently, "I don't need to hear Duart's spin, Alex. That's all."

"But what if he says something important?"

He opens his eyes. "Do you really think that's what's happening here?"

"No, but... we can't be passive."

He gives a little shrug, his head still resting on his pillow. "I'm okay with passive at this point."

Slowly I lower my brush. I place it very carefully on top of the fake wood dresser, as if this matters, as I meet his gaze in the tiny mirror above. "I don't understand," I state clearly and slowly, "why you don't care."

For a second, the very air between us almost seems to shimmer and vibrate. I have the deep-seated and desperate impulse to snatch my words back, stuff them in my mouth, and beg him not to answer. He stares at me steadily in the mirror, his gaze resolutely unblinking.

Neither of us speaks, and it feels as if we are hovering on the edge of something, and I absolutely do not have the strength or courage to look down.

Then Mattie bulldozes into the room, just as she has a thousand times before, her energy frantic and intense and entirely oblivious.

"I don't have any clothes," she moans, half accusation, half lament.

I almost want to laugh, except I really don't. Slowly, like I'm agreeing to a stalemate, I move my gaze from Daniel's in the mirror to turn to my daughter. "I'm not sure this is meant to be a social occasion, Mats."

She gives a theatrical groan. "Mom, you don't understand *anything*."

Except, I think, as my gaze moves inexorably back to my husband's in the mirror, registering the bleakness there, I'm afraid that I do.

TWENTY
DANIEL

Six months earlier
Somewhere outside Brattleboro, Vermont

"Dad, I think she's dead."

Sam's voice is low and strained as Daniel hunches his shoulders and peers through the darkness, his fingers clenched around the steering wheel. He's driving without headlights because it's safer, but it takes a *lot* of concentration, and he wishes he'd thought to bring his glasses, something that hadn't even crossed his mind—over a month ago now—when he'd set out from Ontario for this.

"Who's dead?" he demands in a voice that is just as low and strained as his son's.

"Pauline," Sam tells him. "Granny's asleep."

Daniel breathes out a quiet sigh of relief. Pauline is one less person to worry about, and she was on her last legs anyway. She was the only other surviving resident of the care home where she and Jenny had been eking out an existence for the last four weeks. Amazingly, when he and Sam had arrived at the home four days after they'd left Tom's farmhouse, his mother-in-law had still been, against all his expectations, alive.

Daniel had been bracing himself for the worst, and, in truth, it had been bad enough—there had been twelve residents in the memory unit of the care home, and ten of them were dead, in various stages of decay. He'd left Sam in the car, his son chafing against being treated like a six-year-old but still going along with it. For the four days of their journey, Daniel had hardly allowed him out, save to go to the bathroom, and then only quickly. He was conscious of how close they were to Hartford, how dangerous and damaged everything seemed, in a different way from Utica—no violent gangs here, but instead a steady stream of desperate, frightened people on the highway heading north or west, fleeing the radiation, or at least the fear of the radiation.

As they drove steadily toward Springfield, these poor souls had clawed at the car, or banged on the windows, but Daniel had simply stared straight ahead and kept driving.

Once, Sam had protested, "Dad, you might drive over someone. Kill them."

"They'll move out of the way." He was not about to slow down, to get dragged out of the car, have yet another vehicle stolen from them, not for anyone or anything. His resolve was tested when a young woman, no more than Sam's age, bravely stepped in front of the car, her chin tilted, her eyes flashing, her face covered with the reddened, dry, and peeling skin of radiation burns. Daniel kept driving, and, thankfully, at the very last minute, she moved.

If she hadn't...

It was something Daniel had refused to dwell on. Sam hadn't said a word.

And so they'd traveled to the nursing home—driving at night for safety, sleeping during the day, crawling down Route 90, ignoring the exodus. Four days of tension and fear and purpose, and then, amazingly, they'd pulled into the parking lot of Tall Oaks like they had a hundred times before to visit Granny, steeling themselves for her inevitable decline, noticeable in increments, and always painful.

This, Daniel knew, would be entirely different.

The nursing home had looked as abandoned as everything else; Daniel had been sure he would find nothing but rotting corpses, and there had been plenty of those, but when he'd made it through the secure doors—left unlocked when the power had failed—holding his breath against the stench, Jenny had stirred from a recliner by the blank-faced TV where she'd been wasting away, nothing more than skin and brittle bone, and Daniel had gaped at her, utterly amazed.

She and Pauline had been drinking the bottled water in the memory unit's little kitchen and subsisting on packets of cookies and crackers as well as the apples and oranges in the fruit bowl that were kept out for residents. They'd both been impossibly frail and yet they'd been alive. Jenny had seemed almost regal as she'd risen from the chair, talking to Daniel like she'd been waiting for a taxi that had finally arrived. Despite everything, it had almost made him smile; she was true to form, if nothing else.

But it had quickly become clear that Pauline wasn't as strong as Jenny, and now, just a few hours later, she was dead.

Good, Daniel thought, but he didn't say it aloud. He pulled over to the side of the road and opened the back door, trying not to breathe, just in case. They were about fifty miles from Springfield, heading north on Route 91, somewhere between Bernardston and Brattleboro, Vermont. The crowds had started to thin out maybe twenty miles back; people either hadn't made it this far or hadn't wanted to. Daniel was glad; abandoned roads were easier in all sorts of ways, but they only had a quarter tank of gas left, and he didn't know where they were going to find any more.

Now, as gently and respectfully as he can, he pulls Pauline

out of the car while Sam watches, apprehensive. "Should we bury her?" he asks.

"No."

"Dad..." His son's protest fades away into silence.

"We don't have time," Daniel tells him brusquely, an explanation rather than an apology, although in truth he feels a flicker of guilt. If he were a better man, he'd want to bury an innocent woman, or at least show her some respect. "We have to find somewhere to hole up while I look for gas." By his reckoning, they're a hundred miles or so from Boston, eighty from Hartford—not far enough. Vermont, he hopes, is far north enough to be safer, at least from the radiation. Whether they'll encounter gangs in that green and pleasant land remains to be seen.

Daniel's plan is to find an abandoned house and rest for a few days while Jenny regains some of her strength. He'll find enough gas to get back to Canada, and they'll try to cross in Vermont, up into Quebec.

He leaves Pauline by the side of the road, after crossing her arms over her chest. It's all he can think to do to create a sense of occasion, of seriousness.

"Should you say something?" Sam asks uncertainly.

Daniel tries to summon a prayer, but his mind feels both blank and full of static. "Rest in peace," he finally says, wearily. He gets back in the car and keeps driving. Jenny hasn't even stirred from her sleep. He wonders if she'll remember Pauline, or even notice that she is gone. His head throbs and his mouth is dry; he's trying to conserve water but he knows he should probably drink something. Is a dry mouth a side effect of radiation poisoning? He remembers, when his aunt had radiotherapy for cancer, it dried up her salivary glands so she couldn't even spit. Is that happening to him? Is his body already being destroyed from the inside out? Is Sam's?

"He stayed in the car," Daniel reminds himself. "He stayed in the car."

It is only when Sam asks him if he's talking to himself that Daniel realizes he said it out loud.

They're about twenty miles from Brattleboro when the warning light appears on the gas tank. They're nearly at empty —and at the end of the road.

Daniel slows as he glimpses a barricade that has been set up across the whole road—an impenetrable barrier of oil drums and concrete blocks. An effort has been made here, and Daniel sees why when he spies the bullet-proof vests of the Vermont state police. For some reason, this shocks him; it's the first police presence he's seen since the Canadian Border Services on the St. Lawrence over a month ago.

"What..." Sam breathes.

Daniel brakes. He can't drive through that kind of blockade, and he's queasily apprehensive as a police officer strides toward him. He rolls down the window.

"You'll have to go back," the officer informs him flatly. "No crossing here."

"No crossing...?"

"Vermont is a no-contamination zone."

A *what*? Daniel almost wants to laugh. Does this guy think he can stop the radioactive cloud from rolling onward?

"What does that mean, exactly?" he asks, tensely conscious that the police officer is holding a SIG Sauer semiautomatic rifle, a no-kidding-around kind of weapon.

"It means no one is coming in," the man explains irritably. "We've closed the state borders."

"But why..."

"Because we don't want a bunch of radioactive zombies flooding in," the man snaps. "Now reverse your vehicle or suffer the consequences."

He raises his rifle meaningfully and Daniel nods, rolls up the window, and starts reversing.

"Can they even do that?" Sam demands, outraged, as Daniel does a three-point turn with a dozen armed police officers looking on, and then bumps across the median in the middle of the road to the other side. His mouth is drier than ever.

"I don't know," he says quietly. "They have, anyway." He has no plan now, he realizes. They're almost out of gas. There's nothing but tiny towns, barely more than handfuls of houses, for at least fifty miles in just about any direction. The nearest city of any size is Springfield, from where they came, and it's closer to the radiation. He knows they can try to make their way on smaller roads through Vermont, up to the border, but he's wary of having to drive through so many small towns. It feels like an easy way to get carjacked, and that's without considering the problem of gas.

He drives back down Route 91 to the nearest exit, for Route 10 to Northfield, Massachusetts, and turns off, then stops when he sees the barricade that has been erected at the narrowest part of the road—more oil drums and concrete blocks, even an old truck. He knows he won't be able to shift any of it, and the dense trees on either side make it impossible to drive around. Ostensibly, he could leave the car here and they could walk, but Jenny's not strong enough and without a car they might as well be dead. Besides, what would they be walking to? He doesn't even know if there's a gas station in Northfield, not that he'd find any gas there anyway.

Daniel reverses back onto the highway and keeps driving. He thinks they have just about enough gas to make it to the next exit, for Route 10 south to Bernardston, even though he doesn't want to go any further south. Near the exit, he sees a sign advertising a gas station, a campsite, even a Starbucks and a Dunkin' Donuts. He turns off and comes to another barricade, this one just as impassable as the last. The good people of Bernardston have been efficient, he thinks, as well as determined. He wonders how many other barricades they'll come across, against refugees from radiation that nobody wants to let in.

This time when he starts to reverse, the car sputters and then stops. They're out of gas.

From the back, Jenny stirs. "Where am I?" she asks, her tone more curious than fretful. "Where are we going?"

They are, Daniel thinks, good questions, and he can't answer them. He turns off the ignition and pockets the key as he tries to think. They'll have to get out of the car; at least, he will have to get out of the car. It's probably safer for Sam and Jenny to stay here and wait for him to return.

He swallows dryly at the thought. He really needs to drink some water.

"Okay," he says at last. "Sam, you and Granny stay here. I'll go find some gas, come back and fill up. Eventually we'll find a way off the highway. They can't have blockaded everywhere."

"Why are they doing this?" Sam asks unhappily.

"Because they're scared. And when people are scared, they circle the wagons, proverbially speaking." He turns to his son, dredges up a reassuring smile. "It's going to be okay. I got us a car before. I can get us gas. All you need to do is stay inside, windows rolled up, doors locked, okay? I'll be back before daylight. I doubt anyone will even notice you're here."

Sam frowns, still unhappy. "And if they do?"

"It's been twenty miles since we saw anyone," Daniel reminds him. "No one's coming, Sam. It's going to be okay." He reaches back and grasps his son's hand, squeezes it. "It's going to be okay," he says again. Jenny, he sees, has fallen back asleep.

A few minutes later he is out of the car, his coat zipped up and his hat pulled down over his ears. It is breathtakingly cold, so his chest hurts every time he draws a breath. All around him the forest looms, dark and bare. There's a Dunkin' Donuts less than a mile from here, but it's hard to believe.

He starts walking—head down, hands dug into the pockets of his coat, his boots crunching on the dried leaves, around the barricade and then back onto the road, which leads to an intersection. In the moonless darkness, he can't see a thing in either direction, but a sign on the other side of the road tells him that Church Street is to the right. He turns right, toward the town, and keeps walking—past the white wooden Congregational church, its steeple piercing the night sky, and then another; and then, there it is, a gas station with a Dunkin' Donuts.

The pumps, as expected, have been destroyed, no doubt in an effort to get at the gas, and the windows of the Dunkin' Donuts are shattered, the store looted. He glances around the empty street, wondering where he should go. His first thought is to find an abandoned house with a car and siphon the gas out, but based on the barricade he has a feeling that there won't be as many abandoned houses, and that more will be locked up tight and bristling with hostile residents.

He stands there for a few minutes deliberating what to do, his mind as slow as molasses, so every thought feels like something sliding inexorably away from him, gone before he can even begin to try to grasp it.

Then, in the distance, he sees a light flickering. A flashlight? A lantern? The glow is comforting, beckoning him forward, or maybe that's just his weariness, his hopelessness, because he doesn't know where to go on his own. He puts one foot in front of the other, walking down Church Street, toward the light.

As he comes closer, he sees that it is a lantern, hanging on the concrete porch of a small, weathered building that has a sign in its gravel parking lot—Faith Christian Church. It's a tiny building that looks a little like a dry-cleaners, but as he comes forward someone comes out to stand on the porch—a middle-aged woman with woolly white hair and a surprisingly wide smile.

"Hello," she says gently. "May I help you?" He stares at her dumbly. Her smile softens. "You've come a long way?"

"Yes." His voice is a croak. "Canada, originally, and then from near Utica."

She nods in understanding. "Would you like to come in?"

Daniel nods. He feels as if he is in a dream, and he doesn't want to wake up. He follows her into the church, which is tiny —an entrance hall, a sanctuary that seats maybe twenty, and a room in the back. There's no electricity, but another lantern inside lights the way.

"I have soup," the woman tells him. "And coffee."

He sees she has a two-ring propane stove that she fires up with calm efficiency.

"What..." He can't make sense of this; it really does feel like a dream. "What are you doing here?"

She turns to him, still smiling. "Helping people. There's quite a few who have come through, from the highway. A meal is the least I can offer. I'm afraid I haven't got much more than that." She nods toward a wooden chair by the door to the sanctuary. "Why don't you take a load off?"

"All right." He eases into the chair, amazed at how relaxed he already feels, simply from this single human interaction. "Has there been much violence here?" he asks.

"Some, but this is a small town and people are trying to stay civilized. They had a soup kitchen going, but then a gang from another town came and shut it all down. The military were here a few weeks, trying to organize things, but I haven't seen them in a while. I heard talk that they've all headed out west."

"Yes, so have I." The smell of soup—canned tomato—wafts toward him, and his stomach grumbles. He's barely eaten today, and he's still so thirsty. "What about the radiation?"

She shrugs, seeming peacefully pragmatic. "We won't know

until it happens, will we? But we're only seventy miles from Hartford. There's bound to be something, isn't there?"

"Maybe."

"Not much we can do about it but wait," the woman replies. "I'm Dorcas, by the way."

"Dorcas." He nods a greeting. "I'm Daniel."

"A good biblical name." She speaks lightly, with a smile. "I'm named after the woman in Acts who made clothes for the poor. She died and then Peter raised her to life again. Do you know that story?"

He half shakes his head, half shrugs. "Sort of."

"Well, this is my version of making clothes," she says as she spoons soup into a mug. "Because truth is," she explains with a rusty laugh, "I don't know my way around a sewing machine at all."

"Aren't you worried about being attacked?"

"For a little soup and some coffee?" She raises her eyebrows as she hands him the mug. "When the good Lord decides my day has come, well then, my day has come. Until then, I'll be here, doing what I can."

Daniel is both moved and shamed by this simple statement of faith; his own actions have been so far from it—desperate, calculating, selfish. He doesn't know how to be any different; faith, he reflects, is a nice idea until you have to put it into practice with something—or someone—you really care about. He's not going to risk his son's life for a step of faith of any size. It feels like a holier version of virtue signaling, although that is clearly so far from what Dorcas is doing.

"I'm afraid I haven't got any milk or sugar," she tells him as she hands him a cup of coffee, which Daniel takes with murmured thanks.

He balances both the soup and coffee in his lap. "I need gas," he tells her, blurting it out. She is, unsurprisingly, unruffled.

"Gas is pretty hard to come by," she muses. "The gas stations were the first to be looted, along with the grocery stores. Some people have left already, heading out west, hoping it's better there. They needed the gas."

Daniel nods. "Understandable." He takes a sip of soup, savoring its warmth. He's so tired, he feels as if he could drift off right there, lulled to sleep by the woman's kindness, the warmth stealing through his body.

Dorcas frowns at him. "Are you all right, Daniel?" she asks. "You're looking a little flushed."

"I'm tired," he admits reluctantly. And, he fears, maybe sick. *How sick?*

Dorcas presses the back of her hand to his forehead. Her hand is cool and soft and reminds him, bizarrely, of his mother's. For a wonderful, blessed moment, he feels like a child. "I think you have a fever," she says with concern. "I've got some Tylenol somewhere..." She reaches for her purse, a voluminous bag of fake black leather, and roots around it. Daniel takes another sip of soup, and some of it dribbles down his chin. Until Dorcas said it, he didn't realize just how truly sick he felt, but now it crashes over him, pulls him under, and part of him wants to go. He craves that release.

He blinks fuzzily, the whole world seeming to come in and out of focus. "I'm sorry..." he begins, and she shakes her head.

"It's all right. Take this." She presses two tablets into his hand, and for a second he wonders if he should trust her. Maybe she has poisoned him with her soup—but he knows she hasn't. He's just sick, *so* sick... and he didn't let himself realize it until he was sitting in a warm place, sipping soup.

Now all he wants to do is sleep, forget...

"Daniel..." Dorcas says with concern.

His eyes flutter open, and he tries to focus. "I'm sorry..." he says again, but the words are slurred. The cup of coffee slips from his hand; he hears the thud on the carpeted floor, feels the splash of hot liquid against his leg.

That's the last thing he remembers.

He wakes slowly, blinking in the dim light, conscious that he is in bed, and feeling instinctively that he shouldn't be. Memories trickle slowly through him at first, and then with a sudden, alarming jolt.

Sam. Jenny.

He bolts upright, breathing hard. "Where—" he begins, only to stop in confusion. He's in a bedroom, with a home-made quilt draped over him, and embroidered Bible verses on the walls. *Seek ye first*, he reads before he jerks his gaze away.

"Dorcas!" he calls, his voice hoarse and rasping. "*Dorcas...*"

A few seconds later she comes into the bedroom, closing the door behind her. She is wearing jeans and a fleece, and she is smiling like a nurse who has seen her patient improve. "Oh good," she says. You're finally awake."

Finally...? He's reminded of when he first started this hellish journey; he'd had a fever for a whole week. He'd been devastated to learn just how much time he had wasted, but now, he realizes, it is so much worse. He left his son and mother-in-law in a car, completely undefended, virtually helpless, in the freezing winter. What if they're both dead?

A gasp escapes him, a ragged, desperate breath. Dorcas gazes at him with concern.

"You needed the rest," she tells him, and Daniel shakes his head, frantic.

"My son... my mother-in-law... I left them waiting in a car." He takes a gulping breath. "How long have I been asleep?"

Dorcas frowns, full of sympathy. "About twenty-four hours."

Twenty-four hours! It feels like an obscene amount of time.

Daniel throws off the covers; at least he is still dressed. "I have to get back to them," he hurls at her, like a demand. He swings his head around wildly, although he doesn't even know what he's looking for. His coat? His keys? He doesn't even have keys, never mind a car; he left them with Sam.

"Where's your son?" Dorcas asks, and her voice is steady despite his obvious agitation. "Your mother-in-law?"

"On the exit ramp off 91 South," he replies, and now he sounds miserable. To his shame, his eyes fill with tears, and for a second he thinks he might break down and sob. *If anything has happened to Sam...*

"That's over a mile away," she tells him, frowning. "You're not on Church Street anymore. My friend Cal helped me get you back here, to my house, when you'd fallen unconscious." She eyes him critically. "And I'm sorry to say I don't think you can walk that far."

Daniel knows he can't walk that far. He sinks onto the bed, letting his head fall into his hands. "How could I have let this happen..." He chokes on the words.

"Listen." Dorcas puts a hand on his shoulder, and her touch, solid and sure, is comforting. "I can walk down there and check for you. You stay here and rest."

He looks up, blinking at her in bleary surprise. "You'd... you'd do that for me?"

She smiles, looking almost amused. "I might be entertaining an angel, after all, as the Good Book says," she teases him. At least, he thinks she's teasing him. "Yes, I'll do that for you."

Daniel has forgotten about such sweet, simple kindness. It didn't take very long, he realizes, for most people to descend to savagery and selfishness, but he is so grateful that Dorcas did not. "It's a jeep," he tells her, "about twenty years old, parked by the barricade on the south ramp—"

"I think I'll be able to find it. There aren't many cars parked around here these days."

"Thank you—"

"You thank me by resting up," she tells him sternly. "I don't want you getting sicker, not after I gave you my coffee and soup." She squeezes his shoulder and, as meekly as a child, Daniel climbs back into bed. Those few moments of exertion and anxiety cost him; he's feeling weakened again. By the time he hears the front door close, he's already sinking back into sleep.

He wakes he doesn't know how long later, disorientated and dry-mouthed. Dorcas is standing at the foot of the bed, looking somber. Daniel's stomach swoops.

"Did you..."

Already she is shaking her head. "I'm sorry, Daniel. When I got to the car, it was abandoned. I called out and looked around, but there wasn't anyone there at all."

TWENTY-ONE

Michael Duart's "town hall"—his term—is in the gym, where most of the social events have been held, but this meeting doesn't have the same indifferent amiability to it. As I walk in with Mattie—Ruby and Phoebe stayed behind with Daniel, and Sam and Kyle are going to meet us there—I feel the tension like an electric hum in the air. People are starting to feel angry, and they want answers.

Mattie looks around for Kyle—I haven't asked her about that relationship, but I have the maternal gut instinct that something is going on, or at least could be—while I glance around for Sam. Something in me judders to a shocked halt when I see him in earnest conversation with none other than Nicole Stratton, their heads bent close together, Sam gesturing with what looks from across the room like anxious determination.

It's so incongruous, so *weird*, that for a second I just stare. Was I aware they knew each other? I knew Sam knew Ben from basketball, but Nicole? Why would they talk to each other like this, urgently and secretively?

Mattie heads off to join Kyle, leaving me alone, wondering where to go. I've been at the NBSRC for three months now, but

I still haven't grown close to anyone. Mattie has a circle of girls she hangs out with; even Ruby has made a few buddies. Sam's got his basketball guys along with Kyle, and Daniel talks regularly with Tom; I've seen Tom clap him on the shoulder, smiling and nodding.

As for me? I make chitchat with the other kitchen workers during my shift, and I sometimes exchange barbs or jokes with Nicole, but that's it. I won't be sad to leave here, I think suddenly, and then I wonder why I'm thinking that way, almost as if I'm about to go.

Michael Duart comes to the front of the gym, and I take a seat in one of the folding chairs by myself. Mattie is sitting with Kyle, and Sam and Nicole have both disappeared. I can't make sense of that, and I'm not sure I want to. I focus on Michael Duart, and his so-called spin.

He starts off by welcoming us all as if we're at a dinner party or a corporate meeting, or maybe a cross between the two, introducing himself and his "team"—that's when I see that William Stratton is sitting at the top table, flashing everyone a toothy smile, and the sight of him makes me miss some of Duart's smooth-sounding intro, but I pay attention when he talks about radiation levels, and how we all need to stay at the NBSRC for "the foreseeable future."

That's his plan? And are the radiation levels really that bad? I'm filled with both unease and doubt. If they're that bad, why aren't we in the underground complex that's meant to be the big draw of this place, where we can definitely be safe?

Just then, someone asks that question out loud. His voice is strident without being aggressive, but Michael Duart's mouth purses like he's annoyed.

"The underground complex isn't yet ready for habitation," he explains in a voice that I think is meant to sound careful but comes across as prim. "And you can be assured that we are monitoring radiation levels closely. At the moment, the entire

North Bay area is at acceptable levels, but outside of this area..."
He trails off ominously.

"So you think that might change?" someone else asks—a
dark-haired woman, sounding anxious, her fingers knotted
together.

"It is impossible to say. Of course, levels of radiation dissi-
pate over time, so we are hopeful that in a few months, maybe a
little longer, other regions nearby will be habitable again,
including areas as close as Barrie."

Barrie is just north of Toronto, about two hundred miles
south of here, with a population of maybe one hundred fifty
thousand. Or at least it *was*, but now? Barrie is less than one
hundred miles from Toronto. Maybe everyone there has already
died.

A murmur of speculation ripples through the crowd, and
Duart holds up a hand to forestall any more questions. "The
important thing to remember," he states firmly, "is that the
North Bay Survival and Resettlement Center is the safest
place for all of you to be. It's understandable that some of you
might be feeling anxious or even suspicious about matters,
especially in regard to recent events, and a few individuals'
flagrant disregard of our clearly set out rules." He clears his
throat. "These rules have been put in place for the safety of
everyone at the Center, and for the efficient running of the
site. As soon as we start relaxing rules, we could be dealing
with a whole host of problems that could ultimately endanger
everyone here, especially when you consider what the risks
and consequences truly are." He pauses for effect, his gaze
moving slowly around the room as if to emphasize just what
we're up against—total mass destruction of civilization as we
know it.

A few more questions are asked, but already these are
humbler, almost apologetic. The mood has shifted, and Michael
Duart's smooth manner has won the day.

It's only later, when we're all back at the house, that I find out more.

"I think the radiation levels are fine all around here," Sam confesses, sounding unhappy about it. "Guys in the warehouse crew are going out all the time to get stuff, and I know they've gone as far as the Georgian Bay, and Port McNicoll. That's not that far from Barrie."

"Why is he saying that, then?" Mattie demands.

"To keep us compliant," I venture hesitantly. "If everyone's afraid of radiation, they're more likely to do what they're told, aren't they?"

"I don't think he's a bad guy," Sam continues. "Duart, I mean. I just think he likes being in charge of this place. The next step... it's a big one. It's got to be scary, figuring out just what that is, and when and how to take it."

"And what about the underground complex?" Mattie asks. "Do you think it's really not fit for habitation yet?"

"It must be," Kyle chimes in, surprising us, "because Duart and his guys are living in it. I see them come out in the morning when I'm heading to my shift."

"So, *are* the radiation levels okay?" Mattie wonders aloud.

"Maybe it's just a precaution," Sam says with a shrug.

Or maybe Michael Duart wants to be behind a three-foot-wide steel door if anything kicks off. I certainly would.

The town hall meeting seems to have calmed down the general mood at least a little bit, and the mutters subside to murmurs without any more evictions or, really, behavior that could lead to evictions. And yet something has changed in me—shifted or hardened, I don't know which, but there's a growing part of me that doesn't want to have killed an innocent man for a life of this.

I think of that man more than I'd like to; I took his photo

from the truck when we first arrived, slipped it into my pocket without even considering what I was doing—or why. Now, months later, I find myself taking it out and studying it for clues, as if the faces of his family will somehow tell me what sort of man he was—or, really, he wasn't.

I try to think back to that moment when I pulled the trigger, but it's such a blur of adrenaline and fear that I find I can't remember anything about it at all—I'm only remembering the last time I remembered, and so its shape becomes more damning every time I let my mind linger on it. Soon I'll have convinced myself he was a saint.

One evening in November, just after we've had our first snow, a dusting of two inches that thankfully melted by mid-morning, I end up in the chapel, open for private prayer but only used for Sunday services; I've seen only a handful of people attending, including Tom and his family. The small sanctuary with its blue carpet—the same as in our house—smells of dust and old hymnals. I'm not sure why I'm there, only that I found my way without even knowing where I was going.

I come to sit in a wooden pew, and I take the crumpled photograph out of my pocket. I'm not going to cry; I feel too empty for that. The months stretch on in front of me, and I don't see anything becoming different, at least not in a good way. There are a lot of things I'm not ready to think about—the time Mattie is spending with Kyle and what that might mean, Sam's relationship with Nicole, whatever *that* is, and how unhappy he seems, his face set in discontented lines when no one is looking. Ruby, who is growing up without getting any bolder or louder, and Phoebe, a motherless child I'm learning to love and yet who will always be my responsibility, a prospect that daunts me.

And Daniel. Daniel, who now goes to bed right after dinner, and who seems as if he is drifting through his days, but who, last night, rolled over in bed and, without warning, held on to me tightly, burying his face in my hair. Neither of us said a word.

As I sit in that empty pew, I bow my head. I'm not sure if I'm praying or just being silent, but in any case no words come. Suddenly, I think of my father, his affable smile as he would proclaim in the manner of someone declaring a self-evident truth, "Alex, you've just got to trust. There's nothing you can do about it anyway, so you might as well trust."

I know, Dad, but trust what? And how?

I open my eyes and my gaze falls on a dusty Bible under the pew in front of me. I lean down to slide it out and let it fall open —to Psalm 118, which I skim disinterestedly. *Give thanks to the Lord, for He is good.*

Yeah, right.

I leaf through a few more pages, and it isn't until it falls open at Habakkuk that I realize that's what I've been looking for all along. Did some former Sunday School self remember where it was? It's a short book, only a few pages, and so it doesn't take me long to find the verse the man I killed had written on an index card.

Though the fig tree does not bud and there are no grapes on the vines, though the olive crop fails and the fields produce no food, though there are no sheep in the pen and no cattle in the stalls, yet I will rejoice in the Lord, I will be joyful in God my Savior.

The Bible falls closed, nearly slipping out of my hand, as I bow my head and close my eyes. I don't pray because I still have no words, no thoughts, no semblance of any coherent offering to a deity, or to anyone else for that matter. I don't cry because I'm empty inside, too weary and numb to summon emotion of any kind. I simply sit there, my head bowed as the chapel stretches all around me, quiet and dusty and dark, and let the words reverberate through me, echoing emptily inside.

And yet...

And yet. And yet. And yet.

They are words of hope or maybe just defiance, words that can be so hard and yet necessary to say. And yet I can choose something different. Something hopeful. Something more than the NBSRC has to offer, even if at this moment I have no idea what that could possibly be. Even if so much in my life feels alarmingly precious, precarious, and fragile—my children. *My husband*.

And yet.

Is this the start of something? Is this when I find my resolve, steel my spine, and stride forward into something better? It doesn't feel that way as I close the Bible and slip it back under the pew. I just feel as weary as I ever have, but I hold on to that flicker of something stronger as I leave the empty chapel, closing the door quietly behind me.

It's dark and already below freezing, even though it isn't much past six at night. Curfew was moved to seven o'clock during what had once been daylight savings—could we really mark time that way anymore?—ostensibly to conserve electricity. No one protested much; those mutters really have died out now. We're all too afraid, or maybe we're just too tired.

This, I think, is how dictatorships start. With the promise of safety, of a little bit of comfort, and everyone's weary indifference to anything else.

And yet, as I walk through the quiet darkness back to my little house, those words continue to reverberate through me.

And yet. And yet. And yet I will give thanks, I will try, I will persevere, I will prevail. Admittedly, that is something of a loose paraphrase of a sacred text, but still. I feel it. I want it. Not just for myself, or, really, not for myself at all, but for Daniel, who is already asleep. For Sam, who seems so unhappy and still won't look at me. For Mattie, who is defiantly making a life for herself, one that I'm pretty sure includes Kyle, who I'm also trying for. For Ruby, who in her own quiet way is incredibly strong. For Phoebe, the silent ghost-child I never expected to love.

For all of them, I want to make something of our lives, something more than this, something that *isn't* this.

The realization fires through me, gives me even more of a sense of purpose. My stride quickens, my heart rate too. I have no idea what I'm planning, but, for the first time in a long while, it feels like something.

When I get back to the house, I let myself in quietly, not wanting to disturb Daniel, even though it's just before seven at night, hardly late. Mattie flies toward me.

"Mom." She sounds accusing, afraid, and angry all at once. So typically my daughter.

"What is it?" I ask, keeping my voice light.

"Mom, it's serious," she exclaims, like a reprimand. "Something's happened. Something bad."

She laces her fingers together, knuckles white. From behind her, Kyle hovers, pale-faced and as looking as anxious as I've ever seen him. For a second, I'm reminded of the pathetic little man-child we encountered nearly a year ago, in Corville, and yet he's become so much more than that.

"What's happened?" I ask. Even now, I'm still expecting some variation on a teenaged drama, which, considering the world we live in, is both foolish and naive. Maybe the only way of getting through moments like these is to not always expect the worst.

"It's Sam," Mattie says, and my stomach hollows out.

After the fights and booze fests in the warehouse, I can hardly bear to think what might have happened. "What..."

"Come on." She tugs my hand, and I frown.

"Mattie, it's after curfew. And what about Phoebe—"

"She's asleep, and Dad and Ruby are both here. Come on, Mom. This is *serious*."

With deepening apprehension, I let myself be tugged outside and along the road. I have no idea where we're going, but it turns out it's not that far—a narrower road, little more than an alley between two anonymous-looking buildings, heading toward the mess hall.

In the dark, it takes me a moment to adjust to what I'm seeing—two shapes, one crouched over another lying supine on the ground. The first is my son Sam, looking terrified. The second is William Stratton, looking dead.

TWENTY-TWO

"What..." My mouth is dry, and I force myself to swallow as I take a step closer to the terrible scene. "What *happened*?"

"It was an accident," Sam half whispers, half whimpers. "I swear."

"But..." I stand above William Stratton and gaze down at his gray face. He's unconscious, and there's blood trickling from his lip, but at least not his head. "What happened?" I ask again.

"He came at me," Sam explains. "When I was walking back.'

"Why?"

"Because he thinks Sam is having an affair with Nicole," Mattie states bluntly, and I flinch, because I'm Sam's mother, and the thought of him having an affair with anyone, never mind a fortyish woman, is pretty hard to take.

"Sam—"

"I'm not," Sam says quickly. "I mean, she's *old*. Not that she's... I was just talking to her about Ben, because he's been kind of quiet lately... anyway. Stratton is crazy. He just came at me and I... well, we had words, and then I punched him." Sam cradles his fist, his voice filled with a wary sort of wonder. "I've never punched anyone before. It hurts."

"Did you punch him that hard?" I ask, glancing down at Stratton. "To knock him out cold?"

"He hit his head," Mattie explains flatly. "That's what knocked him out."

I breathe out slowly, my mind whirling. This is bad, I realize. Really bad, as bad as Mattie said. If Stratton is dead—or worse, in a way, if he wakes up—Sam will be evicted from the NBSRC, just like those boys who got drunk, one of whom might already be dead. He'll have nothing, nowhere to go, no way to defend or provide for himself. I can't let that happen.

But what can I do?

My mind runs through several unsavory possibilities, discarding each one in turn: hide the body, if Stratton is dead, and pretend it never happened, or at least act as if Sam wasn't involved. No, I can't behave like such a criminal, and if he isn't dead that's not a possibility anyway. I'm ashamed I even thought of it, and yet I did. The other option is to deny it—leave Stratton where he is and, if he wakes up and accuses Sam, ride it out. But Stratton is vengeful, and I'm pretty sure he'll be out for Sam even if Sam is believed, which he probably won't be, because Stratton is Stratton, and a man of importance in this isolated community who thinks Sam is sleeping with his wife. No matter what, it won't end there.

The third option is in some ways the most unpalatable, and yet almost the most possible: leave Stratton where he is, to be discovered, and run before we're forcibly evicted. I won't let Sam go alone; this is a chance for us all to leave the NBSRC and forge our own futures.

The prospect is utterly terrifying.

"Mom." Mattie's voice is urgent. "What do you think we should do?"

Beneath us, Stratton lets out a groan and starts to stir. Sam and I exchange panicked glances, the first time we've looked each other in the eye in a long while.

Stratton isn't even close to dead, I realize. He knocked his head and maybe has a concussion, but this isn't a one-punch-killer type of situation, more's the pity.

We need to make a decision, now.

"We need to put him somewhere," I say, and Mattie and Sam, along with Kyle, who has been lurking behind me looking anxious, all stare at me in disbelief.

"Put him somewhere..." Sam repeats uncertainly. I feel like he's asking me, in the same way he did back in Kawartha, *Mom, are you a killer?* Not in so many words, but the feeling is there, along with the accusation. *Just what are you capable of?*

I'm not sure I know the answer to that question, but that's not what's going on here. "Just out of the way," I explain. "So we can escape."

"We're not in prison," Mattie puts in sharply. I wonder if she'll miss being here the most, with her friends and her teaching job, a semblance of teenaged normality.

"Prisons don't always have bars," I reply, which sounds like something I might have once read on Instagram. "But after this... Sam will be evicted, Mattie, you know that. He'll have nothing. We have to go with him... and we have to make sure we get to take our supplies."

Mattie is silent for a few seconds, absorbing everything I've said, all it means. "We don't even know where our supplies are," she finally points out. "Or our car."

"I know where the cars are," Kyle ventures. "They're all parked out by the farm fields, near the airport."

Mattie arches an eyebrow. "And the keys?"

I picture the keys in a locked cupboard in Michael Duart's bedroom, like something out of the villain's playbook in a Disney movie.

Kyle shrugs. "We don't need the keys. We can hotwire the car."

"Does anyone know how to do that?" I ask.

"I do," Kyle says, surprising me once again. There's definitely more to this kid than meets the eye.

"And our supplies?" Mattie asks.

"I know where we can get some stuff," Sam says. "In the warehouse. Not our supplies specifically, but…"

"What about guns?" I ask bluntly, and the question seems to fall between us with a splat. Yes, I'm the one thinking and talking about guns.

"They're locked up," Sam replies shortly. "I can't get at them."

I shake my head. "We can't leave this place without a weapon."

Sam looks like he wants to argue, but then he relents. "I don't know what to do, then," he replies with a shrug. *Over to you, Mom.*

"Why can't we just ride this out?" Mattie asks. "Stratton was the one who came at Sam. He was provoked. If Michael Duart wants this place to be the kind of *fair-minded community*"—said with imaginary air quotes—"he says it is, then Sam shouldn't be evicted."

At this, Stratton stirs, blinking up at us blearily. His eyes are reddened, his face twisted with hate. "You are so out of here," he half grunts, half snarls at Sam. "And that's if you're lucky."

Has Stratton been listening to everything we've said? The thought is more tiresome than alarming; something else we are going to have to deal with.

"How can we get a gun?" I wonder out loud. I feel like there must be a solution, but I just can't see it. What I know is I'm not willing to walk out of here without some kind of weapon.

"Mom," Sam says after a moment, his voice almost gentle, "maybe we don't need guns." I stare at him like he's stupid, and he continues, "Dad and I didn't have guns when we traveled back to Ontario. We were without them the whole time because they'd been stolen right at the beginning, like, in the first five minutes. It wasn't easy, but we made it. And anyway, most people..." He trails off, swallowing hard. "They're dead now. Stratton said eighty percent, but I think it's worse out there. People just can't last that long. It's... it's pretty empty out there." He lifts his arm to gesture to outside the base and, really, the whole world, empty as it now is. "I think we go without the guns."

"I think so, too," Mattie interjects with swift decisiveness. "We don't have time to figure anything else out. We need to get out of here. We can decide the rest later."

It goes against all my instincts, to be so vulnerable, but maybe my instincts are wrong. Maybe, in the end, those instincts haven't been all that helpful or even good; a man is dead as a result, and my son is suspicious or maybe even scared of me. Still, the words are hard to say, never mind believe.

"All right," I relent reluctantly. "We'll go without guns."

The next hours pass in a panicked and determined blur. We pick up William Stratton, Sam taking his arms and Kyle his legs, while he groggily protests and tries to shout, and then we lock him in a closet in the mess hall, in a scene reminiscent of *Scooby-Doo*. I'd laugh, if it weren't so deadly serious, but Sam gets the vibe, because as we lock the door he murmurs, "If it weren't for those meddling kids..."

I choke on a laugh, and he gives an abashed grin, and for a second we're just us again; it doesn't last longer than that.

We make it back to the house, managing to avoid the guards who patrol the streets after curfew, their flashlights cutting arcs of light through the darkness. Mattie and I start packing while Daniel stumbles groggily from the bedroom and

Ruby wakes up Phoebe and gets her dressed. Kyle has gone to find the car, and Sam to the warehouse, all of us knowing full well that any moment this could end in the NBSRC equivalent of arrest and imprisonment, eventual eviction, as good as a death sentence.

"What's going on..." Daniel half mumbles, and I try my best not to notice how out of it he seems. It's only eight o'clock.

As briefly as possible, I fill him in on what has happened and what we've decided. He blinks the sleep out of his eyes, becoming alert, his gaze darting from me to Mattie, who is hurling things into bags.

"Leave..." he repeats disbelievingly. "And go where?"

"Anywhere."

"But the radiation—"

"Sam said it's not as bad as Duart makes out," I tell him. "But if you're worried about that, we'll head north."

Slowly Daniel shakes his head. "Alex, it's November. It will be *freezing* up north. And there's nothing much up there, besides some small towns and fishing camps."

"Plenty of space, then," I quip, and there's an edge to my voice, because why is he protesting this? We have no choice. Doesn't he realize that?

"It might be like the cottage all over again," he warns me. "People hyped up, terrorizing the countryside..."

"It might not," I counter, which isn't much of an argument, but I haven't got a better one. "It's more remote out here than back at the cottage," I continue doggedly, "and you know that's saying something. Besides, I'm just not sure how many people are left. If we stay here, Sam will be forced to leave. We can't have that, Daniel."

The painful irony of the situation is not lost on me; a year ago, I was forcing Daniel to leave our safe haven to protect Sam. Now I'm doing the same thing all over again, and I know, for me as well as for Sam, he'll do it—even if he thinks it's dangerous, possibly a death sentence—and this time not just for him, but for all of us.

He heaves a sigh of acceptance. "So where exactly are we going?"

"I don't know. We need a map, I guess." And a lot of other things. "Sam's getting some supplies, Kyle a car. We'll meet up at the warehouse." I make it sound so simple, when I know it is anything but.

"And what about Nicole and Ben?" Daniel asks, and I'm jolted as well as shamed, because the truth is, I didn't even think about them.

"You mean... should they come with us?" I ask hesitantly.

"If they want to."

"I... guess? I don't know if they will." Although if Stratton decides to go for Nicole the way he did Sam... "I don't know where to find them," I say, like an argument, or maybe a reason.

Daniel shrugs. "Maybe Sam will."

"I suppose we can ask him," I reply.

We don't have time to talk any further because we have to go. Mattie takes Phoebe from Ruby and hoists her on her hip; after a sleepy protest, the little girl curls into her, her head on Mattie's shoulder.

"You okay, Rubes?" I ask my youngest daughter gently, putting my arm around her shoulder and holding her close for a few precious seconds. I'm jolted by how tall she is; she comes up to my chin now. She nods, her hair brushing my cheek. "It's going to be okay," I tell her, a promise I know I can't make, but will do my utmost to keep. "It really will."

She nods again, without saying a word. I give her shoulder one more squeeze and then let her go because we need to move.

Adrenaline fuels me forward, gives me a purpose I know I don't really feel, not if I let myself stop and think for two minutes, but I can't now, because how long is it before Stratton is found? Before the game is up and we are tossed out on our own, with nothing, forever? Questions and reassurances can come later, I tell myself, as we hurry down the darkened street and I pretend even to myself not to notice how Daniel is lagging behind, breathing heavily as he tries to keep up.

By some miracle, we avoid any curfew patrols and make it to the warehouse, where Sam is waiting, looking apprehensive but resolute, his breath creating frosty puffs in the cold night air. Nicole and Ben are standing next to him, their bodies both hunched, their arms wrapped around their middles. When Nicole looks at me, I see she has a black eye. My breath rushes out. I guess they're coming with us.

There are several boxes of supplies stacked around Sam; I can't see what they hold, but hopefully stuff that will be helpful. It's better than nothing, anyway.

"How did you get into the warehouse?" Mattie asks him.

"It's just a keycode. I watched the guy lock it up the other day. He didn't seem to care."

I breathe out; can it be this easy? It feels wrong, somehow, and yet I so want it to be easy. Or if not easy, then at least possible. I need it to work, because it's hard enough, not knowing where we're going or what it will be like when we get there.

"And the car?" Mattie asks.

Sam shrugs. "I don't know how that part works. We're behind barbed wire, and I don't have any bolt cutters. There are some weaker points than others, but..." He trails off, shrugging, before continuing doubtfully, "If Kyle hotwires a car, he can drive it here, I guess, but someone is bound to hear it. And then we have to get out of here somehow, and with all this. I don't know how we'll do it." He nudges a crate with his foot.

"Not without someone noticing anyway," Daniel says. His tone is wry but he's huffing and puffing and holding his side in a way I'm trying not to notice. Mattie notices, though; I can tell by the way her eyes narrow, and her lips press together. Just like me, she doesn't say anything. "I'll tell you what," Daniel says, and now he sounds intent, although with a hint of that old wryness. "Let's leave here in style."

"What's that supposed to mean?" Mattie demands, and Daniel just smiles.

"Trust me," he says, and I know we will. It's not like we have another choice.

We find out what he intends just a little while later. Kyle joins us at the warehouse, echoing our fears about the noise of starting a car; he doesn't want to do it until we're ready to go, because there are patrols roving around the base and it will make too much noise.

We decide to take the crates to the car, even though it's at least a ten-minute walk and it's freezing cold plus they're heavy; it feels safer to load up there and then just go. Although how we're going to go, I still don't know, because, no matter what Daniel said about exiting in style, the base is enclosed by barbed wire, all the gates padlocked. I don't let myself think about it too much because there's too much to do, and I'm trusting that Daniel—and Sam—really do have some kind of plan.

Nicole and Ben work silently alongside us, neither of them speaking. At one point, I pause, wanting to say something, but Nicole gives a pre-emptive shake of her head as she hefts a crate. I guess there will be time later, if I even want to share those kinds of confidences with this woman.

Twice while we're hefting crates we hear voices and see the menacing sweep of a flashlight arc across the parking lot, and we all hit the ground, flat on our stomachs, Mattie cradling Phoebe to her. I'm not afraid, even when the patrol is close enough to hear the men's voices; I feel too disembodied to feel fear. In the same way as I was out on that road with the blown-out bridge, I'm separate from myself, a spectator to what is happening, distantly wondering how it will all unfold.

Maybe that's the only way to get through moments such as this one.

The patrol moves on, and we keep working, breath coming in frosty puffs, fingers numb with cold. I'm conscious of time passing, unspooling like a thread, the bobbin bouncing away from us, out of reach. It's been over an hour since we put Stratton in that closet. We didn't even gag him; he could have been discovered by now, and they might already be looking for us, ready to mete out whatever justice Michael Duart's faceless committee decides is appropriate.

Finally we are loaded up and in the car, a battered, black SUV that seats eight but is taking nine, with Phoebe on Mattie's lap.

We wait, breaths held, hearts racing, as Kyle crouches by the steering wheel and starts tinkering with wires. Daniel is at the wheel, and I glance at him, concerned; although he's long since caught his breath, he's still holding his side.

A sputter, two, and then the engine coughs to life and turns over. Kyle flings himself into the back, and Daniel steps on the gas so we lurch forward, and Mattie lets out a little shriek of surprise.

"How are we getting out of here?" Nicole asks in a low voice. It's the first time she's spoken since we saw her outside the warehouse. She has her arm around Ben and he is burrowing into her, looking more like a little boy than I've ever seen him.

"You can't go over it, you can't go under it..." Daniel murmurs and I give him a look. He's quoting the old childhood story of Ruby's, *We're Going on a Bear Hunt*. She loved that book.

"Daniel—"

I break off as Daniel floors the engine and the car shoots forward.

Someone shrieks—maybe even me—as we start speeding

toward the fence, four ragged lines of barbed wire. At least it's not chain-link, I think numbly, just as floodlights suddenly come on behind us, illuminating an armed patrol that is running right at us. Not us, I realize, seconds later, but toward cars. They're not letting us go without a fight.

I barely have time to process that before our car hits the wire, and for a terrifying second I think we're going to ping back like the snap of a rubber band. The car simply isn't strong enough to break the barbed wire or rip the fence posts out. From behind us, an engine roars to life.

No one speaks and Daniel's knuckles are white on the steering wheel and then with a pop the fence flies free and so do we, the car careening down the road, leaving the NBSRC behind us—except, of course, we're being chased by two vehicles, and it's clear our pursuers have guns when a bullet scrapes the side of the car, and I realize they're trying to shoot out our tires.

"Dad," Sam gasps, although I'm not sure what he's trying to say because another bullet shatters the window right by my head and Daniel reaches out and pushes me down so my forehead smacks against the dashboard and for a second I'm stunned, my head pulsing with pain.

Daniel weaves wildly over the road, trying to avoid being hit, while I stay crouched down, scrunching my eyes shut against the pain still thundering in my head.

"Is everyone okay?" he shouts, and for a split second I'm reminded of when we had a fender bender that resulted in our rear window being shattered and Mattie getting a bruise on her leg from being flung forward in her seat. It's the same hoarse and authoritative demand of a father who is determined to take care of his family.

And he's doing it still, I tell myself. *We're going to get out of this.*

"Yeah, Dad," Mattie whispers. "We're okay."

We drive in silence for another minute, maybe two; no one speaks and there are no more gunshots. I finally dare to raise my head from the dash. "Did we lose them?" I ask, risking a look behind us. All I see is empty, darkened road.

"I think so," Daniel replies, "unless they know where we're going and plan to cut us off."

"But *we* don't know where we're going," Mattie points out. "So how could they?"

'They'll figure we're going north," Daniel tells her. "And the only way north from here is Route 11."

"So..." I prompt, trusting he has a plan. "What are we going to do?"

"Go south," Daniel replies with a quick, small grin. "And then head north. We've got half a tank of gas, so we should be okay."

"And when we go north," Nicole interjects, "where are we actually going?"

"I looked in the atlas earlier," Daniel says, passing a hand over his forehead, which I notice is beaded with sweat, and his skin possesses a grayish cast. "There's a fishing camp about fifty miles northwest of North Bay. Red Cedars, it's called. I don't know much about it, but it will have cabins of some kind and it will be on a lake with fishing." He glances at Kyle. "Have you ever gone ice fishing, Kyle, back in Corville?"

Mutely Kyle shakes his head.

"Well," Daniel replies cheerfully, "there's a first time for everything."

We drive south, seeing no one and nothing; Daniel drives without headlights to avoid detection, so it feels as if there's nothing but darkness—dense evergreens lining the road, which snakes like a dark ribbon through the trees. High above us a handful of stars glitter from behind banks of clouds, the only faint light.

Fifteen minutes and ten miles later, Daniel takes an exit off the road and then gets back on it, heading north. Was it long enough? Will they have set up a roadblock or, worse, some kind of trap I can't bear to think about, so our escape is over just as it has begun?

Tension tautens the closed confines of the car as we silently count off the miles, no one saying a word. We pass the exit for North Bay, the old sign for 22 Wing barely visible in the darkness, and then we keep driving. Two, three, four miles. After ten, I begin to breathe easier. Surely there's no blockade, no trap. We're on our way.

In the darkness, Daniel turns and gives me a quick smile. Silently I reach out and twine my fingers with his, giving them a brief squeeze before letting go.

Then I turn my face to the window and the moonless night as Daniel keeps driving.

TWENTY-THREE

I open my eyes to wintry sunlight and a dark-eyed, dark-haired child standing about six inches from my face, staring at me silently. For a confused few seconds, I think it's Phoebe, but then I realize it's an older child—maybe five or six—and a boy.

I sit up, blinking the sleep from my eyes. I'm in a bed in one of the dozen cabins at Red Cedars Fishing Camp, on Red Cedar Lake, fifty miles northwest of North Bay. And there's someone else here.

I look around the bedroom of the cabin and see that Daniel is still asleep next to me, breathing deeply. Last night, we pulled into the darkened camp, half-afraid of what we might stumble across, only to find it looking empty and abandoned. We bypassed the main building and drove to the two cabins farthest from the road; the doors were unlocked, the beds made up, if smelling a little musty. The whole place felt as if it were completely untouched since before the bombs, which was both unsettling and reassuring. I was reminded of Goldilocks, creeping in and trying out all the furniture, and here I was, the next morning, woken by someone who might belong here more than I do.

I prop myself up on my elbow and manage a smile. I tell myself I don't need to be frightened of a child. "Hello," I greet him.

The boy blinks at me. He has dark, silky hair and thick, spiky lashes. His face is an impassive oval. I wait for him to speak, wondering who he belongs to. Who else is here, and are they friendly?

"What's your name?" he finally asks, and I almost laugh at the surreal normality of his question.

"Alex. What's yours?"

"Jason."

"Hi, Jason."

He nods his own greeting, then gestures to Daniel, who is still asleep. "What's his name?"

"Daniel." I pause. "Where do you live, Jason?" I ask tentatively.

He gives me a look like I'm stupid, in the way only a six-year-old can. "Here," he says.

I decide it's time to get out of bed.

Although the cabin has a log-burner, we didn't fire it up last night, and it's freezing as I stuff my feet into sneakers. I went to bed fully dressed, but I grab my parka and zip it up before following Jason out of the bedroom and then the whole cabin. I'm not sure where he's leading me, or where everyone else is; Ruby and Mattie are sharing one bedroom, Sam and Kyle another, and Ben and Nicole took their own cabin next door, but I don't see or hear any of them as I step outside.

I pause for a moment, taking in the pristine and wintry landscape of heavy frost, the whole world glittering and white, Red Cedar Lake stretching out in front of the cabin, half-frozen and frost-covered, fringed by evergreens and leafless trees. The cold air catches in my chest and I breathe in deeply. For the first time since we left the cottage, I feel free.

"Aren't you coming?" Jason asks, sounding impatient, and I turn to this little boy who has somehow become my guide.

"Where are we going?"

"To the others."

Hmm. Not sure how I feel about that, or even what he means, but I let go of my usual suspicious instincts and follow him down the dirt track that connects the cabins, all of them facing the breathtaking view of the lake. The whole world is silent and hushed, the frost so thick it looks like snow. The air is crisp and clear and improbably, considering all the obstacles we almost certainly face, my heart lightens. Leaving the NBSRC was, I acknowledge, the right decision, and one that superseded anything to do with Sam or William Stratton.

Jason leads me to the main cabin and dining room, which, I see now, is occupied. As I look around the camp in the daylight, I realize with a jolt that it is neither empty nor abandoned, as we'd assumed late last night in the darkness. There are quiet signs of life everywhere, from the canoes and rowing boats pulled up on the dock, to the line of laundry strung out between two cabins, to the two beat-up trucks parked behind the main cabin. In the darkness last night, we missed them all.

I follow Jason into the main cabin, which has a soaring ceiling and wood-paneled walls, with a huge picture window overlooking the lake. It's half living room, complete with leather sofas and a huge stone fireplace that now holds a cheery blaze, a deer's head with an impressive set of antlers and a baleful stare positioned above it. The other half of the cabin is a dining room with about a dozen round tables; one is laid out with breakfast items and various people are sitting around a few of the others, eating and chatting. The scene is so relaxed and normal, it takes me by surprise. I find I almost want to laugh.

"Mom." Mattie rises from one of the tables, a mug of coffee in one hand. I'm jolted by her presence, and not just because I didn't realize she was here. There are times in a parent's life when, for no more than a moment, you see your child as others must see them—not as someone who is achingly familiar and beloved, but just as a person in their own inalienable right. And for a second, that is how I see Mattie—her dark hair pulled back into a ponytail, her manner relaxed and assured. She is dressed in a cable-knit sweater and jeans, and someone here must have given her a pair of fur-lined boots because I've never seen them before but they're on her feet.

She'll be sixteen next month and she looks it, or even older —a young woman, fully grown. Someone who, if I'd met her on the street, I'd feel a flicker of interest and admiration for and I'd think to myself she was the kind of person I'd like to get to know.

"Hey." I embrace her clumsily, overwhelmed by everything, and she laughs at me, shaking her head.

"You look like you can't believe your eyes."

"I can't," I admit. I glance at the other people, including Jason, who has joined someone who looks like his dad. Everyone is observing our interaction with a sort of smiling bemusement. "What... what's going on?" I ask Mattie.

"There's a community living at this camp," she replies. "Come and meet everyone. They're all so friendly."

She tugs at my hand, and I walk toward the group, feeling both shy and hopeful. They all *look* nice, but my suspicious instincts are still there, ready to rise to the fore.

"Hey, everyone," Mattie says, "this is my mom, Alex."

Everyone murmurs some version of a greeting in a way that makes me think I've just entered a group therapy session. Why does everyone seem so smiling and relaxed? I feel as if I've entered a time warp or a fever dream. This isn't the way the world works anymore. At least, I thought it wasn't.

"Draw a chair up, Alex," a woman invites me. She is mid-thirties, her long, deep-brown hair pulled back into a ponytail, with a calm, capable manner that makes me wonder if she's in charge. "Have some breakfast." She gestures to the buffet spread out on one of the tables—a tureen of porridge, scrambled eggs, stewed apples, coffee. Where did they get it all, I wonder. How long have they been living at this camp?

I help myself to eggs and apples as well as a cup of coffee— it's instant, but better than anything I've had in a long while. Then I join Mattie and the woman who invited me to have breakfast at one of the tables.

"Last night," I say by way of both introduction and explanation, "we didn't think anyone was here."

"We were all asleep," the woman replies with a laugh. "I'm Vicky, by the way."

"Alex," I say, before I remember she already knows my name.

The others take the opportunity to introduce themselves— Jason and his dad, Adam; a young hippyish couple called Rose and Winn; a single man in his fifties named Stewart, a middle-aged couple, Patti and Jay. They have two kids, a boy and a girl, who are currently fishing.

"There are twelve of us here all together," Vicky explains. "My parents, Sheryl and Don, are out back. They ran this fishing camp before the bombs, and a few months ago, when everything started getting crazy, we decided to pool our resources and form a community here. Help each other out. We're stronger together, that sort of thing."

"And you haven't been... attacked?" I ask cautiously.

"I told them what happened to us at the cottage," Mattie interjects. "But not everyone is like that, Mom."

"There's more space out here," Vicky replies, which is exactly what I'd said to Daniel, although I'm not sure I really believed it at the time. Does simply having more space make people behave more like decent human beings? Is that all it takes? "And people have more resources," she continues.

"Besides, most people know each other around here. We take care of each other." She shrugs. "We haven't had any trouble."

I can't quite let go of my skepticism. "How come there are only twelve of you here?"

"That's all that have wanted to join," she answers with a little laugh. "We're open to people joining, though, as long as they pull their weight." She gives a smiling shrug. "Most people up here have their own outfit. A lot of residents were self-sustaining from before, anyway, and pretty independent about it. They don't need or want to be part of a community."

I think of Daniel's comment, right after the first blasts, about how everyone up here has been waiting for Armageddon, and I smile faintly in acknowledgement.

"Well, it looks incredibly impressive," I tell Vicky as I take a bite of my eggs. "I can't remember when I last had eggs."

"We're fortunate that we've got a few dozen chickens," Vicky explains. "A few of them are still laying, even though it's winter." She goes to refill her coffee before rejoining Mattie and me at the table. "Your daughter said you were at the old 22 Wing base?"

I nod. "Yes, but we... had to leave."

Vicky gives a little grimace of understanding. "They run a tight ship there, I've heard."

I nod again, not trusting myself to say anything that might be taken the wrong way. The fact that Sam punched one of the leaders of the place might not go over so well here, no matter how friendly they seem. "Tell me about this place," I say instead. "Where do you get your supplies? I haven't had real coffee in months."

"Is instant coffee real?" Vicky returns on a laugh before she explains, "We're working toward being as self-sufficient as possible. My parents were already building toward being completely self-sufficient before this all happened. The camp has its own artesian well, and the electricity is run on solar panels. We've got to be careful in winter, obviously, with the limited daylight, but so far it's been okay. My parents grew all their own fruit and vegetables, and we have several greenhouses, so we can produce year-round. Patti and Jay ran a farm nearby and we used their fields last summer for wheat and corn. They also had a couple of pigs and cows we've brought over here, and of course there's always fish in the lake. Plenty of walleye and perch, pike and trout." She spreads her hands wide. "We've managed so far. The instant coffee came from the Costco in Sudbury, though. Right at the beginning, they emptied the warehouse and distributed everything equally to anyone who showed up. We got about one hundred canisters of coffee and oats, and a few other things besides. But it won't last forever, of course."

They did the same thing at the Foodland in Corville, I recall, but it all went badly wrong when the military took over and someone started shooting. A man died, and my daughters were terrified.

But it seems, I reflect, that not every part of the world has descended to wanton destruction and self-motivated acts of violence, which is heartening. I look around the room and I feel as if I've turned back time.

"It all sounds amazing," I tell Vicky sincerely. "What did you all do before the bombs?" I glance around the table, still humbled and gratified by how friendly everyone seems. Why am I hesitant to embrace it completely? *Them?* Have I become that cynical? Of course, I've had more than enough reason to, but... this place really does feel different.

"I was a lawyer in Toronto," Vicky tells me, and for a moment her smiling countenance drops and she turns somber. "I was driving up here when Toronto was hit, a few days after the first attacks. If I hadn't been..."

"I'm sorry," I say quietly.

"Even now, it doesn't feel entirely real. The whole city... gone."

"The whole world," someone else—Patti, I think—puts in quietly.

The others tell me what their lives were like before they came to the camp. Rose and Winn were traveling, picking up jobs on farms or fruit-picking; Patti and Jay ran their farm nearby; Adam, who is Native American, was the doctor on the Nipissing Reserve south of here. His wife died of cancer—she'd been going through chemotherapy when the attacks first started —three months ago. Stewart was the local Anglican minister, of a small, wooden church down the road. He still conducts services.

"And Mattie said there are a few of you?" Vicky resumes once everyone has given me their potted biographies.

"Nine," I admit, like an apology. "They must all still be asleep." I think of Daniel, who didn't even stir when I left. Is he simply exhausted... or is it something more? I could ask Adam to take a look at him, but it feels presumptuous, and in any case, I'm not sure I can handle knowing.

"Well, they're welcome to breakfast when they wake up," Vicky says, "and then you guys can decide if you want to stay awhile, or if it's better to move on." Her voice is friendly, her face open, but I tense all the same.

It feels like there was a veiled threat to those words, but I think that's just me overreacting. At least, I hope it is.

Over the next hour, while I chat to the various residents of the community—Sheryl and Don come in and give me an effusive welcome—the rest of our crew trickle in. First Sam and Kyle, looking wary, and then incredulous when they see the spread for breakfast. Ruby brings Phoebe, and Mattie sits with her to help her eat. Nicole and Ben arrive, looking as hostile and suspicious as I'd expect them to—I don't think Nicole has another setting—but they do seem to soften when they're welcomed just as I was.

It all feels too good to be true, but maybe... maybe, for once, it isn't.

After breakfast, Sheryl and Don insist we all have a tour of the place, which I accept with alacrity, because I'm curious to see how they've managed it all. They've basically done what we tried to do back at the cottage, only bigger and better. It's both humbling and inspiring.

"Where's Dad?" Mattie asks in a hiss as we head out of the dining hall. Guiltily, I realize I hadn't even noticed he hadn't come in, although, I realize, I think I *had*; I just hadn't wanted to.

"He's sleeping," I tell Mattie. "Driving all that way in the dark was a lot."

Mattie frowns, looking like she wants to say more but won't. Or maybe, like me, she doesn't want to say more. Either way, she drops the subject, and I'm relieved.

We head outside into the cold, clear day, Sheryl and Don leading the way through the camp. There are fifteen cabins, and seven are being used. Sheryl and Don have their own house, a little way down the road. As they walk us through the greenhouses, the vegetable patch, now sprouting a few winter parsnips, the solar panels, the barn... I'm impressed all over again. This place really is run well.

Vicky falls into step beside me as we head toward the lake to see the dock and boats.

"Red Cedar Lake freezes hard, but usually not until early December," she tells me. 'I certainly wouldn't walk on it now."

I glance out at the lake. The ice is transparently thin in some places, dark water seething below. The heavy frost of this morning has melted under the sun, but everything still glitters.

"I wasn't planning on testing it," I tell her, and she smiles before cocking her head.

"What do you think so far?"

"I think it's all pretty amazing," I admit honestly. "We tried to do something similar back at our cottage, but I have to say it was nothing compared to this." I shake my head as I give a rueful laugh. "To be fair, none of us had the skills to start with. All we had was a book on sustainable living. My daughter Ruby practically memorized the whole thing."

"She sounds like a smart girl."

I glance at Vicky; as friendly and open as she is, there's a slight reserve to her that I sense rather than observe. "What about you?" I ask. "You were living in Toronto. Will you stay up here forever?"

"There's not exactly a lot of places to go," she replies wryly before her expression turns serious, even sorrowful. "My fiancé died in the Toronto bombing," she explains. "I was driving up here, like I said... I'd asked him to come, but he had an elderly mom nearby and he wanted to stay for her. And the truth is, I don't think either of us ever thought Toronto would be hit. I mean, this is Canada. We're the nice guys. Nobody wants to nuke us, right?" I give a small, sad nod of acknowledgement and she continues on a sigh, "It all got past that, I guess. Too many people with their fingers on the trigger. In any case... there's nothing to go back to, and what we've got here... it feels important. Meaningful. And it's enough for me."

"I can understand that," I tell her.

"And what about you?" Vicky asks. "Were you headed anywhere in particular when you left North Bay?"

I shake my head. "Just away. That place got kind of... oppressive."

She nods. "I'd heard that. We have a radio," she adds by way of explanation. "So we're in communication with a few different groups and we know a little bit about what's going on, although we try to keep a low profile."

"That's probably wise."

Everyone is heading back up to the main cabin for hot drinks, and so we turn from the lake and follow the group. "We try to operate as a true community," Vicky tells me. "Everyone gets a say, a vote. We rule by consensus. I don't suppose it would work if there were dozens and dozens of us, but there aren't." I nod, not sure where she's going with this. "If you were to stay," she continues, "that is, if you were to want to stay, we'd vote on it as a group. Obviously, it would be a big deal for us—you'd be almost doubling our size."

"Right," I reply after a moment. I don't think I'd seriously considered staying here, as great a set-up as it is, although I'm not sure why. "Thank you," I add, although I'm not entirely sure what I'm thanking her for. Maybe just not killing us for descending on their little group.

Vicky gives a brisk little nod and keeps walking. I decide to peel off and head back to our cabin, to check on Daniel. As I slip inside, I breathe out slowly. So much has happened in such a short time, it's hard to process it all.

And yet there's more to come because when I come into our bedroom, Daniel is awake, propped up in bed, gently prodding his stomach with one hand. When he sees me, he yanks down his t-shirt, looking guilty.

I still.

"Daniel," I force myself to ask, "what are you doing?"

"Alex..." He lets out a sigh, a sound of surrender and weary resignation. Everything in me feels fragile, breakable. I walk slowly toward him, barely daring to breathe. He stares at me silently as I lift up his shirt.

He looks the same, I think with relief—the same lean, brown chest I've known all my married life, minus the middle-aged paunch he had before the bombs.

Wordlessly, he takes my hand and guides it to his abdomen, wincing as he prods his stomach with my hand. That's when I feel it—barely at first, and then more insistently, the hard, round shape of it, pressing into my hand.

A tumor.

TWENTY-FOUR

DANIEL

March the previous year
Near Albany, New York

They've been staring at the same peeling wallpaper for over a month. Daniel and Sam have cracked more than a few jokes about it—how ugly it is, maroon and brown stripes in alternating widths, how it must have been picked by someone either blind or a hundred years old, but the jokes wore thin a few weeks ago and now there's only waiting.

They have no car, no food, no water, and Jenny has been too weak to walk or even stand. They came to this run-down ranch house to recover, but it's hard to do that when you have nothing to recover with.

At night, Daniel goes out to forage among the abandoned and ruined buildings of these dismal outskirts of Albany; occasionally he finds food or supplies that might be helpful—a flashlight, a box of Band-Aids, a bag of gummy bears. There's not much left anywhere, but he takes what he can get and is grateful.

"It's the little things in life," he told Sam one time as he popped a gummy bear in his mouth, and his son forced a smile.

It's been two months since that night in Bernardston, when Daniel had thought he'd lost both Sam and Jenny for good. When Dorcas had broken the news to him that the car had been abandoned, he'd stumbled out of bed, reaching for his coat, his shoes, without knowing where he was or how he was going to get back to the car.

Fortunately, Dorcas was willing to help. She drove him with Cal in his car—a giant of a man with a shiny bald head, a shambling gait, and a wide smile. The car was a clunker—a twenty-year-old Ford Fiesta that rattled and coughed the mile back to the exit ramp and the abandoned jeep. Sam still wasn't there, and it was clear the car had been completely looted— the windows broken, the tires slashed, their supplies taken. *Again.*

Daniel had forced his mind away from the grim prospect of starting over with absolutely nothing and shouted hoarsely for Sam, willing his son to hear and respond.

"He would have left the car," he told Dorcas and Cal, knowing he sounded truculent. "He would have left if he'd thought there was going to be trouble, and taken his grandmother somewhere safe."

Left, though, Daniel asked himself, or been kidnapped? But why would they kidnap a young man and an old woman? For what possible purpose?

"Sam!" he called again, desperation turning his voice ragged. "*Sam.*"

And then, finally, a hoarse whisper. "Dad?" Sam crawled out of the woods—his clothes torn, his face muddied, his eyes wide. "Granny's safe," he said, and Daniel sobbed with relief.

It had happened just as he'd told Dorcas—Sam had seen a truck blazing down the exit ramp and decided to abandon the car, taking Jenny into the woods, where they hid while the car was looted, its windows broken, the tires slashed for good measure—and no good reason.

Cal drove them all back to Dorcas' house, where they recuperated with more coffee and soup. Jenny fell asleep in the bed Daniel had vacated earlier, while the rest of them discussed what to do.

"There's a car lot on the outskirts of town," Cal had suggested. "A Subaru place. 'Bout a hundred cars there, I'd say. I haven't checked it out, but surely they haven't all been taken. And I think I could figure out how to hotwire a car, may the good Lord forgive me." His weathered face creased in a wry smile.

A car lot. Daniel couldn't believe he hadn't thought of such a thing before. There were car lots over the state, the whole country. All those brand new, shiny cars—hundreds and hundreds—just parked there, empty and waiting, and meanwhile people were stealing their rust buckets right out from under them. It was both absurd and pointless, but not as pointless as what they'd discovered when Cal had driven him and Sam to the car lot: five hundred cars, just as the old man had said, all parked there, pristine and gleaming in their neat rows—with their windows all shattered and their tires slashed to ribbons, just like the jeep.

Cal had surveyed the depressing scene, scratching his cheek reflectively. "I guess they did it just because they could," he remarked, sounding sorrowful but not surprised.

Because they could. Was that why anyone did anything, these days? The sheer futility of it all, the utter, absurd pointlessness, filled Daniel with total despair and made him want to laugh and sob in exactly equal measure. But worst of all, he realized, succumbing neither to laughter nor sobs, was the fact that he still didn't have a car.

"Well, you're not going to be able to get a car from this place, that's for sure," Cal said, stating the unfortunately obvious. Then he shocked Daniel to a humbled silence when he added as if it were a foregone conclusion, "I guess you'll have to take mine."

"Yyy... yours?" In his shock, Daniel stammered. "I... I couldn't."

Cal smiled, a weary yet knowing curve of his lips. "I think you'll find you could, son."

"But... I mean... you'll need it."

"I don't, as it happens. I mean, don't get me wrong, it's been convenient on occasion. But I don't need a car." He glanced at Dorcas with an almost tender smile. "Me and Dorcas, we've already decided, we're staying put. When the good Lord takes us, well then, He takes us, and that's that."

"Amen," Dorcas murmured, smiling.

Daniel could not believe, or really understand, these two people's peaceful equanimity. But already he knew Cal was right; he found he *could* take the car, and quite easily.

"Are you sure?" he asked, and to his shame he realized he was already holding his hand out for the keys.

"I'm sure," Cal replied, and gave them to him.

The Ford Fiesta lasted for forty miles before it gave out, gasping to its end on Route 2 outside of North Adams as they crawled along the Massachusetts/Vermont border, heading for Lake George, and then up around Champlain to New York's border with Quebec. Daniel had pored over the crumpled ten-year-old road atlas he'd found in the glove compartment of Cal's car, trying to figure out a workable route. Of course, that didn't take into account the far more pressing concerns—food, water, and shelter, none of which would be easy or perhaps even possible to find.

By that point, Daniel was starting to get a better, and grimmer, measure of the situation, at least regionally—refugees flooding the roads, heading either north or west, away from the radiation and the devastated cities, a general lack of food and water, no humanitarian aid or military presence, an atmosphere of toxic fear. Violent gangs were less of a problem than people like him who were so desperate they'd do anything. That felt even more dangerous.

He'd been planning on traveling only at night and holing up somewhere during the days, but it took just one afternoon to drive the forty miles, and then they were carless. They'd already drunk the water and eaten the granola bars Dorcas had kindly given them, and they had nothing. Literally nothing but the clothes on their backs, in the middle of winter, over four hundred miles from home, and with an elderly and frail woman in their care. Daniel didn't think it could get much worse.

The next month had them moving snail-like across a wintry landscape of northern Massachusetts and then upstate New York, sleeping in abandoned houses or barns, with Daniel making sure Sam and Jenny stayed inside as much as they could while he went out and looked for food. Once, he found a looted 7-Eleven with three cans of baked beans forgotten on a bottom shelf. He'd been ecstatic, until he'd realized they had no can opener or anything that could act like one. He'd ended up making a hole in the can with the Fiesta's car key, and they'd had to siphon the mixture out with their mouths, one measly bean at a time. It was better, he told Sam, than starving.

When they found a place Daniel deemed safe and warm enough, they stayed, mainly for Jenny to regain some strength, although it was hard for her to do that when there was so little food. Still, Daniel knew he and Sam needed to regain their strength as well; they were all weakened from the journey.

Jenny struggled to walk for more than a few yards at a time, and he and Sam took turns carrying her, but it was far from easy, especially when they were feeling so weak themselves. They needed a car, Daniel thought, more than once, and each time with increasing hopelessness. They needed a car or eventually, somewhere between here and Flintville, Ontario, they were going to die, whether they found food or not.

Somehow they managed to eke out an existence as they inched steadily—or, really, not so steadily—northwest. Occasionally, Daniel would find something that kept them going for a few days or longer. Once, he snuck into a woman's house to discover her long dead on the sofa, and a cupboard of dwindling food supplies—a sack of rice, a can of corn, another of peas—all of which he took, and without a backward glance at the poor woman's corpse. She was dead, he thought, determined to be ruthless. She didn't need it. She didn't need to be buried, either. He doubted there was anyone left to mourn her.

They'd continued on in this way through January, but in February Jenny developed a fever and Sam a cough. They were too spent to go any further, and Daniel knew they needed to rest for longer—and he needed to find more food.

And so they sat here in this run-down ranch house, staring at the ugly wallpaper while Jenny slept in one of the two small, shabby bedrooms, both of them waiting and wondering what to do, because that was all that was left.

"I could go out," Sam ventures late one afternoon, far from the first time. Outside the sky is already growing dark, and a few mean-looking flakes of snow drift down indifferently.

"No." Daniel's reply is automatic; he has always insisted Sam and Jenny stay inside when they've rested. He hopes— God, how he hopes, praying earnestly every day—that the intermittent exposure will not be too dangerous for either of them.

As for him... well, he'll take whatever happens to him at this point as long as he gets Sam back. Jenny, too, but considering her health and age he isn't holding out as much hope for her.

"Dad, I've been in this place for a month," Sam fires back,

sounding irritated and even angry, more than he has in all their travels. "Come on. Give me a chance."

Daniel shakes his head, an inexorable back and forth. "No." He won't go into the reasons, the dangers, or the justifications, and so Sam just glowers at him. Daniel decides it was time he went foraging.

"You stay here with your grandmother," he tells Sam sternly, knowing his son will never leave her alone. Thank goodness, because he needs him to stay inside. He will never, ever forgive himself if Sam is affected by the radiation, if he gets burned or poisoned or cancer or however it comes for him, which it won't, because he won't let it.

It is fully dark when Daniel ventures out onto the streets of this southern suburb of Albany, run-down and weedy and mostly abandoned. Albany, it seems, isn't far enough to escape; people are heading further north or west, wherever they can go that feels safe... if such a place even exists.

He walks slowly, his feet dragging along the road, weary right down to his bones. He has no idea where he's going to find any food. He supposes he'll do what he's been doing, with limited success, for the last month—sneak into abandoned houses or stores and hope someone forgot to take it all, gather up what scraps he might be lucky enough to find.

It doesn't feel like nearly enough. He knows it isn't. How long can they keep existing this way? He thinks of Sam's cough still rattling in his chest, Jenny's debilitating weakness, his own lethargy and gauntness. Something needs to change—but how?

He's spent hours thinking about possible solutions. Could he find food in a school, a hospital, a warehouse, a farm? Every time he tries to look, all he comes across is broken glass and bullet holes. Nearly three months on from the first bombs, the world is still so very broken—and getting emptier. In the dead of winter, a nuclear war is a disaster. Lack of food and freezing temperatures have added to the horrific death toll. Yesterday, when he went foraging, he came across an entire family, huddled together for warmth—and frozen to death.

Up ahead he sees an apartment building of crumbling brick, its windows mostly intact although the front door has been left wide open, an invitation or maybe just surrender. Daniel hesitates, and then, slowly, cautious with every inching step, he goes inside, having no idea what he'll find.

What he does find, as in so many other places like this, is emptiness and decay. There's a musty, sweetish smell in the air whose source he knows too well. A cold wind blows through the hallway, rustling the trash that carpets the floor in drifts of paper and cardboard.

A few apartment doors are flung open, while others are tightly shut. Daniel steps through the first open door into a shabby three-room apartment that has been completely ransacked. Like so many other places he's seen, it hasn't been just looted but wantonly destroyed—windows and mirrors broken, sofas and mattresses slashed, what has to have been something like a sledgehammer sent through the TV. People high on coke or meth or fentanyl, taking their pointless pleasure or maybe just acting out their terror. Who knows? It doesn't matter, anyway.

There's nothing there, Daniel is sure of it, but he checks anyway, opening every single cupboard. He finds a handful of silverware in the kitchen, which he takes, and a dish towel. He pockets that, too, and then he moves on.

He works his way methodically through the building, going into the empty apartments first and then circling back to the ones with closed doors. Most of them are locked; whether there are people inside he doesn't know and isn't about to find out. He might be desperate, but it would be insanity to come face to face with someone wielding a weapon and defending their home.

He takes what little he finds—a women's sweater, a pair of old sneakers, a blanket, and, best of all, a dented can of spaghetti and meatballs, already expired before the bombs. Never mind; food is food, after all.

On the top floor, he turns the knob of a closed door, and is surprised when it swings open. He steps inside, and stills when he hears the thin, fretful cry of a baby. For a second, his instinct, or maybe just his desire, is to turn around and leave. He can't get involved with an infant, not when he's already got two people to take care of.

But then he hears another sound—the croaky voice of a woman.

"Hello?" she calls out, her voice hoarse and papery. "Is anyone there? Can you help me, please? Hello?"

Still Daniel hesitates. Then, reluctantly, he moves forward, rounding the corner of the narrow front hallway to the small, dark living room, where a young woman lies supine on a sofa, a baby swaddled on the floor next to her.

She is clearly close to dying—utterly emaciated, the bones of her face as naked as a skull, her eyes sunken into her flesh. She reaches one scrawny hand out and then drops it in exhaustion. Her lank, dark hair lies in greasy strands next to her thin, pale face. "Hello?" she whispers. "Can you help me? Please?"

Daniel glances down at the baby, who is just as gaunt, its mewling cry pathetically weak, its tiny form nearly lifeless.

"How can I help?" he asks, and a smile breaks over her face, lighting her sunken eyes in a way that makes him feel wretched because already he knows he can't help. It's too late for her, and most likely for the baby as well.

"I'm trying to get to Buffalo," she rasps. "There's a... a military base there..." She trails off, catching her breath; just those few words have taken too much effort. "It's a safe place. They're letting people in. I need to get there."

Daniel shakes his head slowly, regretful but firm. "Buffalo is three hundred miles from here."

"I have a car," she says.

He stares at her for a long moment. "You do?"

She leans forward, nodding eagerly, then collapses back against the sofa, gasping for breath. "A Honda Civic. It's parked in a locked garage about a mile from here, on County Road. I put it there when the looting started... I figured it would be safe, when I was ready to drive out somewhere, get away from all this... but then I got sick, and Tiffany too..." She gazes down at the baby, her lips trembling as she looks helplessly at her daughter. The baby's face is so wizened it looks more like an alien than a child. Daniel feels a stirring of pity.

"Do you want me to get your car for you?" he asks.

She nods, eager again. "Would you..." She pauses, gulps. "Can I trust you?" she asks, the question of a helpless child.

What other answer can he give? He keeps her gaze as he answers.

"You can trust me," he promises her.

TWENTY-FIVE
ALEX

Neither Daniel nor I speak as I withdraw my hand from his stomach. He gives me a grimace of apology and lowers his shirt while I sink onto the edge of the bed.

"Why didn't you tell me?" I ask in a whisper.

He lets out a little sigh as he straightens his t-shirt. "I didn't want to add to everything, but... I suspected you already knew."

My head drops toward my chest, and I close my eyes. He's right, I did know, even if I was trying my best not to.

"From the radiation?" I have to force the words out.

"I'd guess so." He sighs. "I wasn't as honest with you as I should have been. When I went to get Sam and then Jenny there were a lot of people fleeing the fallout. Some people even had burns... I mean, it's not something you can see, so I was always wondering—is it bad? How bad? Am I breathing it in right now? What will it do to me?" He shakes his head. "I just didn't know. I tried to keep them both indoors as much as possible, either in the car or a house, but..."

I'm both completely unsurprised and deeply shocked. Of course the radiation was that bad. I wanted to believe Daniel's glib assurances, gleaned from sci-fi series and disaster movies, but did I really accept his version, deep down? No, I never did. Which means...

"Do you think Sam..." I begin, and then find I can't finish that sentence.

Daniel gives me a look of mute appeal. "I did my best, Alex, I swear, but of course I don't know. I just don't know." He looks abject, and so very apologetic, and I feel guilty for making him think this could, in any way, be his fault. Dear God, I think, what sort of wife have I been?

In any case, I tell myself, my son isn't sick like my husband. Sam isn't struggling to breathe or to eat; he isn't falling asleep at six o'clock at night. His skin isn't gray; his body isn't gaunt and wasting away.

Silently I reach over and take Daniel's hand. He twines his fingers through mine, and we sit there for a few minutes without saying a word, because it feels like there is nothing more to say.

We can't leave this camp, I realize belatedly, with Daniel this sick. Will Vicky and the others understand, or will they still put it to a vote? And how sick *is* Daniel? I glance at his familiar, beloved face, now so weary and lined. Will it be a matter of weeks, months, more? Or maybe less... maybe just days. Like with the radiation, there's no way to know.

A sound escapes me, ragged and hitching, and Daniel squeezes my fingers.

"I'm sorry," he says.

I shake my head. "You have nothing to be sorry for. I'm the one who should be sorry. I made you—"

"You didn't."

"If you hadn't gone—"

"Then we wouldn't have Sam back."

He sounds so certain, but some part of me is determined to rail against it all, finding fault and blame because for some inexplicable reason that feels easier.

"Still," I insist stubbornly. "I shouldn't have asked that of you."

"Alex." Daniel's voice is gentle, and it forces me to look him full in the face—his tired eyes are full of love and sorrow. "I would have gone anyway."

Another sound escapes me, half hiccup, half sob, and I know I can't take any more, not now. And Daniel can't either, I tell myself, because he looks exhausted. So I change the subject, the switch as abrupt and obvious as a screech of tires, and say, "Let me tell you about this place. It's kind of crazy, but in a good way."

Daniel smiles and settles back against the pillows. "Okay," he replies. "Tell me."

I tell him about the community and all its members, the solar panels and the artesian well, the farm fields and greenhouses, the fishing and the boats, the fact that this place is pretty much self-sustaining, or soon will be.

"Vicky said if we wanted to stay, they would put it to a vote," I finish before adding firmly, "I think we should stay."

Daniel smiles and shrugs. "Well, I don't think I'm going anywhere in a hurry."

I know he's just trying to be realistic, but I can't bear to hear it, and he must see that in my face, for he catches my hand, staying it with his own. "Alex. We need to be honest about this."

I avert my gaze from his, recognizing it's cowardly, but it's the only way to keep from crying. "I know."

"I have no idea how long I'll last," he continues steadily, "but I'm pretty sure this is terminal."

A tear leaks from my eye and trickles down my cheek before dripping off my chin. "Don't..." I whisper.

"I don't mind dying," Daniel tells me as he traces the lines of my palm with his thumb. "Maybe I should, I'm not that old, after all, but I'm not afraid. Tom helped me see that."

I turn to face him. "*Tom?*"

"Yes, Tom, from the NBSRC and before. He's a good man, a man of faith, and..." Daniel pauses, his throat working. "I was feeling guilty about... about something I did. Or really, something I didn't do." He closes his eyes. "And Tom helped me to forgive myself. He assured me that God had forgiven me. And I hadn't even realized I'd needed that until he'd said it."

"Daniel..."

"I don't want to tell you," he continues, his eyes still closed. "Not yet, anyway. Maybe not ever. I'm forgiven. That's enough."

"I killed a man," I remind him, my voice wobbling all over the place. "A good man, a man of faith like your Tom, maybe. And I don't think Sam has forgiven me for it, never mind God."

"I think," Daniel says, opening his eyes, "that you're the one who can't forgive. You can't let it go, Alex, just like I couldn't, for so long. You need to."

I nod jerkily and slip my hand from Daniel's. He's tired, and I really can't handle any more of this kind of conversation. I have to take it in small bursts in order to keep going, and, now more than ever, that's what I need to do. "You should rest," I tell him. "I'll come back in an hour or so to check on you, give you something to eat."

He gives a small, sad smile, and I know he understands why I'm pulling away, but he lets me do it.

"I love you," I blurt. I wonder how many more times I'll have a chance to say it.

"I love you, too," he replies, and then his eyes flutter closed.

I'm feeling too raw to face everyone back at the main cabin, and so I end up going for a walk down by the lake. The ground is frozen hard, the lake a mix of ice, slush, and frigid water. Above the sky is a pale, hazy blue that looks like it might morph into the slate gray that promises snow.

I walk steadily, putting one foot in front of the other, doing my best not to think. As long as I keep my mind full of this buzzing blankness, I'll be okay. I won't give in to the grief, or the regrets that I wasn't the wife I should have been to my husband. That I stayed angry and resentful when I could have been kind and, yes, forgiving. I have a lot to forgive myself for, and I'm not sure I can do it, or even if I should.

Eventually I run out of space; the shoreline becomes impassable, a thicket of fallen evergreens blocking the way, their dead branches looking like hundreds of skeletal fingers. Slowly I turn around, and come, to my surprise, face to face with Nicole.

"Have you been following me?" I demand, my breath a frosty puff of air between us.

She shrugs. "I've been walking in the same direction."

I shake my head and start to walk past her. I'm not in the mood for Nicole's peculiar brand of orneriness, not now.

"What's wrong?" she asks, just as I walk by her.

I hesitate, and then, with my back still turned, I admit recklessly, "Daniel has cancer, from the radiation. He's dying." Saying it out loud makes me feel worse. This is happening, and there's nothing I can do about it. No matter how hard I fight or how fast I run, no matter how many promises I make to protect my family, to forge or force a way through...

Cancer will beat me. *Us.*

"I'm sorry," Nicole says quietly. "That sucks."

A ragged laugh escapes me, torn from my being. "Yeah, you could say that."

She turns and falls into step alongside me, and, by silent, mutual agreement, we start walking back toward the camp. "You're going to stay here, then?" she asks.

"If we're allowed. They have to vote."

"Yeah, there's that."

"What about you?"

A sigh escapes her, long and weary. "I'm running out of road. I mean, I can't cope on my own. I'm fully aware of that. Maybe it's why I stayed with William for so long. And I need to be strong for Ben." She sounds angry with herself, and I feel a stirring of sympathy.

"You're stronger than you pretend, Nicole," I tell her, and she laughs.

"No, I'm actually not. This whole tough-cookie-who-doesn't-care schtick? It's just an act. You've seen me cry." She says it like an accusation. "You know I'm not up for any of this. Plus, I have no idea how to garden, knit, pluck a chicken, skin a... I don't even know, a deer. I'm totally, *totally* hopeless at all that stuff, and, frankly, I've been okay with that."

Improbably, I find myself smiling. "You could learn. I did. Ruby's got a great book that teaches you all that kind of stuff, step by step."

"A book?" She sounds understandably skeptical.

"Yes, but nothing like a little hands-on experience, though, it's true." I turn to face her, summoning a strength of conviction I didn't realize I felt until this moment. "You and Ben could make a good life for yourselves here," I tell her. "Let go of that tough cookie act, put how William treated you behind you as best as you can... This could work out for you, if you let it. If you let go of some of that cynicism—understandable, why you have it, but that doesn't mean you have to keep it—and just... embraced this. What it could be for you, as well as for Ben..." I run out of steam as well as breath.

Nicole cocks her head. "Thanks for the inspirational talk."

"You're welcome."

"Can I have that on a poster?" she asks musingly. "Or actually, a coaster? Too bad VistaPrint isn't around anymore, or you could do a roaring business in the inspirational logo field. I really see this kind of thing taking off."

I laugh. The sound is rusty but real. "Yeah, too bad. I could order a round thousand and sell them out of the trunk of my car. I mean, everyone needs a little motivational slogan in these times, right? To keep you going?"

"What about you?" She drops the joking, her expression turning serious. "You sound like you aren't going to stay here."

"I don't know. We have to for now because..." I can't make myself say it. "But as for the future? The rest of my life?"

Her eyebrows—still elegant—lift. "Can any of us think that way anymore?"

"Maybe not," I allow. "Maybe I just need to be in this moment, crappy as it is, and not worry about the next one, never mind the one after that."

"That sounds like good advice," she replies, sounding sincere for the first time since I've met her, and we walk back to the camp in a silence that feels like solidarity.

I know we need to tell the kids about Daniel's condition, but I'm not ready to have that conversation quite yet. So I help Vicky and Sheryl prepare lunch—pickled beets and bread made from nut flour—and then wash up. *As long as I keep busy*, I think, but I know that's not true.

After lunch, I head back to the cabin to check on Daniel, to find he's asleep and sweating out a fever. When I rest my hand against his clammy forehead, he doesn't even open his eyes.

I decide it's time to face some hard truths and figure out a plan for all of us.

Sheryl offers to keep Phoebe occupied in the kitchen while I gather my troops around me. We're sitting in the living room of our cabin; Kyle started a fire in the log-burner and it lets out a cheery glow as well as a comforting warmth. The door to Daniel's bedroom is firmly closed.

"So," I tell them all. "We need to decide if we want to stay here."

Mattie, quick as ever, answers incredulously, "Why wouldn't we? I mean, where else are we going to go?"

"Remember what the Strattons said about something

happening out in North Dakota?" I remind her. "There might be places, whole cities, being rebuilt out there. If there's a government, they're going to want to restore order." Even if it's almost impossible to imagine life getting back to some kind of normal.

"I don't want to live in North Dakota," Mattie replies, obstinate now.

"You'd rather live in northern Ontario?" I ask with an attempt at a smile.

"I *like* it here." She gives me a look that manages to be both accusing and sympathetic. "People are nice, and it's got a cool vibe. You don't have to keep running, Mom."

Which makes me look at Sam, for some reason, and once again he looks away. "I'm not running," I reply, but my tone is unconvincing, even to myself. "Anyway, that's not the point. I just wanted to know what you guys thought." I glance at Sam, at Kyle, at Ruby. "Do you all want to stay?"

One by one they nod, although Ruby ventures, "I want to go where you go."

"Thanks, Rubes." I give her a quick, reassuring hug. "I'm willing to follow the consensus on this," I tell them all. "If you want to stay, we'll stay, and the community here will put it to a vote. Nothing is guaranteed, unfortunately—"

"Don't I get a vote?"

I turn to see Daniel standing in the doorway, looking terrible. His face is gray, covered with a sheen of sweat, and he's leaning against the door frame like he doesn't have the strength to stand up.

"Dad..." Sam begins, sounding alarmed.

"You already told me you wanted to stay," I tell him, pressing my lips together to keep from crying. I can't stand to see him looking like this, and I'm pretty sure, judging by everyone's horrified faces, that my children feel the same, along with Kyle.

"Yes, but I need to tell everyone why I want to stay," Daniel replies, his voice both steady and gentle. He knows I haven't told them about his cancer, and they need to be told.

I swallow and nod, giving permission, even if I'm unable to put it into so many words.

"Dad..." This time it's Mattie who protests, a wobble in her voice. "What... what's going on?"

"I have a tumor in my stomach," Daniel tells them without preamble. "Probably from radiation exposure, although who can say for sure? But it's been growing and I'm feeling it and eventually it's going to get me. I'm sorry, guys. I really am."

For a few seconds, everyone simply stares. It's like they can't take in what he's saying; it simply won't compute. They won't let it.

Then, finally, Sam says in a faint voice, "You mean... you have cancer?"

Daniel nods, as unflappable as ever. "Yes."

"And..." This from Mattie. "It's going to kill you?"

"Well, it's not like I can get treatment around here." Daniel tries to smile, but then his face collapses with sadness. "I wish it didn't end this way," he admits in a low voice. "I don't want to leave you all. I don't want you to be *left*."

"But..." Mattie gulps. "I thought you said the radiation wasn't that bad."

"I guess I was mistaken." Daniel spreads his hands wide. "I don't think it's as bad now, at any rate, because it's had to have dissipated so much. But back then—when I was getting Sam—I think it was bad then. Worse than anyone realized, at least for a while."

"You knew," Sam says suddenly. His voice is hard, and he almost sounds angry. "You knew, and that's why you kept insisting I stay inside, and Granny too, for all that time."

Daniel gives our son an appraising look. "I was trying to protect you, Sam."

"Well, you shouldn't have!" Sam shouts as tears start from his eyes. "You shouldn't have! You don't have to be such a damned *martyr* all the time." Abruptly he pushes up from the sofa and storms out of the house, slamming the door behind him so hard it feels as if the whole cabin rattles.

For a few seconds we all simply sit there, silent. Then I rise and head to the door. "I'll talk to him," I say, and I go outside.

Sam is striding toward the lake, taking more or less the same route I did a few hours ago. I follow him at a distance, wishing I knew what to say or even how to say it, but I don't. I feel empty inside, used up, and yet somehow I've got to be here for my son —say the right thing, make the whole situation if not better, then at least bearable.

"Sam." I start with his name, keeping my voice gentle, as I come to stand a few yards behind him. He is facing the lake, his hands laced together on top of his head, elbows akimbo.

"I'm not in the mood for a pep talk, Mom," he states wearily.

"I'm not in the mood to give one."

"Good." He drops his hands abruptly, so they smack down by his sides as he continues to stare out at the lake.

"I know this is hard," I begin, wincing inwardly at how feeble I sound. *You think?* I imagine Mattie firing back at me, eyebrows raised, but Sam just sighs.

"It *is* hard. I'm just... I'm so *mad* at him." His voice breaks, and he bows his head as he takes a few shuddering breaths to control himself.

"Sam..." I step closer, reaching one hand out, although I don't touch him. That is not what I'd expected him to say. "Help me understand. I get why you're mad at me, but why... why at Dad?"

"Mom," Sam tells me in that same weary voice as he scrubs at his eyes, "you do not understand anything. Sorry, but it's true. You have gotten it all completely wrong from the beginning."

I blink, absorbing this, trying not to let it sting. "So tell me what I got wrong," I say finally, keeping my voice gentle.

Sam sighs. "You think I freaked out because you killed that guy on the road, right?"

"Well..."

He floors me with what he says next.

"That's not it at all," my son tells me as he turns around. "I wasn't freaked out because you killed that guy... I was mad because I should have been the one to do it."

TWENTY-SIX

Okay, that was *not* what I'd expected him to say. At all. So clearly I did get a lot of things wrong.

"Why..." I lick my lips as my mind spins. "Why do you think you should have been the one to do it, Sam?"

He huffs impatiently, the impatient twist of his shoulders acting as a dismissal. "Because I haven't done anything," he bursts out. "Because I've been acting like a stupid baby since this whole thing started. Dad treated me like one, and I let him." His face crumples and then, like a child, he starts to cry.

I stretch out my arms for a hug, but he spins away before I can reach him.

"Don't," he snarls. "For the love of—Mom, *don't*."

Slowly I drop my arms. Sam wipes his cheeks.

"What do you think you should have done?" I ask quietly.

"Anything," Sam replies savagely. "*Anything*. I just let Dad do it all, basically. He treated me like this little kid who needed protecting from everything. Who couldn't handle the truth, and that's because I couldn't." He draws a shuddering breath and then continues doggedly, "I mean, at first, I know I was acting stupid, like it was all a—a video game or something.

I *know* how stupid that sounds, but I just... I don't know, it all seemed kind of... exciting, in a weird way. I can't really explain it, but it was kind of... cool." He flinches, even before I've said anything. "I know how that sounds, I know, I know—"

"Sam," I interject gently. "It's okay." I can completely appreciate how unreal everything seemed back then, especially at the beginning. I'm hardly about to begrudge my son having more or less the same reaction I did—the incredulity, the suspended sense of surreality, like it wasn't really happening, or at least, it wasn't really happening to me.

"But then... I *wanted* to do stuff," he continues, his voice rising. "To help. I offered to go out and look for food, or a car, when we needed one. But Dad always said my job was to look after Granny. She was... well." He grimaces, and I can imagine. My mother had an immense strength of spirit, but at the end she was frail, vulnerable, and suffering from dementia. It was a miracle that Daniel managed to bring her back.

"I know, though," Sam continues, "that that wasn't it, at least not all of it. He was just trying to protect me from the radiation. And I never really argued about it. I just let him... because the truth is..." Sam blows out a breath, his shoulder slumping. "The truth is, I was scared." He gives me a guilty look, the kind of frightened glance he might have given me at six years old, when he'd done something naughty. "I didn't want to risk getting burned or zapped or whatever. I wanted to stay safe, so I let him do it all and I pretended it was his idea."

"And Dad wanted you to stay safe, too," I return quietly. I hesitate, trying to feel my way through the words, to say what Sam needs to hear. "I can understand why you feel guilty, Sam, but, please believe me, you don't need to. Dad certainly wouldn't want you to, and especially now. Keeping you safe was his absolutely number one priority—"

"But it's not like I was six," Sam burst out. "Mom, I was

eighteen. I should have dealt with it. I should have... manned up."

"But Sam," I protest, "you have your whole life ahead of you—"

"And Dad doesn't." Sam's expression and voice both turn bleak, and I fall silent, the reality of Daniel's condition reverberating through the emptiness inside me. "How am I supposed to live with that?" he asks, like he needs to know the answer, as if I could possibly have it. I don't know it for myself, never mind my children.

But Sam's situation is different from mine; it is, I realize, the same dilemma Mattie has been facing, with Kerry. How do you accept that someone willingly gave their life to you—in Kerry's case, the matter of a single second; in my husband's, month after treacherous month? Both were incredibly courageous and noble sacrifices... but they can be hard to accept.

"I don't know," I admit. I think of my trite words to Mattie—*make it count*—and yet they're true. Aren't they? Surely they need to be. "Just with gratitude, Sam, and not with anger or guilt. Dad would have never wanted that."

"He did something bad," Sam confesses in a low voice. "Something he wouldn't tell me about. In Albany, he found a car. He came back with it and he was... crying." He sounds like he still can't believe it. "He was trying not to show it, but..." He trails off, shaking his head. "I don't know what, but I knew it was something. Something had happened. Or he had done something to get it. I don't know."

My stomach cramps with anxiety but I keep my voice steady. "Whatever Dad did, he did it willingly, for you. It was a choice he made."

Sam gives me a level look. "Like you killing that guy?"

I do my best not to flinch. "I thought I was protecting everyone," I admit quietly, a sorrowful agreement. "It's been hard—really hard—to accept that maybe... maybe I wasn't. That maybe

I made a mistake, and that guy was just trying to be nice." Even after all this, it's hard to admit. To accept... and yet I know I need to.

Sam cocks his head. "While holding a gun."

"Well, we were all holding guns." I swallow and force myself to tell him, "I thought you've been distant from me these last few months because you were so... so sickened by what I'd done. Killing someone in cold blood, without even considering they might be okay."

Sam is silent for a long moment. "It wasn't that," he finally says. "I mean, that was part of it, maybe, at first. Like, when I found that Bible verse and photo and stuff... well, it would have been easier all around if those guys were bad news, right? But I didn't blame you, Mom, or Dad. Not for that, for any of it... I was just... I was *ashamed*." His face crumples and he gulps several times, staring down at the ground. This time, he can't meet my eye, but I know it's not because of me. "Like, that whole time," he continues in a choked voice, "I was just hiding in the backseat."

"Oh, Sam." I step forward and this time he lets me hug him. He clings to me, or maybe I cling to him, and neither of us speaks. Part of me wonders why we couldn't have had this conversation earlier, made these strides sooner, while another part acknowledges the stark truth that it simply wouldn't have been possible. Daniel's condition, his inevitable death... that's what has forced these painful truths out at last. It's a blessing amid the grief and tragedy, and one I'm grateful for, but...

Though the fig tree does not bud and there are no grapes on the vines, though the olive crop fails and the fields produce no food, though there are no sheep in the pen and no cattle in the stalls, yet I will rejoice...

The verse ripples through my mind, quiet yet insistent; I

know I'll never forget the words. This time though, instead of the usual churning sense of guilt, they leave a surprising and unexpected peace in their wake, a feeling that is not as elusive as it once was. Everything feels so hard, and it's going to get so much harder...

And yet.

Two words I can choose to live by, even though it's not easy. *Especially* though it's not easy.

Slowly I release Sam and step back. He sniffs, running his wrist along his nose, before giving me a shamefaced smile. "Sorry."

I smile faintly. "I wish I had a handkerchief."

"Dad would have one."

"You're right, he would have."

We are, I realize, already talking about him as if he's dead, but he isn't. He *isn't.* "Let's go back and talk to him," I tell Sam, and together we walk back up to the cabin.

That night the community votes on whether we can stay; it only takes ten minutes, but it feels like the longest ten minutes of my life. If we have to move on, I don't know how we will, or where we'll go. I'm worried it might hasten Daniel's death, a prospect I can hardly bear to think about.

Fortunately, that's not how it turns out. Vicky emerges from the main cabin, smiling.

"Come inside and get warm," she tells us. "It was unanimous."

The relief is palpable and sweet. I go back to tell Daniel, and he girds himself to join us by the fire in the main cabin. Vicky makes hot chocolate, an unimaginable treat, weak and watery as it is. This is a beginning of something, yet with a terrible ending wrapped inside it, but I'm still choosing.

And yet.

As we sip our hot chocolate, Vicky takes us through our days. We won't be assigned jobs here the same way we were back at the NBSRC, but we will all have to chip in and if we aren't pulling our weight someone will, she tells us with good humor, certainly let us know about it.

"So far, we've kept it casual," Vicky explains. "Based on goodwill. We don't want to turn into some work camp where you have to carry out orders. That's not the point of life, even this life, such as it is."

Daniel and I exchange amused glances; it's almost as if Vicky overheard me complaining, back at the NBSRC. My sense of relief deepens; this was definitely the right choice, and I think we all know it.

Over the next few days and weeks, we fall into a rhythm of work—making meals, cleaning up, trapping and ice fishing, weeding the boxes in the greenhouses, harvesting the winter parsnips, mending both tools and clothes. Sheryl teaches me how to sew and I darn sheets for an entire afternoon, sitting by the fire, feeling like Ma Ingalls. Sam and Kyle become obsessed with fishing, and Ruby spends every moment she can in the greenhouses with Rose, who is our resident green thumb. Phoebe follows Mattie like her little shadow, and Mattie takes to the kitchen, learning tips and tricks from both Sheryl and Patti about how to make a couple of potatoes and a single swede go a long way.

Nicole and Ben find their place too, albeit a little more slowly. Ben has to drop his too-cool-for-this attitude, but soon enough he's fishing with Sam and Kyle, and even gutting and cleaning the walleyes he's caught. Nicole, unsurprisingly perhaps since she was an interior designer, knows how to sew and helps me with the darning.

Life both slows down and speeds up; the days pass in a blur

of productive activity without anything feeling frantic or rushed, and yet they pass, and, as they do, I feel Daniel begin to ebb away.

I know better than to pretend it's not happening. Time is too short and too precious for such pointless deception but oh, how it hurts, not to pretend. To be forced to acknowledge the reality that creeps closer every day.

At first, he went down to the lake to watch the boys fish, applauding when they caught a perch or a walleye or the occasional pike. It brought me such joy, to see him there, to hear the mingled laughter.

Then he stood on the deck, wrapped up well, and cheered them on from there, his hoarse voice carrying on the still winter air while the boys smiled and gave him a thumbs-up. Then it was from inside, in a chair by the big picture window, where he could still at least see them. And then it was by the fire, where he couldn't, asking me how they were doing, his voice faint and hoarse.

And then it was back at the cabin, in bed, where he started to sleep all the time, stirring only to smile at me faintly and pick at the food I brought him. It was only a matter of weeks from the first to the last; by mid-December, I knew he wasn't going to get out of bed again, not for any extended period of time, at least. How could something happen so fast? How could I let it?

And yet I was powerless, we all were, and that was part of the pain.

Adam didn't have much to give to ease Daniel's obvious suffering, but he'd kept some codeine from his practice and he offered it to Daniel, who, in typical fashion, refused it.

"Save it for someone who really needs it," he told the doctor, who shook his head, smiling sorrowfully.

"Don't you think you do?"

"Not for long," Daniel quipped, his grin turning into a grimace.

"How bad is it?" I ask him one night while I sit with him. Everyone else is up at the main cabin, where they tend to congregate in the evenings. "Really?"

"I can handle it, Alex."

"You don't need to be strong for me," I tell him. "Not anymore."

He lets out a tired laugh as he leans his head back against the pillow. "You were always the strong one in our marriage."

"No." My eyes fill with tears and resolutely I blink them back. "You were. I just acted like... like a bitch." My voice wobbles with recrimination.

He laughs again and reaches for my hand, pressing it against his cheek. "No, you didn't. You're strong, Alex. Stronger than you realize. You always have been." He pauses, still holding my hand against his cheek. "Promise me you won't forget that."

What can I do but promise? "I won't," I say, but Daniel must sense my hesitation because he continues more fiercely,

"I mean it. You're a doer, Alex, a leader. You've never thought you are, but I've seen it, time and time again. You rise to the challenge. You get things done. After I'm gone..." He holds my unhappy gaze. "You know we need to talk about this. After I'm gone, I don't think you should stay here, hiding away. This is a good place, a safe one, but it's not the end for you." He smiles faintly as he adds, "Never mind Michael Duart, *you* can be part of the rebuilding of the world. You have it in you. I know you do, and I want you to be part of whatever's next... for my sake. For our children's."

"Daniel..." I shake my head helplessly, because how can I promise such a thing? Daniel is full of fine words, but do I believe them? Can I?

"Do you promise?" he demands, and, unable to speak, I nod again, because I know I'd promise him anything now, and maybe he's right. Maybe I do have it in me, even if I feel so far from that in this moment.

"I promise," I whisper. Then I continue, feeling like I have to say it because my chances to are slipping away with every passing day. "The whole thing with the house back in Connecticut, from before..." I begin stiltedly. "Your job..." It feels so long ago, and it's basically become irrelevant to our lives now, and yet... it's still there. It's always been there, between us in one way or another, because I've made it so. "I shouldn't have been so angry," I say quietly. "I'm sorry. So sorry."

Daniel shakes his head, still holding my hand. "Alex... I basically lied to you for six months. I would have been angry if you'd done that to me. I would have been furious."

And yet I don't think he would have been. He would have been sad, and maybe disappointed, and he would have tried to understand why I'd done what I did... an understanding I never even tried to afford him. "Why did you lie?" I ask, without an iota of the bitterness and resentment I carried self-righteously for so long. "It's so unlike you. You're the most honest person I know."

Daniel is quiet for a moment, considering. "It started out not so much as a lie as a prevarication," he explains finally. "I was going to tell you when I had another job. I didn't think it would take that long. I'd tide us over by using our savings and moving assets around... I kept telling myself it would work out, and then I'd be able to explain everything, not even eventually, but soon. Really soon. And I told myself it was because I didn't want you to worry, but really it was because I didn't want you to look at me like I'd failed, which, of course, I had."

He speaks matter-of-factly but with deep sorrow, and it tears at me. "Daniel—"

"But I should have trusted you with that," he continues, cutting me off with determination. "What's a marriage if we can't share our failures as well as our successes? If we can't bear each other's burdens all along the way? I know," he adds, his voice choking a little now, "that it was the lying that was the hardest part for you. Not the loss of money, or even of the house, hard as all that was. And I'm sorry for that, because choosing to lie, to live in that lie, was the worst failure of all."

I shake my head, cupping his gaunt cheek with my hand. "We don't need to be sorry anymore," I whisper. "For anything." He smiles at me in response, his eyes filling with tears, and for a moment neither of us speaks.

A thousand memories are tumbling through my mind in a kaleidoscope of poignant fragments—our wedding day, when he choked up during the ceremony. Getting the keys to our first apartment in New York and eating pizza on the floor because we had no furniture. My labor with Sam, when Daniel kept telling me to breathe until I screamed at him, and then he didn't speak for an hour. When Mattie had pneumonia, and he sat up with her all night. My dad's funeral, when we held each other and cried. Laughing so hard over a joke nobody else would understand, until my stomach ached and tears streamed down my face.

Tears are streaming down my face now, as well as Daniel's, as we simply sit there and bask in each other's presence, as twenty-two years of marriage slip by in the blink of an eye.

TWENTY-SEVEN

In January, when the snow is three feet deep and Red Cedar Lake has frozen hard, when the weather is so breathtakingly cold I don't move an inch at night lest I encounter the icy bed sheet, when darkness descends on the camp before five o'clock, Daniel dies.

Death, I have found, always comes as a shock. My dad had terminal cancer for months and yet, when he actually died, it jolted me as if he'd been perfectly healthy all along. That's how it is with Daniel.

He continues to ebb away, sleeping more and more, and being less alert and present when he's awake. We take turns sitting with him, coaxing him to eat, but by early January he starts refusing all food and that's when I know the end is looming. Even then it feels like a shock, an insult, because death isn't natural, I've found. It's wrong. At least, it feels wrong, something to rail against even as you have no choice but to accept it, however you can.

I'm sitting next to Daniel when he dies. For the last few hours, his breathing has become more labored and sporadic, the deep, even breaths of sleep now sudden, gasping breaths, with longer and longer spaces between each one. I'm holding his hand, which feels limp but still has the warmth of life in it—his heart is beating, blood is coursing through his veins, he is *alive*.

And then he isn't. It takes me about a minute to realize he's already taken his last breath. And then just a minute later, he feels very much dead; his body is completely still, immovable, the warmth already stealing away from it. I slip my hand from his and I kiss his cool forehead and then I walk quickly from the room because I know I don't want to sit with my dead husband.

I want to remember him as he was—alive, funny, thoughtful, giving, warm.

I don't cry. Some things, I suppose, are too deep for tears, and in any case I know they will come later. For now, I focus on practicalities. I head toward the main cabin, where a handful of people are sitting by the fire—Mattie, Ruby, Sheryl, and Patti. The boys are fishing, and everyone else is somewhere around the camp. I draw a breath, and Mattie gives me a sharp, knowing look.

"He's gone?" she says, not quite a question.

I nod. I feel my composure start to crack and I have to take another breath, this one more of a shudder, to keep it in check. "I'm sorry." I come over to my girls and put an arm around each of them, and for a few minutes we simply sit there, clinging together, no one able to say a word.

This is the beginning, I realize distantly, of a new life, a *lack* of life, a life I didn't want, and yet here we are.

The next few days pass in a blur of activity, a haze of grief. The ground is too frozen for a burial, but then Kyle remembers how we buried Darlene, just over a year ago, by burning the ground and loosening the soil. He and Sam do it together, and I watch from the main cabin, their solitary figures silhouetted against a wintry sky.

We have a funeral out by the lake, and Stewart, the minister I haven't yet gotten to know, reads a Bible verse while I stare straight ahead and try not to break down in front of everyone.

"Though the fig tree does not bud and there are no grapes on the vines..."

My head jerks up as I stare at him in shock. That verse? Now? Then I realize that Daniel must have read the index card stuck in the sun visor too, and it must have resonated with him just as it had with me. He must have told Stewart about it and planned to have it read here. It's something we never shared with each other, as there are now so many things we won't share, and that realization is enough to have me doubling over as grief finally forces me to break.

I'm not that strong, after all. Not like Daniel thought. I'm weak, horribly weak, and it's on show to everybody.

Sam, Mattie, and Ruby all put their arms around me as the sobs rack my body, impossible to stop. Grief can't always be contained or controlled and mine rises up and overwhelms me while everyone watches, and I don't even care because I simply have to cry. *Daniel*. My Daniel. Even now, especially now, I can't believe he is gone, that I won't get to tell him again that I'm sorry, our gazes won't meet, full of wry humor as we know exactly what the other person is thinking. I won't rest my head on his shoulder, he won't hold me in his arms. I won't become annoyed by the way he crunches his cereal or clears his throat before answering a question. How can I not have all these things, forever?

The sobs continue to shudder through me, and my children hold me up until I can stand again, wiping my face, whispering my thanks, and Stewart continues reading from Habakkuk.

Afterwards, we head inside for refreshments, of a sort; Sheryl made a cake with precious flour and sugar, although I find I can't eat anything. My stomach is both hollow and churning, and the future has never looked bleaker. I can't face the next hour, never mind the next day or week or month. And what's the point, anyway? What future am I hoping to forge, anymore, without Daniel by my side, holding me up and urging me on in his sure and quiet way?

I end up slipping away from the muted gathering and heading outside to the lake, where I can breathe, even though it's icy cold. I carefully walk down the cleared path through the snow to the dock and stand there, breathing in the freezing air, my face tingling with the cold, staring out at the blur of blazing whiteness that is the snow-covered lake.

Daniel...

I can't think about the future; I can't think at all, and so I simply stand there, and let myself empty out. Then I hear the crunch of boots on snow behind me, and then a voice.

"I know you probably want to be alone."

Nicole. I close my eyes, tilt my head to the sky. Yes, I very much do.

"I also know there's nothing I can say right now to make this remotely better. I just..." She blows out a breath. "I admire you, Alex. I know I haven't acted like I did, but... I do. And... you're not alone in this, okay?" I hear the hint of a smile in her voice as she adds, "And that is absolutely all the sappiness you're going to get from me."

"Good," I manage to reply even though my voice is hoarse from crying; I'm an empty husk, blown on the wind. "Because that is definitely all the sappiness I can take."

A month passes, I'm not sure how. Days slip by and I immerse myself in work—sewing, cleaning, baking, sinking my hands into the soil of the greenhouse. Whatever I can do to keep busy, not have to think, or, worse, remember.

For a while it works, but then it stops, and it feels like all I can do is think—and remember. I see Daniel everywhere; I hear his voice, I know what he'd say in any given situation, I can picture his wry smile perfectly. At night I know exactly how it feels to have my head resting on his shoulder, his arms loosely clasped around me. When we're sitting around the dining table, I can picture perfectly his cocked eyebrow, hear his dry remark...

Strangely, this is no longer a torment but a comfort. It almost feels like he's there, this ghost version of him that walks by my side. But in the meantime, as much as I long to, I can't live in this shadow world of grief, because I have five children to think about—my own three, as well as Kyle and Phoebe.

And life, for them, needs to go on.

The first flicker of something new happens in early March, when the snow is still deep but the days are warmer, if not actually warm. Vicky comes to find me in the kitchen, where I'm peeling carrots with Sheryl.

"Alex." There's something deliberate about her tone that gives me pause, the peeler in my hand.

"What is it?"

She glances at Sheryl and then says, "I just had a radio communication from a place in Winnipeg. They heard that the U.S. has set up a temporary government in Watford City, North Dakota."

"Watford City..." I haven't heard of it, but I recall the rumor from the Strattons that the government had moved to North Dakota. "I heard they might be doing something out there," I say, unsure why she's telling me this in such a deliberate way, with such emphasis.

"Not just that," Vicky continues. "They've put a kind of callout to American citizens. They want to populate several communities up there, restart civilization, as it were. They're going to collect people from various places. Mackinaw City is one of them. That's about three hundred miles from here." She stops then, deliberately, and waits for me to catch up.

I stare at her, sensing where she's going with this, and yet resisting it out of both instinct and fear.

"Do you... do you want us to go?" I ask uncertainly.

"No," she replies quickly. "It's not about what I want, Alex. But you're American, and... maybe I'm wrong here, but I always got the sense that *you* would, one day. That you wanted to be part of something like this, eventually. Something bigger than what we're doing here." She pauses before admitting, "Daniel told me as much."

Daniel, heckling me from the grave, pushing me forward even as I resist. The thought almost makes me smile, even as I am accosted by both fear and grief. "I suppose I did," I admit slowly. "Once. But when it actually comes down to it, now..."

"You can think about it for a little while. If you decide to do it, we can contact them by radio, learn a little more, as well. And we can give you enough gas to get you to Mackinaw City."

I shake my head. "You need it—"

"No," Vicky returns, smiling. "I don't. I'm staying here. We all are. We're happy here. But you..." She pauses, considering. "Alex... I think Daniel really understood you. He knew you needed something different."

I think about it on my own for three days, my thoughts pinging around like the proverbial little metal ball in a pinball machine. Vicky gives me a little more information she's gleaned from the radio: there are twelve settlements that are going to be the start of a new United States of America, and the government is building more infrastructure to support them.

For the moment, the entirety of the United States is concentrated in northern North Dakota, and they will expand from there. There's estimated to be less than five percent of the U.S. population still alive, around just seventeen million people scattered across the wasted country. Before the bombs,

North Dakota had a population of less than a million. There's going to need to be a lot of building. Of growing. Of hoping. Of believing. But it's also going to be hard, and unknown, and I really don't know if I'm up for it. Yet for my children's future... for the chance for them to have a life that is more than survival, as pleasant as that has sometimes been here at Red Cedars...

Can I risk it? Do I want to?

I decide to put it to everyone else. We gather in the cabin, everyone looking as serious as if I'm about to read a will—and, in a way, I am. This is Daniel's legacy, I know it is.

We can make a life for ourselves here...

He always had more vision than I did. Then, back at the cottage, when he saw us homesteading and I dismissed it as playing at pioneers, and now, when I'm facing something that terrifies me but that he believed I could do—and he told me so. This is as much about Daniel as it is about me.

"Mom," Mattie asks, sounding urgent. "What is it?"

Haltingly, I tell them about Mackinaw City, North Dakota, these new settlements that will form the bedrock of a new America. About the idea, the hope, of helping to build something bigger than ourselves. I tell them about the schools that will be starting, the towns that have already been founded. It's not what we once knew, but it's an approximation of it. It's *more*.

For a few seconds, all I get back are silent stares. No one looks particularly impressed or enthused by all I've said, and I can't blame them. We've faced so many unknowns in the last year. Do we really want to face another one, and one as big as this?

"What do you guys think?" I ask uncertainly.

"It's not going to be like the NBSRC but just... *bigger*, is it?" Kyle asks, sounding distinctly unhappy about such a possibility.

"I don't think so," I reply, "but the truth is, I really don't know. I think, at least I hope, it will be more an attempt at—at living real life again, but... in North Dakota."

"This is real life," Mattie shoots back, sounding fierce. "This is very much real life, to me."

"Of course it is," I murmur. "I just mean... more the way things used to be."

"We can never," she declares, "go back to the way things used to be."

Inwardly, I sigh. When Mattie is in a fighting mood, it is impossible to say the right thing. "You're right," I tell her, and even that makes her glower.

"I think it's worth a shot," Sam ventures after a moment. "I mean, it's pretty great here in some ways, but it feels... like summer camp." He glances around at all of us, caught between guilt and excitement. "Or, I don't know, like a time out of reality. I'm not... I'm not sure I want to spend the rest of my life at Red Cedar Lake."

Mattie looks like she wants to argue, but Ruby gets in there before she does. "I want to go with you," she says softly, staring at me. "Wherever you go, I want to go."

Mattie is glaring at me accusingly, like I've turned everyone against her. "Mattie?" I ask gently. "What do you want?"

She gathers Phoebe to her, holding the little girl closely, her expression both defiant and afraid. "I want to stay here," she declares, her voice trembling. "I'm *going* to stay here." She glances at Kyle, and I watch as some silent communication passes between them, and then he gives a little nod.

"I'm going to stay here, too," he says.

I deflate, a little; I realize I'm disappointed. As scared as I feel, I know by my reaction now that I wanted to go to North Dakota. I wanted to try this. For Daniel's sake, but also for my own. But I can't go without my daughter, and I of all people know when Mattie won't be moved.

"Okay," I say after a moment. "Then we won't go."

Sam deflates, his breath leaving him in a defeated gust, and Ruby tucks her knees up to her chest. I realize then that I am not the only one who feels disappointed.

Then Mattie lifts her chin, her eyes flashing as she gazes steadily at me. "This doesn't mean, Mom," she states, "that you can't go."

I stare at her blankly. "What are you talking about, Mattie?"

"You can go," she reiterates, her voice coming out stronger now. "All of you. You want to, and you should. But Kyle and Phoebe and I... we're staying here."

I let out a huff of disbelief. "I'm not going without you." I'm certainly not leaving my sixteen-year-old daughter alone, living out some romantic fantasy with her maybe-boyfriend.

"I'm sixteen," she tells me. "An adult."

"No, you're not—"

"In this world, I am." She cuts me off, sounding very certain. "I can make my own choices, and so can you. And Sam and Ruby can, too." She glances at both her siblings. "If that's what you want, you should go. I mean it. I get it, there's a life for you out there, and you should take it. But I'm staying here."

I shake my head slowly. The Mattie I know and love would have been up for it, I realize. The challenge, the adventure. What has changed?

"I don't want to keep running," she tells me, a tremble to her voice. "I'm happy here. Kyle and I are happy here... together, with Phoebe."

He puts his arm around her, and my jaw slackens. I suspected something was going on, but... this? This much, at their age? I should have had that conversation with her. I should still have it.

"I'm not going," Mattie says again. "I don't want any more than this. I really don't."

And now she sounds like Daniel. Can I blame or begrudge her for her choice? I know already that I can't. And yet... what about Sam, Ruby? What about what they want, what life can they make for themselves?

And what about me? There's no way I can leave my daughter. Everything in me cries out against it, and yet...

And yet...

"Mom," Mattie says, and now her voice has turned achingly gentle. "I really think you should go."

TWENTY-EIGHT

DANIEL

March the previous year
Outside Albany, New York

Carefully Daniel fits the key into the padlock and unlocks it, and then pulls up the roller door of the garage with a loud clatter that echoes on the still, wintry air. Inside the musty-smelling space is a Honda Civic, maybe five years old. He breathes out deeply, hardly able to believe it's really there. It feels like a miracle, except of course it isn't, it's a responsibility, and one entrusted to him by a woman whose name he doesn't know, whose very life depends on him bringing her car back to her.

Next to the car are five five-gallon jerry cans of gas. It's enough to get to Buffalo or Flintville... but not both.

An hour earlier, Daniel made a deal with the woman gasping for breath on the sofa, her baby next to her.

"I need to get out of here, too," he'd told her. "Not to Buffalo, though, but up north. I'll get your car for you, but I'll have to drive my son, and my mother-in-law along with you, at least as far as Syracuse."

As he said it, he didn't know if he was being ruthless or just realistic. Surely it wasn't too much to ask, to accompany her as far as he could? She nodded, already agreeing, but then Daniel realized that they couldn't go that way, because both Syracuse and Rochester had been hit. The only safe way—if it was indeed safe—to get to Buffalo, would be to go south. Take Route 88 all the way down toward Binghamton, maybe, and then start cutting across west, through northern Pennsylvania, before heading back up to Buffalo. It would double the mileage, at least, and it was also in the opposite direction of where he needed to go. There definitely wouldn't be enough gas.

"Are you sure there's a base at Buffalo?" he asked, sounding doubtful, wanting to change her mind. "It's so far away..."

She nodded again, eagerly. "Yes, I'm sure of it. My cousin told me about it. He owns the garage I mentioned. He went a couple of weeks ago, but I was too sick. But he knew about it... it's the only place I know to go... I'm going to meet him... I have to get there..." She trailed off, closing her eyes, clearly exhausted.

Daniel hesitated. He needed to look at the atlas again, but, if he drove this woman all the way to Buffalo, maybe he could cross into Canada at Niagara, and then make his way north and east through Ontario, avoiding Toronto, of course, but getting there steadily. It would add a lot of time to the journey, maybe even months, and he didn't have the gas for such a long trip, but he knew he didn't have any other options.

"Will you get the car for me?" she asked, opening her eyes and gazing at him in desperate appeal. "Please? You can ride with me. Hell, you can drive the car." She let out a raspy laugh that ended in a rattling cough. "I'm not well enough."

"All right," Daniel said slowly, the word drawn from him reluctantly. He didn't want to link his fortunes to this woman's, but she was the one with the car. "Where's the car exactly? And the key?"

With halting, painful breathlessness, she told him where the keys were, both to the garage and the car, hidden in a box under her bed. The garage, she said, was at 122 County Road, tucked behind a house with a front porch with green posts.

"It'll be abandoned, but the car should be safe. The garage is made of concrete and the door's padlocked."

"All right," Daniel said again. He found the keys just where she'd said they were and pocketed both sets. Then he headed back into the living room and gazed down at the woman, who had fallen asleep, her mouth hanging open, her breath coming in slow, rasping breaths. The baby had stopped crying; her eyes were open, and for a second Daniel wondered if she was dead, but then he saw the faint rise and fall of her tiny chest.

He turned away from them both and went to get the car. It took him over an hour to find his way to County Road, and then walk along the side of it until he came to number 122. It was nearly midnight, the sky inky black, and he'd been gone for hours. He needed to get back to Sam and Jenny. He needed to get back with a car.

He walked around the clapboard farmhouse just as the woman had instructed and there was the garage, tucked behind, locked up tight and looking safe.

And now here he was, just past midnight, the garage unlocked and open, the car right in front of him and he had the keys in his hand, and it would be easy, so easy, to get in that car and drive back to Sam and never think of that woman and her baby again. He clenches the car key in his fist, so that it bites into his palm, hard enough to hurt. He welcomes the pain because part of him can't believe he's willing to think this way. And not just think but do.

He's going to do it. He's going to take—*steal*—this car and drive back to Sam. He's going to condemn this woman and her innocent baby to death.

"They'd be dead anyway," he mutters, but the words sound

petulant and frightened even to his own ears. They aren't dead now.

A shuddering breath escapes him as he loads the gas into the trunk, and then slides into the driver's seat. He rests his hands on the steering for a few minutes and just breathes. Then, steeling himself, he puts the key into the ignition; the car starts with a cough and then the engine turns over. Daniel reverses out of the garage and heads back down County Road, toward the ranch house where he left Sam and Jenny.

He drives for a few minutes, his knuckles white on the wheel, muttering under his breath, "They'll be dead anyway. They'll be dead anyway." It sounds like the worst kind of prayer.

The dilapidated ranch house where his loved ones wait comes into view. Abruptly, Daniel slams on the brakes. Without even realizing he is going to do it, he swings the car around and starts driving back to the apartment building, his face set in grimly determined lines.

He pulls the car around to the back of the building, glancing around furtively, praying no one is watching him. He *needs* this car to be here when he gets back. Then he locks the car and heads inside. The smell of decay seems worse as he walks through the empty, garbage-strewn halls, but maybe that's just his imagination. On the top floor, he knocks once on the apartment door and then steps inside.

"Hello?" he calls out. There's no answer. He walks slowly into the living room, where the woman is still lying on the sofa, but even from across the room Daniel can tell she is dead. His first, irrelevant thought is he wishes he'd thought to ask her name.

He walks over to stand next to her, staring down at her slack face, feeling a stirring of pity, but not much more. Then his gaze moves to the baby, who, he realizes, is still alive, her blue eyes open and seeming to stare straight at Daniel.

Tiffany. He knows *her* name, this motherless child who has no one, absolutely no one, in the world but him right now. Slowly he stoops to pick the baby up. She is far too light, her bones seeming as hollow as a bird's, and, with a forgotten father's instinct, he brings her to chest, his palm cradling her tiny head. She lets out a feeble cry, barely more than a breath. She is tiny, wizened, starving... and alone.

What on earth is he going to do? He glances again at the woman. Her eyes are wide open, her body motionless. She is most definitely dead.

Holding Tiffany, he goes through the apartment to find anything he can take with him—diapers, a bottle, baby clothes, *something*. There's nothing but a few changes of baby clothes, all of them filthy. How long had this woman and her child been living here, alone, with nothing? Considering how empty the apartment is, it must have been a while.

He goes through the woman's drawers, but what few clothes there are are too worn and dirty to bother with. A tangle of cheap jewelry lies on top of the dresser, worthless. There isn't even any soap or shampoo in the tiny bathroom; everything has been used up.

All he can take with him, Daniel realizes, is the paltry stuff he found in the other apartments—and the baby.

His heart is like a lead weight inside him as he gathers the few things he found and puts them in a plastic shopping bag. The baby in his arms has gone silent and still, and for a second he wonders, half-hopes, that—but no. He can't be the kind of monster who hopes that a baby is dead.

And yet... a *baby*. How on earth is he meant to care for a baby? He has no diapers, no bottle, no milk, no food... and this baby needs all of those things, fast. He considers bringing her back to Sam and Jenny, and can already imagine Sam becoming anxious, accusing. *Dad, it's a baby! We have to stay in Albany and find some milk...*

Already Daniel knows that getting Jenny was most likely a mistake. If he hadn't listened to his son, if he hadn't felt guilty and wrong for not being willing to go all the way to Springfield, they might already be back safe at the cottage. He might not have exposed them to as much radiation as he fears he has. Yes, they rescued Jenny, but Daniel can see with his own eyes, feel it in his gut, that his mother-in-law most likely doesn't have that long left. Hopefully long enough to make it back, but...

Was it worth it? And would it be worth it to bring this baby along, slow them all down, expose them to more radiation, danger, starvation, who knows what else? There are so many risks, and he's not strong enough to face them all.

He leaves the apartment, the unknown woman's burial chamber, and heads down the hall, the baby cradled in one arm. Her eyes have closed, and her breathing is shallow. She is so very light.

Daniel's steps slow. Falter. Briefly, he closes his eyes. He thinks of Sam, of Jenny, of the four hundred miles between him and home. For a moment, he lets himself think of Alex, of Ruby and Mattie, his family, waiting for him. Are they safe? Are they *alive*? He's been gone for over three months. He needs to get back to them, to protect and care for them as he swore to do...

He glances down at the baby in his arms, now barely breathing. A choked sound escapes him and then he gently lays her down in a doorway. Her eyes flutter open, stare straight at him, and then close again.

"I'm sorry," he whispers, his voice choking, and then he walks quickly away.

He drives back to Sam and Jenny without taking any of his surroundings in. It isn't until he comes back into the ranch house that he realizes he has been crying.

Sam, hunched on the sofa, looks up at him, startled. "Dad... what's wrong?"

Daniel wipes his cheeks, hardens his heart. He will not let

himself think of that baby now, and maybe not ever, even as he already acknowledges he will always be thinking of her. *Tiffany*. She is part of him, now.

No.

He wipes his cheeks, nods once. "Let's go," he says. "I've got a car."

"You do?"

"Yes," Daniel replies without explaining, and then he turns away.

He's sold his soul, he thinks, and he'd do it again for his family, no matter how wrong he knows that is. But it's done now, he's crossed that Rubicon, and the only way now is back home... to Alex.

He forces himself only to think of her as he and Sam load Jenny into the back of the car, and then they head north, to home.

"I can't believe you got a car," Sam marvels. "Where did you get it?"

"It was in a garage."

Sam glances at him uncertainly. "Dad... are you okay?"

Daniel wipes his cheeks again. "Yeah, I'm fine." He feels, with a surprising certainty, that they're going to make it back. He will not let himself have done something so despicable as leaving a baby to die without it meaning something. He nods, makes himself turn to Sam and smile. "I'm fine, Sam," he says, and then he sets his face toward the road, the future, bleak as it seems, and keeps driving.

TWENTY-NINE
ALEX

It takes me three weeks to decide. At first, I don't even consider it. I'm not going to leave Mattie, it's as simple as that, and she clearly won't be moved. She tries to move me, but it turns out I'm just as stubborn as she is.

"Mom... it's not like we'd be saying goodbye forever," she huffs in exasperation, as we peel potatoes in the kitchen and outside it snows steadily. It's March, and Kyle and Winn are leading the maple syrup making. "If the world is getting back to normal, at least in North Dakota, you'll be able to come back or I'll be able to visit. We might even be able to email, or, I don't know, Skype." She rolls her eyes, but I can't share her certainty.

"You and Kyle," I say instead, because it's a conversation we need to have. "Is that a thing?"

"A *thing*? Mom. Ew."

I put down my peeler. "Mattie, I'm serious."

She stares at me for a moment. "Fine, then, so am I," she says. "And yes, we're a thing. But we're not... like, don't give me *that* lecture, okay? I don't think I can take it." She rolls her eyes again, even more theatrically. "It's early days. And he's not the reason I'm staying. I just... like it here. I liked it at the cottage, too. And I really, really don't want to live in North Dakota." She gives me a glimmer of a smile then, along with a tilt of her chin, and I realize my defiant Mattie is still there; she's just choosing something different. Something right.

And I need to, too. I talk to Sam, who has been on the radio with Vicky and has learned about the college that is starting, with six hundred students.

"Six *hundred*," he marvels, and I realize how hungry he is for socializing, for friends. Ruby, too, loner that she's been, lights up at the thought of a school with real grades, a science class, an art room. Things we thought were gone forever but have now—maybe—been given back to us.

It occurs to me then that maybe I'm being selfish, insisting that we stay because I don't want to lose Mattie. And maybe I won't lose her even if I go. The thought is terrifying, but it also feels weirdly right. I can almost hear Daniel whisper his encouragement, spurring me on.

Another week passes, of sleepless night and anxious days, wondering whether I'm the worst mother in the world, or just a pragmatic one, or maybe even a noble one. Vicky gets more reports on the radio about the new settlements in North Dakota—they will be self-sustaining in terms of food; they already have a lignite coal mine back in production. The internet is up, too, and the water and sewer systems are working. Everything feels like a miracle. "It's like pioneers," I told Vicky, "but with infrastructure."

I ask Mattie again if she's sure she wants to stay.

"Yes, I'm sure." She sounds exasperated, almost amused. "Mom, come on. Stop nagging me."

"I haven't exactly been nagging—"

"I really won't be mad if you go." Her voice gentles. "I think you should. And Sam and Ruby, too. They want to. I know they do."

I'm still sitting on the fence about it all when Stewart

approaches me. I'm down on the dock, staring at the lake, which is now breaking up from the ice, the loud cracks of it echoing across its expanse. Dark water swirls and surges and huge chunks of ice bob in its eddies.

I smile a cautious greeting because, even though Stewart took Daniel's funeral and was so kind about it, I haven't really gotten to know him. Maybe I'm keeping my distance for a reason; I don't want his pious sympathy, and I also don't want to be pushed into anything, which says more about me than him, I know, but I still feel it.

"I've heard you have a big decision to make," he remarks, his kindly face creasing into a smile, as he comes to stand with me on the edge of the dock.

I eye him a little warily. "Yes..."

"If you want to talk about it..." He leaves that suggestion open, and I manage to give him an apologetic smile.

"I'm not sure how much there is to say. I'm still thinking about everything."

He nods equably, not quite taking it as the brush-off I meant it to be. "There's a speech by Martin Luther King Jr.," he remarks after a moment, which seems to come completely out of left field. "A sermon, actually. He gave it in Chicago to the Women's Auxiliary."

"Okay..." I wait for more, because clearly he must be going somewhere with this.

"It starts with him declaring that it's midnight in our world today." He pauses, his face tilted toward the sky, and then quotes, "'Man is experiencing a darkness so deep that he can hardly see which way to turn. The best minds of today are saying that our civilization stands at the midnight of its revolving cycle.'"

"I'd say that's pretty much true today," I remark after a pause when he seems as if he isn't going to say anything more.

It's certainly a dark and dangerous world out there. Midnight, as it were.

"He goes on," Stewart continues, "to say that it is midnight in the social order, the psychological order, the moral order. And in this midnight hour, the darkness is interrupted by a knock on the door." Another pause. "King was talking about the world knocking on the door of the church. But I see it another way, too. The only way out of that darkness, any darkness, is to open the door... to whatever is there, waiting for you."

I stare at him for a moment, trying to figure out what he's trying to say. "So you think I should go to North Dakota?" I finally ask, surprised he'd give me such one-sided advice. What about the community here? What about Mattie? And Kyle and Phoebe too, and even Nicole and Ben, who are both choosing to stay? I'd be leaving them all behind, and for what?

"I think," Stewart responds, "you should open that door."

And as I stare at him, still longing to resist, I realize he's right. I need to open that door, but I also need to close the one to the past: the world as I once knew it, the cottage I once loved—and the man I killed, whether he was good or bad or something in between. The past, with all its regrets and longings, can't hinder me now. For the sake of my children, as well as myself, I have to look forward.

A week later, I do it. It's not easy, it's not even exciting, to open that door. It's just terrifying and faintly wrong and yet... *and yet*, unsettlingly right, like a settling in my bones, in my very self. Daniel made me promise I'd do something like this, and now here I am, doing it.

Mattie hugs me, happy for me even though it means saying goodbye to her, at least for a while, although we make promises to keep in touch via the radio and maybe email, and if we are able to visit, we tell each other, we will. I say goodbye to Kyle and Phoebe too, along with Nicole and Ben. Nicole hugs me tightly and whispers to me, fiercely, that she's glad I'm being brave. I can't believe I'm leaving them, that they're letting me, that I'm letting myself.

Sam and Ruby are, of course, sad to leave Mattie, but I see the excitement in their faces about the future. A future that isn't about running, or hiding, or just surviving. They're ready for this attempt at real life, just as I am, even as every joy will now be tinged with sorrow. Mattie. *Daniel*.

They will both come with me, in their own ways; I know I will think of them, miss them, every single day. And Mattie is already planning her visit, once the world opens up again, which it surely will, now that it is the midnight hour, and the knock is at the door. We have heard it, and we are answering. And I will come back, I tell her fiercely. One day, I will come back. *I promise*.

But for now... we go forward. We leave Red Cedar Lake behind, and all the community there, everyone waving as we take one of their cars, so kindly given, and head down the rutted dirt road, toward the future.

The drive to Mackinaw City is surprisingly uneventful, three hundred miles through western Ontario and then south through Michigan. There are signs everywhere that normality is something that can be reached for, maybe even grasped—houses being built, signs along the road offering food and water and medical aid, a phone number you can call if you're in distress. We pass a dozen or more cars; when I catch a glimpse of the other driver, she smiles at me. The world is finally reawakening to what it once was, or at least a shadow of it.

In Mackinaw City, a military plane is waiting for us, along with two dozen other people who have also decided to settle in North Dakota, everyone looking wary and hopeful, and more than a little shell-shocked, too. As we board, a man in military uniform greets me gravely.

"Good to see you here, ma'am."

I find myself, suddenly and surprisingly, near tears.

We settle in the plane, all the passengers offering each other shy and uncertain smiles; we all seem similarly emotionally moved, as if we've been evacuated from a war zone. We're being rescued, I think, and then I correct myself.

We are rescuing ourselves. We are choosing this, whatever it is. Whatever lies ahead of us.

Ruby slips her hand into mine and Sam gives me an excited and slightly shamefaced smile; he's like a little kid and he knows it, but that's okay. That's how I want him to be. I give them both smiles and hugs and then I take a deep breath as I think of Daniel, of Mattie, of the pain I carry with me that is now part of me, and always will be. But maybe that kind of pain can make you stronger, or at least wiser.

Then I think of the cottage, picturing it as if it is still there, tranquil and solid, with the sun setting over the placid lake, the comforting sound of the whippoorwill as twilight falls on the peaceful, eternal scene. I remember Kawartha and the NBSRC, the community at Red Cedar Lake, the journey we took without ever knowing where we were going or how long it would be.

And now this... the future, whatever it holds. Whatever happens, we're ready for it.

I turn to the window and tilt my face to the sky.

A LETTER FROM THE AUTHOR

Dear reader,

Huge thanks for reading *The Midnight Hour*; I hope you were hooked on Alex's journey. If you want to join other readers in hearing all about my new releases and bonus content, you can sign up here:

www.stormpublishing.co/kate-hewitt

If you enjoyed this book and could spare a few moments to leave a review that would be hugely appreciated. Even a short review can make all the difference in encouraging a reader to discover my books for the first time. Thank you so much!

The Last Stars in the Sky was inspired by my family's time at our own cottage (which is very similar to the one in the story!) in Ontario, and it was so wonderful to continue Alex's story beyond the cottage in *The Midnight Hour*. If a nuclear Armageddon scenario really did happen, I hope and pray that there would be people like some of the characters in this story who genuinely want to help others. Hopefully none of us will have to find out!

Thanks again for being part of this amazing journey with me and I hope you'll stay in touch—I have so many more stories and ideas to entertain you with!

KEEP IN TOUCH WITH THE AUTHOR

www.kate-hewitt.com
substack.com/@katehewitt

f facebook.com/KateHewittAuthor

X x.com/author_kate

instagram.com/katehewitt1

linkedin.com/in/kate-hewitt-38b44521a

ACKNOWLEDGMENTS

Many thanks, as always, to my editor, Kathryn Taussig, as well as Vicky Blunden, who worked on the manuscript while Kathryn was on maternity leave. Also to Jacqui Lewis for copy-editing and the rest of the team at Storm. I'm also very grateful to Oliver Rhodes for believing in this series in the first place. I also would like to thank my fellow writers Emma Robinson and Jenna Ness, who talked through the story with me at various points. Lastly, a huge shout-out to my family for being so supportive—and interested—in this series. And special thanks to Cliff, my dear husband, who loves the cottage as much as I do. You are not Daniel! At least, you are the best parts of him. Love you!

www.ingramcontent.com/pod-product-compliance
Lightning Source LLC
La Vergne TN
LVHW030603220125
801792LV00005B/285

* 9 7 8 1 8 0 5 0 8 7 0 3 8 *